CM01583165

HELEN ... AUGHTER

"A fantastically done portrait of royal life in pre-Classical Mycenae, Sparta, and surrounding lands...a vivid journey through the lives and experiences of some familiar characters of legend." – L.M. Ironside, author of *The Sekhmet Bed*

"Captivating from the beginning...filling in the blanks from previous tales and spinning a wonderful plot." –Lauren Johnson, *A Write To Review*

ALSO BY LAURA GILL

THE ORESTES TRILOGY

The Young Lion
The Outcast
The Warrior

KNOSSOS

Helen's Daughter

Laura Gill

Helen's Daughter

Copyright © 2011, 2014 by Laura Gill
All rights reserved

Cover Artwork by Laura Gill
Copyright © 2011, 2014

ISBN-13: 978-1466382626

ISBN-10: 1466382627

Disclaimer: No part of this publication may be reproduced, stored into a retrieval system, or transmitted in any form (electronic, mechanical, photocopying, recording, or otherwise), without the prior written permission of the copyright owner

EPIRUS
Ephyri
Iolkos
PHTHIA
AITOLIA
Delphi
Krisa
Cirrha
PHOCIS
EUBOEA
BOEOTIA
ITHACA
Aulis
Orchomenos
Gulf of Corinth
Thebes
ELIS
ATTICA
Corinth
Athens
Nemea
ARCADIA
ARGOLIS
Mycenae
Argos
Tiryns
SPARTA
MESSENIA
Therapne
Helas
Pylos
GREECE
1250 B.C.

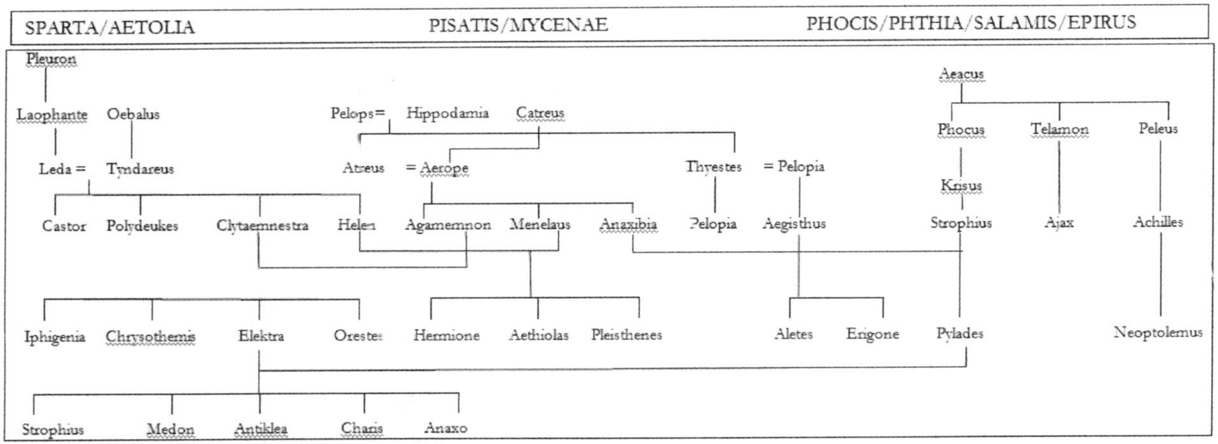
SPARTA/AETOLIA
PISATIS/MYCENAE
PHOCIS/PHTHIA/SALAMIS/EPIRUS
Pleuron
Laophante
Oebalus
Pelops=
Hippodamia
Catreus
Aeacus
Phocus
Telamon
Peleus
Leda =
Tyndareus
Atreus
= Aerope
Thyestes
= Pelopia
Krisus
Castor
Polydeukes
Clytaemnestra
Helen
Agamemnon
Menelaus
Anaxibia
Pelopia
Aegisthus
Strophius
Ajax
Achilles
Iphigenia
Chrysothemis
Elektra
Orestes
Hermione
Aethiolas
Pleisthenes
Aletes
Erigone
Pylades
Neoptolemus
Strophius
Medon
Antiklea
Charis
Anaxo

CHAPTER ONE

"HERMIONE!" ELEKTRA BURST INTO THE sitting room in an air of agitation, dragging her older sister behind her. "Come with us to the great gallery."

Chrysothemis shot me a desperate look, warning me that whatever my cousin intended to see or do in the megaron's great gallery meant trouble.

I laid aside my shuttle of bright blue wool. "What's going on?"

"Father's on his way home right now," Elektra said.

"She thinks she saw his chariot," Chrysothemis added quietly.

"Shut up!" Elektra's snub nose crinkled, and she bared her large horse teeth. A tall, strapping young woman with shocking red hair, she should have been born a man; even her husky voice sounded mannish. "I know what I saw."

I knew better. As always, she knew only what she wanted to see. Elektra was impatient to see her father return in triumph, and to denounce her mother as a whore, as though my uncle did not already know he was a cuckold. "I don't think you should go," I told her.

Chrysothemis seized upon my advice. "Listen to her, Elektra."

But Elektra disregarded her. "So you won't come?" she asked me.

"I want no trouble," I said, "and you're bent on causing it." I retrieved the shuttle.

Seizing her sister's arm, Elektra hustled her from the room. I watched them go, Chrysothemis dragging her heels and complaining. Elektra had been restless all through the autumn and winter, ever since the beacons announced the Hellene victory at Troy. We had endured six months confined with her, suffering her moods and interminable pacing back and forth; we might as well have been caged with a brooding lioness.

Let her wait a little longer. Agamemnon would arrive home tomorrow, and that was soon enough.

But when he did come, he would expect a hero's welcome. Harried scrub maids, laundresses, and cooks had been laboring hard ever since word arrived two days ago that the High King's ships had landed at Tiryns.

My cousin was mistaken. Had Agamemnon intended to come home today, Aunt Clytaemnestra would have been overseeing our toilette, scrutinizing our jewelry, hair, and dresses before herding us downstairs to line up in the megaron like so many painted cult votaries.

Clytaemnestra must have granite nerves to remain as calm as she was. She had had six months to contemplate how she was going to get back into her husband's good graces after cuckolding him with his rival kinsman, yet she had not even sent her lover away.

I wanted to be a hundred miles from here, away from my aunt and uncle, and their bitter quarrel. Since the beacons had blazed, I prayed for Hermes to speed my father home so he might send for me, but there was no word except that he had quarreled with my uncle and left Troy while the spoils were still being divided. Poseidon's wrath struck the fleet hard, sending many ships with their crews and Trojan riches to the bottom of the Aegean, but I knew deep in my heart that Menelaus was still alive. Perhaps he had wanted to raid elsewhere before going home, and was even now stepping ashore on a Spartan beach.

Clear yellow sunshine slanted through the narrow window, flooding the sitting room with warmth and light but scant comfort. Dwelling on my father's whereabouts inevitably conjured unwelcome thoughts of my mother. Clytaemnestra's messenger, bringing further news about the sacking of Troy, told us that Menelaus had not killed Helen, but took her back as his wife and queen without recriminations. I burned with shame, unable to believe it. My mother had abandoned her home and family, sparked a ruinous war, and my father was just going to let her live after all the horrible things he vowed to do to her?

Speculation buzzed among the nobles and court ladies. Maybe he was saving her for a special execution, or maybe she had beguiled him with her naked breasts just as the messenger said. I could not bear to listen to their talk.

Elektra's agitation pierced me like a dart, banishing my earlier calm, making it increasingly difficult to concentrate. And weaving on the small loom left my mind free to wander, to spin webs of the mind. Had Chrysothemis stayed behind, we could have worked together, talked of inconsequential things, and forgotten our troubles. Alone, I grew anxious.

At last, I hung the shuttle on a wooden peg beside the loom and ventured outside.

I found myself heading down the service stairs, and through a rear corridor which led toward the megaron. An oil lamp burned at the end of the dim passage, near the door leading into the vestibule. A crack in the door would let me observe anyone entering the megaron, and slip away again unnoticed should there be trouble.

Orestes might be there, too, spying on the messengers who were arriving with the king's baggage. My youngest cousin was curious about the father who had left him so many years ago, but also very anxious.

"What are you doing here?" Clytaemnestra's authoritative voice echoed back along the passage. I froze. "Didn't I order you to stay out of the way?"

"Father's on his way home. I saw his chariot coming up the road." My heart sank. "He's going to kill you!" I winced at Elektra's recklessness, taunting her mother like that.

Then I heard the sharp slap, my cousin's outraged yelp, and my aunt's reprimand. "Insolent child! Go back to the women's quarters and stay there!"

Someone's hand suddenly clamped down on my shoulder. I stifled a startled cry. A servant would not dare surprise me like that.

"What's this?" Apprehension knotted my belly at the man's low voice brushing against my ear. Strong arms turned me about. "Hermione, my dear, should you be here?"

Aegisthus savored my name with a leer that choked me with revulsion. I kept my eyes on the wall to avoid his lascivious gaze. "I heard someone might be coming today."

"And who told you that, little bird?" Aegisthus's long fingers inched down my exposed throat. I swallowed hard. Would he venture even lower and brush against my breasts under the pretense of admiring an embroidered band or straightening my dress? "Whoever it was, they are mistaken." His hand left my throat to cup my cheek. "Go back to your loom."

"Of course." I would seize any excuse just to get away from him.

Aegisthus leaned in close enough to kiss me. He exuded sexual hunger like a foul odor. "Of course, what?" he pressed.

I choked out the hated word he forced me to use. "Yes, Uncle."

His thumb grazed my lips. "Such a good girl, Hermione."

When he released me, I sidled away with his ravenous gaze crawling up my spine, suppressing the urge to run. How could my aunt, who saw and heard everything else, not know about her lover's advances toward me?

I crept back up the side stairs, taking a different route which led past the empty gallery. Clytaemnestra made swift work of banishing my cousins, but she might yet be nearby. Hoping to avoid her, I quickened my pace.

Then I heard the megaron's heavy oak doors swing inward on their oiled hinges, and a man's thunderous bellow carrying to the rafters. "Where is that whore who calls herself my wife?"

Agamemnon was here! Elektra had been right. It could not be anyone else. Shocked, I retraced my steps, ducked through the curtain into the gallery, and peered down to get a better look at my father's brother.

Built like a bull, the king of Mycenae towered over the servant he had shoved aside. Gray streaked his black beard, and bitter lines twisted his mouth and scored his brow. Several armed companions and a pregnant woman in a threadbare gown accompanied him into the megaron.

And down in the megaron, fragrant pinewood burned upon the great central hearth, and green garlands twined its four supporting pillars. Purple cushions and a tawny lion skin graced the throne upon the dais against the far wall. A royal welcome for a king who was not supposed to arrive until tomorrow.

"My lord, you wound me!" Clytaemnestra swept into view with arms outstretched. She wore her finest raiment, her dark hair swept up in oiled ringlets, and gold roundels sparkled on her flounced skirts. "I am overjoyed to see you safely home. All Mycenae rejoices."

"Then why has Mycenae not turned out to greet me?" Agamemnon grumbled sourly. He wanted his hero's welcome, with cheering crowds and fanfare. "People seem surprised by my arrival."

"We thought you were returning tomorrow." Clytaemnestra managed to sound genuinely contrite. "Forgive me. It seems your messenger made a mistake."

Bronze rasped against leather as Agamemnon drew his sword. As he advanced toward her, I held my breath. "But I see garlands hanging and fine cushions upon the throne, and you all dressed for company. So who are you expecting, wife? Is it that snake Aegisthus? Hoping for one last indiscretion before I cut your throat?"

I would have thrown myself on my knees to plead for mercy, but Clytaemnestra never flinched. With the sword tip wavering mere inc
from her throat, she fearlessly reached out and grasped the blad
its macabre dance over her collarbone. "Have your spies
my lord? I threw that lecher out months ago. You were

But Aegisthus was still here! He had accosted m
hour ago. Elektra would have shouted it out an
as the liar she was, yet my voice refused to

Agamemnon leaned closer. "It took
he spat. "I thought you had more se

"I am at your mercy, my lor
of Night blinded me with a
you, and that beast to

lling
d you,
out him."
arter of an
d her mother
s to realize that?"
ate and the Daughters
nter. I was so angry with
weakness." Clytaemnestra's

voice quavered on the verge of tears. Agamemnon could not possibly be taken in by her outrageous performance. “It took me this long to see him for the snake he was, using me to get revenge against you.”

An audible sob escaped her as she kept going, “When we heard the news from Troy, he took me to bed and whispered his plan in my ear. He planned to murder you and Orestes, and make himself king. That abomination fouling the throne of Mycenae? How could I possibly let him sit where better men like you and Atreus have sat? How could the mother of your son have gone along with his schemes?”

She was so good she almost had me believing her.

“Forgive me for lying, my lord,” Clytaemnestra said. “I withheld the news for fear of your anger. I did not want our children to see their father kill their mother the way you and Menelaus saw your father murder your mother.”

Slowly, Agamemnon lowered the blade. A knot formed in my throat, rendering me mute.

Clytaemnestra extended a welcoming hand. “Come, my lord. Your daughters have missed you. Orestes wants to hear your stories. It is all he talks about.”

Agamemnon sheathed the sword, though his scowl remained. “Menelaus might be swayed by a pair of tits, but you’re no Helen. I will …the and make the offering, and then we will see. Meanwhile, attend to m… …ncubine. Cassandra is a woman of royal blood.”

…emnestra acknowledged the pregnant woman with contempt. “Is th… …t she is?”

… nothing to say about it.” Agamemnon began fumbling with the … of his bronze cuirass.

“I see,” … between her teeth. I knew that tone, knew she was seething wit… …artbeat away from exploding.

“Do I d… of willfulness?” Agamemnon snorted his contempt. “An… pretty talk about making amends! I’m beginning to thin… …ly mean it.”

Clytaemnestra … …ite and loving wife to the hilt. “My lord, you honestly c… be happy about the woman.” She ventured a step forward. "Let me get that for you. It must be new leather to be so stiff. Orestes chose the finest lamb from your flocks for the sacrifice, and I have a magnificent purple robe laid out for you to wear once you have been purified."

Agamemnon's sour grunt passed for acknowledgement as, still struggling with his buckles, he pushed past her toward the royal ritual bath. Like a dutiful wife, she followed. I heard the door close after them.

As I began to back slowly toward the curtain, armed men filed into the megaron and surrounded the hearth. Three blocked the entryway with their spears and towering ox-hide shields. The companions looked around them, and at each other, apprehension graven on their faces. The pregnant woman, Cassandra, wrapped her arms over her belly; her eyes grew huge with fear.

And then, the storm broke. Muffled shouts and shrieks from the lustral bath jarred the air. My heart lurched to realize the king was being attacked. Clytaemnestra's wild hollering competed with Agamemnon's outraged bellows and shouts for help.

Aegisthus was in there, too. I choked back a cry, hearing his voice shouting Agamemnon down. "Die, you dog!"

My brain struggled to work. No wonder Aegisthus had not fled the moment Agamemnon beached his ships at Tiryns. No wonder he intercepted me in the passage. They had planned this all along! I crammed my fist into my mouth, realizing that I had almost walked straight into the slaughter.

At Agamemnon's first wounded cry, all seven companions surged toward the bathroom door, weapons drawn, but not a single one made it past the great hearth. The guards swarmed them at once. Metal clashed amid savage curses and grunts. Bones cracked as tall shields rammed men down and lethal bronze punched through leather and flesh.

Cassandra shrieked and crouched beside the hearth, arms clasped over her head. Bodies hit the floor all around her. Blood streamed across the painted stucco tiles and pooled around heads, torsos, and severed limbs. It spattered the regal frescoes, [illegible]ing across the wall.

Seeing the carnage, my every instinct [illegible] at me to escape, but shock rooted me to the spot. I could not make my body move.

When it was done, the attackers seized the woman's arms, hauled her whimpering and struggling to her feet, and held her fast between them. All the companions lay dead except one man whose twitching fingers clawed at the floor; a spear through the throat brought a gurgling end to his agony.

Clytaemnestra and Aegisthus emerged from the bathroom spattered with blood. She held the sacred labrys, he a knife. Slowly, they advanced toward Cassandra. I doubled over, biting down on my knuckles and pulling ragged breaths to keep from vomiting.

Clytaemnestra said something to the woman. Cassandra was sobbing and pleading in a foreign tongue.

Panic gave me the strength to break away. On my hands and knees, I scrabbled to safety, yet not fast enough to escape the sounds of the woman being murdered behind me.

Once I reached the hallway, I staggered to my feet and stumbled to my room, where I shut the door and huddled whimpering in a corner.

Hours crept by. I dared not stir from my corner. No one sought me out. Elektra and Chrysothemis must be under guard with their maid. I did not know where Orestes was. Clytaemnestra might have been telling the truth when she said Aegisthus meant to kill him, too. I whispered prayers to Athena and Hermes, hoping the gods had shielded my cousin during the carnage, and whisked him far away.

Twilight's blue-black shadows crept in, banishing the sun. No one came to bring me clean water or food, or to light the lamps. Night closed around me like a shroud, deepening my fears.

I kne[illegible] I could not face Clytaemnestra or Aegisthus without betraying myself. W[illegible]at they had done was too sickening, too terrible for me to hide behin[illegible]n ignorant façade. They were practiced liars and murderers, snakes who [illegible]ew how to taste the air with their forked tongues. They would smell [illegible]terror.

In the da[illegible]ss where my imagination ran riot, I pictured my aunt and her lover s[illegible]ing along the corridor like a pair of vipers, dripping black blood fro[illegible]eir fangs, slipping into each room to dispatch its inhabitant. Serp[illegible]devouring their young. Chrysothemis. Elektra. Orestes.

Hermione.

CHAPTER TWO

I SHOULD HAVE EXPECTED THIS.

Savagery and treachery ran in my father's bloodline. We were cursed, we Atreidai. The gods despised us.

Mycenae's stones remembered the crimes of my forefathers. It had begun a century ago with the curse my great-grandfather Pelops incurred when he unjustly murdered a man. That curse followed his youngest sons, Atreus and Thyestes, who vied for Mycenae's throne after the last Perseid king had died childless.

Thyestes had seduced his brother's wife and tried to usurp the kingship. Atreus executed his unfaithful wife, but afterward burned with a fierce rage against the man who had robbed him of the woman he had loved. And so, his bitterness had led him to devise the cruelest revenge his mind could conceive.

Atreus sent his exiled brother splendid gifts and messages of reconciliation, and invited him to return to Mycenae. While he took Thyestes out on the boar hunt, his men slew Thyestes' three young sons, quartered them, and cooked them into a stew Atreus served that night to their unwitting father. Atreus then had the servants bring out the last course: three severed heads and three pairs of hands and feet garnished with gristle and swimming in blood.

A horrible story, it gave me nightmares when my Spartan nurse first told it. Thyestes had wept and vomited. Then he cursed Atreus over the remains of his slain children.

Forget the image of venomous serpents slithering along the corridor devouring their young. Aegisthus was man enough to avenge the deaths of his half-brothers by seizing Atreus's grandchildren. There was nothing to stop him now. He would smile that smug, lascivious smile as he cut our throats and cooked us in a stew, and all my father would ever get back would be my severed hands and head.

I forced myself to take a deep breath and think, to be braver than these tears. I was a princess and grown woman, not a child to be frightened by old stories. Aegisthus would not dare try such a thing with my father.

Muffled footfalls in the corridor alerted me. Whoever it was paused right outside my door. I gave a start. My gaze darted to the window, to the bed, to the blackness, seeking a hiding place. There was nowhere to go.

It would be Aegisthus with his dagger and my aunt with the bloody labrys. I held my breath as the latch turned.

When the door cracked open, I blinked at the rushlight wavering in someone's hand. Then a boy's uncertain voice pleaded with me. "Please, let me in."

My eyes stung as they adjusted to the light. "Orestes!" I hurried over to him, and yanked him inside.

Orestes maintained his composure long enough to set down the light, but after that, after the door was shut and the silence and leaping shadows threatened to close in around us, his lower lip started to quiver. As his composure deserted him I gathered him into a tight embrace.

"They killed him!" His sobs were muffled against my clothing. "He came home, and they killed him."

I rocked him my arms, glad to have him safe, but hurt to see him this distraught. "I know."

"They murdered him in his bath." Orestes gasped for breath. "I saw it. I saw them do it."

Astonished, I drew back and raked him up and down with critical eyes, taking in the dried blood on his hands, legs, and clothing, but it was not his; he was not injured at all. I choked back a gasp upon realizing whose blood he was wearing. I took his hand. "Come, sit down on the bed and tell me what you saw."

Orestes brushed his hand across one cheek then the other, smearing them with his father's blood. He climbed onto the bed, dangling one leg over the side. His lower jaw trembled with the effort of holding in his grief.

"I saw the garlands in the megaron and the servants carrying hot water and linens into the lustral bath. Something wasn't right. I don't know what, but it felt wrong. Mother was arguing with Elektra up in the gallery. I didn't want them to find me there, so I ducked into the bathroom and hid behind the curtain in the privy."

He hesitated, wrestling with his tears. I urged him to continue. "I heard shouting outside in the megaron. I knew it had to be him," he said. "Then he came into the bathroom and undressed. He got into the water, and when his eyes were closed, that's when Mother did it. She threw a net over him, and grabbed the labrys, and starting hacking at him. He shouted for help. He tried to break free, to stop her, but he couldn't. And then Aegisthus came in, and took the knife from the altar, and..." Orestes broke down again.

"I heard the shouts," I said softly.

Agony and fear distorted his square face. "I think Aegisthus heard me behind the curtain. I thought for certain he was going to murder me. Mother grabbed him and told him it was a mouse, and they had other business to finish."

She was not stupid; she must have known it was not a mouse. "How did you escape?"

"I was trapped in there for hours," he said numbly.

I shook him hard to get his attention. "Orestes!"

Orestes struggled with his recollections, grimacing and repeatedly shaking his head, until at last he was able to get the words out. "There was so much blood. It was on the walls, the floor, even on the ceiling." He started crying again as he recalled the details. "Father was lying in the tub with the net over him. The water was red with his blood. I thought he was dead, but then he moved a little. He saw me. He looked right at me. I swear, he gasped my name. I crawled over to him, to help him, but there were so many wounds." He moistened his lips with his tongue. Tears streamed down his face.

I stroked his hair, smoothing it back, with a forced smile on my lips. "It's all right." How could I lie thus to him? No, it was not all right. Orestes had just seen his father slaughtered right before his eyes. "Did he say anything to you?"

"Yes. I had to bend down to hear him, he was so weak. There was blood running from his mouth, but he said 'Orestes, avenge....'" I heard the words stick in his throat; he forced them out, anyway. "And then he died." In a rush, he pushed on. "I took his ring because I thought he'd want me to."

Orestes fumbled for an oblong object, a golden seal ring depicting a pillar between two rampant lions. Agamemnon's insignia. I took it, feeling the weight in my palm, and ran my thumb over the encrusted blood, scraping at it with my fingernail. "Now, what did you do next?"

"Went back to hide. Some men came to take Father away, then they came back to scrub the room. I stayed hidden till they were gone." Orestes swallowed an emerging sob long enough to finish. "I wanted to find Timon, but there was someone watching his door. I think men are waiting for me in my room, too."

"You were smart," I assured him. Orestes had kept a more level head than his sister would have. Now I had to get his mind on more urgent matters, like escaping. "Stay here. I'm going to get some water and clean you up."

Fetching a cloth from the washbasin, I bathed away his father's blood. He accepted my ministrations in numb silence, then his eyes suddenly widened in horror; he bit down on his knuckles and moaned. "Oh, no! No!" Orestes pulled his knees up to his chest and curled up in a fetal position on the mattress.

"What is it?" I asked.

Orestes kept shaking his head. "I can't do it! I can't! Avenging him means killing *her*."

He did not have to explain. Mothers were sacred. A man who murdered the woman who bore him, no matter what the circumstances, was shunned as a matricide, forever pursued by the dreadful Erinyes, the Daughters of Night.

Clytaemnestra should have considered that before she struck out, but she had chosen her lover over her husband and children. All I could do was comfort Orestes with caresses and endearments, something better suited to a child than a twelve-year-old boy now shouldered with adult responsibilities.

I gave him a few more moments to grieve. "Orestes, listen to me. You have to get away from Mycenae."

"I know," he mumbled. "I tried Timon, but..." His gaze roamed the room, darting back and forth as his mind raced. "I can't go back to my room to get my things."

"Where can you go that's safe?" I pressed.

It took a while to get him to think, but when he did, his mind worked rapidly. "Father's men might still be at Tiryns, but... No, Aegisthus might be watching that road, and the road to Sparta." A pause. "He'll never expect me to head north, to my kinsmen in Phocis. It'll be rough going, though. Corinthia and the Isthmus are wild country. There are—" Orestes sat up with a start. "You have to come with me. You can't stay here. It's too dangerous."

For a moment, I seriously contemplated the idea. My every instinct urged escape from this haunted, blood-soaked place, but it was not feasible. Orestes would have enough to do surviving in the wilderness and staying ahead of any pursuers without a woman adding to his troubles. Old Timon had prior experience hiking and negotiating the wilderness during his pupil's frequent outdoor excursions. I would only hamper his progress.

"I can't go with you, Orestes," I said. "But my father is on his way home, and he'll soon send for me. Now finish washing up and go find Timon. You haven't much time."

The world was changing, falling to pieces all around us, and only the gods knew what would happen tomorrow. Orestes' hands trembled as he bent over the washbasin to rinse away the last vestiges of his father's blood. I walked him to the door and, slowly turning the latch so as not to make too much noise, peeked out into the corridor. All was dark and silent. I nodded to Orestes.

He hugged me one last time. "I will come back for you."

I sent him on his way with my blessing, for the mother who should have blessed him had just murdered his father.

CHAPTER THREE

NO ONE CAME FOR ME THAT NIGHT. At dawn, a servant brought breakfast and clean linens. I noticed her shaking hands and the way she averted her eyes. Even my own maidservant, who came in to comb my hair and attend my other needs, did her best to remain inconspicuous.

Down the corridor, Chrysothemis's hysterical weeping heightened the morning's funereal air.

Elektra screamed with the daylight, and kept screaming. Ceramics shattered against the wall. Furniture overturned, crashed, and through it all she howled, shrieked that her mother was a murderer. I heard footfalls hastening along the corridor, then the queen's servants trying to silence her.

Inertia kept me rooted to my bed. Fear knotted my tongue. All I could do was lie very still atop the coverlet, breathe in and out, and concentrate on the warm sunlight slanting across my bed. Only by lying still and basking in the heat and light would the terror stay away.

I knew why Clytaemnestra had done it. Iphigenia. Agamemnon had stained his hands with his own child's blood.

Why had I been so blind? After almost eight years, I should have known better than to believe my aunt would ever send Aegisthus away and try to regain her husband's favor. Clytaemnestra's hatred for

Agamemnon was a mother's anguish for a slain daughter. Her outrage demanded vengeance, not reconciliation. She could not have made that more obvious than when she took Aegisthus into her bed.

THE DEEPENING AFTERNOON angled the sunlight away from my bed, leaving me in the cool shadows. Elektra and Chrysothemis were still, except for the occasional muffled sob.

Memories rolled over me, like ripples engulfing a pebble. Agamemnon's murder was the old double curse claiming yet another victim. Iphigenia's sacrifice had been the curse, too. It was always the curse, going back through the generations.

I was nine years old when my mother went away, taking my baby brother Pleisthenes with her, and almost twelve when my father left Sparta to retrieve them. For two years, Menelaus had brooded through fruitless negotiations with the Trojans and Hittites. There had been several minor skirmishes along the Anatolian coast while Agamemnon mustered allies and requisitioned transport and materiel for a massive assault on Troy.

At last, a Mycenaean messenger arrived carrying the official summons for my father to muster his host and join the Hellene fleet at Aulis. Because the news made him happy, it made me happy, too. Had I known he would be gone for so many years, I would have cried instead and begged him to stay. Losing my father was not worth getting my mother back.

On that last morning, my father's manservant helped him into his silver-studded bronze cuirass and fastened his greaves upon his shins. Menelaus bent down to let me pin on his cloak. My brother Aethiolas set the boar tusk helmet with its flowing horsehair crest upon his head. He exchanged final words with my grandfather, then held out his arms to gather me and Aethiolas in a crushing hug, making us a solemn promise that he would bring our mother and little brother home.

His blue cloak fluttered behind him in the breeze as his charioteer drove him south to the port of Helas. I did not see him again.

Six months after my father left for Troy, my grandfather sent me with my old nurse to Mycenae. How I dreaded going after hearing all those terrible stories! But Tyndareus insisted. It was for my own good as a princess and future queen, he said. With my mother gone and grandmother dead, only my aunt could provide me with a royal woman's proper education.

I cried when the mule cart carried me away from Therapne, and wept again when I boarded the ship and learned that sailing made me seasick. Princesses were not supposed to heave their breakfast over the side, no matter how polite and sympathetic the captain was about it. I wanted to go straight home, even when my nurse reminded me that Mycenae was a grand place. Did I not want to see the wonderful Lion Gate my grandfather Atreus had built, and the tomb of the hero Perseus?

"No!" I cried.

"Hush now, child," she chided. "You also have three princess-cousins who are going to be your friends."

Mycenae crouched aggressively on upon a low hill below Mount Charvati; it exuded an ominous air. On the southeastern side, the citadel faced a precipitous ravine, while farther to the south and west there was a sizeable, walled lower town containing multi-storied tenements, workshops, sanctuaries, an agora, and two massive tholoi, the larger one belonging to my grandfather Atreus, and the smaller one to my uncle Agamemnon.

I was secretly glad that Agamemnon was absent. On those few occasions when he had come to Sparta, his brutish physique and saturnine demeanor—inherited, people said, from his father and grandfather—intimidated all, including his brother's young children.

The Lion Gate made me think of him. No matter that the famous lions were lionesses, and the gate dedicated to Mother Dia, the structure had a hulking masculine aspect about it. The lionesses stood rampant upon an altar, guarding the sacred pillar-tree that was the royal house. Steatite heads faced outward, jaws agape in mid-roar. Real amber and obsidian had been set into the eye sockets, so that when the light caught them they gleamed like flame and honey, always watching those who came and went from the citadel, always threatening.

A third lioness dwelt in the citadel. She was flesh and blood, and awaited me in a painted antechamber at the summit of the palace.

To look upon my aunt, one would never realize that her sister and mother were such small and delicate beauties. No one ever praised Clytaemnestra for her good looks. Her hair was chestnut brown, and her cold gray eyes were set in a square, fleshy face. She was big-boned and imperious, and had been a strong athlete in her youth. One felt her formidable presence everywhere, from the storerooms to the galleries, and no one wanted to cross her. Although she had borne four living children, she was not a maternal woman, and made it clear from the first that she was taking me in only because duty demanded it.

Her maid brought me upstairs to the queen's apartment, where she welcomed me by dismissing my nurse. "An eleven-year-old girl is practically a woman," she coldly explained, "and does not require such attendants." Then she set down strict rules: there would be no running around the palace unattended, no excursions to the agora in the lower town, and no fraternizing with the servants.

My girl cousins came out to meet me. Iphigenia and Chrysothemis were lovely, with their mother's chestnut hair, and seemed nice, the kind of girls who liked dolls and dressing up, just like me. Elektra had the bright red hair that she and I, as well as my father and brothers, had inherited from Atreus and his mother Hippodamia. Elektra also had her mother's stolid looks, a face full of freckles, and greeted me with an impish, gap-toothed smile.

Clytaemnestra addressed me again once they left the room. "Your father and uncle have decided you will marry your cousin Orestes," she said matter-of-factly. "Mycenae and Sparta are to be united through one bloodline. Do you understand what I am telling you, young lady?"

I had always known one day I would make an important marriage with someone my elders chose, but Orestes was seven years younger than me, practically a baby. It would be like marrying Pleisthenes. "Yes, Aunt," I croaked.

She caught my reluctance and tightened her mouth disapprovingly. "You will learn to be a faithful wife. You will be useful. I will not tolerate a daughter-in-law who idles about or causes trouble. There's no room for your mother here."

My eyes stung with involuntary tears. It was not my fault my mother had run away with her lover! "Yes, Aunt."

Clytaemnestra barked an order at her lady-in-waiting, bidding her bring Orestes, then she turned back to me. "Dry your eyes, young lady. Princesses do not snivel." She thrust a linen cloth at me.

The lady-in-waiting went out, then returned with a middle-aged woman leading my youngest cousin by the hand.

I struggled to conceal my disappointment, while studying the little prince with his freckles, blue eyes, and reddish-gold hair. Orestes was just a baby. I wanted to marry a handsome hero, not a willful four-year old who picked his nose!

Orestes had not the slightest clue what was going on. When directed, I took his clammy little hand and walked with him to the queen's private altar. Orestes fussed and fidgeted. Getting him to repeat the oath took colossal patience and effort.

I settled into my new life at Mycenae. Clytaemnestra continued my lessons. Atreid kings believed in educating their children, sons and daughters both. We learned to read, calculate figures, and write the script the palace scribes used to make the tallies, because such a skill would give us a useful advantage where most people, even other kings and queens, were illiterate.

Iphigenia was the brightest, blessed by Apollo with the gift of music. She had a nightingale's voice, and could play the four-stringed phorminx, which I could never master; she even composed her own songs and sang them for guests in the megaron. Eleven-year-old Chrysothemis was pretty, with clever fingers for working wool and plying a needle. However, she was woefully empty-headed, unable to read and write much beyond her own name, a lack for which her mother constantly berated her.

Nine-year old Elektra could not read or write much, either, but she was terribly good with figures and always knew what was in the storerooms and how much; she was not so timid as Chrysothemis as to care what her mother thought about her lack of literacy. She was loud and mischievous, and delighted in lewd jokes and boyish pranks: catching lizards and spiders, slipping worms into Aegisthus's shoes, and snakes into Chrysothemis's sewing basket. When I told her how Spartan girls were allowed to exercise, and run outdoors and hunt, and even compete in their own athletic games, she envied me. "I want to follow hounds, but Mother won't let me." Elektra scrunched her freckled nose. "*She* does, you know."

Orestes was still too young for the schoolroom. I taught him how to count on his fingers and tried to teach him some signs, but he kept scribbling nonsense on the floor with the charcoal stick. He seemed bright enough. Maybe it was just best to play cat's cradle with him and let his pedagogue handle him when the time came.

Clytaemnestra scrutinized my every word and action. I had never tried harder in my life to please someone, to no avail. It was Iphigenia who did everything right, because she was her mother's favorite. Another girl with such beauty and talent might have become an insufferable bitch, but not Iphigenia. I liked her at once. She showed me around the palace that first day, and did all she could to make me feel welcome. What I did not like was having to compete with her. Iphigenia did not like it, either, and tried to reassure me. "Mother is very strict," she said. We exchanged sister-tokens and vowed to be friends forever.

Perhaps I would not have to stay long. The Trojan king Priam would surely relent once he saw the Hellene forces massed on the plain below his city. Once the war was over, my father would return with my mother and Pleisthenes. Then I would be able to return home to Sparta and have everything the way it was before.

AT THE HEIGHT OF A BLISTERING SUMMER when the grass on the citadel heights withered, Agamemnon's herald arrived bearing a letter.

The High King informed his wife that their daughter was to come straightaway to Aulis to marry Achilles. So Clytaemnestra sent for Iphigenia to tell her the news. I came along as far as the gallery, hoping my father had sent a message, too.

Fourteen-year-old Iphigenia glowed when Talthybius described how handsome, and noble her bridegroom was. He even presented her with a golden necklace that Achilles wished her to have as a bride gift. From then on, she talked of nothing else. I envied her the brave hero she was getting.

But Clytaemnestra was too level-headed to be enticed by handsome princes or beautiful jewels. After dismissing her daughter, she asked Talthybius a dozen hard questions, berating him like one of the servants when he hesitated or gave seemingly contradictory answers.

She asked why Agamemnon could not bring the bridegroom to Mycenae instead. "Is he so tied to this Trojan expedition that he can't spare a few days at home for his own child?"

Talthybius possessed a courtier's sly silver tongue. "Not at all, my queen! With the winds blowing against the fleet, the king needs to boost morale among his allies. What better way to accomplish this than with a royal wedding? He wishes to show his love for the princess by making her a happy bride, and to remind his followers that they are fighting for the faithful wives and daughters those vile Trojans would steal away."

"Hah! Agamemnon knows perfectly well that our sister was a willing accomplice in her so-called abduction." Clytaemnestra's disdainful exclamation rang through the megaron. "And where, exactly, does he plan to find the food and wine to hold this sumptuous wedding feast? We thought the men at Aulis were starving."

"The king has requisitioned wine, grain, and meat from his own estates to supply the feast."

Clytaemnestra might have yielded then, except for two glaring points.

First, Agamemnon did not want her to attend the wedding. "How absurd!" she remarked. "I am Iphigenia's mother, and a bride's mother always attends. Who else is going to help my daughter to her bridal bed?"

Talthybius kept his head bowed. "My queen, the king deeply regrets the necessity, but he relies upon you to rule in his absence. There is no one else he trusts with this important duty."

Snorting, she made a dismissive gesture. "And Agamemnon does *not* trust that squinting, senile old fool he appointed to chaperone us?" Lord Mekisteus, the distinguished fool in question, grumbled from his place near the dais. Clytaemnestra ignored him. As Talthybius started to speak, she silenced him with a warning finger and raised her other objection. "Does our husband know that Prince Achilles already has a wife and young son on Skyros. Does he plan to set her aside to marry Iphigenia? Her father will be greatly offended to have his family's honor so slighted."

Here, too, the herald had a ready answer. "Achilles does not live with the lady, my queen, and her father is but a petty king. King Agamemnon will compensate him with lavish gifts."

By now, it was obvious my father had not sent me any message. My handmaid hustled me away to bed, for it was very late. I wished she would have let me stay to hear the rest, because afterward I never knew exactly what the king's herald had said or done to convince my aunt to relent.

Iphigenia's excitement was contagious. On her last night at Mycenae, we enjoyed singing and dancing in the women's sanctuary. My cousin dedicated her doll to Lady Artemis and slept wrapped in fleeces on the floor before the altar.

At dawn, the priestesses led her from the sanctuary crowned with a diadem of scarlet poppies and wheat ears, and robed in yellow as soft as the morning sunshine. Iphigenia said goodbye to us all, then she climbed into the mule-drawn cart with her mother, who was determined to accompany her to her wedding whether Agamemnon liked it or not. Four dozen Mycenaean warriors armored in gleaming bronze had been dispatched to escort them. With them went livestock and carts laden with pithoi of vegetables, grain, and oil, and stacked with amphorae of wine for the wedding feast.

Aulis was a long distance from Mycenae. Timon showed us on a map sketched by a mariner on a yellowing old hide the route Iphigenia would have to take by both land and sea. He explained that it might be well into autumn before she and her mother returned.

Clytaemnestra knew that the winds at Aulis were blowing northeast, against the fleet and delaying its departure, but neither she nor anyone else at Mycenae ever suspected that those winds had anything to do with Iphigenia.

*****

I SAT ON A STONE BENCH at the edge of the great court, combing wool with my cousins and maid. The enclosed court with its smooth white stones and shady plane tree was a pleasant retreat in the afternoons when the petitioners had all gone home. The savory smells of baking bread, roasting meat, and frying onions came from the nearby kitchen. Orestes played by himself with a wooden stick and hoop; he stoutly refused to play with us because Elektra had humiliated him the other day when she tricked him into wearing girl's clothes and accompanying her across the crowded court.

All was serene until a shriek suddenly pierced the air, echoing around the courtyard. A ghastly wail that went on and on, like the scream of a wounded pig, and it came from the lower citadel. I sat straight up, stiff with horror. Chrysothemis's distaff fell from her hands. Orestes let his hoop roll and topple over, and rushed over to us. Elektra turned her head this way and that. "It's coming this way," she said.

Along the aithousa, the sentries came to attention. Our maid and Orestes' pedagogue started to usher us inside. "Someone has let loose a demon," Althaia said.

Clytaemnestra then appeared. She emerged from the purplish shadows of the south-facing stairs, and stumbled ashen-faced and disheveled into the court. She was robed in black tatters. Her hair hung loose and wild. Chrysothemis shrank back with a whimper. Orestes started to shake. I saw the crowd which had gathered around the queen, which was still growing, acquiring its own momentum. Catching up to us, it swept us along and up the stairs into the megaron. I held onto Althaia's hand, while protesting being jostled and shoved hither and thither.

I saw my aunt standing upon the dais like some terrible goddess of death and destruction. As I studied her, she cut the air with a single swift gesture, commanding silence.

"Iphigenia is dead!" she groaned. Dark circles ringed her swollen, bloodshot eyes. "She's dead. *Murdered by her own father!*" Her face twisted into something demonic. She shrieked again and clawed cheeks already scored with the marks of her fingernails until the blood flowed again.

Then she pointed a finger at the hearth and snarled, "I curse you,

Agamemnon, son of Atreus! I curse your limbs, I curse your breath, I curse your bones, I curse the very blood in your body!"

Amid the horrified gasps, the regent Mekisteus hobbled forward on his cane in a foolish attempt to correct her. "My lady queen, you have our heartfelt condolences for the princess, but to curse—"

"Shut your mouth!" Clytaemnestra rounded on him. Mekisteus flinched back. "Agamemnon is a child-killer. He's a backstabbing, infant-murdering pustule! I curse him with a mother's curse. Let him die as sudden and horrible a death as he inflicted on his own daughter."

"Stop saying those things!" Elektra dashed up onto the dais to confront her mother. I held back a gasp. "I don't believe you!"

Clytaemnestra viciously twisted her ear. "I don't care *what* you believe, you insolent brat!"

"You're a liar!" Breaking free, Elektra escaped howling from the megaron. Chrysothemis followed close on her heels in a flood of tears. Orestes started bawling because everyone else was shouting and crying; he clearly did not understand what was going on, except for the fact that his mother was very, very angry. His pedagogue lifted him up and carried him back to the nursery, leaving me alone with the maid in a maelstrom of insanity.

Iphigenia could not be dead. Agamemnon would never, ever murder his own daughter. Things like that only happened in the old stories. No. This was all a terrible mistake, an illusion. I was dreaming. Clytaemnestra was a nightmare creature. In a moment I would awake, and Iphigenia and her mother would still be on the road from Aulis.

It was no dream, though, but harsh reality. The pedagogue Timon later gave us the details. "The winds that plagued the fleet would not abate," he said. "Calchas the seer read the omens, and discovered that Lady Artemis had a grievance with the High King. Agamemnon killed a white hart near her sanctuary and then boasted he was a better hunter than she."

Again, it seemed illusory. Such cruel twists of fate only occurred in the stories; no real person would ever be so foolish. Timon went on to explain that Artemis had demanded the blood of Agamemnon's eldest daughter. The very goddess who looked after children, who protected virgin girls, ordering an innocent slain on her altar! "Artemis would never demand such a horrible thing!" I protested. "Iphigenia was consecrated to her service."

"Do you think the lives of insignificant mortals mean much to the gods? Even kings are nothing but playthings to them." Timon shook his head. "I heard that your father resisted until the captains threatened to seize the princess and cut her throat themselves. Then he gave in. Agamemnon invented the ruse as a kindness to his daughter, so she would not be afraid."

"But when she saw the altar and knife, and no bridegroom!" Chrysothemis exclaimed. "What, then?"

"I am sure he explained it to her before then," Timon answered, "so she would consent to the sacrifice."

"And what did Mother do?" Elektra wanted to know.

Timon often lost his patience with her, but the unusual circumstances and her obvious hurt made him sympathetic. "I am told she was held under guard until afterward."

Artemis might have demanded the sacrifice of Iphigenia. The gods might not regard us mortals as worthy of compassion, but the grieving, outraged Clytaemnestra could turn to the primeval powers of the earth for redress. Any woman could summon them who had just cause and the nerves for it. She could not punish Artemis, for even queens had to obey the gods. She could, however, turn the dark goddesses against Agamemnon.

Clytaemnestra had become a handmaiden of the Erinyes, that trio of dreadful goddesses who spoke for the wronged dead, on the journey from Aulis. She kept the citadel awake that night intoning terrible curses. Exhaustion brought a brief silence toward sunrise, but the quiet was fraught with tension. No one questioned that Clytaemnestra had the right to crave vengeance for her murdered daughter, but her frenzied rites and hoarsely voiced vows to make Agamemnon suffer could not possibly help her. He was her lord and husband. Even a woman as strong-willed as she had to obey.

Just before noon, the goddesses woke the demon inside her again. Marching down to the cult house, her women anxiously following at a distance, she removed the sacred labrys from its plinth and embarked upon a orgiastic whirlwind of destruction. Anything belonging to the king fell under the double axe: his furniture, the frescoes on the walls of his apartment, his painted vessels and intricately woven hangings. His servants, who tried to stop her, discovered to their detriment that she could wield that labrys with a man's skill, strength, and utter ruthlessness.

Chrysothemis fled sobbing in terror when a young groom left his entrails on the stuccoed floor. Timon had already hustled Elektra and Orestes to the safety of the nursery, once again leaving me alone with the maid Althaia, who in her fright could do little more than flatten herself against the wall and hope not to be noticed; she was useless.

I should have run after my cousins, yet some curious impulse compelled me to stay and see what would happen next. So I joined the queen's maids, and hoped to disappear among them.

Clytaemnestra finished hacking Agamemnon's kingly headboard with its decorations of inlaid lapis and ivory to pieces. She was heaving great breaths like a bellows. Her face was flushed from exertion. Sweat glistened on her brow and dampened the neck of her blood-spattered smock. Feral triumph glowed in her eyes as she scanned our horrified faces. "That's how it's done!" Her voice was hoarse and rasping.

And then she recognized me, hiding among her women. "You!" Her lips curled into a snarl. She drew her arm back, and the next thing I knew something heavy thudded into the doorjamb beside my head. A woman behind me screamed. I thought Clytaemnestra had thrown a footstool at me and missed. Then I saw it—the labrys, its bronze blade quivering in the plastered jamb a mere three inches away—and almost lost my bladder.

"Come here!" she snarled.

I edged forward. Clytaemnestra grabbed my shoulder and shoved me toward the splintered bed where she dragged the embroidered scarlet and blue coverlet from what was left of the mattress, and dumped it on me. "Take this."

I staggered under the weight. Agamemnon's bed had been almost seven feet long, and the coverlet had been woven upon one of the great standing looms in the weaving house; it was the months-long work of half a dozen women. Clytaemnestra ordered her maids into the room, shoved split cushions and torn wall hangings at them, and directed them downstairs. As if in sympathy, she took the coverlet from me, and replaced it with a more manageable fleece rug. "Go!"

In the megaron, my aunt hefted the coverlet onto the great hearth, without considering how all that heavy wool would smother the fire. Smoke billowed into the chamber; it stung my eyes and caught in my throat, but that did not deter her. Clytaemnestra called for more torches. She seized linens and cushions from the maidservants to heap onto the hearth. "Burn it all! And bring those bitches!"

At first, I did not know who she meant. But then she turned on old Lord Mekisteus, who had come down to try to reason with her, and said, "Fetch his sluts. Have them hurled them into the ravine."

"But, great queen, only condemned criminals and—"

She fetched him a blinding slap across the face. "Throw those bitches off the walls!"

My stinging eyes would not let me see anymore. I was crying. Clytaemnestra was going to kill the king's concubines. She was not going to stop with wrecking his rooms and burning his things. Not even killing one of his servants had satiated her bloodlust.

One of the queen's maids finally took pity on me and helped me escape the megaron. Safe in the nursery with my cousins, I heard women shrieking for mercy elsewhere in the citadel. Agamemnon's concubines, whom I had never seen. I kept visualizing the labrys stuck in the doorjamb beside my head, and replaying the thud it made as it struck. Clytaemnestra had wanted to kill me, too. What had I ever done to her?

Mekisteus fled Mycenae that very night.

Chapter Four

IPHIGENIA HAD BEEN BURIED in the sanctuary of Artemis at Aulis, as befitted a sacrificial victim. But Clytaemnestra ignored the priestesses who warned her not to disturb the goddess's precinct. She scorned their criticisms, their febrile efforts to console her, and had Iphigenia disinterred from her grave to rest near those who had loved her most.

On a gloomy autumn day, Iphigenia's funeral procession threaded the short distance from the palace to Agamemnon's tholos tomb. Rain had deluged the citadel during the night, and the distant thunderheads lowering over the mountains promised another storm before dusk.

Swathed head to toe in black, her face painted chalk-white, Clytaemnestra presided like the goddess of the dead over the funerary rites. She was calm now, grim and silent. Only the professional mourners dared utter a sound, and then those women sounded like harpies with their ululating shrieks.

People tossed cypress and late-blooming flowers before the funeral cart. Iphigenia had had no prothesis rites before the burial; she had arrived from Aulis already shrouded in her grave clothes. Because Iphigenia's corpse was no longer fresh, the women of the palace could not wash and anoint her, dress her in her finest garments, speak gently to her spirit, and open the megaron doors to let the mourners see her—all the careful, tender little ceremonies designed to ease the dead into the hereafter. We glimpsed her only at a distance, her shrouded corpse lying in the bed of the cart surrounded by all her grave goods.

The procession reached the open area before the tomb. A brisk breeze fluttered our skirts and veils, making us draw our cloaks closer. Here and there, blooms tumbled from the cart. The professional mourners with their wild hair and raiment and torn cheeks ceased their wailing.

Clytaemnestra turned to face the dromos, the long sloping passageway leading down into the tomb. Crouching, she slapped the flagstones with the flat of her hand, summoning forth the dark powers of the earth. "Persephone, dread queen! Hades, dreadful dark lord!" she cried. "Attend us!"

Six pallbearers, all of them distinguished lords of the court, moved forward to shift Iphigenia's bier from the cart bed and onto their shoulders to carry her into the tomb.

"No!" Clytaemnestra flung out her arm, commanding them to halt. I did not understand what she was doing. Why was she interrupting the rites? Iphigenia's eternal repose had already been disturbed once. She had to be laid in the tomb, or else her restless shade would haunt the living.

Clytaemnestra began to circle the cart with slow and stately steps, her black draperies billowing around her. And as she moved, she sang in her rough and throaty voice Demeter's lament for her lost daughter Koré. No green shoots would burst forth and flower, no harvest would be gathered, not until the grieving mother found her daughter again. Winter would reign forever, and starving mortals wail in anguish as Clytaemnestra the queen of Mycenae cried out now.

On the final circuit she abruptly halted, braced both arms on the driver's ledge, and hauled herself up into the cart so she was standing among the vessels and garlands surrounding her dead daughter's body.

I had never seen anyone interfere with the deceased, before or since. My grandfather had paused over my grandmother Leda's bier as the pallbearers lifted her from the funeral cart and thoughtfully touched the shroud as though inspecting the linen. But this was not like that. Whatever demon had inhabited Clytaemnestra on her homecoming, it manifested itself again, so she forgot all propriety and dread, and loosened the yellowing linens to gaze upon her daughter's decomposing face.

Her howls shattered the air; the mother and maenad inside her was screaming, oblivious to the scandalized exclamations and gasps from the crowd. I shuddered as she lifted Iphigenia in her arms and clasped the corpse to her breast. Iphigenia's chestnut tresses spilled from the shroud; it came away from her skull in clumps. As the wind shifted, it wafted an odor of putrescence toward us.

Orestes whimpered next to me, reminding me that he was present. He should stayed behind, or at least his nurse should have been with him—oh, where was that absentminded old woman? I bent down to pull his small body against me, simultaneously urging him to bury his face in my skirt so he would not have to look anymore. Timon reached for his hand to hold it.

Above the moans, we heard a chariot's clattering wheels and harness bells jingling in the distance, signaling a late arrival. A nobleman's chariot rolled past the amazed townsfolk who were compelled to form a hasty aisle to accommodate it, and wheeled to a halt.

Timon grunted when he saw the chariot's dark-haired passenger step to the ground. The man removed a magnificent purple cloth, slung it over his arm, and approached the cart with its two occupants, one living and one dead.

Clytaemnestra obviously knew who he was, because she savagely rejected his advance. "Get away from my daughter, you vile spawn of incest! Crawl back to your lair where you belong."

Elektra yanked on Timon's sleeve. "Who is he?"

"Aegisthus." The old pedagogue spat out the name like a curse.

I recognized the man's name. He was my second cousin.

Aegisthus was an abomination with a history. He was the sole surviving son of my great-uncle Thyestes, who had ravaged his own daughter to sire the boy. According to the tale, Atreus married the princess shortly thereafter without realizing she was his niece; she must have been fostered elsewhere for him not to have recognized her, or maybe he simply forgot that his brother had a daughter. So Pelopia's belly had swelled with her father's monstrous seed, which Atreus naturally assumed was his. When the child was born, so the story went, Pelopia tried to abandon it, and her private shame, in the Chavos ravine. Atreus's herdsmen had found the infant and returned him to his father.

Aegisthus had later learned the secret of his birth and helped his real father murder Atreus; he was only seven years old then. I heard he took immense pride in his name, Goat-Strength, which had been given him because, it was said, a nanny goat had suckled him in the ravine.

That was the tale told in Sparta. In the Lion Court of Mycenae, everyone kept their mouths shut.

Aegisthus had nothing to boast about. When Agamemnon and Menelaus took back their birthright, the thirteen-year old bastard had escaped with his father and lived with him in penurious exile on some remote island until old Thyestes finally expired. Nowadays, Aegisthus moved among powerful friends throughout the Peloponnese. He was always careful never to stay in one place too long, and skillfully exploited the laws of hospitality to shield him from Agamemnon's retribution.

He must not have feared Agamemnon too much, now that the High King had gone overseas to fight at Troy. At the very least, he felt secure enough to return to Mycenae for the day.

It was not surprising that Clytaemnestra maligned him, for most people, when they mentioned him at all, spoke Aegisthus's name with derision. All the slanders and ghoulish stories had led me to form a mental portrait of a stunted man with cloven feet, pointed yellow teeth, and huge pimples cratering his face. Therefore, it came as a complete shock to discover that this ill-favored second cousin was quite the opposite.

Aegisthus was about thirty years old, sinewy and narrow-waisted and clean-shaven in the Cretan style, with the serpentine lovelocks favored by the young men of that island. Charming and intelligent, he was also vain and cruel; his monstrousness came from within.

Kneeling on the flagstones, he extended the purple robe to my aunt. "Gracious queen, I have not come to trespass on this sad occasion, but to mourn with you. I, too, know what it is to suffer Agamemnon's cruelty." His quavering voice rose toward a crescendo; it sounded so contrived, so wheedling and transparent that even a babe would have seen through his act. "Like his father, he feels no remorse in the slaughter of children, while you—"

"Shut your mouth!"

Aegisthus touched his forehead to the ground, but it seemed to me that he smiled as he did so. "Forgive me my outburst. My only intention in coming here was to commiserate with your loss." When his voice broke, I imagined a perfectly timed tear sliding down his cheek. "Banish me if you must, but take this robe to cover your daughter with. She should not go into the dark tomb in that shabby linen, but be shrouded like a princess in royal purple and gold."

Aegisthus's coaxing worked its magic. Clytaemnestra began to relent where no one else had been able to comfort her. That was the last time she wept openly for her daughter.

Clytaemnestra moved to the driver's seat to accept his gift, then allowed him to assist her to the ground. As the pallbearers lifted Iphigenia's bier onto their shoulders and the procession began to move down the dromos, he offered my aunt his arm and spoke tenderly to her, urging her to disregard any slanders regarding his character. Of *course*, he was at her service. He would do absolutely *anything* he could to assist her in this troubled time.

How could she listen to him? Aegisthus was a walking curse, an abomination. Nothing about him was sincere. His presence would taint the tomb, Iphigenia's remains, and everything else he touched.

A light drizzle started to fall. Shivering in my cloak, I drew my hood over my veil. Soon we would all be able to go indoors again, where it was warm. Elektra scrunched up her nose as she craned her neck trying for a better view down the passageway, yet to no avail. All one could see from the head of the dromos were shadows moving against the glow from the oil lamps burning within. Had we been a little older, my cousins and I would have been allowed to carry the offerings into the tomb and arrange them around the bier.

Afterward, Clytaemnestra carried out the customary blood sacrifice, as Agamemnon would have done had he been present. Aegisthus assumed a position near the altar as a priestess-acolyte from the cult house poured the purifying water from an ewer over my aunt's hands. A second priestess sprinkled the sacred meal over the sacrificial heifer's head. Hyrtios, the high priest of Zeus, waited with the mallet behind the heifer.

Clytaemnestra took the labrys—the very same double axe with which she had almost split my head in two—from the high priest's attendant and held it aloft where everyone could see. "Hades, dread king of the world below," she intoned in a loud, steady voice. "Persephone, dread queen of Hades. Receive this blood offering for my daughter, Iphigenia."

Yet she did not wait for the mallet. The heifer's feed had been drugged that morning, so it should not have mattered except as a matter of custom, but at the last second the animal moved. The labrys gashed the heifer's shoulder rather than severed her spine. As she lowed, tossing her head, her mortal wound spattered blood onto Clytaemnestra's gown and Aegisthus's tunic. The meaning was clear: she had not consented to the sacrifice.

People cried out at the bad omen, hissing Aegisthus's name. Clytaemnestra shoved the labrys at the high priest, and seized the sacrificial knife from one of the priestesses to end the heifer's agony. A swift cut and the heifer dropped to her knees. Acolytes swarmed in to dismember the carcass for the burnt offering.

I gulped back my shock. Clytaemnestra was the paramount high priestess of Mycenae and knew very well how to dispatch a blood sacrifice. How could she make such a colossal mistake at such a crucial moment? For the sacrificial animal not to consent offended the gods. For Iphigenia's afterlife, it meant her ghost would find no rest.

Worst of all, Clytaemnestra invited Aegisthus to the funeral feast. Within the week, he had moved his possessions and servants into the palace.

When Agamemnon heard the news, he sent a furious missive chastising her for disturbing Iphigenia's burial. He ordered her to evict the bastard son of Thyestes from his hearth and take Mekisteus back as her advisor, or else there would be dire consequences. Clytaemnestra simply ignored the message and pretended not to receive any subsequent ones, even when the High King's herald placed them directly into her hands.

Meanwhile, Aegisthus stayed on as her most honored guest. Clytaemnestra lavished him with presents, seated him beside her at feasts and festivals, and allowed him access to the megaron on those days when she received petitioners. At night, the entire citadel could hear their lovemaking.

Elektra and I occasionally crept into the queen's empty sitting room when the guards were gone and her maids were asleep. We spied on the lovers through the bedroom curtain. Sometimes, we discovered them heaving and groaning, their bodies fused together to make some grotesque, two-backed, eight-limbed monster, but more often than not we had to wait so long to venture out that we arrived too late to watch them rutting and instead had to settle for their post-coital conversation.

Aegisthus often expressed his frustration at not being able to ride out on the hunt; the moment he left the protection of the citadel, Agamemnon's agents, lying in wait for just such an opportunity, would murder him.

Clytaemnestra remained unsympathetic. "You took that risk when you came here."

Once, he talked to her about his youth: his confusion and loneliness at a court where his half-brothers were much older than he and hated him; his mother's madness, for which he had been mercilessly teased, and her eventual suicide; and his resentment for the high position and power he thought he had been denied. Hearing him speak, realizing his sarcasm and oiliness were calluses he had grown against those who had hurt him, one could almost feel sorry for him. My pity for him never lasted, for like a wounded animal Aegisthus lashed out at everyone.

One night, he lay naked in bed with his arms tucked behind his head, and expounded on a thoroughly different subject. "It's too bad Calchas didn't tell Agamemnon to sacrifice Elektra instead. Such a brat!" Beside me, Elektra hissed sharply between her teeth. "Did you know the child called me a snake just this afternoon?"

Clytaemnestra said harshly, "You must have deserved it."

"Now, how can you say such a thing?" Aegisthus's mock-astonishment was palpable. It was a confusing and distasteful game they played with each other. "I absolutely *adore* your children."

She twisted around to smack his cheek. "Shut up. You *are* a snake." Then she hunkered down on her side, facing the wall, and hugged an embroidered cushion to her ample bosom. "Elektra might be a brat, but she's mine, and don't you ever forget it. Next time, let Menelaus give up his own daughter."

I did not want to hear any more.

I never again went with my cousin to eavesdrop on their sexual encounters. Who knew what other hurtful things they might say? I judged it better not to chance overhearing.

Although we never discussed it among ourselves, my cousins and I were all afraid. Iphigenia's death and Aegisthus's arrival had awakened our collective terrors, making the gruesome old stories that much more real. I suffered nightmares about Agamemnon sending another messenger, a harbinger of death wearing Aegisthus's face, bearing orders to select and bind a second princess on the altar. It was always me he chose, pointing his finger and leering. *Come here, little bird.*

Aegisthus had started calling me that, embellishing his pet name for me with spurious affection.

I knew what he did with little birds. He liked to wring the necks of sacrificial doves, twisting off their heads ever so slowly, savoring the way the fragile bones cracked, relishing the way the bird struggled in its death agonies before going limp in his hands.

Chapter Five

Clytaemnestra ordered laborers to open Agamemnon's tholos, air out the burial chamber, and prepare a place for the slain king and his companions. Though it was a wife's duty to prepare her husband's corpse for the prothesis, she left the washing and anointing of the corpse to menials, and canceled the viewing.

My maid Althaia gleaned gossip from the queen's maids and brought me additional details. "She's even going to bury the king's followers and the foreign concubine with him."

Clytaemnestra hired the finest professional mourners in Argolis. She sent to Midea, the king's own estate, for foodstuffs and wine to furnish the funeral feast, and selected the grave goods. Yet when presented with the immense, glittering Trojan treasure that had been Agamemnon's share of the spoils, she suddenly became stingy, mixing in old, disused furniture, chipped vessels, and battered armor with the better items. In the meantime, I saw her wearing new jewels, and Aegisthus flaunted gold and silver ornaments, a silver-studded sword, and a gold drinking cup—wedding gifts they gave themselves from the Trojan spoils.

Hypocrite. While Clytaemnestra denounced my mother as a whore, she openly consorted with her lover, who would become her husband the very night of the funeral feast; she could not even wait a decent interval.

A scathing reprimand from the ruling body of the Argive assembly went unheeded, even when they sent a royal envoy. Aegisthus delighted in playing the hospitable king. He heaped the envoy with the traditional guest-gifts and lent a polite ear to the assembly's grievances as though he seriously meant to take their advice under consideration.

Plasters and painters returned to the king's apartment to retouch work they had begun before Agamemnon's return, only now the bright frescoes and rich furnishings belonged to a usurper.

Aegisthus's supporters came to the wedding feast and received lavish gifts from him and the queen. Agamemnon's gold went to the men who had helped murder him. I despised those ruffians, the way they insulted us princesses and mocked the absent Orestes. I hated how they molested the servant girls, who clearly did not like them, either. Clytaemnestra tolerated the nuisance as long as his retainers did not break anything or kill anyone, and Aegisthus himself kept his indiscretions with the servant girls private.

On the funeral morning, dozens of noblemen and their wives poured in from throughout the surrounding area, cramming the citadel to capacity. Clytaemnestra received the mourners in the megaron, where for the first time before an audience she spun the elaborate fiction she had crafted to explain the deaths.

"Faithful Talthybius told me my dear husband was in such a terrible mood that day." Talthybius had told her nothing; he had not even been there. "We never even expected him that afternoon, but the next day. What happened was all a terrible misunderstanding!"

"Indeed," commented Cylarabes, Argos's Lord Ambassador to Mycenae.

Clytaemnestra blotted a theatric tear with the corner of her black-edged veil. "What a horrible scene! There has always been bad blood between Lord Aegisthus and King Atreus's sons, but this was a terrible, tragic accident. Lord Aegisthus was merely acting as a loyal kinsman, advising us in matters where a woman's soft hand would not suffice. He would have been gone when Agamemnon arrived, had the timing not been so bungled."

"Yes, I can imagine just *where* a man's firm hand might be useful," Cylarabes observed drily. Behind him, a pair of ladies covered their mouths with their hands to stifle their titters.

Clytaemnestra stared him down. "It came to blows, right here where we're standing." Her scarlet mouth twitched at the corners, curving into a poisonous little smile. "Agamemnon's poor concubine! That unfortunate Trojan princess miscarried from sheer fright and died right there."

She related all these details, knowing her audience was not at all taken in by her playacting. And why should they be? By now, everyone knew how she had cursed Agamemnon after Iphigenia's death, and how she had carried on her affair with Aegisthus.

"Where is Prince Orestes?" Cylarabes asked. "A man's faithful son and heir should be the one to preside over his funeral rites."

Clytaemnestra provided a ready explanation for that, too. "The commotion startled him. He has gone into hiding, as frightened little boys will do."

Aegisthus made his entrance just in time for the first libation, amid much grumbling and muttering. He, too, wore black, along with a contrite expression. When addressed, he repeated Clytaemnestra's story almost verbatim. No one believed him, either.

Pallbearers brought the king's bier into the great court for the procession, which stretched from the palace to the royal tholos: a shuffling line of black-clad courtiers, ambassadors, priests, merchants, and scribes who had come to pay their respects to the dead king.

Agamemnon's tholos tomb gleamed in the sunshine, its whitewashed apex thrusting up against a clear blue sky. At the end of the dromos, a monolithic façade of red porphyry and mottled green Laconian marble inset polished double doors standing fifteen feet high hinted at the splendor within.

No amount of alabaster and marble and bronze could disguise the fact that this was a tomb; not even a High King's riches could defeat death. Dozens of flickering lamps allowed a macabre play of light and shadow upon the walls. I could barely make out the vaulted ceiling worked with interlocking spirals, rosettes, and acanthus leaves. Myrrh and crocus oil perfumed the space, and the doors had been left open since yesterday to banish all rankness, but death had a very distinct odor and nothing could mask the putrescence of a grave sealed for seven years.

Chrysothemis reached for my hand, clutching it tightly as we entered the tomb together.

Elektra was not with us. Yesterday morning, Aegisthus's men had dragged her from the palace and taken her away. They had pulled her hair and struck her like a common slave as she dug in her heels to resist them. The entire citadel had heard her shouting obscenities against her mother and Aegisthus, accusing them of sacrilege, regicide, and denouncing them as usurpers. Chrysothemis and I were too afraid to intervene, to ask questions. Better to remain inconspicuous lest we find ourselves dragged away, too.

A short time later, Clytaemnestra had called us to her sitting room to explain, although not before she reprimanded Chrysothemis for her hysterical weeping. "Calm down, you foolish child. You should be rejoicing. This is Elektra's wedding day!" Clytaemnestra exclaimed. "She has married the prince of goatherds and moved into a thatch and mud palace." In the ensuing silence, the queen allowed herself a venomous smile. "I understand he's quite handy with the rod."

In the tomb, Chrysothemis leaned against me and sobbed. I drew my veil over my nose; it did little to shut out the horrible stench, but concealed my disgust with Aegisthus. Already playing the king, assuming the role of chief mourner and using Agamemnon's own golden rhyton to pour the customary drink offering.

"Hades, dread lord, and Persephone, dark queen," he intoned, "receive this libation for the shade of Agamemnon Atreides, High King of Mycenae, Argos, and Achaea, overlord of the Islands, and conqueror of Troy." Dark red liquid splashed like blood onto the floor beside the king's shrouded bier.

Aegisthus next drew Agamemnon's sword from its red leather sheath, slid the blade under his right foot, and bent it double.

Orestes should have been the one to pour the libation and dispatch his father's sword. Aegisthus's trackers had not found him or we would have heard. Let swift Hermes continue to watch over him, I prayed, so he might return one day and deal with his father's murderers!

It was so cramped in the burial chamber that we in front were pressed against each other and in danger of falling across the bier. Agamemnon's corpse was shrouded in white linen so gossamer-fine that one could just start to recognize the dead man's features underneath. I heard a woman nearby remark about the lack of smell, and a man explain to her that when a corpse bled out first the stink was much less. When he next started to relate an anecdote about a prince's burial where the corpse had been so ripe that it was nothing but a mass of seething grave worms, she and several other women swiftly hushed him.

I tried to breathe while averting my gaze from the corpse. Agamemnon's shroud revealed more shadow than detail; my aunt would have made certain that no one could see his many wounds. Yet in her miserliness and spite, she had not provided the traditional royal death mask. I overheard people commenting on the lack thereof, complaining about the flouting of custom.

We started to disperse, making way for the kinsmen of the slain companions. Those men had been cremated to conceal the true manner of their deaths, and their funerary urns arranged in places of honor around the king's bier. Chrysothemis, still crushing my hand in hers, directed my attention toward the tomb's other occupant. Iphigenia's burial had been moved to one side. Fresh garlands lent color to her moldering shroud. "It's so sad," my last remaining cousin whispered in my ear. "Iphigenia should have been here with us."

"If she had been," I whispered back, "then there would have been no funeral today."

Just before we exited the funereal gloom, I noticed the Trojan concubine's plain urn standing alone in a corner. Cassandra had no grave goods and no mourners to provide food or drink offerings. It saddened me to think that my aunt nursed such spite against my uncle's unfortunate captive that she could not have spared even a strand of cheap beads or a plain wooden spindle to help speed Cassandra's shade to the hereafter.

Chapter Six

Late spring showers kept us indoors.

Chrysothemis took it badly. Having spent the frigid winter months gossiping with the maids, spinning and weaving to her heart's content, she now panicked over a single day's confinement. She hated silence and gloomy things, and had no strength to confront the ghosts of Mycenae. Sometimes she let her spindle fall idle and stared blankly at the wall, tears streaming down her face.

After Elektra left, Chrysothemis took no pleasure stitching the bright embroideries she worked so well. And she refused to weave as it meant facing the wall where someone could surprise her from behind. She grew pensive and wary. Her hypervigilance, mingled with my own fears, convinced me to keep a lamp burning at night while I slept. A true daughter of kings ought to be fearless, but in the end a princess was still just a woman.

As the days passed, Chrysothemis sometimes broke the silence with soft utterances. "I wish Mother would let me get married." She twisted yarn between her fingers, drawing out a fine, even thread as the spindle twirled. "I'm more than old enough."

Chrysothemis's desire to marry and leave home was a familiar refrain, though now she dared not ask her mother for the privilege. Rumors were going around that Aegisthus intended for his bastard son, a bad-tempered eight-year-old brat he had sired on a slave woman, to succeed him as king of Mycenae. King Aegisthus. The whole notion sickened me.

I strove to hold my distress in check when the bastard boy barged into Orestes' chamber to rummage through his things. Aletes knocked over the gods on his rival's altar, took his jewelry, and tore up his cherished letters from Agamemnon. Gods forgive me for not having rescued them! I had not wanted to violate the sanctity of my cousin's possessions.

Chrysothemis opened her mouth to keep talking, yet only a choking gasp emerged, and her gaze was fixed on a point beyond my shoulder. The doorway, I surmised. I turned to see what was amiss

Aegisthus. Acknowledging us with his peculiar brand of mock courtesy, he entered the sitting room and stopped beside my chair, but it was my cousin he was looking at. "I see a certain lady's tongue is as busy as her hands," he said. "What are we chattering about today, Princess?"

Chrysothemis stared at him with large, terrified eyes. Aegisthus took a perverse satisfaction in toying with his inferiors, like a cat tormenting a mouse before making the kill.

"Ah," he drawled, after giving her a moment to answer. "As usual, nothing at all."

His fingers clamped down on the back of my chair. "My dear little bird, your aunt wishes to see you."

I choked back sudden panic. "She does?"

"You say that as though you've done something wrong." Aegisthus bent down to regard me with a knowing little smile. I felt his hot breath on my neck. "I can't imagine *what* you could've done."

A true daughter of kings was fearless, I remembered. "Has she said why?" This time, my voice sounded steadier. "She never sends for me."

"'Why' is irrelevant, young lady. You are to come at once." Straightening, he extended his hand to me. Lacking another option, I set aside my embroidery hoop and got to my feet without his help.

He stopped me in the deserted corridor, claimed the hand I had refused him, and raised it to his lips while holding my gaze. "Dear Hermione," he breathed, lingering much too long over my knuckles. "I wonder who is going to claim you now that your fiancé is gone."

Revulsion tempted me to wrench my hand away, yet caution kept me still. Aegisthus's lips curved in a sly smile as he turned my hand over to flick his tongue over my palm. My fingers twitched with the urge to curl into a fist and make it impossible for him to continue his disgusting attempt at seduction. "That is for my father and grandfather to decide."

"Hmm, but you are here and your grandfather is in Sparta." The point of his tongue teased the hollow of my wrist. It was like being licked by a lizard. "Your father has not yet returned home."

"I thought my aunt wished to see me."

His lips, replacing his tongue, grazed my pulse. "There is no rush."

I concentrated on pulling my scattered thoughts together. "Should an uncle be meddling with his niece?"

Aegisthus released me, though not entirely. He braced his left arm against the wall, trapping me on my right. "Ah, but you're Helen's daughter." With his free hand, he traced his fingertips over my left breast. I suppressed a shiver. "Does she have the same lustrous red hair and creamy white skin as you?" He leaned in, so his voice caressed my ear. "But you are much younger than she is, a virgin girl. I wonder..."

Then, laughing, he chucked me under the chin and drew away, leaving me speechless. "Let's not keep your aunt waiting."

I was still trembling when he led me into the queen's apartment. Clytaemnestra's sitting room was luxurious. Inlaid tables, painted vessels, and embroidered scarlet hangings and cushions worked with gold thread made this the most sumptuous chamber in the entire palace. I used to be envious of this room in the days before my nightmares daubed the walls with blood.

Clytaemnestra held a wax tablet and stylus in her hand as she perused the citadel accounts. "Sit down, Hermione." She indicated a high-backed chair across from her. "I have news from Sparta."

Those five words cut through my apprehension to offer hope. "Has my father returned?" Aegisthus had just claimed otherwise, but I preferred not to believe anything he said.

"No, not quite." Clytaemnestra handed me a sheet of papyrus. Papyrus meant a letter from an important person, for only the wealthy could afford to import the costly Egyptian writing material. "It's from your grandfather. Winter storms diverted your parents to Egypt, where they are now guests in Pi-Ramesses while Menelaus finshes repairing his ships. But when he does come home, he will expect to find you there waiting for him. So Tyndareus has sent for you. You will be leaving within the week."

"Parents" meant my mother was still alive. I perused the missive to verify the news. Tyndareus wrote infrequently, even though Clytaemnestra sent regular reports about me. The letter he wrote now was terse, laconic, a mere paragraph informing my aunt that my father had been delayed, and that it was time for me to come home and assume a woman's responsibilities.

Ten words or fifty, it did not matter. I was leaving Mycenae, escaping, going home.

"I hope you speak well of your time here," Clytaemnestra said.

I caught the ominous note in her voice. Aegisthus's presence loomed behind me. Flustered, I fumbled for words. "Of course. I-I am very blessed to have had your hospitality."

Clytaemnestra bestowed an enigmatic smile upon me. "This has been a very difficult time for all. I'm sure that you've heard many rumors about your uncle's death, but the bloodshed that day was a terrible accident." Aegisthus braced his hands on the back of my chair. I imagined him throttling me the moment I gave a wrong answer. "I've been told you were wandering near the megaron just before the trouble began."

Denying it would have exacerbated the situation; Aegisthus must have told her everything. "Elektra said men were coming." I focused on keeping my composure, on not betraying any more than necessary. "I went downstairs to see if it was true." I sucked in a breath. I was shaking all over. Surely Clytaemnestra could hear my pounding heartbeat. "Uncle Aegisthus found me. He told me I was mistaken, and sent me back to my room."

"She's *such* a sensible girl." Aegisthus smothered every word in honey. "So obedient."

Yet Clytaemnestra kept watching me, scrutinizing me like a serpent contemplating its prey. "Indeed. But as I recall, her room is within earshot of the megaron. I'm afraid she must have heard something."

Her clinical detachment pricked my fear to even greater heights. I knew the next few moments would determine my fate. All those sleepless nights I had lain awake rehearsing possible answers should anyone question me, yet now it took all my will to remain calm and remember. "Yes. I heard a terrible commotion coming from the megaron." My aunt must have heard my voice shaking and my teeth rattling. "Men fighting. It frightened me."

"You were wise to stay away. Agamemnon always had such a hot temper. Besides, a brawl between rival kinsmen is no place for a woman. That poor concubine was proof enough of that." Clytaemnestra's smile softened slightly. I had given the correct answer. I had passed the test.

CLYTAEMNESTRA AND AEGISTHUS loaded me with gifts suitable for a marriageable young princess and arranged a modest feast in my honor. I received new clothes and jewels, iris oil, new bronze needles, and ribbons for my hair: more treasures in one day than I had received in the last seven years. I saw the gifts for what they were. My guardians were trying to buy my silence.

On my last day at Mycenae, as the servants decorated the megaron with fragrant garlands and the cooks roasted meat and baked bread for that evening's feast, Clytaemnestra took me down to the cult house to petition the gods to safeguard me during my voyage home.

Mycenae's cult house contained a network of chambers: a room for the entire pantheon upon a painted altar, another for the bloodless offerings, a storeroom for the ritual vessels, a lustral chamber with a ceramic tub where purification rites took place, and an area where the house snake dwelt. On the other side of the building, men had their own rooms for worship.

Iphigenia used to assist with the offerings, as the eldest daughter of the house always did. Those duties now fell to me. Clytaemnestra had never turned to her surviving daughters to help or comfort her.

My aunt began arranging the deities upon the altar, selecting those who most required appeasement. "In Sparta, tending the immortal gods will be your responsibility."

I acknowledged her comment with a nod. Clytaemnestra poured milk and honeyed wine onto the three-legged offering table before the altar, and repositioned several of the ceramic votaries so they faced the gods in perpetual worship. Then she raised her arms, palms facing outward. I mirrored her actions as befit an attending priestess.

"Swift-running Hermes, receive this sweet libation of milk and honey," she intoned. "Watch over this woman Hermione, the daughter of Menelaus and Helen, during her journey home. Poseidon, Earth-Shaker and Father of the Sea, receive this sweet libation of milk and honey. Watch over this woman Hermione, daughter of Menelaus and Helen, during her journey home."

Then it was my turn to placate Artemis. I saluted the goddess's image with an uncertain heart. Even though I kept faith with her as every virgin girl must, Lady Artemis was also the goddess whose anger at Agamemnon had claimed Iphigenia. "Artemis, Mistress of the Winds," I said solemnly, "receive this sweet libation of milk and honey. Watch over me." Dare I trust her safeguard me? "Bless my ship with favorable winds on my journey home."

Together, we bowed deeply to the immortals then left the chamber to let them feast upon the libations while we offered milk to the house snake in the sunny inner court.

Once we finished the morning rites, Clytaemnestra did not lead me back to the palace but onto the circuit wall above the ancient Perseid grave circle. A light breeze played over the ramparts. As I wondered what we were doing there, she spoke, "I see very little of your mother in you."

Coming from her, it was a compliment. I kept my mouth shut, knowing her observations were more her thinking out loud than an invitation to engage her in conversation.

Clytaemnestra gazed out over the tiled roofs of the lower town. "Menelaus should have killed the slut. But no, he waited a moment too long to run her through. Men are so weak when it comes to beautiful women. One look at your mother's tits was all it took, I hear. The sword between his legs rose and the one in his hand fell."

Again, she was thinking aloud, repeating a crude joke Aegisthus had told several months ago. "Oh, I know," she continued. "He must keep her alive if he wishes to remain king in Sparta. But no one ever said he couldn't beat or disfigure her. She ought to have that perfect face slashed, and be flogged through the streets of Therapne. She deserves to have a daughter taken from her, as mine was taken from me."

A chill passed through me that did not come from the morning breeze. I had never thought to hear that sentiment voiced again after so many years. Her words recalled the labrys striking the doorjamb mere inches from my head. She wanted me dead.

I surreptitiously studied the drop from the wall to the jagged rocks below. A powerful woman like Clytaemnestra could easily heave me over the crenellations. No one would stop her.

But it was not my life she wanted; her quarrel was with Helen. Keeping that thought in mind, I gathered enough courage to open my mouth and try to deflate her angry musings. "Perhaps my father is saving her for some special punishment."

"I doubt it," she observed dryly. Then she shifted her gaze to the mountains of Arcadia. They rose like a bulwark to the west; snow still dusted the highest peaks. "I fear for Orestes out in the wilderness, hungry and cold, his head filled with perverse ideas."

Then she looked sidelong at me. "You understand my meaning." She lifted a jeweled finger to command my silence when I would have protested my ignorance. "I think you and Orestes both saw and heard more than you should have. In fact, my followers tell me they saw a redheaded woman hiding up in the gallery that day. I wonder, who that could have been?"

"It was an accident." My explanation tumbled out in an uncontrollable rush. "Agamemnon arrived before I could get away."

"Hermione!" she snapped. "Stop behaving as though you're about to be punished. You were on your way back to your room when it happened. Of course you heard the commotion. Perhaps you even saw a little bloodshed and it was a terrible shock."

Clytaemnestra moved in closer, her gold bangles and rings glittering in the sunlight as she clamped a firm hand on my upper arm. My heart jumped. Was this it? Was she about to drag me to the wall and shove me over the edge? "Agamemnon does not deserve your pity. You never knew what a monster he was. He courted me by butchering my first husband and dashing my baby's brains against the wall. Then he threw me down and took me while my child's body was still warm." Feral rage dripped from her like acid. "You can't know what hate truly means until you've had a man violate you and murder your children before your very eyes. Hate is something the immortal gods can never take from you."

Releasing me, she sucked a deep breath through her nostrils. "I have lost two children. As for the rest, it's murder a child or be murdered by him. Hah! What a conundrum! Sometimes it doesn't matter what you do, the gods will curse you either way."

CHRYSOTHEMIS WAS DEVASTATED at losing me, her last true friend and confidant, and insisted on spending the final night in my bedchamber. My aunt, however, refused her the comfort. "It's time you stop whining and cringing like a kicked dog and start behaving like a princess."

Abashed, Chrysothemis's lower lip quivered with burgeoning tears. I squeezed her hand, then led her out to the stairwell to offer what encouragement I could. "There's no reason to be afraid."

"Everyone's leaving," she complained. "I'm going to be all alone here, and you know how Mother hates me."

Although I did my best to reassure her, her fearful whisperings and gossip would have kept me awake all night. I kissed her goodnight, then, yawning, retired to my room to undress. I had eaten and drunk a bit too much at the feast, and my eyelids were drooping. Althaia, too, was sluggish, fumbling as she removed my paint and finery. She had better be awake and alert in the morning. I had to rise early.

A faint noise outside my door roused me from a disjointed dream about the cult votaries attending the feast, and calling with reedy little voices for more milk and honey. I listened for the sound again above Althaia's rhythmic snoring, heard nothing, and dismissed it as a mouse or some other night noise. I yawned and sank back into a snug, blissful slumber.

Sudden lamplight stung my eyes. Someone had entered the room. I heard shoes thump to the floor, then what sounded like fingers undoing a belt. Squinting, and hazy with sleep, I tried to make out the figure looming beside the bed. A man. Sluggish fear stirred in my belly. "Althaia," I groaned.

A powerful hand came down on my wrist. "I don't think so, little bird."

Aegisthus, still holding me fast, dragged aside the coverlet and sat down beside me; the mattress sagged under his weight. He was naked. Panic banished my sleepiness. "No!" I twisted in his grasp and cried out again for Althaia, snoring on her cot. Why would she not answer me? "Let me go."

"Your maid is sound asleep." He leaned over to lick my earlobe. "I'm afraid she drank a bit too much tonight."

I tried to collect my scattered wits. "Get off me."

Ignoring my protests, Aegisthus kissed my throat, his stubble scratching my skin. A scream started in my throat, but he anticipated me by covering my mouth with his. I bit down on his lip, tasted his blood, and a moment later tasted my own when he backhanded me across the face. Rough fingers grasped my throat. "Don't make me beat you into submission," he hissed. "It would ruin your pretty face."

My lip throbbed where he had struck me. "I don't want you."

Aegisthus responded by tearing open my linen shift. Feeling his erection pressing against my belly heightened my terror. Sobbing, I tried yet again to escape him, but all my thrashing and squirming did was give him a chance to get between my legs.

"You're Helen's daughter. You were born for this." The taste of my blood soured his kiss. When he thrust his tongue into my mouth, it was all I could do not to gag or bite him again. His erection prodded my thighs.

I kept crying as he sucked the blood from my lips and moved down to kiss my breasts. His slimy tongue on my nipples filled me with disgust. "Stop!"

When he began to move against my body, I knew what was coming. His chest mashed against my breasts, his hands pinioned my wrists above my head, except for the moment when he reached between my thighs to guide his shaft into me. I could not move to struggle, except to turn my head away from him and close my eyes.

Aegisthus pierced me with a single, vicious thrust and kept going, deep inside me, ignoring my pain. He tore me open, again and again, and with every thrust he pounded me into the mattress. I could not move for the agony, or breathe for the weight crushing me. I could not even cry out except to whimper incoherently.

It went on and on, with him grunting and groaning into my neck, claiming sloppy kisses from my mouth, telling me how good it felt. Sweat poured from his body. His masculine odor filled my nostrils. I gagged back vomit.

Finally, he shoved into me one last time, and then, with a strangled groan, he emptied his seed into me. Once he finished, he continued to hold and caress me as though we were actual lovers.

He kissed me on the mouth, lingering with his tongue. Perspiration dripped from his brow onto my breasts. "It's a shame you have to leave so early tomorrow," he purred. "I would like nothing better than to stay and enjoy you again." Groping hands squeezed my buttocks.

Tears leaked from my eyes to run down my sticky cheeks. His slime oozed from the aching void between my legs. "Just go. Get out."

Obliging me, he rose and dressed, but just before he left he tugged the sheet out from under me and roughly wiped away the seed and blood staining my thighs. "I will take this with me." Wadding it in one hand, he picked up the lamp with the other. "Go back to sleep now, little bird."

I curled my lips into a snarl. "Stop calling me that."

"Ah, but it's my favorite endearment for you." Aegisthus leered down at me. "It's what my father used to call my mother when she was a little girl."

CHAPTER SEVEN

I SPENT THE REST OF THE NIGHT curled up in a little ball, sobbing into my pillow. It hurt too much to move. A pulsing ache burned my thighs. My body felt bruised where he had pinned me down and my lip throbbed, but that was nothing compared to the wound in my soul.

The first hints of sunrise streamed through a crack in the shutters. Dogs barked down near the Lion Gate. Sandals slapped against the paving stones below my window. The citadel had begun to stir. A servant would soon bring me my breakfast. Porters would come to take my belongings to the waiting cart. I tried to focus past the hurt and anger. Today, I was boarding a ship, going home to Sparta, far, far away from Mycenae. Aegisthus would never be able to touch me again.

With that thought, I brushed my hand across my eyes and forced myself to climb out of bed to wake my useless chaperone. "Get up, you lazy slug." I shoved her, then punched her arm when she did not respond fast enough. "Get up!"

Althaia, bleary-eyed and yawning, did her best to comply. Her eyes bulged when she saw me crouched there with my bloodshot eyes and a split lip. "Mistress, what happened?"

"What do you think?" Bitterness poisoned my reply. Her sluggishness—no, her uselessness—had led to this.

She wobbled from her cot to fetch a washcloth from the basin. I flinched from her initial attempt to dab the clotted blood from my lip, then my resolve evaporated and I crumpled sobbing into her arms.

"Everything will be all right." Althaia rocked me like a child. "Sotera will be with you. She knows what to do."

As she said this, she kissed my forehead to reassure me, then released me to open the shutters so the daylight could flood in. I washed my face in the basin as she ordered hot water for a sponge bath and made me choke down the porridge and cheese the servants had brought. "You have to be strong," she said. "Remember, you're a princess."

A harsh laugh escaped me. Princess. That word was beginning to lose its luster.

The hot water arrived with a sea sponge and a soft woolen towel. I bathed the blood and seed from my thighs, then washed my breasts and everywhere else Aegisthus had touched me. I practically rubbed myself raw with the sponge, and still it was not enough.

A soft knock at the door brought a stout, older woman. Sotera. Althaia drew her into a corner where they spent the next several moments whispering back and forth, gesturing to me as they did so. It aggravated my patience. "I will not have you gossiping."

Althaia turned toward me. "Mistress, she must know the truth," she explained. "But the walls have ears."

It should not have bothered me at all, for the servants always spoke in hushed tones so as not to disturb us, but I could not think straight.

Sotera did not say a word as she toweled me dry and dressed me in a clean linen shift. Clytaemnestra had chosen her for her competent, no-nonsense manner. Althaia seemed to have faith in her trustworthiness, but that was no guarantee the older woman was not also a spy for my aunt.

"Hold up your hands, Mistress." Althaia slid thick bracelets over my wrists to conceal the bruises. She hung golden lilies from my earlobes as Sotera mixed scarlet ochre with goose fat to dab over my swollen, split lip and ground dry white clay into powder to mask the purpling marks on my face and throat. Last of all, she outlined my eyes with kohl.

I stared at my visage in the polished bronze mirror Sotera held up for me, knowing that no amount of art could conceal my bloodshot eyes or put a smile on my face. The women dressed me in a blue woolen dress and sturdy shoes for traveling. A cloak of gray went over my shoulders.

Porters arrived to carry my chests downstairs, then Althaia and Sotera accompanied me down to the great court; they flanked me like bodyguards. I walked slowly, doing my utmost to swallow my pain, and remembering to keep my shoulders thrown back and chin raised like a proper princess.

I maintained the illusion with relative ease until I saw Aegisthus standing beside Chrysothemis. *Rapist!* Beaming, he held out his arms like a loving uncle. *Monster!* He left me no choice but to accept his repulsive embrace and to pretend he had not violated me just hours ago.

"Farewell, little bird." Aegisthus kissed both my cheeks, lingering a moment longer than he should have. Naked hunger still gleamed in his eyes. "I fear your aunt drank a bit too much last night and could not be here this morning. I will give her your love when she wakes."

Twining my fingers in my skirts, I fought an overwhelming urge to claw out his eyes and denounce him, for all the good that would do. I had no kinsmen to take my part and avenge my honor, and Aegisthus, standing there with that smug smile plastered across his face, knew it.

When it came her turn to say goodbye, Chrysothemis clung weeping to me, far too distraught to notice anything was amiss. Typical. I wonder whether she even noticed her mother's absence.

It took my last ounce of self-determination to wobble down to the Lion Gate and, taking my leave of the faithful Althaia, climb into the covered mule cart with Sotera.

I felt as tremulous as a cobweb. Breakfast sat like a millstone in my gut. The cart's jouncing motion did nothing to alleviate the soreness between my legs. Tears streamed down my face, running tracks through my white paint.

Mycenae and its sheltered valley receded into the distance. I never once looked back.

In the mid-afternoon, Tiryns on its high rock reared up over the Argive plain. I clung to the cart for support as it ascended a steep incline to enter the citadel's imposing eastern gate. As I was expected, a steward met me in the outermost courtyard. He offered his hand to help me from the cart and escorted me to the great court where the queen of Argos awaited me.

Aegialia cut an elegant, imposing figure standing amid the scarlet pillars of the aithousa. Clytaemnestra had cautioned me not to talk to her while passing through Tiryns, for the two queens despised each other despite their common cause. Aegialia, too, had taken a lover and deposed her husband, but it had been a bloodless coup. Diomedes had fled into exile when the Argive lords denied him permission to come ashore, and revoked his kingship. Aegialia had married her lover, a scion of the Argive royal house, and installed him as king.

Almost at once, she noticed something amiss, but waited until she had escorted me upstairs to the women's quarters to inquire. "Princess, should you be wearing paint and jewels on the road?"

At first, numbed by exhaustion and shock, the question did not register. Then Aegialia gestured to my face with its sticky tear-tracks, and to my mouth where the red ochre had worn away to reveal my split and swollen lip.

Clapping a hand over my mouth, I bolted into the bathroom. Sotera hurried after me. I crumpled to my knees on the floor beside the stone seat and lost my breakfast down the privy hole.

Aegialia found me doubled over, gasping back dry heaves, with Sotera rubbing soothing circles across my back. Flounced skirts flowing around her in a fragrant mass, the queen knelt down and lifted my arm to tug off the bracelet.

"Please, leave me alone." I started to wrench my hand back, but it was too late. Aegialia had already seen the bruise encircling my wrist.

"I don't think that would be wise." Aegialia snapped her fingers at the maids crowding the doorway. "Draw the princess a hot bath."

I wiped my hand across my mouth and, leaning on Sotera's sturdy arm, staggered to my feet. A maid flushed the vomit down the privy with water from a jug. "I didn't sleep well last night."

"Don't lie to me, young lady." Aegialia slapped her hands against her skirts. "I know what I see when I see it. You're going to have a long, hot bath, and then you're going straight to bed."

Servant girls filled a ceramic tub with steaming water, then the queen's maids undressed me despite my protests that Sotera could attend me, and I wished to be alone. They helped me into the bath, and scrubbed and scraped me clean. I relished the opportunity to soak my bruised body and wash away the filth, and I lingered until the skin on my fingers wrinkled from the hot water. Sotera wrapped me in a soft woolen towel, then held me to her breast when, still feeling dirty, I broke down again. The queen's handmaids pretended not to notice.

Aegialia had left me alone to bathe, but returned in time to find me weeping on Sotera's shoulder. She dismissed the maids while she gathered my dripping hair in a towel. "I have chamomile tea waiting for you."

She made me drink the tea while Sotera dried and combed my hair, then she tucked me into bed between lavender scented sheets. A maid drew up a chair for the queen. "There's no need to tell me who did this," Aegialia remarked softly. "Only one man in your aunt's household would have dared."

I laid my head against the pillow. Clytaemnestra was wrong. The Argive queen was a warm, caring woman, not at all the vicious harpy my aunt had made her out to be. "I tried to hide it."

Aegialia arched a meticulously plucked eyebrow to let me know exactly what she thought about my efforts. "Of course you did, but you're new to this. It takes a very skilled woman to conceal a man's abuse."

All Mycenae must have noticed. My sorry attempt to hide the evidence had only drawn attention to it, and that did not bode well for my going home. "What do I do now?"

"Don't wear any more paint, except maybe a little on your lips." Aegialia bent over me to stroke my cheek. "Sleep, child. There's no need for you to be afraid or dwell on this any further. Remember, you've escaped. He can't hurt you anymore—"

"Yes, he can!" I had tried to tell myself the same thing earlier, but it was not true. "I still feel him all over me."

Sighing, she arranged the embroidered coverlet over me. "I know you do. It's normal for a woman to feel that way until she becomes strong enough inside to let it go."

"How?" I asked.

"Let the great goddesses be your allies. When you get home, confide in a priestess you know you can trust, and ask to be purified. If we had time, I would take you through the rites myself, but your grandfather would question the delay. However, there might something else I can do." Aegialia straightened, then snapped her fingers at the nearest maid. "Enyo, bring the Athena from my altar."

It sounded so easy, and yet at the same time I was not sure anyone or anything could help me overcome my fear and self-loathing. "How do you know so much about these matters?"

Aegialia evaded the question. "I assume your aunt knows nothing about this?"

"I did not see her this morning."

"Well, I will not be the one to tell her. She knows exactly what kind of viper she's taken into her bed."

When the maid returned with the goddess's image, Aegialia set it down on the little table beside my bed, then raised her palms and urged me to sit up and do the same. "Holy Athena, battle-goddess of Argos, watch over this woman Hermione, daughter of Menelaus and Helen. She has been taken against her will. Cast your tasseled aegis over her."

I drew strength from the prayer. Aegialia kissed my forehead when we finished. "I will give you an amulet to keep you safe on your voyage, and a packet with certain herbs," she said. "When you get home, take the herbs in a tea to purge your womb."

It had not occurred to me before now that there might be a baby. A whimper escaped me at the horrible possibility.

"Don't worry," she said. "I am a high priestess of Hera and Athena and know what I am doing. Give yourself over to your patron goddess and let her heal your hurts. The man who did this to you has no lasting power over you or your womb." Aegialia bestowed a second kiss upon me; she smelled like sandalwood and bread, and other womanly things.

She stayed with me as my eyelids started to droop.

I slept through the night, waking at dawn when Sotera roused me. I dressed and joined the queen in her apartment, where she forced me to eat a little porridge and dried apples. She sat alone, with her shutters open to catch the sea breeze. I had not seen her new husband, or any man since the steward had taken his leave yesterday. A maid told me that King Cometes was conferring with his advisors in Argos, and that the queen did not care for the noise and intrigues of the court, and preferred to stay at Tiryns for her health.

Aegialia set bread and a wedge of goat cheese before me. "Eat," she urged. Once I choked down enough food to satisfy her, she handed me the promised packet and a gold amulet depicting Dia, the Great Mother Goddess from whom all other goddesses sprang.

"A woman gave this to me a long time ago," Aegialia explained. "I admit, I do not keep the old Mother Goddess, but Dia owns many altars in Sparta. Perhaps you are the one she was meant for." The queen pressed the amulet into my hand. It felt warm from her touch.

After breakfast, Aegialia walked with me as far as the outer court and kissed me farewell on both cheeks. The captain of the guard assisted me and Sotera into the cart that would take us down to our ship, a merchant galley which would be escorted by two pentekonters.

I had no stomach for traveling. Poseidon's blood did not run in my veins. Seasickness laid me low soon after the ship set sail. I spent much of the five-day voyage lying in a musty claustrophobic cabin with a cold compress over my eyes, trying very hard to remain calm and not focus on the ship's rolling, swaying pitch, the rank odors, or my own misery.

I asked Athena to watch over me and Mother Dia to comfort me. Artemis had done nothing to help safeguard my virginity—not that I had trusted in her protection since Iphigenia's death. She was irrelevant now; Artemis took no interest in ruined women.

Aegialia's Dia amulet left its sweaty imprint in my palm as I clutched it to my breast. I kept telling myself the seasickness would pass. I imagined the pleasures of taking another hot bath and sleeping in a soft bed once we made port, but my mind always leapt ahead to what would come next. I agonized over my homecoming. Would my grandfather notice anything? Groaning, I flung my arm over my face. Tyndareus was an irritable old man. He would not understand anything beyond the insult to his family's honor.

Sotera nursed me with dried fruit and bitter-tasting but nourishing Egyptian beer. She also emptied the chamber pot and did what she could to lift my spirits. Her stomach seemed cast in bronze. I envied how easily she weathered the trip.

By the fourth day, my nausea subsided enough to let me hold down my food. I could even go ashore for exercise when the crew beached the ships for the night. But, fearing the strange sailors, who were rough men, I never lingered long.

Just before we reached the port of Helas, Sotera rummaged through the baggage and found me a clean dress, a comb, and hand mirror. I dreaded seeing my own reflection. Dark circles ringed my eyes. Sweaty, tangled hair framed my pallid face. Mottled yellow replaced the purple of my bruises. A scab crusted the cut on my lower lip, though Sotera was quick to point out that the swelling had gone down. "You look much better," she said.

"Don't lie," I chided. "I don't look like a princess at all. Grandfather will notice."

"No one will say anything, Mistress," Sotera answered confidently. "I'm sure you'll be able to wash before you see him."

She helped me wash and fix my appearance as best she could, but in the end the only remedy was to throw on a cloak and draw up the hood. An armed escort met my ship on the beach. Their leader, a florid Spartan nobleman, came up the gangplank to help me onto dry land. Crewmen assisted the porters loading my baggage onto a mule cart; they had only begun working when the gentleman took me into his chariot and drove me to the governor's residence overlooking the harbor. Here, I would spend the night before setting out for Therapne in the morning.

I heaved a relieved sigh to discover Lord Echemus was an elderly widower with failing eyesight who did not notice anything except an exhausted princess requiring a comfortable room, a hot bath, and a proper meal. He paid his compliments like a doting grandfather before leaving me alone to rest.

Sleep refused to come. I tossed and turned despite the comfortable bed, and rose at dawn feeling thoroughly miserable. Sotera arranged my hair in a simple style and dressed me in my favorite gown, scarlet banded with horizontal black and taupe stripes. Then she pinched my cheeks to bring out some color and dabbed red ochre on my lips to conceal the scab.

She sat beside me in the covered mule cart as we progressed north, following the river Eurotas from its marshy estuary into a countryside lush with olive groves and fields. Sotera was not a talkative woman. I thanked the gods for her silence, knowing how much harder the trip would have been had she been one of those garrulous servants who repeatedly inquired after my health or mood. Instead, she let me be, limiting her intrusions to grasping my hand whenever the stress began to show.

Returning home should have been a cause for celebration rather than dread, but seeing Therapne spread once more across its three hills inspired no joy in me at all. Aegisthus had polluted me with his foul essence, and now it spoiled everything. "Sotera," I asked, "do you think anyone will notice?" Regardless of what she had said yesterday, I found her reassurances hard to believe.

"No, Mistress," she said. "They will think you're tired."

Sotera was right. Meeting me on the portico overlooking the outer court, my grandfather dismissed my pallor as the effects of seasickness. "Women don't belong out on the sea," he grumbled. Then he banished me to my chamber for the remainder of the afternoon. "Lie down and rest, child. Later, you can make yourself pretty and come visit."

It shocked me to see the changes in him. Tyndareus had always been tall and vigorous. Nowadays, he stooped a little and leaned on a cane. He had always been choleric. Now, he barked constantly at the servants and complained about almost everything.

Foremost on his mind that evening were my mother and aunt. "A man ought to have a devoted daughter to tend him in his old age, but what do I have? Two sluts I'm ashamed to own." Tyndareus patted my hand as I laid a snowy fleece over his knees. "Hermione, be a dear and bring a brick for my feet. Make sure it's warm. Those lazy slaves either bring me a cold lump or burn my toes."

I did as he bade, only leaving his chambers when his manservant arrived to turn down his bed.

Despite the late hour, there was one more thing I needed to do before going to sleep.

My new apartment had its own private altar, a painted platform on which to arrange the gods. Sotera sent a servant girl for hot water to make tea. I knelt down, kissed Aegialia's amulet, and prayed for strength while waiting for the water to arrive. Once Sotera hustled the girl out and shut the door, I emptied the queen's packet into a cup and prepared the draught.

For a long time, I sat staring at the cup. I wanted Aegisthus's seed gone, flushed out, but dreaded the pain the medicine would surely bring; the gods never sent their gifts without demanding some sacrifice in return. And it was dangerous. Only a high priestess who truly knew her art could properly measure out the herbs without killing the woman she was administering them to. Clytaemnestra might have known those secrets, but she had not imparted them to me.

Most women chose to endure the travails of pregnancy rather than risk the medicine.

Yet I did not have that choice. Less than a handful of people knew my shame; to the rest of the world, I was still a virgin. Whatever monstrosity Aegisthus might have planted inside me must die. It must be either the medicine or a willow twig dipped in juniper between my legs.

I drew in a deep breath before raising the cup to my lips; my hands were shaking. High priestess as well as queen, Aegialia would have known how to prepare the herbs. It was a bitter brew, as foul as the thing I was doing, but I drank it down, nevertheless.

Sotera took the cup away and dimmed the lamps. I lay down amid the soft fleeces to pray and wait, trying not to think about the rape that had been or the pain that was to come.

An hour passed before the medicine took effect. When it did, it brought on the heaviest bleeding and fiercest menstrual cramps I had ever experienced. Doubling over on the mattress, I fought the urge to send Sotera for cramp bark tea, but I did order a heated leather pad to alleviate the pain. I let the warmth penetrate my womb, and concentrated on the image of a loving goddess with a face like my grandmother's. I imagined Dia sitting with me, stroking my hair and telling me everything would be all right.

I thanked the goddess again and again while weeping miserable tears. Sotera arranged the coverlet over my body. She stayed beside me through the night.

Tyndareus assumed the bleeding was my normal menses. "Seasickness and now this," he commented. "It's a wonder women can get out of bed to cause as much trouble as they do." He demonstrated a grandfather's gruff concern, ordering a hot brick for my feet and admonishing Sotera to give me white willow tea.

Sotera laid the hot brick against my feet, while my grandfather sat in his chair mumbling about the weakness of women. Just having him near, grumbling and doting over me like a sick child, here in my childhood home, triggered an overpowering urge to confide in him.

But he was a man, a warrior who had once fought with Herakles, and he despised my mother and aunt for spreading their legs indiscriminately. Even if he did believe me, he would have sputtered and raged like Agamemnon, offering no comfort at all. Then he would have taken down his worn shield and sword, and hobbled to Mycenae to demand restitution, broadcasting my shame to the world. Confronting Aegisthus at his age probably would have cost him his life. I was not even sure I could have told my father. A man could not give back what another had taken.

"Grandfather," I said wearily. "Please stop fussing. I go through this every month."

Tyndareus gave me some pretty faience beads he thought might lift my spirits, and let me alone after that. Once my bleeding ended, I asked him for an escort to Dia's sanctuary below the palace so I might receive ritual purification.

"Whatever do you need to do that for?" he asked. "There's a place right here in the palace for your women's rites."

I had rehearsed my speech beforehand. "I know, Grandfather, but I have never had my woman's blood here in Sparta. I should observe the customary rites and be initiated."

"Ah, I see." He gave me a dry kiss on the cheek, while I cringed inside for misleading him like this. "Well, then of course you can have an escort."

A lady of the court assured me that Dia's high priestess had overseen all the rituals of the royal cult during my absence. I remembered Polycaste as a nice older woman who used to visit the palace and spend long hours spinning wool and talking with my grandmother. She was a royal kinswoman, my grandmother's first cousin, and had served Dia since she was young. Polycaste used to dandle and kiss me, and give me sweet treats, but that was long ago. She did not know me as a grown woman, the Hermione who was now. After so many years, she might as well have been a stranger. Yet, heedful of Aegialia's advice to find a priestess I could trust, I went to Polycaste, anyway.

Polycaste examined the packet, turning it this way and that, and sniffing the residue. I held my breath. Her thin gray eyebrows pulled together, and then her eyes widened. "Princess..."

Forgoing all ceremony, she grabbed my arm to whisk me into an empty antechamber, where she shut the door behind us. "Now, did you take this because you were foolish, or because you were forced?"

Sotera assumed a protective stance behind my chair as I poured out the truth for this diminutive old woman with her white hair and wizened apple face. I had been so long without a mother figure, without someone to watch over and love me! When Polycaste embraced me and began rocking me back and forth, it was like crying in my grandmother's arms.

"You're not to blame, Hermione." Polycaste's breath stirred my hair. "You did everything you should have. Here, blow your nose, dear." She gave me a linen cloth. "You are not a whore."

I dabbed my nose dry. "I'm not my mother."

"She's not a whore, either."

Her assertion stunned me. "She left my father for her lover," I said.

"No, she did not."

"How do you know?"

Polycaste remained adamant. "Paris seized her against her will. Don't ask me how he did it, because I do not know for certain, but abduct her and your young brother he did. I told your father so before he set out."

That was not so. I saw how it was. The old priestess was just saying that to be charitable, because she still considered me a child for whom the truth would be too difficult. "Father said he would do terrible things to her."

"That was only in the beginning, when he first came home," Polycaste said. "Do you remember how he stopped raging against her, and promised to bring her and your little brother home? He knew she hadn't gone willingly." She stood up then, brushing imaginary lint off her robe, and reached for my hand. "But you're not here for her today."

The high priestess escorted me to the sanctuary's lustral bath, a sunken basin called an adyton. It was floored with gleaming marble and surrounded with colorful frescoes. A corner altar held a cult statue of the goddess. Dia stood ten feet tall. The priestesses had draped her in embroidered robes made sweet with saffron. She cradled her naked white breasts in both hands, and around her feet were arranged all the goddesses representing her various manifestations. Her inlaid eyes stared into empty space and her reddened mouth held a fixed smile. I felt no warmth from her, no indication that she was there with me.

Polycaste prepared a douche of vinegar and water, and let me flush myself out behind a wooden screen. Novice priestesses brought in jugs of tepid water. I stripped naked and stepped down into the adyton with them so they could purify me.

"Lady Dia, Great Mother Goddess who safeguards women, receive Hermione, daughter of Helen, daughter of Leda, into your sacred embrace." Polycaste stood on the topmost step, arms upraised to summon the goddess; the confines of the tiny chamber amplified her voice. "She has been violated outside the holy blessing of marriage, without her consent. She has bled away the seed planted inside her." I shivered as the novices poured the water over me, but welcomed the discomfort that would exorcise the last of my rapist's malignant spirit.

Polycaste clapped her hands together. "Great Goddess, remove the impurities from this woman's body. Make her spirit whole." Her chant soared. "Sing, Hermione! Sing your prayer to the goddess!"

I raised my arms in supplication. "Great Goddess, let me be made pure again!" Water dripped from my scalp, tracking rivulets down my breasts and belly. "Drive out the evil and let me be whole!"

"Great Goddess, hear this woman's plea!" Polycaste swept her hands inward to cup her small breasts through her robe. I clasped my naked breasts, squeezing them, invoking my holy womanhood. "Let her be consecrated!" Polycaste cried "Let her be one with your servants, so that she may go forth as a princess and high priestess and spread her abundance upon the land."

After the novices dried me with soft linen cloths and rubbed me down with scented oil, Sotera dressed me in clean garments. I tingled all over. Clean, at last.

Polycaste bestowed the kiss of peace on my cheeks, then grasped my hands in her dainty, wrinkled ones to lead me from the chamber. "Look at you! All grown and beautiful, and with such glorious hair! Come, let us make goddess cakes together and sing the sacred chants to celebrate your womanhood."

CHAPTER EIGHT

IT WAS A QUIET WORLD of storerooms and sanctuaries, the world of the mistress of the house, the domain which was my birthright and now my sole responsibility.

My day began early, in the kitchen giving orders to the cooks preparing my grandfather's breakfast, and ended late, spinning upstairs with my women. I was responsible for managing the palace's many stewards, laundresses, and scrub maids. I maintained the household ledgers, oversaw the storerooms with their rows of pithoi containing lentils, grains, oil, and vegetables, and supervised the women in the weaving house.

Although Clytaemnestra had given me a thorough if indifferent education in organizing all this chaos, a princess could not run such a large establishment without intermediaries. So Tyndareus appointed a personal secretary to assist me. He was a middle-aged, knobby-kneed scribe named Iphinous whose mild-mannered exterior hid a shrewd mind and no tolerance for laziness or excuses from his subordinates. A man cut from the same cloth as my aunt. I would have been lost without him.

In addition, my grandfather assigned me two highborn young handmaidens, Monime and Thebe, and gave me a golden seal stone such as queens used. It was engraved in meticulous detail: a seated goddess shaking opium poppies under a laurel tree with a sun and moon. One could wear it as a ring, but it was very heavy and cumbersome. I wore it upon my wrist, and sometimes like a pendant, hanging from a silver chain between my breasts.

Another woman might have grasped at her newfound wealth and authority with eager hands and played the haughty queen. I had no wish to become Sparta's goddess-on-earth before my time. Acting as Mother Dia in all her various aspects, taking responsibility for the abundance of the land and its people was a weighty thing. Despite Polycaste's reassurances, I was not altogether certain I was worthy enough to serve Sparta or the goddess.

I kept Aegialia's amulet close, invoking Dia's protection like a shield against the evil memories that threatened my tranquility.

Polycaste warned me that would take time for me to grow into the mantle of a high priestess and sacred heiress, and to accept that Aegisthus had no power over me in my own domain.

The familiar female chores of spinning and weaving eased my mind, and the traditional rites as performed by the daughter of the house offered a welcome diversion from my many cares. I swept around the altar in the palace's cult house, poured out the libations each morning, and set out milk for the house snake.

I tended the family tombs twice a month, dedicating blood sacrifices and drink offerings to my grandmother and maternal uncles.

Castor and Polydeukes had died together in a botched cattle raid three months after my mother's abduction. Always restless, they had spent so much time away from court that I did not remember them well.

Not so my grandmother, who had died not long after my father left for Aulis. Leda had been a mother to me. Helen might have borne me, but it was Leda who had first taught me how to spin and sew a straight seam, how to honor the goddesses, and how to preserve the sacred ways. It was she who had given me my first terracotta doll and let me sit before her dressing table to try on her ornaments. How I missed her still!

Had she lived, Tyndareus would never have needed to send me to my aunt at Mycenae.

To this day, he regretted his decision. "Had I known what a murderous bitch Clytaemnestra would turn out to be," he snorted, "I'd have kept you at home and let Polycaste see to your proper rearing. Or I'd've sent you to your cousin Penelope in Ithaca."

Some evenings, he banished Aethiolas and my young half-brothers, my father's sons by a concubine, from his apartment so he could speak with me alone. I dreaded those private interviews, for while I enjoyed doting on him as a dutiful granddaughter he sometimes asked me questions I preferred not to answer. Foremost among them was what I knew about Agamemnon's murder. "There are a dozen different versions, and most make no sense. Let's see now." Tyndareus sourly ticked off various death scenarios on his fingers. "Aegisthus simply *happened* to be there when Agamemnon got home, and it was all a terrible misunderstanding. Aegisthus and Clytaemnestra slew him in his bathtub. No, they did it in the megaron. No, they butchered him and his companions at a feast Aegisthus gave, though why Agamemnon would ever set foot in that reprobate lecher's house is beyond me. It goes on and on. Hah! All I know is that they murdered him, and it was no accident."

I diligently threaded blue wool onto my needle and bent over my embroidery to hide my distress.

"I heard she married Elektra off to a goatherd." Tyndareus expelled a sardonic grunt, phlegm ratting in his throat. "Speaking of marriage, if your father doesn't come home soon I'm going to have to be the one to break off your engagement to young Orestes, assuming he's still alive. I suppose it's too much to hope the gods will be kind and let Aegisthus cut Clytaemnestra's throat before the boy has to do it."

I found it increasingly hard to focus on my embroidery. Why could he not drop the subject and focus on something more pleasant?

"You understand that you can't marry a matricide, don't you, girl?" Tyndareus plucked little wool sausages off his blanket; they littered the floor around his chair.

I poked my needle through the intricate pattern of spirals. "It will be as you decide."

"I was a fool to choose Menelaus. Oh, your father's a good man, but he brought with him that terrible curse." Another clump of wool sausages drifted to the floor. "I let Agamemnon's wealth and prestige influence my decision. I should have known better."

A dutiful granddaughter did not interrupt. I blocked in a bright blue spiral and tried to shut out thoughts of the curse while feigning attentiveness.

"Orestes would bring murder to this house," Tyndareus concluded. "I realize it's no fault of his and that you've grown fond of him, but the gods haven't been kind to the Atreidai. You understand, don't you, girl?"

I waited until I was certain I could keep an even tone before answering. "Of course, Grandfather."

ALL WENT WELL WITH MY FATHER in Egypt until the raiders came. One moment, Menelaus and Helen were honored guests of the king, then prisoners the next, for the ships which devastated the villages of the Nile Delta were manned by Hellene mercenaries. The Egyptian king responded with force; his patrols caught two raiding vessels, burned them down to the waterline, and took the crews captive.

Ramesses did not understand that our people had many kings, and that my father had had nothing to do with the raid. I wrote to him, as my father's loving and loyal daughter, to ask that he release my parents and let them come home again after so many years away.

Ramesses never answered.

WHENEVER MY GRANDFATHER SPOKE of finding me a suitable husband, I wondered whether he meant to have a traditional marriage contest such as the one in which he won my grandmother, and the later, more famous one, in which he gave away my mother.

Everyone knew about Helen's marriage contest; the bards still sang the tale at wedding feasts.

Twenty years ago, three dozen princes and noblemen had converged on nearby Amyklai to compete for my mother's hand in marriage. To keep the peace, Tyndareus had exacted a most solemn and dire oath that they would honor his decision and defend the marital rights of the man he chose. To sanctify that vow, he had sacrificed a horse. Later, Agamemnon had used the Horse Oath and my mother's abduction to compel the suitors to join his coalition against Troy.

I wondered who would come, should my grandfather decide to hold another such contest for me. So many potential suitors had died fighting overseas that there was almost no one left to compete for my hand, even had they wished to come. I overheard the whispers in the court, among the visiting dignitaries and merchants: Spartan princesses either cuckolded their husbands or murdered them, and were no longer worth the trouble.

A generation ago, it had been different. A Spartan princess had been a prized commodity back then.

Sparta took its traditions from Crete, with its powerful priestesses and multitude of female deities. A Spartan royal woman was a vital force in her own right. I learned this shortly after my return. On my way to and from the cult house, common women held out their hands to touch my clothes, bent to kiss my sandaled feet, and asked me to sanctify their kourotrophoi, the little mother-child fertility figurines hopeful mothers placed on their altars.

Polycaste observed all this without the slightest hint of surprise. "You carry the holy aura of your foremothers. It is your kharis that they crave."

Kharis meant far more than mere physical beauty, grace, or charm. It encompassed the raw sexual energy the gods sometimes bestowed on a woman. A woman blessed with kharis turned heads whenever she walked into a room. Other women might envy her, even though she might be far plainer than they, but were inexorably drawn to her in hopes of drawing some of that divine radiance into themselves. As for men, they would gnaw their livers with desire for a charismatic woman, and duel each other to the death to possess her.

Aegisthus had desired me so fiercely that he had been willing to risk all for a single hour with me. My kharis had driven him to rape me. As I moved through my duties, passing sentries and servants and scribes, I could only wonder how many other men were struggling with the same temptation.

Sex and violence. I had observed early often those threads wove together. A mystery a princess and high priestess must unravel. So it was that Polycaste instructed me in the offices of the sacred labrys she had kept in trust since my grandmother's passing.

The queen's labrys was many generations old, having been brought by my foremothers from Knossos to Sparta in the years after Poseidon's wrath had devastated Crete and destroyed the island of Thera. Its bronze twin blades had been sharpened countless times over the centuries. Its haft was cracked with age, but the labrys was priceless, because it carried within it the essence of all the royal women who had ever wielded it.

Clytaemnestra had never permitted me or anyone else to touch Mycenae's holy labrys, even though as an Atreid I owned a stronger right to it than she. Yet I had observed her enough times to know what words to speak, how to wash my hands, and where to strike.

For my first sacrifice before the people, Polycaste and her priestesses painted my face with white clay, and painted my mouth and the sacred stars upon my cheeks with red ocher. We called it the moon-mask, the inscrutable face of the goddess. Once the mask dried, they dressed me in the traditional open bodice, which was cinched in by a painted leather corset, and tied a sacred knot at the nape of my neck. A priestess's apron was tied over my seven-tiered flounced skirt, and a round headdress surmounted by a dove crowned my head. By degrees, the mortal woman who was Hermione vanished behind the façade of Sparta's paramount high priestess.

I felt the change come over me. "Mother Dia, Great Mother Goddess!" I projected myself toward the people gathered for the sacrifice. A groan went up from them, at once reverent and fearful. Hundreds, including my grandfather, lifted their hands to their brows, palms facing outward, for the customary salute. Such was my power as goddess-on-earth to inspire the people's dread and worship. I relished every moment.

I held up the labrys so the sunlight glinted off the twin blades. "Receive this nourishing blood with our fear and gratitude!" The animal was an unblemished heifer, garlanded, sluggish, consenting to the sacrifice. "Grant us your blessings in our fields and groves. Grant us your blessings in our pastures and vineyards." People raised their hands as if hoping to touch the labrys. "Bless our flocks, our hearths, and our children."

The double axe now weighed almost nothing in my grasp, where earlier it had been very heavy. A plaything of the gods, I mused. Shifting my grasp on the haft, I raised the labrys over my head, waiting for the priest to stun the heifer with the mallet. Then I brought the labrys down behind her broad neck.

A strong woman like Clytaemnestra could drop a heifer with a single, well-executed blow, but I lacked her experience, and in my nervousness had not put enough muscle behind the stroke; the labrys's seeming lightness was illusory, fostered by my own glee at playing the goddess. The heifer's forelegs folded under her and she went down twitching and snuffling, her huge dark eyes dilated with bewilderment.

Quickly, I did it again, to sever her spine and end her suffering. Polycaste claimed the bloodstained labrys from my hands, switching it for the sacrificial knife to finish the ritual. Without hesitation, I sliced through the artery to let the warm blood stream out. Priestesses swarmed in to collect the liquid in great basins, while I stood there panting and flush with the essence of the goddess. I stared at the knife, at the blood sticking to and congealing upon my hands, and saw it as the stuff of life and death. I could bless and nourish whole peoples with this. I could lay my sticky hands upon a barren woman and her womb would quicken.

Life.

Yet there was also Death. I could wither a mortal man's potency and revoke the blessings of life. Had he stood there before me at that instant, I could have brought Aegisthus whimpering to his knees. I could have cursed him, unmanned him, made him outcast.

Afterward, when I described all this, Polycaste cautioned me against going too far. "You must put your personal grievances and prayers aside when you play the goddess. You make empty yourself to make the perfect vessel. Your feelings are imperfection."

I bit down on my lower lip before retorting, "Is the goddess not my protector? Why should I not turn to her for justice? I want him to die. If I were a man, I could march back to Mycenae and run Aegisthus through with a sword. I could tear out his heart, and hack him to pieces, and hurl his carcass into the ravine for the dogs and vultures to devour!" A killing rage burned through me. I heard my voice grow in volume.

"Hermione!" Polycaste said sharply.

I did not stop. "I am the sacred queen. I am the Great Mother Goddess from whom all other goddesses spring. I am the Mistress of the Spartan Royal House, the Lady of the Labrys. I give life and bring death!" My naked breasts swelled with my every breath. Although the novice priestesses had washed the blood from my hands, I still wore the moon-mask and high priestess's costume. Power yet flowed through me. Polycaste would not tell me what to do.

Shaking now, I stood up from the chair where I had been sitting. "I curse you, Aegisthus, son of Thyestes. I curse the breath in your body. I curse your limbs, your eyes, your mouth, your blood. I curse your hands, your feet, your heart, your stomach. I curse your manhood. Let it wither like a dead branch, so you never violate a woman again. I curse you with misery and death. Let Mother Dia and all the gods upon Olympus witness these words and give them weight."

I glanced around the sanctuary anteroom for a knife to draw blood to seal the curse, and saw the sacrificial dagger lying on the offering table before the altar. Polycaste at once saw my intentions. She rose, but was not swift enough to stop my snatching up the blade.

Sharp bronze stung my palm as I scored it across the soft flesh. Blood welled from the cut. "Mother Dia, witness this offering!" I cried. "Let my blood seal my words."

Then Polycaste was there, seizing my wrist to apply a clean cloth to the wound. "That's enough, Hermione!" she barked. "A queen's charge is to bless and preserve, not to curse. Your aunt has already done plenty of that, and look where's it gotten everybody."

"He violated me!" I helped her apply pressure. "He deserves to die in the most horrible way possible." Uttering the curse left me simultaneously elated and drained, a sure sign that the goddess had been inside me. She would grant my words weight. Aegisthus would suffer.

"You must never do it again," Polycaste said firmly. "Curses can rebound and poison the maker. Do you think Clytaemnestra will profit long from the blood she's shed? A king's blood is sacred blood. She's unleashed a terrible evil. Don't emulate her. There are already too many curses in your family."

But all those curses had come from men stained with dark deeds and blood. Clytaemnestra had repaid Agamemnon for his abuse. I hated that she had taken Aegisthus as her lover, but was she not in justified in punishing the murderer of her daughter? What else could she have done under the circumstances? She had already suffered the loss of her firstborn son to his cruelty. They could never have been reconciled after Iphigenia.

And besides, what murders had *I* committed? What oaths had *I* broken? I sat down again, convinced that it could not be a crime to send evil back to its source.

SPARTAN MEN SOMETIMES PARTICIPATED in the women's rites. These were ceremonies in the ancient tradition: ecstatic dances and life-renewing orgies. As the sacred queen, I should have led the people in their worship, and taken a consort from among the young men, but times had changed and new ways were replacing the old. Princesses no longer danced and mingled with men around the holy bonfires, and no amount of explanation would have sufficed to convince my grandfather that the sacred revels had nothing to do with base prostitution.

Tyndareus need not have feared on that account. I cherished no desire to lie with a man, no matter how young and handsome, no matter even if he was a consort chosen for me by the gods.

But I would still attend to grant my blessing to the revels and see the land made fruitful. Polycaste's novices dressed me as in Mother Dia's aspect as Aphrodite, the goddess in the fullness of her allure.

Bonfires blazed against the hot midsummer's night. Drums in the twilight throbbed a primal beat. Half-naked men and women gathered in the firelight. I was not permitted to go among them, but must remain on the dais flanked by an entourage of priestesses and palace guards whose task it was to shield me from any amorous adventurers.

Polycaste brought me the pyxis containing opium granules. "Sacred Queen, receive this gift of the poppy. Let the great goddess enter into you so she may observe the rites performed in her honor."

Poppies were the goddess's special gift to women, enabling them to cross the boundaries separating worlds to speak directly with the gods. Although I had never entered into a poppy trance before, Polycaste had instructed me on what to do, and cautioned me in how I might react and what visions or sensations I might experience. After praying and fasting all that day, I was anxious. Would I feel blissful and content, elevated by the sacred substance, or would it grant power to my innermost demons? Could Aegisthus's malevolent spirit contaminate the life-giving essence of the ceremonies?

Polycaste heated the raw opium in a vessel over the coals. As they began smoldering, I bent over the tripod to inhale the smoke through a ceramic pipe, breathing it in slowly and normally as Polycaste had directed me, stopping only when my head reeled.

I sat back on my wooden throne, blinking, turning my head this way and that seeking cool air, water, anything to alleviate the night's stifling heat. The roses in my floral chaplet were wilting; their scent was cloying, nauseating. Sweat formed in the valley between my painted breasts. A priestess pressed a cup to my lips. I gulped down cold spring water flavored with barley and sprigs of mint; the sacred kykeon dribbled down my chin to burn a freezing path down my gullet. I did not feel like a goddess, rather like a helpless, insignificant creature imprisoned in a place where she did not belong.

"Aphrodite comes!" Polycaste cried. "The goddess is among us!"

Earlier, she had shown me a goddess crowned with poppy heads and wearing a beatific smile. She had urged me to relax, to become an empty vessel, but stepping outside the mortal realm frightened me; it felt like drifting away attached to a cobweb that would surely break, leaving me lost in the labyrinth between worlds. I was not accustomed to communing with the gods.

Euphoria and sweet visions eluded me. A maelstrom of carnal desire ruled the night. Firelight and shadows playing against the heaving naked flesh sprawled around the bonfire, transforming men and women into grotesque creatures. I saw a meadow inhabited by demons. Where I might have screamed, the poppy dulled my senses, so I could only sit haplessly and pray that none of those creatures of the night noticed my presence.

Then one man stood up, gripping a prodigious erection, and undulated his body like a serpent while leering at me. Panic lanced through my opiate haze. He became Aegisthus, licking his lips and stroking himself, and meanwhile my bodyguards did nothing. I gripped the armrests of my throne, hyperventilating and unable to cry for help. Aegisthus twirled in a lazy circle, flapping both arms. *Little bird.*

I squeezed my eyes shut.

A moment later, Aegisthus was gone.

At dawn, my chaperones escorted me home. I was by then wobbly and very nauseous, and twice leaned from the litter to vomit onto the roadside. My head ached fiercely. I trembled all over. Yet it was blessedly cool in the palace, where my handmaidens undressed me and sponged away the sweat and cosmetics. Sotera helped me lie down and placed a compress over my eyes to ease the headache. Soon, the morning grew sultry, and the cool sheets became damp with my sweat. Polycaste had warned me opium would make me sick. Monime and Thebe took turns fanning me, while I dreamt of fire and writhing bodies and rape, and was miserable throughout the rest of that day.

Aegisthus lurked everywhere, tainting the goddess's gifts. I might not be able to take a consort during the revels, but one day I would have to marry and submit to a husband. What would happen on my wedding night when my bridegroom, whoever he was, tried to touch me? Aegisthus had not just taken my virginity; he had violated every other part of me, too.

Let Mother Dia give weight to my curse and make him suffer. Let him die a horrible, gruesome death.

"Sex is not rape," Polycaste explained. "Rape is for small-minded men who despise women and their mysteries. They cannot create, only destroy, and so in their anger they twist our goddess-given pleasure into something dark and terrible. Sex is natural and good. Always remember that. Never be ashamed of your pleasure. Aphrodite grants it to you to compensate for the pains of childbearing."

I gazed down at the table where we were sorting through the dried herbs used in the sanctuary: herbs for preventing conception, inducing miscarriage, stimulating a mother's milk. Polycaste had taught me the recipe for Aegialia's medicine. "He's always in my thoughts."

"Then you must fight him," she answered firmly. "Understand that to utter a curse is to unleash greater evil. It does nothing to heal the wound. Look at Clytaemnestra. She might have relished killing Agamemnon, but if she doesn't realize what she's done now, she'll soon learn when Orestes returns to avenge his father's death."

"You believe he's still alive out there in the wilderness?" I had not heard Polycaste mention my cousin before today.

"Oh, yes." She measured a handful of acacia seeds into a jar. "He's an instrument of the Erinyes. They will preserve him until he fulfills his appointed task, then they will hound him in turn." I heard the seeds showering into the ceramic vessel. "The Fates are cruel, entangling us in dark webs we did not weave for ourselves.

"As for you, Hermione, Mother Dia punishes the man who violates a woman according to her own time. But she cannot help a mortal woman who refuses to help herself. If you want to become a whole person again, then you must learn to shut the gates upon your tormentor. Build a wall to keep him out. Let it be whatever you wish—a chasm opening under his feet to pull him into Tartarus, Athena's great shield, a thunderbolt. Anything at all that diminishes his potency. Do as the queen of Argos told you and make the goddesses your allies. Keep them near you."

She was right. I could either defend myself or let him go on raping me in spirit. "Polycaste," I began softly, "has a man ever injured you?"

"No, I have been very fortunate to have had nothing but blessings from the goddesses." She secured the jar's lid with wax. "But I have seen many women who have suffered a man's anger. I have seen women broken and lost, and women rise stronger than they ever were before. The world is changing, growing darker and more violent." A sigh escaped her. Regret deepened the furrows in her wrinkled face. "I see it in my own grandchildren. My grandsons all want to be soldiers. People have started to turn their backs on the goddesses of old. They say it's become a man's world now, that giving women too much power is asking for trouble, and all they have to do to make their point is mention your mother's name."

CHAPTER NINE

AUTUMN BROUGHT A PHOCIAN MESSENGER bearing letters for both me and my grandfather. Unable to contain my curiosity, I left the wine press where I had been supervising slave women treading the grapes, and went outside where the light was better.

A breeze buffeted the papyrus sheet in my hand. I knew that handwriting! Orestes was alive.

"Dearest Hermione, you must be wondering where I have been and what happened to me." Yes, indeed! "It took Timon and me almost two months to reach Phocis. We had a rough time of it, because Aegisthus sent trackers after us. All that is behind us, though. Timon and I are now safe and sound in the citadel of Krisa, under King Strophius's protection.

"Krisa is a very large citadel, with a splendid view all the way to the sea. And Mount Parnassus is the biggest, most marvelous mountain I have ever seen!" Orestes loved mountain climbing, and during his many boyhood adventures had explored the many foothills near Mycenae. "Krisa sits atop one of its spurs, and there are many valleys and forests. Parnassus is sacred to Apollo and the Mother of the Mountains, but the pilgrims who travel to Delphi have to be careful, for they say there are as many bandits on the mountain roads as there are goats."

Orestes ought to be telling me how he had escaped Mycenae and eluded Aegisthus's trackers. I forced myself to relax and take my time with the letter, knowing that he would explain everything once he settled down and focused.

A paragraph or two later, however, and it became obvious that Timon had not only stood over his pupil's shoulder to correct his grammar, but had also censored the letter. I had sensed the pedagogue's interference earlier, but it stood out even more strongly now, with Elektra's story.

"She was in an unfortunate situation, evicted from the palace, and married to some lowly goatherd," Orestes wrote. "I was very upset. Strophius was kind, though, and sent our cousin Pylades to fetch her here." I doubted that a sense of altruism had anything to do with the Phocian king's actions. A princess of Mycenae was a valuable commodity, virgin or not. "Elektra was ill for several days after she arrived. I am not certain what was wrong with her. She does not want to talk about it."

I hoped Pylades had run his sword through that wretched goatherd.

Orestes offered no further details about his sister's mysterious ailment, except to say she was feeling better, and had married Pylades at the harvest festival. I wanted to hear more about her. How was she managing, pressed into a royal marriage with a stranger so quickly after being liberated from her abuser? Whenever I thought of the nameless goatherd, I pictured Aegisthus. Did Elektra despise Pylades, or had she befriended him?

"I am worried about Chrysothemis," Orestes continued, "because she is alone now, and there is no way to bring her here. I cannot even get a message to her, to see how she is. If you have any news, please send it to me."

He said nothing about his father's murder. I knew the shock and horror must still weigh heavily on his mind. Perhaps he could not discuss it yet, or his pedagogue censored all references to it. I suspected all was not well beneath those neatly formed words.

All those details were interesting, but still not the information I sought. Frustrated, I skimmed the letter through, only to find nothing about how an adolescent boy and an old man had survived those weeks in the Corinthian wilderness. How strange, I mused, when that was precisely the sort of adventure Orestes enjoying talking about.

"I hope you are doing well, Hermione. Has your father returned home yet?" he wrote. "I wish you were here for my naming day. Strophius gave me a farm with seven slaves. Pylades will take me to visit next spring.

"Mother wrote to me, and sent gifts, too. She begs me to come home, swearing that she is crying rivers of tears worrying about me. Hah! She never cries. Aegisthus sends me letters, too, full of advice I do not want, and pretending to be my friend. Meanwhile, he calls himself king and sits on my father's throne. Vile usurper!" At last, Orestes let his true feelings show. I felt his anger. "I wish Strophius would tell them to stop writing me, but he will not get involved except to advise me to be very careful in writing back. Timon is helping me write this letter."

That came as no surprise. Timon was also a stickler for stilted syntax. "I have told Mother that it is good for a young man my age to spend time away from home learning about the world." Either Timon or King Strophius must have dictated that response, because Orestes himself would not have been that calm with Clytaemnestra after what she had done. "I am doing well, and hope to be able to visit you soon in Sparta. Your loving and faithful cousin, Orestes."

Orestes sounded well enough, except for the undercurrents of restlessness threading through his prose; he dared not say half the things that must have been on his mind. Later, when I wrote back to him, I would also have to guard my tongue, not because a pedagogue was standing over my shoulder censoring my letter, but to shield him from certain harsh truths that were not his concern. Orestes had his own battles to fight.

Hoping to cast off my strange mood, I returned to the wine press to finish supervising the slaves.

That night, Tyndareus banished my brothers from his sitting room so he could speak with me alone. My half-brothers Megapenthes and Nikostratos went without complaint. Poor Aethiolas! Our grandfather silenced him the moment he tried to talk politics or war, grumbling that the only thing a sixteen-year-old had any business doing was keeping his mouth closed and listening to his elders.

"It isn't fair, Hermione." Aethiolas wore a sour face all the way to the door. "You're a girl. You haven't got anything interesting to say."

I shooed him out. "Would you rather listen to all that boring talk about grapevines and wine pressing?"

"Oh, please!" Aethiolas's freckles crinkled along with his nose. "I know you're going to talk about Mycenae."

"Out, boy!" Tyndareus's reprimand brought an abrupt end to our back-and-forth. "Hermione, come here. I've told that lazy slut time and again, but she never wraps the brick properly."

Sparing an apologetic look for my brother, I shut the door and attended to my grandfather's hot brick before sitting down with my sewing basket. "Aethiolas doesn't like being excluded," I commented. "He's not a child anymore."

"Young lady, I know boys far better than you. Used to be one, you know." Tyndareus hawked the phlegm in his throat. "His voice breaks, he grows a few inches, and all of a sudden he thinks he's old enough to be included with the men. This doesn't concern him." A letter bearing the Phocian king's seal appeared in his hand. "Strophius writes. He says Orestes is doing well."

I selected a skein of turquoise wool from the sewing basket and snipped off a length to thread onto my needle. "That's good."

Tyndareus grunted. "At least now the young man has a protector and doesn't need to come here."

Only a graybeard like him could get away with such choler. I wetted the thread between my lips before saying, "You say that as though you don't like him. You've never even met him. He's no miscreant but a well-mannered boy. He's committed no crime."

"What has that got to do with his future? It's a bleak thing, his fate. He's no criminal now, but he will be. Even Strophius admits he hasn't got much of a choice. Doesn't mean Strophius will offer the lad sanctuary once the deed is done, though. Orestes will have to face the Argive assembly's judgment or flee as an outlaw." Tyndareus started fussing with the blanket. "I told that useless slut I wanted the blue woolen one you made."

"Do you want me to fetch it?" I started to shift my sewing off my lap.

Tyndareus screwed up his face. Sometimes he seemed to complain just for the sake of complaining, so the young people would not shove him into a corner and forget him. "I'll box her ears tomorrow."

"Grandfather..." I hesitated. "Perhaps someone else should kill Clytaemnestra first." I took a risk venturing this suggestion. However justified she might have been, Clytaemnestra would have to die for the regicide she had committed. Agamemnon's kingly blood was sacred blood. "All Orestes would have to do is kill Aegisthus, and there would be no crime."

"Is that so?" Tyndareus harrumphed at the notion. As a woman, I had no business expressing my opinion—which made me wonder whether he would have dismissed the suggestion so quickly had he heard it from a man. "And who do you suggest ought to remove Clytaemnestra? Surely you don't expect me to strap on my armor to deal with that ungrateful bitch? Strophius? Doesn't want to get involved. Menelaus? Your father's detained abroad. He quarreled with Agamemnon before he departed Troy, and he's not going to want to do anything but enjoy his homecoming when that stubborn Egyptian bastard releases him. Aegisthus? He didn't go to the trouble of climbing into that whore's bed just to cut her throat. Clytaemnestra stands between him and being ousted altogether. Who do you think runs things at Mycenae—him?" Tyndareus wiggled his feet under the blanket. "Whatever else he may be, Aegisthus isn't a fool."

Perhaps matters would change once my father came home and had time to rest and deal with whatever business awaited his attention. Agamemnon had been his brother, and honor bound him to avenge his murder. Surely he would help Orestes. "Clytaemnestra isn't young. She might die from an illness or have an accident before Orestes is old enough to seek revenge."

"It's not your concern, young lady." Tyndareus shoved the brick away from him with his foot; he was done with it. "Of course you can write to him and Elektra, but you're to be careful what you say. You're not going to marry the boy, so don't you lead him on."

What gave him the impression that I would toy with a thirteen-year old youth? It was perfectly reasonable to caution a young woman to guard her tongue so she did not hurt a rejected fiancé's feelings, but to assume I was leading a besotted youth by the groin? That stuck in my throat. I was not my mother. Could he not at least credit me with having scruples?

Yet Tyndareus had always held women in low esteem; his wife had been the one great exception. Nevertheless, I stabbed my needle through the linen stretched taut across my embroidery hoop. Pull the thread into place. Jab again. I was no slattern. "As you wish."

OVER THE NEXT TWO YEARS, it gradually became clear that my grandfather was procrastinating.

He had dithered in sending for me after the war ended, and now he sat on his hands again, delaying breaking my betrothal to Orestes. What was wrong with him? I wondered. It was not as though he was senile or indecisive in other matters, so why now?

"Ending your engagement would bring a hornet's nest of suitors," Tyndareus grumbled, "and who wants to suffer through another tiresome marriage contest? It's become too much fuss to give away a girl. That shows you what's wrong with things in Sparta. Let your father deal with suitors and marriage contests and all the knotty problems they bring."

Just like him to say that when he knew full well that Menelaus, detained indefinitely at the Egyptian royal court in Pi-Ramesses, was in no position to deal with anything.

One year passed, then another. The Egyptian king's bureaucrats kept finding excuses to detain my parents, although Ramesses did allow them to communicate with the outside world.

Menelaus maintained a regular correspondence with my grandfather, who kept him informed about various matters. My brothers and I wrote polite notes inquiring about his health and expressing a desire to have him home. Aethiolas and I refrained from mentioning our mother or asking about our little brother because we did not know how to phrase those queries. Pleisthenes must be dead. Had he been alive, we would have known.

It overjoyed me when Menelaus answered back. A laconic note scribbled on papyrus: "Dearest daughter, I hear you have been a comfort to your grandfather and brought much honor to your family. Your mother and I will come home when we are able." It did not even matter that Aethiolas had received a near-identical reply. My father remembered me! He was proud of me! I kissed the slip of papyrus and tucked it into my jewel casket.

Not surprisingly, my mother had nothing to say. She probably did not even remember that she had a daughter.

I wrote often to my cousins in Phocis. Elektra, who had never mastered her letters, did not write back very often, and was standoffish when she did. Last summer, she had borne a son named Strophius, and was now pregnant again. According to the various messengers who brought news, motherhood had not softened her disposition at all.

Although I kept my grandfather's bitter admonitions in mind and never encouraged him, Orestes sent me trinkets such as a fifteen-year-old boy would send his girl: colored ribbons, copper bangles, glass beads. Strophius obviously had not sat him down to explain the situation. In return, I sent gifts appropriate for a woman doting on her younger kinsman: leather gauntlets and belts, cloaks, and tunics woven by my own hands, or embroidered bands to embellish his clothing because Elektra was not a very proficient needlewoman.

As for my other relations, I occasionally wrote to Chrysothemis. When she answered, which was rarely, her colorless phrases told me that someone was standing over her shoulder.

"Mycenae isn't your concern, young lady." Tyndareus smoothed the rug over his lap and stretched his hands toward the brazier. "I know you like your cousin—Chrysothemis sounds like a very nice, biddable girl—but it's best to let an angry beehive like that be. Now stop dwelling on it and open that shutter a bit more. It's too dark in here."

AN ARCADIAN AMBASSADOR ARRIVED at court the next afternoon. Tyndareus hobbled out on his cane to meet the man while I ordered servants to prepare a hot bath, refreshments, and a guest room. A royal kinsman like Agamedes could not be expected to sleep on a cot in the aithousa.

My handmaidens decked me in jewels and spangled flounces, and accompanied me downstairs to formally bid the ambassador welcome. Servants had arranged two inlaid chairs and a pair of three-legged tables in the megaron. They brought wine and mixing bowls. I stayed long enough to offer Zeus and Mother Dia libations, then withdrew with my women to the gallery above.

Agamedes voiced his king's concerns. "You must know by now how bad things are north of the Isthmus. The Dorians have completely overrun Thessaly. Oh, King Peleus and young Neoptolemus made a brave stand against them, halted them in Phthia, but they've lost Iolkos. It's only going to get worse from here. Troy was a waste." Agamedes smacked his fist in his palm. "*This* is the war Agamemnon should have fought."

"Indeed." Thus far, Tyndareus was keeping to his habit of saying little at the outset; he always let petitioners and ambassadors state their business first, and watched them squirm a bit, before weighing in with his answer. Once, Polycaste confided that he had done that with my father and uncle when they had first arrived seeking sanctuary after Atreus's murder.

"You'd think there would be Trojan gold to make up for the losses," Agamedes continued, "but half of it's lying at the bottom of the Aegean, along with far too many ships and good men." Tyndareus grunted, a sign that he was paying attention. "Agapenor was lucky to survive that shipwreck. Menelaus caught the tail end of that storm, and it blew him straight to Egypt." Agamedes tossed down his morsel of oil-dipped bread with a long draught of wine. "Thank the gods it didn't sink him. Only Nestor escaped it entirely, that lucky old dog. Didn't waste any time loading his ships with spoils and leaving Troy, did he?"

"I'd have done the same."

"Things are too uncertain now. Agamemnon could have rallied us against the Dorians, him and Diomedes. Aegisthus isn't worth a shit as king. He'll sit on his hands like his father did before him, wasting his time with wine drinkers and troublemakers, while the unrest brewing in Argos spills over our borders. It's already started in the mountains."

"And King Cyanippus does nothing about it?" Tyndareus asked in a cautiously indifferent tone.

"That useless old pustule never stirs himself except to scratch his balls and take his supper. Sure, he deposed Aegialia and Cometes, but that was to further his own interests. He's not going to tangle with Aegisthus or Clytaemnestra. I hear he's more afraid of her than him Hah!" Agamedes held out his cup to a servant to be refilled. "You Spartans must be favored by the gods to enjoy such peace. Menelaus is sure to come back soon, and in the meantime you've reared a fine grandson. That's all a man can ask for, to die an old man in his own bed and leave behind a full treasure house and strong male heirs."

Tyndareus belched as he swallowed his wine. "Do you take me for a decrepit fool? Do I look like I have one foot in the tomb to you?" His outrage was for show, a jest between two aging men. "I can still hold the reins and lead men to war. I've still own all my wits."

Agamedes chuckled. "Ah, I can see that."

My grandfather shook his head. "Women's foolishness has been all our undoing. You name some trouble and, gods know, there's a woman behind it. Helen spread her legs and went off for the first stranger who whispered sweet nonsense in her ear. Clytaemnestra got herself a little taste of power and then decided she didn't need her husband. Same with that whore Aegialia. Hah! Who do those sluts expect to protect them when the Dorians or some other enemy come hammering at the gates? Clytaemnestra might be able to wield a fisherman's net and a double axe against an unarmed man, but she doesn't know the first thing about war." Tyndareus snorted disdainfully. "We Spartans have our troubles, same as everyone else. Women expect too much around here, with their athletic games and sacred rites and their grand notions about power when they ought to shut their mouths and mind their proper business of bearing children and keeping house."

I did not like the turn this conversation was taking. Tyndareus heaped an old man's embittered scorn upon the ancient ways every chance he got, never mind that swearing to uphold those very traditions was what had made him king of Sparta in the first place.

"Ah, I forgot," Agamedes mused. "You let your daughters inherit before your sons."

"It's the hidebound fools ruling the Spartan assembly who allow it. I have nothing to do with the whole sorry business." Tyndareus irritably motioned for more wine. "I know what you outsiders say among yourselves about the Spartans, that we have the most beautiful girls in all Hellas, that we're ruled by queens whose bloodlines go back centuries to the Cretan kings at Knossos, but—" Just as the servant started to refill his cup, my grandfather's gesticulating caused the wine to slosh out onto the stucco floor.

Tyndareus barked at the youth to clean up the mess and leave the wine jug. "I have nothing but stupid and clumsy servants these days." He kicked the unfortunate server as he knelt down to mop up the spilled droplets. "About the queens, it's all nonsense, except the part about Spartan girls being beautiful. Ah, that they are! Leda was a vision of loveliness, a sweet girl with the right breeding, but her mother was no queen, never mind what the priestesses say. You know how women lie." Leaning forward, he refilled Agamedes' cup from the jug, then his own. "Her mother's father Pleuron was a minor landowner whose ancestors migrated into the Eurotas valley from Arcadia, and her father's people were displaced Aetolian nobles."

Polycaste had shown me the sacred scrolls kept in the sanctuary. Leda's father was indeed an Aetolian nobleman, but that was where Tyndareus's version of the truth ended. I bit back a fierce urge to stand up, right there in the gallery, and deny my grandfather's fiction.

Tyndareus took the lie further, much to my disgust. "The Spartan inheritance comes down to my granddaughter through *my* bloodline. My paternal great-grandfather was the hero Amkylas, and his mother was the lady Sparta, who gave her name to this entire region." But Amyklas had been *Leda's* maternal great-grandfather, a Cretan nobleman who had dedicated a shrine to the year-king Hyakinthos near the town which now bore his name.

It should not have surprised me, for like other Hellene kings my grandfather was an adept liar. For years, he had been disseminating tales about his mother Gorgophone's ancestry, claiming she had been Perseus's daughter of the same name. Everyone knew he claimed Perseid lineage to honor his friend Herakles, but how could he go so far now as to attack his beloved Leda by usurping her ancestors, and *then* dismissing her as lowborn? How dare he!

Tyndareus dabbed his mouth with his napkin. "Hermione's a well-bred young lady. She's content to run the household and mind the altars, but finding her a suitable husband will be a chore."

"Your granddaughter certainly has a splendid pedigree to go along with her beauty, but no one wants a wife with her pretty head stuffed full of strange ideas," Agamedes commented. "Agapenor will be relieved to hear of her industry and proper piety."

Had he come to propose an alliance between Arcadia and Sparta? Gods, no. Agapenor was my grandfather's age!

Tyndareus echoed my sentiments. "How so? Agapenor's a bit old to be looking for a new queen, isn't he?"

Agamedes picked his teeth with a probing finger. "What, he's still fit enough."

"Hah! He came home with gout and an arthritic shoulder, don't lie to me. And he didn't send you all this way to propose a marriage alliance without suitable bride gifts."

"When he hears of her suitability, he'll be more than willing to heap your granddaughter with treasures."

I held my breath. Arcadia was a poor backwater where the people clung to their primitive language and customs. Agapenor's wealth was counted in goats and olive trees, not gold or silver or arable land. "I will consider it," Tyndareus replied, "but Menelaus will have to agree to the arrangement. I will tell you this much: I've had enough of Mycenae and its endless blood feuds. We should never have become entangled with the Atreidai."

Agamedes grunted. "We've all suffered under the High King, and it's no better now that he's dead. The clashes between Aegisthus's men and Agamemnon's followers get worse every season. Cyanippus sits on his hands at the Larissa of Argos and the Argive assembly hasn't got the collective balls to urge him to man up and act. It's obvious they're all waiting for Prince Orestes to solve their problem for them. Pah! What do they expect a green youth to...?"

Monime chose that particular moment to hang over the balustrade to get a better view of my grandfather's beefy bodyguard Enops. Curse her foolish shuffling! I could not hear a thing.

"Sit down," I hissed.

Although she obeyed at once, it was too late. Agamedes and Tyndareus were talking about the profitability of the olive trees in western Arcadia. I had missed everything.

Angry, I turned upon my chastened handmaid. "Don't you *ever* interrupt me again."

Monime's quivering lips and moist eyes betrayed her hurt. Subdued, she hung her head and did not utter another word until much later, as she helped me prepare for bed. "Forgive me, Mistress. It's just that Enops is so handsome. I want him to notice me."

"You have no excuse," I said sharply. "A proper noblewoman does not make such a spectacle over a man in public, especially when he's lower born than she."

"But there are so many handsome young men at court, Mistress," Monime exclaimed, half-pleading like the adolescent girl she was. "Don't you ever admire them?"

It was an impertinent question. Clytaemnestra flogged her handmaidens for less. Of course, I liked love songs and sweet, sad tales that made me cry, but that was only natural for a woman. I wanted nothing more than that. And a princess of Sparta could not afford to moon over handsome sentries and bodyguards, especially when people considered her mother the most infamous whore in the Aegean.

"Never," I said firmly, realizing even then how prudish I sounded. "Your husband will be chosen for you, and he will look nothing like that hulking stallion guarding the king." I thought about old King Agapenor with his gout and arthritic shoulder.

Thebe brought over a silver basin and a sea sponge to wipe off my cosmetics. "Surely there's no harm in looking."

"As long as that's all you ever do." I closed my eyes to let her wipe the malachite off my eyelids. "You must submit to your husband, no matter how old or sour or impotent he is, or how much you dislike him. My mother started a war by abandoning her husband for her young lover, and now everyone hates her. You don't want to be a Helen."

Thebe wrung out the sponge. An uncomfortable silence permeated the air. Certain topics were taboo in the royal household. Monime and Thebe were much too young to remember my mother sneaking away in the night with Prince Paris and the contents of the Spartan treasury.

I was not.

I had been sick the week the Trojan delegation came to Therapne, and only saw Paris once from a distance. As far as I could recall, Priam's second son was not the youthful, charming prince of beauty the bards sang about, but a much older and harder man. So why did I refer to him as young? Perhaps because everyone else did. Or perhaps because Paris's supposed youth and beauty made my mother's betrayal more palatable.

During the days leading up to the abduction, no one had cause to complain about my mother's behavior with the Trojan prince or anyone else. Helen was the perfect hostess and deferential wife, remaining in the background until an urgent message from Knossos obliged Menelaus to leave to attend my great-grandfather Catreus's funeral. Tyndareus was away trying to cool a blood feud between my uncles and the sons of Aphareus. So Leda had assisted my mother in entertaining the Trojans while they awaited my father's expected return. Surely my grandmother would have noticed if anything was amiss, and surely she would have said something if she had. Leda never raised the alarm as far as I knew.

Late one night, however, she entered my room with my nurse, bundled me in warm fleeces, and took me to her chamber. Another nurse brought six-year-old Aethiolas. The atmosphere in the palace was rife with tension. Leda refused to explain what was going on or why we had to stay with her. She sent out many messengers but would not speak to us at all except to urge me to drink the sleeping draught she had prepared.

At daybreak, the high priestess Polycaste arrived. I overheard her and my grandmother whispering like cicadas through the thin wall, something about my mother and Pleisthenes, who had never joined us in Leda's chambers. I could not recall what they said in any greater detail, because my head was congested from my cold and the poppy juice my grandmother had given me, and Aethiolas was making such a fuss at having to stay indoors.

Leda later bathed my forehead with a scented cloth and assured me that my grandfather and uncles would be home soon. Polycaste urged me to eat a honeyed sesame cake, but neither woman would explain anything. Did they think me so naive? I saw the guards stationed at the door and in the courtyard below the window, and knew they were there because some danger threatened. I also knew very well how adults always tried to withhold bad news from children, but I was nine years old, almost a woman, and no amount of lying could convince me that something terrible had not happened.

Only when my grandfather returned home that evening with my uncles did Polycaste gather me and Aethiolas to her and explain that the Trojans had taken my mother and baby brother with all her women, and emptied the treasury, too. As she related these misfortunes, Castor and Polydeukes were already on their way out again, their booming voices breaking the gloaming serenity of the valley and their chariot wheels creaking as they charged into the night, but it was far too late to intercept the Trojans. They returned empty-handed and in a sour mood, and spent the next day drinking.

Polycaste told me and Aethiolas that the Trojans had taken my mother by force, but everyone else, including my grandparents and uncles, behaved as though she had gone willingly. My brother and I did not know what to believe.

I knew when my father had come home from the outraged bellows echoing up from the megaron. All Therapne could hear the terrible things he said—how he would flay my mother alive, shove hot pokers into her every orifice, and leave her carcass for the vultures. Frightened, Aethiolas dashed into my room to hide.

Menelaus found us, anyway. Filling the doorway like a raging beast, he caught a squealing Aethiolas in his rough grasp and inspected him all over while my brother bawled. This was not our father playing the Minotaur for our squealing amusement. Real fury blazed in his eyes when he barked at my brother to shut up and shook him. I expected him to give me the same treatment, and trembled with dreadful anticipation. I did not want him wrenching aside my clothes and groping me like that.

Instead, Menelaus addressed my grandmother, while the nurse carried a sobbing Aethiolas into the next room to soothe him. "Examine her." He jabbed a thick finger in my direction. "I want to be sure."

He left without laying a hand on me. Leda did nothing, but a short time later Polycaste came and took me aside, and gently explained that she was going to look between my thighs. "Your father wants to know if the Trojans hurt you there, but of course he does not want to frighten you by inspecting you himself. That is a business strictly for women."

I lay back on the bed with my dress hiked up to my waist as she directed. "Did the Trojans do that to Mother?"

"I do not know what they did with her," she replied, though I could sense even then she was not telling me everything. "But they insulted your father's honor by stealing her and your brother, and raiding the treasury. Breathe deeply and relax, Hermione. I will not hurt you."

She talked to me throughout the examination to put me at ease, but even her gentleness could not erase my embarrassment. I did not have to be old enough to be initiated into the women's mysteries to comprehend that no one's hand but mine belonged down there.

It was not painful, just a slight probing. I supposed Polycaste was satisfied with whatever she found—in those days, I had not explored there to learn what my maidenhead felt like—because no one scolded me afterward. She gave me a cloth to wash myself with and left me alone. I hugged my knees to my chest and brooded. Servants in the palace had begun slandering my mother, saying she had spread her legs for the Trojan prince and gone willingly with him to escape a boring husband. That last part was a vicious lie, because my father was neither stupid nor boring. Menelaus was the most wonderful man in the world!

An endless stream of gossip spilled through the corridors. Helen was a born slut. Servants and courtiers alike whispered that as a girl she had done it with the hero Theseus, and had had a secret baby by him that died. I felt nauseous inside, and wept angry tears at the growing certainty that my mother had abandoned me for some stranger who was not my father.

My grandparents refused to speak my mother's name. They would not even answer my questions about the rumors, except to shake reproving fingers at me and admonish me to always be a good girl. "Stay away from any man who's not your kinsman, young lady," Tyndareus said gruffly. "Don't look at them and don't talk to them, and don't you ever spread your legs wantonly unless it's for your husband."

His accusatory tone made me feel guilty. Polycaste had touched me there, but then my father and grandmother had sent for her, and Polycaste herself had assured me that I had done nothing wrong.

My father sent for me and Aethiolas. Menelaus was no longer the raging Minotaur. He gathered us close and assured us that we had not misbehaved. "I had to make sure you were safe," he said. "The Trojans have no honor, abusing my hospitality, dishonoring me, and shaming my house."

"Are you going to fight them?" Aethiolas asked.

Menelaus tousled his hair, then stroked my curls. "I'm going to get your mother and brother back," he said firmly. "Your uncle Agamemnon is going to help me."

Two days later, he left for Mycenae.

I FOUND MY GRANDFATHER berating his attendant, a harassed-looking girl who gratefully fled the apartment the moment he shooed her out. "That stupid slut can't do anything right," he muttered.

Considering her master's perpetual fussiness, Aketa did the best she could. I humored him. "What did she do now?"

Tyndareus, hard-pressed to name anything in particular, grumbled under his breath. "Everything's either too hot or too cold, or too rough or not clean enough. Useless slut."

To soothe him, I inspected the fleeces covering his couch. I had the laundresses air them out every week. "Did you enjoy your supper with

Lord Agamedes?" Tyndareus mumbled an affirmative. I licked my lips, pulling a fortifying breath before asking, "Why did you tell him that story about King Amyklas? Wasn't he Grandmother's great-grandfather?"

Tyndareus shuffled over to the shutters to inspect the rag keeping out the draft. "Sometimes you have to lie about things to change them."

"What is it you're trying to change?" I asked cautiously.

He looked at me. "I know you women like your sacred traditions, but they're a nuisance. If you heard me talking about Amyklas, then you also heard what I said about the Dorians. Just because they've taken Thessaly and Magnesia doesn't mean they'll stay there forever. Their Herakleidai allies want their birthright restored, which means that sooner or later they'll cross the Isthmus." He nodded shortly. "You're a good girl, Hermione, but a queen can't lead men to war. Aethiolas has had the training. He ought to be king when your father dies. Instead, it'll be whatever man you marry. An outsider like me, like your father. A fortune seeker, a mercenary."

Tyndareus left the shutters to return to the couch. I took his arm to help him lie down, then covered his legs with a fleece. "Agapenor's a good king," he said, "but there's nothing worse than an old man with a pretty young wife. It's an invitation to trouble."

Did he think me so loose, then? "Grandfather..."

"A pretty young woman with an ailing old husband and a kingdom to give away is bait for the young wolves of the court," he continued. "You want a hundred mercenaries sniffing around your skirts, like those leeches hounding Penelope?" The mere suggestion sent hot-cold shivers of revulsion coursing through me. "It would happen, whether you liked it or not, and there wouldn't be much you could do about it. You need a strong man at your side, a strong king and a fighter, but Agapenor's not the one."

Long ago, as I recalled, he had looked down at me sitting on my grandmother's lap, patted my plump baby cheek, and commented what a headache it would be finding me a husband. I had been five years old then, and had not understood what he meant. Thirty-six suitors sought my mother's hand; there would surely be a prince or king for me. I had not realized there were other considerations, that for a princess of Sparta marriage was not as simple as a good man bringing bride gifts to my kinsmen

Tyndareus shook his head. "The Spartan laws are all backwards."

Polycaste had warned me that a day might soon come when men trod all over my birthright as well as my sacred womanhood. "Grandfather," I said, "it's one thing to change the old ways, but there are other things you can't change. Your ancestors are written in your very blood and bone."

Tyndareus laughed. "Hah! Nothing is written that can't be unwritten. Kings have their bards invent new tales all the time. It's an old trick." A phlegmatic cough rattled his chest. "We call it politics."

CHAPTER TEN

TWO MORE YEARS PASSED. A subtle yet steady change marked the letters Orestes sent me. They became less grammatical and more passionate, the signs of a maturing young man lacking proper supervision. With his pedagogue dead, no one was censoring his correspondence, and he had begun using his own seal and messengers.

Seventeen was a glorious age for a young man, ripe with adventure without any real responsibilities. I found it hard to reconcile my memories of Orestes the boy with Orestes the young man. Though I imagined him narrating his letters in his boyhood voice, I knew his voice would have broken by now. The Phocian ambassador and the various messengers who brought Orestes' letters described him as tall and broad-shouldered, with a bullish neck and knack for boxing and wrestling, and a deep voice. All I could conclude with any certainty was that Orestes would have liked Aethiolas, given their shared passion for the outdoors.

"Dearest Hermione, Pylades and I have returned from exploring several caves high on Parnassus. Pylades has a fascination with caves and long-ago things, whereas I prefer the open heights. We went looking for deserted caves where Phocian ancestors might have lived once.

"Three of the four caves we explored were empty but for animal droppings and some old nests, but in the fourth we found signs that men had been there before, and that it was a sacred cave. The arrowheads we found there were made of stone, not bronze, and the god relics were very strange. That cave must have been used by people before Prometheus taught them how to build houses. Do not worry about our committing sacrilege. We did not disturb anything, except to pour out a libation before we left.

"Needless to say, I was grateful to be out in the open air after the darkness and strangeness of that cave. I am sending you some flowers from the alpine plateau, where they grow in abundance. I regret that they were crushed in my pack on the way down."

With a chuckle, I set the dried, smashed mountain daisies and campanula on the table beside me. Count on Orestes to send me wilted flowers.

"Dearest cousin, there is something which weighs heavily on my mind, which I must mention. I beg your forgiveness that I even have to trouble you with it."

Orestes' apology set me on edge. Was it the unresolved betrothal? Tyndareus continued to dither, but his was not the only hand in the game. Strophius as king of Phocis and my cousin's legal guardian could also have canceled Orestes' obligation. No, I did not think it could be that. Orestes would have mentioned it earlier, to say how sorry and hurt he was. This had to be something else, something much more vexing than Elektra's perpetual scolding.

"Aegisthus sent me..." I knew deep inside then what was coming. I had to compel myself to keep reading. "Aegisthus sent me a letter, along with a very strange gift, a sheet stained with old blood he says was yours from when he enjoyed you." *Enjoyed* me. So he could not say outright that he had *raped* me, for fear the letter would be read by my grandfather, and from there passed onto my father in Egypt. Sooner or later Menelaus would come home, and Aegisthus was not quite stupid enough to hand him the knife to cut his throat with.

"I destroyed the letter and the sheet before anyone could see them. I swear to you by blessed Athena, I will not utter a word about this matter to another soul.

"I do not believe the story, anyway. Aegisthus knows Mother's gifts and letters will not lure me home. He knows his servants cannot kill me, so now he sinks to base slander to incite me. He wastes his efforts. I know you have always despised him. And I am not going to run back to Mycenae like some hotheaded fool and fall into his trap. This latest insult only strengthens my resolve to see him dead."

Was Orestes so thickheaded that he did not realize Aegisthus's "enjoyment" could have been rape?

As a boy, he used to bring me wildflowers whenever I was sad or got sick. I imagined him doing it now, appearing at my door with wilted daisies and campanula, except that rape was not a cold; it never went away. It was not something that a young man's flowers or trinkets could fix.

Unable to read the rest, I folded the letter, stowed it in my pocket, and stood up. My movements aroused the attention of my maids. "Mistress, are you all right?" Monime asked.

Not at all. "I need air."

Nonetheless, that did not mean I wanted a gaggle of attendants on my heels. I would rather have gone alone, but a princess of Sparta never went anywhere without her chaperones. Dismissing Monime and Thebe, I had Sotera accompany me to the inner court. At least she was discreet and not overanxious to please.

That evening, Tyndareus inquired about the letter. Bless him for his failing eyesight, for it meant he could not snatch the papyrus from my hand and inspect it himself. I showed him the pressed wildflowers and read aloud the portions about the sacred caves and Parnassus. Tyndareus mumbled his appreciation. "I used to do the same thing as a young man with my friends." Reminiscence overtook him, prompting him to shake his head somberly. "That was so long ago. They're all gone now—Eubalus, Herakles, the whole lot of them. The older one gets, the smaller the world becomes. Smaller and smaller till it shrinks in on you, and you can't get up anymore. You can't see or hear anything, and then all you're left with is a tomb."

"Don't talk that way, Grandfather." I hated listening to his gloomy speeches. "Would you rather be dead?"

"Wait till you're my age, then the prospect of drinking from Lethe and becoming a shade won't sound so bad." Thin lips puckered together. "Ah, but shades don't need hot bricks, now do they?"

I waited until morning to write back. "Dearest Orestes, your flowers arrived quite dead, but I like them all the same. They remind me of the old days when you used to come home from your adventures with a bunch of half-wilted primroses and daisies crushed in your fist.

"Let me get the unpleasantness out of the way first, so you can enjoy the rest of this letter." I twirled my stylus while considering what to say next. Should I lie to him, just this once? Indecision needled me. I could not tell him the truth, and yet could not bear feeding him an outright falsehood, either. "You know as well as anyone how Aegisthus tries to goad you. Do not give him the satisfaction." It was an equivocating answer at best.

"Next time you write, I want to hear more about your visit to this strange sacred cave and the things you found there. Last year, a woman from Mount Taygete showed me a little fertility figure her great-grandfather found in a cave up on the mountain. It was very crude, a pregnant woman with large breasts and thighs, and like nothing I ever saw before. It was not a kourotrophos, because it held no child, but the woman told me the people in her village worship it as Eleuthia. Was that what you saw? If so, you may be quite right in guessing those things came from the time before Prometheus."

Encouragement flowed from my stylus, interrupted only by the need for more ink. "Grandfather likes hearing about your mountain climbing and other adventures. He is starting to lose his eyesight, and does not move around as much as he used to. It makes him short-tempered, so anything that lifts his spirits will be appreciated." Orestes had never met Tyndareus, but liked hearing about his Spartan relatives. "I am sending you instructions on how to properly press flowers, so you do not have to keep apologizing for mangling them, and I can keep them forever. Your loving and faithful cousin, Hermione."

CHAPTER ELEVEN

One late spring afternoon, a messenger delivered the breathless news to my grandfather that my father's ship had landed at Helas. The king and queen of Sparta would arrive in two days.

Although we had known there was always the possibility that the latest round of negotiations with Ramesses might succeed, after seven years everyone had stopped clutching at false promises. I had overheard many say they would only believe the news when my father's pentekonter beached on Spartan shores and Menelaus stepped down onto the sand.

That day had now come.

Tyndareus issued orders, grew short with his servants, and fretted over his infirmities. I instructed his manservant to humor him.

There was so much to do! Iphinous delegated the tasks. First, the royal apartments had to be opened, aired out, and scrubbed floor to ceiling. Scrub maids descended on the megaron to sweep the hearth, scour away the soot, and lay down fragrant wood, while other servant women sat in the inner court weaving garlands. Cooks' assistants brought back cartloads of fresh fish, mussels, and spices from the market.

Noblemen began to arrive bearing amphorae of wine and livestock for the feast. The butchers worked into the night cleaning and quartering the carcasses for the roasting pits. Mouthwatering aromas of cooking meat and baking bread soon enveloped the palace.

I tried to be everywhere and have a hand in everything, only to find myself becoming as peevish as my grandfather. Iphinous urged me to relax, reassuring me that he and his subordinates had the situation under control. I found it impossible to take his advice, however, for the need to impress my parents preoccupied my very waking thought, as did the nagging fear that they still considered me the child they had left behind so long ago.

I did not sleep well the night before. After a quick breakfast, I bathed then donned the raiment I had selected the previous day. My handmaids anointed me with scented oil before dressing me in a blue linen shift. Over that went an embroidered cream bodice and a blue flounced skirt cinched with a white leather girdle. Sotera fastened golden lilies in my ears and a matching necklace around my throat. Thebe painted my face, and Monime dressed my hair. Elegant pin curls looped across my forehead and long ringlets cascaded down my back.

I assessed the result in my hand mirror. Anticipation knotted my stomach. What would my parents think, seeing me for the first time as a grown woman?

Aethiolas also wore his best, and voiced similar sentiments when I met him downstairs in the megaron. "Do you think Mother even missed us?" he asked quietly. "She never wrote."

Not knowing the answer, I glanced aside, contemplating the hearth. Purple cushions graced my father's throne and the two chairs reserved for my mother and grandfather. "She'll want to take over the household. I suppose..."

"You think she'll find fault with you?" Aethiolas kept his voice low amid the swirl of men and maidservants standing on our orders. Visiting nobility had begun drifting to the outer court to catch a glimpse of the royal procession. "If it's worth anything, I would give my right arm to have you manage my house."

At twenty-three, Aethiolas was now a wealthy man in his own right. Tyndareus had invested him with two estates. He often traveled throughout the kingdom as our grandfather's deputy, and regularly visited King Agapenor's court as an unofficial ambassador.

A triton sounded from the walls, alerting us to the royal cortege's arrival. Aethiolas offered an arm to escort me onto the portico.

Our half-brothers joined us outside. Megapenthes and Nikostratos were slight and dark-haired like their dead mother, and very sly and secretive. One often found them sitting with their heads together, muttering in low tones. I found them to be haughty and disdainful, but Aethiolas somehow got along with them.

Eighteen-year-old Nikostratos greeted us by muttering a caustic remark under his breath, "Father ought to have tied a rock around that bitch's neck and dumped her in the deepest part of the Aegean." He shared a malicious smile with Megapenthes. "I hope he at least beat her black and blue."

It amazed me how much they hated Helen, as neither young man was old enough to remember her. Clearly, they had learned to despise her at their adoptive grandfather's knee, and so obedient to his will were they that they even believed in his manufactured pedigree. "Stop that, both of you," I said sharply.

Megapenthes challenged me with an frosty smirk. "Your mother should be ashamed to show her face in Sparta again."

He did it to needle me, because I was the eldest and exercised too much authority for his liking. "She's the queen," I answered, "and Father has forgiven her, so not another word."

We found Tyndareus waiting on the garlanded portico overlooking the lower citadel and gatehouse. Three dozen sentries stood at attention along the crenellated ramparts. Richly dressed courtiers, priests, and scribes thronged the terraces, awaiting the appearance of the royal procession. The first lookout had already sounded the alert. A quarter-hour, maybe less, and then...

Another triton sounded. All conversation ceased. The world went still. I could hear the breeze snapping through colorful banners overhead, and birdsong in the trees greening the terraces. I swallowed past a throat suddenly gone dry. It would be any moment now.

At length, we heard distant harness bells jingling. A dust cloud rose up from the lower town, then a wave of sound rolled toward us, cheers erupting from the onlookers lining the route. I tensed, my fingernails digging crescents into my palms. Father was coming, he was really coming home, and he was so close now, it would just be another heartbeat.

A shout erupted from the bastion above the gate. Bronze and wood clanged together as the sentries drummed their spears against the paving stones. A two-wheeled chariot passed under the gate, then another, and four more after that—the royal companions accompanying their king. I recognized my father at once, in his splendid blue cloak and boar tusk helmet with its tall crest and plume. He drove his own chariot, as he had always liked to do.

Abundant gray salted Menelaus's red beard and his skin was weathered from the windy Trojan plain and relentless Egyptian sun, but he had retained his massive stature. Sunlight glinted off his embossed bronze cuirass, and his helmet's scarlet horsetail crest stirred in the breeze.

I caught the silly, joyous grin spreading across my face and suppressed a girlish desire to wave and call out to him.

Removing his helmet, my father handed it to a groom before extending his hand to assist a woman from the chariot. Mother. A sudden chill froze the smile on my lips, and my happiness dimmed. Expectant murmurs passed through the crowd. Tyndareus, leaning on his cane, shifted his feet and grumbled an unintelligible obscenity under his breath.

Holding her head high, Helen let Menelaus escort her across the courtyard and toward us as easily as though the hundreds watching her were nothing. She must have been accustomed to all the scrutiny by now.

Seeing her legendary beauty for the first time with an adult's eyes, I was not impressed. Helen was dainty and dark-haired like a woman in a fresco, but she was also cool and impenetrable. Why in the world had so many men wasted their lives fighting in her name, or had they even known what they were dying for? *I* would not have died for her.

Nevertheless, Helen compelled one's gaze, even mine. She possessed true kharis. Studying her with a careful eye, I saw that she was not beautiful because she had creamier skin or blacker, glossier hair than other women, or even because she had kept her looks and slenderness past forty. No, not that. She was beautiful because a god's hand had pulled those features together in a rare balance of perfect symmetry.

I scrutinized her dress, too. She wore a vivid scarlet and yellow costume edged with gold fringe and rows of carnelian and amber beads. Not a single flounce or fringe was askew. Even her hair was perfect. Either she had excellent maidservants, or the gods had decreed that she must never, ever be allowed to be imperfect, ordinary, mortal.

My father formally presented her to Tyndareus, who acknowledged her a look that said he would rather slap her across her pristine white cheek. Helen inclined her head, then coolly shifted her gaze aside.

Tyndareus and my father clasped arms as they exchanged greetings. Standing to one side, my brothers and I watched with unbearable anticipation. Ten thousand butterflies fluttered inside me.

Finally, Menelaus turned toward us. Shaggy eyebrows shot up, his eyes bulged, and a huge grin split his face. His jovial roar echoed around the court as he held out his arms to us. "Come here!"

Laughter and polite applause rippled down from the terraces, reminding us that we were all on display, and that it would be undignified for us to swarm upon him like small children.

We might as well have saved ourselves the effort, as our father cared nothing about propriety. Lumbering forward, Menelaus enfolded each of us in a crushing hug, starting with Aethiolas, moving on to our half-brothers, and finally ending with me.

"Is this fine young lady the little girl I used to bounce on my knee?" His cuirass bruised my ribs as he squeezed me to his chest. After several breathless seconds, he released me and held me at arm's length. "You've grown very pretty, Hermione."

My mother followed in his wake, all frost and subtlety to his bluster. Because she was so dainty, I had to bend my head to receive the frigid peck she bestowed on my cheek. My nose twitched at her overpowering fragrance. Did she feel nothing at all for me? She gave Aethiolas the same aloof greeting, and ignored Menelaus's bastards entirely.

After my father presented the royal companions to my grandfather, who thanked them for their loyal service to Sparta, the men went apart to offer the customary thanksgiving sacrifice. My mother's handmaids closed ranks around their mistress. Drawing a deep breath, I approached them. "Would you like to retire?"

Helen and her women swept past without acknowledging me.

She might as well have stabbed me through the heart with a weaving pin. Dismissing me like a servant rather than her own daughter, that left me thunderstruck, then angry. If that was how she wanted to be, then let her choke on her frostiness.

At noon, we went into the megaron for the feast. Helen occupied the queen's seat, making it clear to all that *she* was mistress of the house, no other. Her coldness smothered my appetite.

She did not eat, either. She picked at her supper like a bird and drank almost nothing, and sat there like a cobweb woman, chill and glittering, while the conversation flowed around her.

Not once did she acknowledge me or anyone else. I knew I should confront her, say or do something, but I had not the slightest idea what. Should I ask whether she enjoyed the dishes? She obviously was not hungry. Or perhaps I should inquire about her journey. I hoped she had spent the entire voyage seasick. If she had not run away to Troy with her lover, I would not have been sent to Mycenae, and Aegisthus never, ever would have touched me. I had nothing at all to say to her.

Menelaus dominated the conversation at the high table. Everyone drank up his stories about Egypt, Crete, the Hittite lands, Canaan, and Libya, where the lambs were born with horns. As I listened, I forgot my grievance with my mother long enough to recover some appetite, and tucked into the fruits, nuts, and honey-drizzled sweets the servants set out. Yet as the night wore on, I noticed how my father's shoulders slumped and his mood darkened. "So many dead," he said, sighing.

Helen took his malaise as her cue to leave. Menelaus let her go with his blessing, kissing her hand. Her handmaidens rose with her, jostling me with scarcely an apology.

I excused myself to accompany them out. Helen did not notice until we reached her apartment, but when she did she brought me up short. "I do not need you to follow me. As you can see, I have sufficient chaperones." Gold flashed on her slender fingers as she indicated the three young women.

At that, I squared my shoulders and lifted my chin. How strange it felt, towering inches above my own mother. "I am your daughter, not your servant."

"Yes, I know who you are," she answered coolly.

"Do you?"

An immaculately plucked eyebrow arched up like a raven's wing, and her mouth tightened. At last, she had displayed some reaction! But then the mask returned, leaving her once more cold and enigmatic. "Come see me in the morning, Hermione," she said. "I have gifts for you."

I withdrew before her maids could shut the door in my face. She could keep her jewels and perfumed oils. I wanted nothing from her except the one thing she refused to give.

Returning to the megaron, I found Menelaus deep in conversation with Tyndareus about my mother. "It hasn't been easy these last seven years. We..." Then, noticing me slipping back into my seat, he abandoned the subject. "Listen to me, going on about my troubles when my children have been so attentive and patient." He called over his shoulder to his manservant. "Asphalion, tell the servants to bring in the gifts."

Royal gift-giving was its own unique spectacle, the quality and quantity of the presents an indicator of the giver's esteem. Courtiers leaned forward in their chairs to evaluate the items the porters piled by the central hearth.

My father rose from the high table and took the hearthside chair the servants had set out for him. Starting with Aethiolas, he called his sons forward one at a time, to assume the place of honor upon the footstool beside him. His largesse that night seemingly had no limits as he heaped silver-studded swords, inlaid daggers, armor, painted vessels, bronze cauldrons, chariots, jewelry, and fine garments upon my brothers. Aethiolas and Nikostratos were so overwhelmed they were dumbstruck. Megapenthes broke down and wept.

"What is this?" Menelaus exclaimed. "Have my sons been so neglected that they have to weep?"

After my brothers, it was my turn. Laughing, Menelaus called me forward, slapping his thigh as though he expected me to sit on his lap. As with my brothers, treasures piled up around me: an inlaid box containing alabaster cosmetic jars, brushes, tweezers, and polished silver mirror; bolts of scarlet and purple wool from Sidon, and sheer linen from Egypt; a painted casket brimming with Egyptian faience and semiprecious jewelry; an ivory spindle with an amber whorl set in gold; a carved cedar chest; and lotus-scented hand cream. I understood now why Megapenthes had wept. I did not want all this, did not want to see our father trying so hard to fill the void left by his absence. It frustrated and embarrassed me, because it was both too much and not enough.

"You have been a blessing on this house." Menelaus leaned down to plant a kiss on my cheek. Then he selected a splendid necklace, an outlandish Egyptian collar glittering with jewels, and made me stand and turn around so he could fasten it behind my neck. "This is to remind you that a good woman is worth more than gold."

The necklace spread its ponderous weight across my shoulders and collarbone; its counterweight nudged my spine. I hated both it and the metaphor it conveyed, with its subtle reprimand for women who did not mind their place. I did not need a yoke around my neck to keep me from becoming my mother. She was reminder enough.

CHAPTER TWELVE

HELEN NEGLECTED HER DUTIES as mistress of the house, leaving me to continue to manage the servants, consult with the scribes, and oversee the storerooms. Once she moved her belongings into her apartment and unpacked, she became a solitary creature, spending her days weaving at her loom, taking long walks along the riverbank, and gathering herbs in the hills, playing queen only when the occasion or her husband demanded her presence.

I observed from the gallery as she received the war veterans who came to visit and reminisce with Menelaus; since they had fought to recover her, he would not let her slight them by her absence. So she welcomed them with refreshments and a wooden smile, and sat among them with her spindle to endure their stories in silence. She might as well have been a ceramic votary for all the enthusiasm she showed.

Then she did something so strange my eyes caught it at once. When she rose to replenish the wine, she sprinkled a mysterious powder into the krater. What was she doing? Surely she could not be trying to poison my father and his guests. I held my breath as a server refilled the wine jugs from the krater, and the men drank.

No one died. It did not take me long to realize my mother had used opium, perhaps mixed with something else to counter the telltale drowsiness and euphoria. I knew the signs. Polycaste had taught me how to distinguish between the poppy species growing throughout the valley, how to harvest the milky sap, seeds, and straw, and prepare them for various uses.

As the men continued to talk, recounting the savage battles they had fought and friends they had lost, all their bitterness and sorrow and even laughter evaporated, yielding to a numbing apathy. I saw them again the next morning, refreshed and seemingly unaware that they had been drugged. What had my mother done to them to leave them so content? When had Helen the queen become Helen the sorceress?

She admitted nothing when asked, and she maintained a straight face while suggesting that the shadows and high vantage point must have confused me.

On the second occasion, I watched my father instead, marking how he set aside his gold cup without taking another draught, and how he alone remained unaffected. It took me far longer to read the subtle interplay between them and realize that she dispensed her drugs against his wishes.

Again, she denied it. She did not even seem insulted by the suggestion. Perhaps she had imbibed her own drug. How else could one explain her woodenness, her self-imposed solitude, or her propensity for staring into empty space, not so much deep in thought as locked in a trance? Nothing excited her curiosity or her anger. Her women told me she was always like that, always serene, never smiling, laughing, or crying. Nothing. How could anyone live like that?

Part of me still resented her enough to wish that she had never returned, while another part wanted to untangle her mysteries in the hope that I might yet find something to love. At night, I lay awake contemplating all the horrors she must have endured to be driven into such deadness. No one was born that way.

My old nurse once told me that people entered this world like newly turned pots which still required painting and firing. Her metaphorical pots occasionally cracked in the kiln, but sometimes the fatal flaw was so infinitesimal that it was not noticeable until someone tried to use the vessel. It might still be beautiful, but it was broken inside and too fragile to handle, and no one could determine how it had been damaged. That was my mother, as lovely and brittle as the antique black eggshell cups my ancestors had brought over from Crete.

Paris had not been the man to break her inside, because she had been distant even before he came to Sparta. Father would never have harmed her. Perhaps it was Theseus, then. No one talked about that abduction now. It was ancient history, but I sometimes wondered what my mother must have felt when the old hero hustled her into his chariot and took her north to Attica. She was only a child, not even a woman yet, and to contemplate that a man my grandfather's age might have forced himself on her...

All these ruminations meant nothing unless I could come out and ask her for the truth, but she never gave me the opportunity. We were never alone together, and she was not a woman for confidences.

Her isolation had made her eccentric. It showed in her long silences, her outlandish taste in decoration, and the way she dressed. In public, she wore a Hellene noblewoman's bodice and flounced skirt, but in private she favored Anatolian dress: an embroidered linen gown and fringed wrap fastened over one shoulder, pointed leather shoes, and a veil for her hair. She had collected costumes from Egypt, Anatolia, and Canaan. She liked long Babylonian shawls sparkling with beads and pleated Egyptian linen. On a wooden form on her dressing table she displayed an elaborately braided, beaded wig made from human hair such as the court ladies wore at Pi-Ramesses.

Sheer scarlet draperies hung at her window, tasseled purple and scarlet cushions adorned an Egyptian couch with leopard heads, and patterned Luwian rugs carpeted her chamber; she told me that people in the eastern lands spread their weavings on the floor. An Egyptian board game called *senet* stood on an inlaid table, and a curved Egyptian headrest sat beside her bed; it looked as uncomfortable as it was bizarre. Strange gods with wings and animal heads cluttered her altar.

When the mood took her, Helen bestowed gifts upon me: embroidered fabrics, carved ivory, faience jewelry, veils clinking with wafer-thin appliqués, and scented oils from Egypt and Babylon. And with each present came an expectant air, an unspoken question, as though we were bartering for my forgiveness, my love. *Is this oil of roses enough? Will this amber necklace tip the scale in my favor?* As she was my mother, I had no choice but to accept, while choking back the words I desperately wanted to say.

Aethiolas did not want Helen's gifts, either. She treated him like a stranger, an honored guest for whom she put on a charming smile while she sprinkled her numbing potion in his cup. He was astute enough to realize something was not right. Afterward, he avoided her company, refused to take food or wine from her hands, and would have quit court entirely had our father not insisted on keeping him close. I envied him the confidences and adventure stories Menelaus shared with him, and would gladly have traded all my mother's glittering presents to have been able to spend one such evening with our father.

It stung that Menelaus had not invited me to his sitting room, although I did not necessarily want to listen to Megapenthes and Nikostratos fawning all over him like the oily sycophants that they were.

"You shouldn't spend so much time in the sun," Helen advised. "Use the Syrian cream I gave you. It's made with crushed pearls, to keep your skin white and soft. We used it all the time in..." She caught herself before she could tell me where.

I ventured a guess. "In Troy?"

Her needle-thin eyebrows drew together. I could almost see the regret on her face. "Yes," she said shakily. "It was very windy." Then, bringing the quaver in her voice under control, she changed the subject. "Your father wants me to inspect your jewel casket and wardrobe, and your dower goods." She drew out the fibers from her spindle. "He is drawing up a list of suitable bachelors."

This was the first substantive thing she had said to me in days. Yet I did not want her poking through my belongings, invading my world. "I am still betrothed."

"Your father has broken your engagement to Orestes." Her painted spindle whorl twirled a tight circle as she flicked it between her thumb and index finger. "He sent the message yesterday."

My father had not said a word to me on the subject, preferring instead to pet and dote on me like a little girl. "Was he gentle about it?"

"I did not see the letter." It was tantamount to a verbal shrug. How could she sit there oblivious to my feelings? She could not possibly be that obtuse. "I believe he sent rich presents to soften the blow."

"Father should have told me first," I said.

"You expect to be consulted?"

Grinding my jaw, I focused on the perfectly even thread she twisted between her fingers. Did this woman *ever* break her thread or place a wrong stitch? She was even better at women's handiwork than Chrysothemis. "I don't want to have to hear about it later, like an afterthought. I'm beginning to suspect you and Father will surprise me at the altar with some drooling old dotard."

Helen pursed her lips, while the rest of her face betrayed no emotion. "Sarcasm does not become you. It leaves ugly scowl lines."

"Stop it!" She was unbearable, with her cosmetic tips and soulless observations. "I don't *care* about wrinkles or Syrian face cream or what color looks best with my hair!" I cried. "I'm twenty-six years old. I know how to look after myself. How can you sit there so blind?"

Her mouth twitched. After a moment, she answered, very quietly, "I am neither blind nor stupid, Hermione. A mother is supposed to say those things."

"You know nothing about your children, and you don't even care to ask!" I shot back. "You never once wrote to me or Aethiolas when you were in Egypt"

With a little sigh, Helen grasped the spindle whorl to stop its rotation. "I'm not one for writing letters. It is difficult finding the right thing to say to someone who isn't there. Your father is the same way. It takes him forever to start a letter." She set her spinning tools aside. "But we're sitting here together now, aren't we? What would you like to talk about?"

Talking to her like this was impossible. "Nothing."

I left her apartment frustrated by her coolness and agitated over my broken engagement. She did not understand anything.

Menelaus proved much more approachable, despite his initial befuddlement over my objections, and invited me to sit with him beside the brazier. "I realize how fond you are of Orestes," he said, "but it is a fondness between kin, a woman and a boy she has helped foster. Do not think of him as a husband. This marriage can't go forward. It's best to settle the matter as quickly as possible. Strophius will break the news gently to him."

"I know, but..."

"You can't set your heart on things, Hermione. We kings forge alliances for the sake of politics and then we break them. The only certainties in this world are death and suffering." My father leaned back in his chair. "That's not something a young person like you wants to hear, is it? I take it your mother didn't have much to say on the subject."

Complaining about one parent to the other seemed like such a childish thing to do, so I chose my words carefully. "She hardly says anything to me at all."

Menelaus made an empathetic noise in his throat. "Don't expect too much from her." Thoughtful, he stared into the glowing brazier. "She's not like other women. She moves in her own world. Always has."

Questions hung on my lips, and now a persistent inner voice urged me to confide in him, to tell him about Aegisthus. "Father..."

"Yes, dear?"

Hesitation crept over me, fed not so much by my shame as by the slump in his shoulders, the world-weariness reflected in his voice. He had come home after fifteen years of war and now he wanted to enjoy a little peace. I could not bring myself to ruin that. "It's nothing, Father. Never mind."

A DAY CAME when my mother surprised me.

Summer's heat baked the valley, enveloping the palace heights. Servants tacked wet linen across the windows to catch the slightest breeze, and the ladies abandoned their cosmetics to swelter bare-faced in the shade of the inner court. My mother liked to escape with her handmaidens down to the Eurotas. On one occasion she invited me to join her.

Perspiration was trickling down our faces by the time we reached the riverbank. Grandmother Leda had told me many times how the riverbank was a favorite haunt of Spartan princesses. I had become too accustomed to Mycenae's dry hills to think about the Eurotas as a place of escape, so when the time came to accompany my mother the notion seemed quaint.

My mother's maids spread out blankets under a plane tree where the air was coolest. Helen signaled permission for our guard to sit in the shade. People were either in the fields or the agora at that hour, and not likely to disturb us on such a sweltering morning.

Helen took off her sandals and sat down on the blanket. She wore a girl's cool linen smock, with her hair coiled and pinned atop her head. A maid gave her a covered basket with bread for the swans gliding nearby. Helen shredded a flat round into pieces and flicked a few crumbs into the water. Four swans converged on the spot to snatch up the offering with their long beaks. "Your grandmother used to come here all the time."

"It was a long time ago," I said.

Helen gestured to the youngest maid and whispered in her ear. Adreste hurried down the bank to where a swan's feather dangled among the reeds. Phokas, the guard, immediately went after her, cautioning her not to venture too close to the tangled foliage or mud until he probed them for snakes with his spear. I think he liked her, even though she was far above his station. He ended up retrieving the feather for her.

Adreste brought the feather to my mother, who fingered the white quills. "You must have heard the story claiming that I hatched from a swan's egg," she said.

I took a few crumbs from her pile and tossed them in the shallows. When I was small, my nurse used to tell me the story all the time. Surely my mother ought to have remembered that.

Helen continued, "When your grandmother was pregnant with me, an Egyptian envoy came to court bearing many gifts, including an ostrich egg from the land of Punt. She kept it until I was born, then dedicated it to Eleuthia at Amyklai as a thanksgiving offering for an easy delivery. No one whispered about swans then. It was only later, when people saw that I was not like my siblings, but small and perfect, like a girl in a fresco, that they started to murmur about the egg. They began rumors that your grandfather wasn't my real father, that Zeus had entered his body to sire me on midsummer's night the way he had fathered Herakles with Alcmene.

"Others noticed how your grandmother liked to visit the swans. They whispered that the god had attacked her on the riverbank. They pointed to the ostrich egg hanging in the sanctuary and said there was the proof." Helen uttered an ironic little laugh, a sound so unexpected that it startled me, because I had never heard her laugh before. "What nonsense! Have they never seen a swan's egg before?"

I watched Phokas sprawl out in the shade for a nap. "Zeus doesn't sire daughters with mortal women, only hero-sons. But Herakles went mad and murdered his family, and Perseus killed his grandfather," I said slyly. "Imagine what a daughter would do."

Helen leveled a reproachful look at me. "I did not cause the war," she answered tightly. "Agamemnon wanted to control the narrow strait through the Hellespont so his ships could bring back gold and grain from the lands around the Euxine Sea. I was just an excuse, a pretext for war." Her mouth worked soundlessly as she started to speak again. She stopped and shook her head, struggling with whatever it was that she could not say. At last, she heaved a great sigh. "I'm only going to tell this story once, because you're my daughter, but never again."

For a storyteller, she certainly took her time about starting her tale. A warm breeze ruffled my hair without seeming to touch hers. *She moves in her own world,* my father had said. *Always has.*

"Do you remember the Trojans?" she asked. "I think you met Paris once."

"I remember an older man with long black hair and a scar on his cheek. He had a very cruel look."

Helen affirmed my recollection with a curt nod. "His real name was Alaksandu. He came on Priam's behalf to negotiate certain matters with your father. That is how it was in those days. Men tried to use your father's influence with Agamemnon to gain favors or concessions. But I didn't like Alaksandu. Oh, he was polite, but he had a peculiar way of gazing at me whenever your father's back was turned. It made my skin crawl." She gave a visible shudder.

"Your father had to leave suddenly," she said. "Your grandfather was away interceding between my brothers and the sons of Aphareus, and your grandmother had her own duties to attend to. I was alone and anxious, but asking your grandfather to return home, or your father to forsake his obligations simply because a Trojan prince made me nervous would have been out of the question. I was the queen of Sparta. I had a hundred guards to protect me, not that it should have been necessary. The Trojans observed the same customs of hospitality as we Hellenes. Alaksandu would never dare violate his guest-right by trying to lay hands on me."

Just as her narrative built suspense, just as she was about to reveal what had truly happened the night the Trojan prince abducted her, she abruptly stopped and gestured to her maids. "Phylo, bring us some wine."

The young woman retrieved the jug from its tether in the cool shallows; the other maids brought the water jug and mixing bowl. Helen mixed her own portion, then got up, and on bare feet padded to the river's edge. "Let us offer libations to Zeus, Hera, and all the immortal gods."

At this rate, she would never get to the actual story. I watched her tip droplets of dark wine into the Eurotas; an inquisitive swan glided over to inspect the drink offering. Maybe she did not want to tell the tale at all and only did so to refute my halfhearted allegation that she had caused the war.

Then she sat down again, dipped a piece of bread into the wine, and ate. Did I have to wait for her to finish her meal, too? "Are you going to tell me the rest?" The afternoon's relentless heat compounded my frustration with her, making me snappish. "Or are you going to sit there and drag this out?"

Helen sipped her wine. "Such impatience is unbecoming a princess of Sparta." Now she was toying with me. She drew out the anticipation a moment longer to make it abundantly clear who was in control, then resumed the narrative. "People believe I went willingly because Alaksandu did not abduct me through brute force, but clever men have ways to secure a woman's compliance without beating her senseless. Alaksandu laid his plans very carefully. Once your father's ship sailed, he bribed a servant woman to slip into the nursery and take your baby brother. Then he got me alone and told me I would do exactly what he said or I would never see Pleisthenes again.

"Of course, I argued with him." She refused to meet my gaze, keeping her eyes on the grass, the river—anywhere but my face. "I tried to explain how he was violating his guest-right and endangering the very negotiations he had come to conduct, but he twisted everything around, saying my husband and father obviously did not value me very much to leave me alone like that. He spun webs around me, confusing me, playing on my fear for my child. So, yes, I went with him in the end, but only for your brother's sake."

I drew a sharp breath. It had never occurred to me that *both* versions were right, that she had been taken forcibly *and* gone willingly. "What became of Pleisthenes? He did not come back with you."

Helen took another fortifying sip of wine, another delaying tactic. "Alaksandu gave him back to me once we were far out to sea." She glanced over at her handmaidens, all of whom had fallen dead silent to listen to her narrative. "His ship moored overnight at a rocky islet. While we waited for the tide to change, he led me to an isolated spot amid the razor-sharp rocks, spread out his cloak, and...and..." She compressed her lips into a tight pucker. "Afterward, I told him to take me back, now that he'd had me. For a long, long time, he didn't say anything, just stared at me with those cold, dead eyes. Finally, he shook his head and said I was soiled, that my husband and father would execute me. But *he* was kind, you see. *He* would take me back to Troy and make me his wife."

Rustling reeds drew her attention to the riverbank. Helen watched a small brown snake slither among the reeds. I mopped the sweat from my brow. "Tell me the rest," I urged.

Her face fell, but she swiftly recovered the thread of her narrative. "He let me have my son during the voyage, but his men never left us alone together for fear that I would take my child and jump into the sea. Once we reached Troy, he took Pleisthenes away and gave him to his mother to look after. I learned then that he was already married, but he put his lowborn wife aside and married me. Then he got sons on me. Many sons. Sometimes he let me see Pleisthenes, to keep me obedient, but my baby boy had become a little Anatolian prince who thought Alaksandu was his real father. He never knew the truth."

Moisture glittered in her eyes. I sensed the coming tragedy, having always suspected in my heart that my youngest brother was dead. "One winter night, a servant woke me to tell me Pleisthenes was dead, that he'd stopped breathing in his sleep." Helen clamped down on a quivering jaw until she got her emotions under control again. "When I knelt down to gather him in my arms, I saw blood staining his lips and little droplets on the pillow beside him." She swiped her hand over her eyes, obliterating her tears before they fell. Flies buzzed around us in the somnolent heat. "I knew what Alaksandu had done. I hated him then as deeply as a woman can hate a man." Her tone dripped with rancor; it might have been Clytaemnestra sitting beside me. "I nursed that poison in my breast. I cursed him in secret. I wished death upon Troy and every living thing inside its walls."

Alaksandu had survived until the final year of the war, when the hero Philoctetes had shot him with the poisoned arrows of Herakles; she did not need to tell me his fate. "What happened to those other sons?" I asked.

Helen held out her empty cup for Adreste to refill. "There was an earthquake near the end. They were crushed in their beds." Her voice was a monotone, disinterested. She drained the cup in a single long draught. "I suppose it was for the best that Poseidon claimed them. Your father would have dealt with them as Agamemnon and Odysseus dealt with Hector's son."

The handmaidens sat speechless. Phokas dozed on, his snores competing with the buzzing flies. "Is the story true?" Like Helen, I felt nothing for those nameless boys, those Anatolian half-brothers. "You know the one..."

"You mean the story where your father raised his sword to kill me but stayed his hand when he saw my beautiful breasts?" Helen gave an inelegant snort. "You've never seen my body under these clothes. My breasts and belly are lined with stretch marks. That's what happens when a woman bears seven children. I asked him to kill me, to end my suffering. I even tried to guide his blade, but he would not do it. And so here I am."

A heaviness thicker than her dejected sigh settled over the riverbank. Then her mask slipped flawlessly back into place. She plucked the last crumb from her lap and tossed it into the water.

Chapter Thirteen

Dearest Hermione, I received your father's letter some days ago. It has taken me this long to recover from my shock at losing you. Strophius warned me years ago that it might come to this, so the blow was not unexpected, yet it stings the heart."

I hated the way my parents had dashed my betrothed's hopes just as he faced the most difficult trial of his life, and I read his letter in a sympathetic spirit. "Give Menelaus my very best wishes," Orestes said. "I would tell him myself, but every time I sit down to try to compose a letter, my mind goes blank. I know what I should tell him, but cannot make the words come. And with this blood oath hanging over my head, he may not even wish to hear from me." That was not true. Unlike Tyndareus, Menelaus always had a kind word for Orestes. I was certain he would have wanted to hear from him.

"This may be my last letter to you for a long time. The situation back home has become untenable. I cannot wait much longer."

I reached the bottom of the first page, and turned to the second. Orestes not only wrote with a large hand, but had the bad habit of folding each page separately, creating more work for me. "Pylades and I traveled to Delphi late last summer to consult the oracle. I had to know for certain what the gods wished me to do. I would prefer to have

Mother take her own life rather than kill her myself. It would be a lesser sin. The Pythia returned a troubling answer. I am doomed to murder the womb that bore me, and to be tormented afterward with madness and wandering. I should never have consulted the god! Mortal men were never meant to know the future."

Murder. Torment. Madness. Each dire word struck me as if with a knife. Must the gods be so cruel? Orestes had not done anything to deserve the burden the Fates had spun for him.

I came to the end of the second page, and started to unfold the third and last. "There is no going back. I swore an oath. I must go through with the deed. Aegisthus deserves to die. Mother deserves to die along with him, but I have no illusions that killing her will do anything but placate Father's restless shade." *Orestes! Please, don't talk like this.*

"Gods, I want this to be over! I want the ghosts to leave, and the blood to wash away, but it will only get worse from here." Orestes' handwriting became erratic, betraying his emotions. "Duty is such a cold, unyielding thing. It sits like a stone in my belly. All I truly want is five minutes alone with you, to see your lovely face again. Maybe it isn't the correct thing to say now that we're no longer betrothed, but I don't care. It's what I feel. If you were here with me, you would put a finger to my lips to shush me, the way you used to do, only this time I would kiss that finger and then your sweet lips to tell you that yes, yes it is the right thing to say!"

His stricken words had me blushing right down to my scalp. He was speaking to me as a man, a lover, rather than a kinsman. I was touched, inappropriate though it was. "Orestes, you dear fool." I unfolded the bottom third of the papyrus to continue reading. A pressed yellow daisy rested in the crease.

"What is this?"

Focused on the letter, I had not noticed my mother's entrance. Now Helen stood over my shoulder. My handmaidens laid aside their needlework and started to their feet to acknowledge her, but she ignored them.

Helen picked up the daisy. "I heard you received a letter from Phocis. Now it seems someone has sent you a love token." She stretched out her hand. "Let us see who this mysterious admirer is."

I surrendered the letter because she gave me no choice, and sat burning with embarrassment as she perused it. Clytaemnestra had said she could not even read; that obviously was not true. She had to know the sender was Orestes, but of all the letters she had to inspect, why did it have to be this one?

"Is Orestes always so passionate?" she finally asked.

"No, he..." I struggled to find the right words.

"Do you write back to him with the same passion?"

I shook my head. "Of course not. It would not be appropriate."

Helen folded up the letter, but did not return it to me. "Are there any other letters?"

"In the clothes chest, in a little wooden box under my skirts," I answered thickly. She was going to take them all away. "It is not as you think. He's my cousin. He tells me what he does in Phocis, about the places he's been, the people he's met, about Elektra and Pylades and their children. The daisy is nothing. He's always given me wildflowers, even when he was little."

"I will let your father decide what is appropriate," she said. I followed her into the bedchamber, where she rummaged through my chest to retrieve the letters. "Has he sent you any gifts?"

From another box, I produced the glass beads, copper bangles, and other trinkets Orestes had sent over the years. She poked through the collection before dropping the packet of letters inside, shutting the lid, and taking the box with her.

Once she left, once I could sit down and gather my thoughts, it occurred to me that the letter mentioning the bloody sheet was among those she had taken. I had not destroyed it because I enjoyed rereading the paragraphs about Parnassus and the sacred caves. A knot choked my throat. What would she and my father think when they read what Aegisthus had said?

That evening, I forced myself to go down to supper and eat. My half-brothers dominated the conversation, hounding our father with questions about Hittite chariots. Aethiolas was away at his estate. Tyndareus slurped his lentil broth and pointedly ignored my mother.

After the dessert course of honey cakes, I excused myself and retired upstairs to sit by the brazier and await my mother's return. Or would it be my father this time, to interrogate me about Aegisthus's slanderous claims while forbidding me to continue an inappropriate correspondence with Orestes?

I let my handmaidens retire early and stayed up late waiting, trying to remain calm while wondering whether anyone would come.

Near midnight, Helen returned. "You will not write to him again," she said in a hushed voice. "I'm sure you behaved with discretion, but you are no longer betrothed, and he is too old and too filled with passion for this to continue." She handed me the packet, now reduced by a third. "You may keep these."

She left without ever mentioning Aegisthus. I untied the packet and leafed through the remaining letters. Parnassus, the sacred caves—it had to be here somewhere. Nothing. I searched again, but the letter was gone. My parents had confiscated it, they had read the passage about Aegisthus, and yet my mother had not said a word.

AETHIOLAS GRINNED AT ME. "I hear you've been sending love letters to Orestes."

Where a moment earlier we had been talking about his recent excursion to Amyklai, the mood in the sitting room abruptly darkened. "I don't know where you heard that." I lanced my needle through the linen to secure it and set the embroidery frame aside. "There were never any love letters."

"You liked him, though." Aethiolas stretched out his long legs and gave my maids a fond glance.

"Leave me alone!"

Aethiolas perked up at my raised voice. "I was just teasing."

"It's not a joking matter!" Why did he have to spoil an amicable visit with his playing? I could no longer comfort Orestes, and it wore on my nerves. Trust my mother to meddle where she was not wanted! "You know why the engagement was called off."

Abashed, he shifted over to sit beside me and drape a consoling arm around me. "You're right. I shouldn't tease you."

I held out a moment longer, then leaned my head against his shoulder. "Orestes shouldn't have to bear this alone."

Aethiolas gave me an affectionate squeeze. "I know what you're thinking. Father should help him avenge Agamemnon, but it isn't so simple. Father has just come home from a long war. Do you expect him to raise his host again and attack Mycenae? He's tired, Hermione. His men are tired," he said. "And Orestes is the one everyone's looking to. He's the one they want."

"But it's matricide," I protested.

"Clytaemnestra gave him no choice" Aethiolas stated firmly. "Aegisthus stole another man's wife and murdered that man in his own home. Orestes should kill them both and take back what's his."

His vehemence surprised me, for he had never before expressed an opinion regarding the subject. I stared at the floor, studying the way the sunlight streaming through the window knifed across the painted stucco. Thousands might applaud Orestes as he went after the usurpers, but how many would succor him later? "Would you do it, if it were you instead of him?"

Aethiolas did not give it a moment's thought. "Yes. If I didn't, I could never again hold up my head and call myself a man. That's why Father won't get involved. Orestes has to be his own man."

DISTANT THUNDERHEADS ROLLED in over the Taygetus Mountains. Lowering gray skies and the sharp tang of ozone in the air presaged a fierce storm before nightfall. A high wind rattled the leaves from the trees. Autumn was losing its mildness as it faced the onset of winter.

I supervised the slaves dyeing threads in the shed attached to the weaving house. Wool colored in shades of rust and brown hung from the wooden drying racks. Madder dripped from the damp skeins onto the packed earth floor.

A palace servant hobbled into the shed and made his obeisance.

"Princess, the king says you must come to the megaron at once."

"At once" gave me no time to change into more appropriate attire. Scarlet dye smeared my skirt and streaked my fingers where I had sorted through the skeins to ensure the color had spread evenly. I smelled of the vinegar the women used to make the colors fast.

I did my best to rinse my hands and straighten my clothes before going up to the palace. At this time of day, the megaron should have been a bustling center of activity, with petitioners crowding the great court and vestibule, yet it stood desolate, a precursor to the ominous solitude within.

My father, wearing a dour look, occupied the throne. An open letter sat upon his lap. My mother and grandfather sat close by. A servant shut the vestibule curtain, then withdrew, leaving us alone.

Father's manservant Asphalion conducted me to the empty chair beside my mother's. I sat down, folded my stained hands in my lap, and waited.

"Daughter, I have some very grim news to share with you." Menelaus held the letter up to the firelight emanating from the hearth. "This just arrived from Mycenae. Prince Pylades—"

I gave a start. "Orestes?"

Helen hissed under her breath at my impropriety.

"Yes," he said. "Clytaemnestra and Aegisthus are dead. Pylades has written to me to describe what happened." My father rattled the papyrus sheet, cleared his throat, and squinted. "Here, let me read:

"'Orestes and I entered the citadel disguised as pilgrims. We found Aegisthus loitering near the workshops. Orestes ascended the ramp first, to take the high ground, and waited for Aegisthus to make his way back toward the palace.'" I felt faint. Why had Orestes not written his own letter?

"'Aegisthus called out, but no one came to his aid, as we had sent our men to secure the walls and terraces beforehand.'" It was getting hard to breathe; there was no air in the megaron. "'Orestes fought Aegisthus at the top of the ramp, first with bronze, then with his bare hands. Aegisthus went down, and Orestes struck his head off with a single blow. It rolled down the ramp...'" I gasped for air. "Hermione, are you ill?"

Trembling, I let my head droop, only to notice the scarlet dye staining my skirt and fingers. Blood. A low cry left my lips.

Menelaus called for Asphalion. "Bring the princess strong wine and a cool compress. Helen, do something to comfort your daughter."

My mother placed a hand on the arm of my chair, nothing more. Was I a child who required coddling? "Father, I don't need wine or a cloth. Please, go on. You're keeping me in suspense."

Tyndareus rumbled from his chair, "Are you sure, girl? Menelaus, you should have given her the wine to strengthen her nerves before you started."

They were going to dither like this till Asphalion came back, and meanwhile all I knew for certain was that Orestes had gotten into Mycenae and slain Aegisthus, and that Pylades for some reason had written the letter. "No," I croaked. "I want to hear the rest right now. Please, Father."

Menelaus hesitantly continued, "'Once Aegisthus was dead, I went on ahead to the palace and caught the queen coming downstairs to see what the commotion was. I herded her maids and daughter into a side room and shut them in. Orestes entered. I never intended to leave him alone with his mother, we had sworn to let her take her own life and avoid the sin of matricide, but circumstances drew me away from his side at the crucial moment. Aegisthus's son Aletes and a few of his father's followers engaged our men in the great court. I went outside to take command, and cut down the usurper's son. Forgive me. The mistake was mine.'" *What have you done, Pylades?* My mind raced. *What horrible thing did Orestes do while you were gone?*

"'I found Orestes on his knees beside his mother's body, weeping into his hands like a child." Oh, no! No! "'I swear to you, he never intended to kill her with his own hands, but Ares possessed him when he slew Aegisthus on the great ramp, and the god was still raging in his blood when he sought out his mother.'" I heard the words, cold and precise, yet the horror had become so great that they rolled over me without quite registering. "'Her death was as swift and painless as Aegisthus's was brutal, I assure you. The blade went straight through her heart, and killed her instantly.

"'I released the women from the closet and instructed them to attend the dead. Orestes was in no state to speak with his sister. He was inconsolable and immovable.'"

I sat frozen. *Weeping into his hands like a child. Inconsolable and immovable. Curse you, Pylades! You swore to look after him.*

"'Orestes and I arranged for loyal and competent men to take charge of the citadel and safeguard the royal ladies while he sought purification for the killings. We are now heading north toward the Gulf of Corinth, where my retainers have a ship waiting for us. Orestes has been insensible since we left. He begs me to kill him and end the curse on his house. I cannot bring myself to do it. Elektra would never forgive me.

"'We are not returning to my father's house, as he has made it clear he would not succor us if Orestes committed the ultimate sin. However, he will grant us safe passage to the sanctuary of Delphi. Orestes has entrusted me with Agamemnon's seal, and letters authorizing me to act as his regent until this matter is resolved. I will return to Mycenae once he is safe within the god's sanctuary, and will send for Elektra and the children once she recovers from childbirth. I am your servant, Pylades Strophides.'"

Asphalion appeared at my elbow to press a cup into my hand. I thrust it back and took the wet cloth instead, burying my face in it. All I could do was weep, softly at first, then louder, letting it all out, wailing into the damp linen till my throat ached.

Papyrus leaves rustled. I heard my father's joints creak as he stood up, then his footfalls as he crossed over to me. I glanced up to find him standing over me, arms held wide. Rising, I fell sobbing into his embrace.

I hated how my tears left great wet patches on his embroidered tunic. "Orestes had no choice. His father made him swear."

"Look at me, Hermione." Menelaus grasped my shoulders to hold me at arm's length. "How could that possibly be? Orestes wasn't there when Agamemnon was killed."

I hung my head, sniffling. Tears slid down my cheeks. "Yes, he was. He saw it all." I had to force each word out.

"He told you this?"

Squeezing my eyes shut, I nodded. "I saw it, too. I was hiding up in the gallery. I heard the shouts. I saw them murder the companions in the megaron, and the Trojan woman. Cassandra. They murdered her, too."

"Helen!" Menelaus barked at my mother like a guard captain reprimanding an errant sentry. "Come here and comfort your daughter. Take her to her chambers and attend to her."

Numb, I let my mother and her maids escort me back to my apartment, but resisted when she instructed my women to undress me and tuck me into bed. "I don't want to sleep."

"Don't be difficult." Helen opened a packet of herbs while her maids set up a tripod and small bronze cauldron in a corner. Sotera shuttered the window against the drizzle spattering the sill.

"It's not even noon."

She pinched herbs into a cup. "You're in no condition to go back to the dyeing shed. Let Iphinous manage the servants. When this tea is ready, you will drink it. An Egyptian priestess gave me the recipe. It will give you a deep, restful sleep."

A narcotic fragrance wafted past my nostrils when she showed me the herbs powdering the bottom of the cup. Was she brewing the substance I suspected she was? Did she think I would let her drug me that easily? "I don't want your foreign potion." I waved it away. "Just let me be."

"You want to lie awake all night weeping bitter tears? This is much better, believe me." Helen placed the cup on my dressing table, then stooped over the cauldron to stir the simmering water with a bronze ladle. "Stop being stubborn and listen to someone who knows what it's like to be tormented by—"

"Stop treating me like a child!" I raised my voice. "You think I don't know what it's like to be afraid, to see blood shed, to be abused by a man?" I never meant to confide in her like this, never meant to divulge my secret to her at all, but she had provoked me. "I saw the companions and that poor woman murdered! I thought I would be next. And then, when Aegisthus raped me the night before—"

"Be silent!" Helen's reprimand cut like a dagger through my hysteria. Dark eyes blazing, she came over to me. "Who else have you told?"

At least Aegialia and Polycaste had let me talk, while my mother, who above all people should have heard me out, did not even want to hear it. My handmaidens stood white-faced in the doorway until Helen ordered them to get out. "Sotera and Polycaste," I growled. "Queen Aegialia, because she saw the bruises. No one else." I held onto my anger as a shield against more tears. "I took the medicine and tried to forget about it."

Helen's nostrils flared as she sucked in a long breath. "You never told Orestes, when Aegisthus wrote to him about the sheet?"

So she *had* noticed the passage. "I let him think it was malicious slander."

"And you never thought to tell me?"

She made it sound like a personal affront. "You saw the letter, you know what it said. Why didn't you ask about it?" Let her reproach me all she wanted, but she was not going to burden me with guilt for that.

"I had no idea it was anything more than Aegisthus's feeble attempt to provoke Orestes to violence," Helen answered stiffly. "You should have told your father and me straightaway."

"I didn't tell you because you care nothing about me, and because you would have gone straight to Father with it. You think I wanted him to go to war again, to broadcast my shame to the world?" The simmering water had begun to boil; my mother ignored it. "Do you think it makes any difference that Aegisthus is dead? It doesn't change what happened. It doesn't take away the hurt."

Helen acknowledged that statement with an almost imperceptible nod. "No, it doesn't." She went to the cauldron to ladle steaming water into the cup. As the herbs steeped, a soporific vapor suffused the room. "I will have to tell your father that the charge was true. It won't affect your marriageability. Most men are willing to overlook a bride's missing hymen when there's a rich kingdom to be had."

Dumbstruck, I watched her stirring the hot tea. She had just learned her only daughter had actually been raped, and this was her reaction?

She blew into the cup as she brought it over to me. "No one has to know. It isn't always easy to tell, anyway," she added. Steam curled and wisped about her face. "As for this ridiculous business about my not caring, when do you ever come to me with your troubles? Did you think

I would blame you for what happened? Foolish child! You don't know shame until your parents blame you for leading a man on. Theseus was fifty, I was ten, and the only thing I did wrong was be polite and ask to hear more of his stories." Helen extended the cup to me. "Drink this."

I recoiled from the bitter-smelling brew. "It's what you give Father's guests to make them forget the war."

"Yes, it's called nepenthe. Drink it and the Minotaur himself could come crashing through the wall to devour you and you wouldn't care." A secretive smile curved her lips. "You will come to appreciate this gift. I wish I had known about it at Troy."

Heat radiated through the ceramic cup into my hands. After I drank, Helen smothered the flame burning below the tripod and added lavender sprigs to the brazier. Sotera waited to take the empty cup from me, while my mother slipped into the sitting room to chastise my maids. I overheard every stinging word: "I am sure you are sensible, well-bred girls who know better than to spread gossip, but I will tell you anyway, for your own good. You will not breathe a word of anything you heard here this afternoon. If you do, I will send you straight home to your families dowerless and disgraced. Do you understand?"

A peculiar deadness crept over me along with the requisite drowsiness. I felt no sympathy for Monime or Thebe, or any resentment toward my mother for usurping my authority. There was nothing. Nothing. I was not certain I cared for that taste of oblivion.

Closing my eyes, I hovered in the hazy realm between dreams and wakefulness, listening to my mother's skirts rustle when she came back into the room, and to my maids weeping on the other side of the wall. I should have said something, raised an objection, asked Sotera to bring the girls in, and apologized to them, but with each passing heartbeat went the energy to do any of those things, until exhaustion muffled me in deep sleep.

When I woke, Sotera brought me warm mashed apples and black barley bread. "It was a bad storm, Mistress. You slept right through it."

I regarded the food with disinterest. "It didn't last very long."

"You've been asleep more than a day," she said.

Yet I still felt lethargic. Yesterday's peculiar apathy lingered. I stared into space. My thoughts dribbled past me in a sluggish current, yet I could not focus on a single one. Sotera ordered a hot bath. "It will make you feel better, Mistress."

Monime and Thebe were still moping as they washed my hair. I summoned enough energy to address them. "Ignore my mother. She has no business..." And there went the thread. My eyelids started fluttering in the warm, foggy air. "I feel..."

Somehow, they got me out of the bath, dried me with towels, and put me back into bed. I must have dozed a little, because the next thing I knew a hot brick lay snug and toasty against my feet, and my father was sitting in the chair beside me.

Menelaus pressed a shushing finger to his lips. "Don't stir. I wanted to make sure you were resting."

"What time is it?" Had a second day slipped without my knowing it?

"Almost midnight." Leaning forward, he stroked my cheek; his calluses grazed my skin. "Your mother told me about Aegisthus." He spoke slowly, as though gauging my alertness. "I wish you had come to me and told me first."

Although I still felt sleepy and strangely disconnected from my emotions, I found myself clearheaded enough to follow him. "I wanted to, but..."

"Did you think I would get angry and blame you?" He screwed up his mouth to contain his hurt. "Hermione, you're my daughter, my precious little girl. Had you only told me, I would have mustered the Spartan host and shown Aegisthus the true meaning of pain."

And tongues throughout the Aegean would have wagged. *King Menelaus can't keep other men's hands off his wife or daughter.* "I didn't want to do that to you. Another war..." My limbs felt leaden. "Father, what's wrong with me? I can't feel anything."

Menelaus nodded his understanding. "Your mother's drugs are very powerful. It's unnatural, that stuff. Mortals should feel what the gods send them to feel." He harrumphed for emphasis. "She told me you were angry with her. I know it seems that she doesn't care, but you can't expect her to coddle you like your old nurse. She's become so used to hiding behind veils and spinning her webs that she's forgotten how to love." Sighing, he leaned back in his chair. "That's how she is, Hermione. But I don't ever want you to be afraid to come to me."

I wished I could feel enough to give him the answer he deserved. "Orestes. What's going to happen to him?"

Menelaus acknowledged my question with a warm smile. "You're very fond of him, aren't you?" He grew thoughtful. "Perhaps the priests can purify him, so he can walk free again and claim his inheritance."

I let my idle fingers explore my pillowcase's scalloped needlework edge. Chrysothemis could do fine work like that. "May I send a letter? Just through the priests, to ask how he is?"

"Of course you may," my father answered. "You can even write to him, as his concerned and loving kinswoman, but keep in mind what Pylades said: he isn't well. You may not get an answer." Grimly, he shook his head. "I wanted to take you away from Mycenae—you should know that, Daughter—but it's not so easy to think about your children back home when you're lying exhausted in a dusty tent after a hard day's fighting, or when you're busy trying to feed and shelter your men. War is a dreadful business." Then he slapped his hand against his outer thigh. "Well, then. Tomorrow your mother wants you to spend the morning with her. Try to be patient with her."

Visiting my mother could be an excruciating experience, depending on her mood. She was like a fussy old woman when it came to her treasures, and would not let the scrub maids dust her costly imported furniture. That left her handmaidens, who fared no better under her remorseless scrutiny.

"Adreste, that Isis was a gift from Queen Merytamun. It's priceless. Phylo, you'll ruin that mother-of-pearl inlay if you get oil on it." I pitied the poor girls. Monime and Thebe no longer wanted to go anywhere near my mother.

Helen's needle flashed in the sunlight streaming through the window. She was always sewing, spinning, weaving; her hands never stopped working. Scarlet horses pranced across the band she was embroidering for my father. I replaced my spindle in my wool basket and leaned in to watch her work.

"You seem pensive, Hermione." Helen poked the needle through the taut linen. "Alcippe, be careful with that box. It's heavy."

I kept my father's advice in mind. "You're hard on them."

"Girls should have a strict education in what to expect as wives." She remained focused on her work. "A husband wants his wife to fetch his slippers, prepare his broth just so, have his clothes laid out the way he likes—and he expects her to do it all with a cheerful countenance."

I rolled my eyes. "Maybe, but your women must be wondering which is worse: waiting hand and foot on a decrepit old husband, or being nagged to death by the queen of Sparta."

From the corner of my eye, I saw young Adreste smothering her laughter behind her hand. My mother regarded her with a tolerant look, then her gaze returned to me. "You would not make such acerbic remarks if you knew anything about the realities of marriage."

A little sarcasm did wonders for helping me keep my patience with her, though. "Marriage is probably the last thing I will ever have to worry about."

"That's nonsense." Helen secured and snipped off her thread. "Your father will find the very best eligible men and invite them here."

Scowling, I turned to the window. A call from the south watchtower interrupted the morning birdsong. "How delightful. I can hardly wait to meet the whole arthritic, drooling lot of them."

Helen made a little noise at my caustic observation. "I have no idea where you inherited your sharp tongue. It certainly wasn't from me." She selected a skein of darkest umber to outline the horses with, while shaking her head disapprovingly. "Why are you not working? Idle hands breed trouble."

"I get bored spinning and weaving all day." I watched her moisten her thread between her lips. "Where did you learn to embroider like that?"

"Troy." Helen held the needle up to the light to thread it. "Anatolian women are very skilled weavers and embroiderers." She fastened the threaded needle through the linen border to secure it before getting up.

"Alaksandu appointed a woman to teach me, so the other royal women wouldn't mock me as a Hellene rube."

Then she took me into her bedchamber, where she showed me cushions blooming with vivid scarlet poppies, white lilies, and wild roses. Her window was framed with sheer linen draperies bordered with curling vines dripping rich purple grapes. Linen veils spangled with honeybees and gold bullion sunbursts emerged from a cedar chest. Although I had seen these treasures before, I had assumed they were among the many curiosities she had collected; it never occurred to me until now that they were her own handiwork.

"In Troy, I spent my days weaving a tapestry depicting the deeds of the heroes." Helen folded the veils and laid them in a glittering pile. "I imagine it burned with the city. Ah, look here." She spread out another veil, pale green glittering with cobwebs. I jumped at the large black spider crawling across the fabric; my heart continued to race even after I realized it was a cunning facsimile. Helen draped the gossamer stuff over her head. Black widows framed her face, clung to her arms, and hung down her back. "You see? Arachne is always weaving her webs."

All those spiders unnerved me; she had even rendered the scarlet hourglasses on their backs. "Black widows kill their mates."

Her faint smile vanished, and she dragged the veil away from her head with a sigh. "That's exactly what your father said."

TYNDAREUS DIED A MONTH LATER. During his last days, he requested my company. I spent long hours spinning and listening to his youthful reminiscences. Often, he forgot where and when he was, and he carried on long conversations with Herakles and others long-dead. "Castor's going to break his neck racing like that." Sometimes, he looked strangely at me. "Leda, my dear. When did you dye your hair?" I simply held his hand while waiting for the episode to pass; he was so far gone into his twilight world that very little reached him now.

Once, near the end, he became lucid again. "Hermione."

I bent closer, and placed my hand into his clammy one when he groped for it. "Yes, Grandfather?"

He squeezed my fingers ever so slightly. "You should have told me." His wispy voice labored to be heard; it was getting harder for him to breathe. "I would have gone to Mycenae to avenge you. I fought with Herakles, you know."

That afternoon, he slipped into an unwaking slumber and died two nights later. Menelaus kept vigil with me, while my mother waited with her maids in the sitting room. That was as close as she ever came to visiting his deathbed. Yet afterward she washed and anointed the corpse, and arranged for the professional mourners.

On a blustery winter morning, we accompanied the bier down the sloping dromos passageway into the royal tomb. The smoky lamplight threw shadows against walls covered in green Laconian marble and illuminated the tomb's other occupants in their painted larnakes, with their grave goods piled around them.

Menelaus's retainers eased the funeral bier onto the floor. Ululating wails echoed through the chamber as we arranged the grave goods. Megapenthes placed the yellowing boar tusk helmet with its flowing blue crest at the bier's head, and Nikostratos the worn wasp-waisted shield at its foot. Menelaus set the traditional death mask of beaten gold upon the king's face. Then he drew Tyndareus's silver-studded sword from its sheath, stepped on the blade, and bent it after the ancient custom.

Aethiolas was not with us. As Menelaus's ambassador, he had gone to Mycenae to consult with Pylades and the Argive assembly, and would not return until spring.

I lifted the shroud to tuck a hot brick wrapped in leather against my grandfather's feet, a small, intimate gesture amid the many ceremonial gifts. Menelaus poured the final libation, we toasted the dead and broke our cups, and then withdrew from the tomb, leaving the oil lamps burning in their niches and the clay incense burners wafting their sweet smoke. The retainers sealed the tall, bronze-bound doors.

That night, we feasted my grandfather's memory. Antimachus the bard strummed a doleful melody on his seven-stringed lyre. Old councilors shared anecdotes about the dead king. Wine flowed minus the usual cheer. It was an excruciatingly grim evening.

Midwinter brought the frost, covering the mountains with a pristine blanket of snow. Icy winds rattled against the shutters. I spent most evenings weaving or practicing the new embroidery stitches my mother taught me.

Menelaus invited me to dine in his apartment, to console my grief and discuss my marriage prospects. "We won't hold a contest," he said. "Too much trouble these days." An indirect allusion to the war. "It's best done quietly."

A marriage contest would have been absurd given the short list of candidates. "It's too bad about your cousin Telemachus," he told me. "He would have been a good match, but with his father gone his position is too tenable. He has no battle experience, no men under his command, and all his wealth is being squandered by his mother's suitors. A man has to be able to defend his lands and his women, or he's no good. Now look here." Menelaus tapped his finger against three names inscribed in the clay tablet before him. "These are Nestor's younger boys. He's raised some fine lads. Perhaps we ought to invite them to visit in the spring."

Spring felt very distant. Winter's gloomy weather always made me sad. Recent sorrows further weighed on my spirits, and I found it difficult to feign enthusiasm for the princes of Pylos.

Chapter Fourteen

As spring began, we celebrated the festival of Plowistos to honor Poseidon and persuade him to open the sea lanes. My father sacrificed fifteen splendid black bulls, then my mother and Polycaste drew the women apart and led them into the cult house to honor Dia and the reborn year-king.

Aethiolas returned from Mycenae three weeks after the equinox.

He gave us his colorful impressions over supper. "Prince Pylades had no trouble flashing Agamemnon's seal and getting the Argive assembly to recognize him as regent. The old men have been nervous ever since Orestes killed the usurpers. Shitting themselves, I would say, for all the gifts and courtesies they've sent to compensate for having stood by for seven years and done nothing while Aegisthus and his ruffians ran amok."

"What is Pylades like?" I asked.

"An excellent administrator," Aethiolas said. "He measures his words and says little, but when he does talk he has the thickest Phocian accent you ever heard. I'm not sure the Argives understand him half the time. Elektra and their children are with him. Two handsome boys, well-mannered and intelligent. The little girls are charming. And there's a newborn, another daughter called Anaxo."

"Ah!" Menelaus exclaimed with delight. "Is the new mother doing well?"

"I'm not sure," Aethiolas replied. "I kept waiting to see the formidable harpy everyone talks about—I admit, I was even looking forward to it—but she was very subdued. Pylades refuses to have anything to do with her. I couldn't get a straight answer from either one of them, but others tell me she blames him for not watching over Orestes during the coup, and he blames her for exacerbating the situation with her nagging."

"It's true," Chrysothemis added. "She's miserable."

Aethiolas had brought not only news, but my cousin as well. When she encountered me earlier that day in the outer court, Chrysothemis had wept with joy and flung herself into my embrace.

I waited till a passing servant replenished the wine in my brother's cup before asking, "Has there been any news about Orestes?"

A sharp cry of alarm called attention to the white-faced girl seated at the end of the table. Aethiolas had introduced her to us as Erigone, daughter of Aegisthus. Chrysothemis doted on her, addressing her in soft, almost coaxing tones as though she were a skittish puppy. Her muteness and excessive shyness confounded me.

"Don't say his name around her," Chrysothemis hissed at us. "Some spiteful servant girls started a rumor that he's coming back to murder her. She's terrified."

Coolly, Helen appraised the girl. "Does the child not speak?"

"I've never heard her say a word," Aethiolas said. "Clytaemnestra made her live below stairs as a servant. Aegisthus ignored her. Pylades suggested she might do better here, away from Mycenae."

"She seems rather simple."

Clearing his throat, my father shot my mother a reproving look, then spoke to the girl with the utmost kindliness. "Young lady, you have my word of honor as the king of Sparta that no one in my domain will hurt you." Another remonstrative glance toward my mother. "Or insult you."

After supper, I escorted our guests upstairs. Chrysothemis had requested that Erigone share her chamber, and explained why when the girl went into the bathroom to relieve herself. "She will not sleep alone in the dark." Chrysothemis sighed. "I know she seems simple and dumb, but she's not. She hasn't uttered a single word since that awful day."

"Did she see anything?"

"The entire *citadel* saw Orestes kill Aegisthus." Chrysothemis lowered her voice still further. "It was savage. Erigone was so hysterical she couldn't even help with her father's funeral."

"Why in the world didn't you bring Althaia?" I asked.

"She's gone." Chrysothemis shook her head in bewilderment. "One day she was there, the next, no one could tell me where she was. She just...vanished."

I felt a pang of regret, hearing that. Aegisthus must have murdered her to keep her from talking.

Aethiolas visited me later in my sitting room. "I'm sorry I wasn't there for the funeral." He hugged me tightly. "Grandfather didn't suffer much, did he?"

"There was no pain." I invited him to sit, as my women discreetly withdrew to the next room to give us privacy. "He just slipped away. Father and I were with him when he died."

"Mother wasn't there?"

"She waited outside." I took my seat. "I don't know why she didn't come in. Grandfather was so far gone by the end that he wouldn't have known."

Aethiolas's expression tightened, banishing his earlier levity. "She shouldn't have said that about Erigone. Poor girl doesn't deserve it."

A disquieting silence descended over the sitting room. My brother chewed on his thoughts while I mulled over what to do with my rapist's bastard daughter. "Aethiolas," I finally said, "you didn't answer my question about Orestes."

"Pylades receives messages from Delphi." Aethiolas paused for a moment before continuing. "Right now, Orestes is very, very sick. Completely broken down."

I felt my stomach drop. "He's mad?"

"Not raving insane, no." Aethiolas discounted the suggestion with a wave of his hand. "Tormented with guilt and broken down from exhaustion. Pylades told me how difficult the last few years have been for him." He stroked his beard to a point between his thumb and forefinger. "Pylades has loyal Phocian and Mycenaean guards stationed around the sanctuary to protect him from the priestesses of Hekate who want justice for Clytaemnestra, and anyone else who wants to see the matricide put to death. But there won't be a trial or execution until he's well enough to face his judges."

Aethiolas stayed a while longer, keeping me company while wild thoughts raced through my mind. When he finally left, we shared a goodnight hug at the door.

I went to my altar to contemplate the god I had recently added to my pantheon. Apollo was a naked youth, a kouros, with serpentine black ringlets spilling over his shoulders. Gilded serpents twined around his supple arms, a not-so-subtle reminder that he had subjugated the ancient goddess cult at Delphi and made its chief priestess his oracle.

Apollo was not native to these lands, but had come over from Anatolia a century ago wearing an enigmatic smile and foreign air. Even though his priests had given Orestes sanctuary, I did not expect Pythian Apollo to take pity on the son of the High King who had destroyed his altars at Troy.

Had he committed some other crime, Orestes could have approached any altar and received absolution from the local priest-king. Strophius could have purified him, and guided him through the rites of penance, sacrifice and cleansing, but there was nothing our Phocian uncle could do or he would have done it. Matricide was too great a sin, the blood pollution too dangerous for even a priest-king to contend with.

Yet surely there must be something mortal men could do!

I called for a dressing gown, tied my hair back with a ribbon, and set out for the king's apartment.

Asphalion admitted me to my father's sitting room, where a flickering oil lamp illuminated a boar hunt splashed across the wall. Menelaus nursed a cup of wine beside the glowing brazier; he set it aside when he saw me. "Hermione, young lady, you are up late."

As I accepted the cushioned chair, I kept his admonition firmly in mind. *Don't ever be afraid to come to me.* "Father, I have a favor to ask you. I would go to Mother, but I don't think she would listen to me."

"So you want me to ask for you?" Menelaus regarded me curiously. "Well, let me hear what the favor is first, and then we'll see."

"Could you get her to send her nepenthe to Orestes?" I hung on his reaction; his posture and guarded expression urged me to continue while at the same time it kept me on edge. "I realize that we're no longer betrothed, and that he's committed a terrible crime, but he's still my kinsman and friend, and he's very, very sick. Perhaps deadening his pain will help him recover."

My father drew in a sharp breath, indicating this was not a subject he wanted to discuss. "I sympathize, but asking me to get involved..."

How many times had I heard this excuse? "No one wants to get involved, or help, or do anything but judge."

"Pylades has been a great friend," Menelaus pointed out.

"But who else has been there for him?" I knotted my fingers around the armrests. "If I could, I would be sitting with him right now at Delphi."

Menelaus gave me a troubled look. "Those are the words of a mother, or beloved wife."

Flustered, I caught the subtle reprimand in his voice. "I only meant..."

"I will not have you pining for a man you can't have."

I was not pining! Yet the accusation lingered, gnawing at me. Yes, I did love Orestes, after a fashion. How could I not, having been bred to accept him as my future spouse? "Orestes is my cousin. I used to watch him as a child!"

Menelaus listened, stroking his chin and nodding occasionally. "Is that all this is, you acting as a devoted kinswoman, doting upon a boy she used to dandle upon her lap? I will not have you distracted when Nestor arrives with his sons."

"I will wed whatever man you choose for me," I said haltingly. "Can you blame me for wanting to help?"

Having had my assurances, he sent Asphalion to bring my mother.

A quarter of an hour later, Helen arrived draped in a loose robe, her hair rolled up in ribbons and unguents smeared on her face. When she heard, she balked at the request. "Are you mad? You want me to give a centuries-old secret recipe entrusted to my care by a high priestess of Isis to the priests at Delphi for the sake of a matricide?"

"Mother!" I exclaimed.

"Helen, your pig-headedness is trying my patience. First, you insult that poor girl at my table, and now this?" Menelaus set his teeth, his earlier affability wearing to shreds before my eyes. "Your daughter is asking for this one little favor. Why shouldn't I grant it? Just because I broke off the betrothal and denied Orestes sanctuary does not mean I have to turn my back on him altogether. He's still my nephew—and yours, too, damn you. The least you could do is have a little sympathy."

Helen suffered his tirade in unflinching silence. "Aren't *you* the one who always insists that a man ought to feel whatever pain or joy the gods send him to feel?"

"Right now he feels *too* much!" Menelaus's roar was thunderous enough to wake the entire palace. Helen's eyes widened a fraction, and she gave an almost imperceptible start. "Now shut your mouth and send the priests your sorcerous potion, and *don't* give me some feeble excuse that those foreign priestesses swore you to secrecy or that poor Clytaemnestra's ghost is wailing for justice." He wagged a reproving finger in her face. "Curse her shade! She chose her vile lover and vengeance for a dead daughter over her husband and living son. She let that snake loose in Mycenae where he murdered my brother and raped our daughter. Let her suffer the consequences."

CHRYSOTHEMIS FLOURISHED IN HER NEW, unconstrained surroundings. Erigone was another matter altogether.

When I sent Sotera to assist their maid, she came back with a scathing report. "Would you believe that child knows next to nothing about using a lady's toilet or tub? She'll learn, but her wardrobe is hopeless. She owns nothing suitable for a princess."

Never mind that she was Aegisthus's daughter, or that my mother had snubbed her. *I* was going to be kind to her.

Outfitting Erigone as a princess meant cutting and sewing new clothes, but getting her down into the storerooms to select fabric and trinkets proved an ordeal. She hung by the stairwell, balking like a frightened toddler at going any further.

Chrysothemis lit a second lamp to further banish the darkness. "Come on, it's all right." She coaxed Erigone downstairs, one laborious step at a time. "It was Mother's maids that did this," she told me. "They locked her in a storeroom once and left her all alone in the dark."

Between the two of us, we persuaded the girl to venture into the passage and had her walk between us until we came to an oak door. "Erigone, this is my private storeroom," I said encouragingly. "I keep my treasures, personal revenues, and dower goods in here."

I entered first, placing my lamp in a stone niche, and crossed over to the bolts of dyed wool and linen stacked on the shelves. Soft blues, greens, and a pale rose wool suitable for an adolescent girl passed under my fingers. Then I opened a painted chest and let the lamplight play across glittering Egyptian faience and gold. "Come over here and choose something."

Erigone gawked at the jewels, yet kept a wary distance as if she expected me to box her ears simply for looking. Chrysothemis, on the other hand, combed through necklaces, bracelets, and earrings with a woman's natural delight. "Do you ever wear these things, Hermione?"

I laughed at her covetousness. "Go ahead. Pick whatever you like." A strand of gradated green beads caught my attention. "These would be nice for Erigone."

Chrysothemis and I selected silver bangles, glass beads, and plain gold hoops for Erigone's ears, because she steadfastly refused to choose anything. It was the same with the embroideries and woven bands, which we bundled into a basket along with a bronze hand mirror and ivory comb, and a spindle—the necessities for a woman of good birth. Erigone helped Sotera carry the fabric when we left; the task distracted her from her fear of the dark.

I made certain to lavish her with praise once we deposited the items in the guest apartment. "That was well done, Erigone. Why don't we go down to the river and feed the swans?"

My handmaidens assembled blankets and food for a picnic, and we enlisted the guard Phokas to escort us down to the riverbank, where a soft breeze sweetened the spring afternoon. Chrysothemis removed her sandals to wiggle her toes in the grass as my maids spread out the blankets.

When she saw the swans, Erigone exclaimed over their curving necks and snowy plumage. I took a flat round of sourdough from the basket, tore it into pieces, and passed them to the girl. Two swans glided over to claim the crumbs. Erigone watched their every movement with rapt enthusiasm. I sent Phokas to fetch a swan's feather caught among the reeds twenty yards away.

"Mother had such terrible nightmares the week before she died." Chrysothemis plucked a blade of grass and folded it lengthwise. "You wouldn't have recognized her, she changed so much."

An odd subject to darken the afternoon with. I lay down on my side, propping my cheek on my elbow, and let my cousin talk. Obviously, she wanted to unburden herself.

"Mother sent me to Father's tomb with a wreath three days before," Chrysothemis continued. "She was so frightened, she refused to come with me. I'd never seen her afraid like that before. Why, she even had to take juice of the poppy to sleep at night, but still it didn't keep the dreams away. That very day, the morning Orestes came, she woke screaming, and ran up and down the corridor crying for light even though it was already dawn."

That did not sound like the Clytaemnestra I remembered. "Did she tell you what those dreams were?"

"Only about the last one, and only an hour before...you know." Chrysothemis reached for another blade of grass and started to curl it around her index finger. "She dreamt that she gave birth to a viper that sank its fangs into her breast to nurse on her blood. She told me Orestes and Elektra were coming home to murder her. I didn't want to hear her talk like that, but she made me stay and listen. She gave me some jewelry and said how sorry she was that she'd ever married Aegisthus or treated me so badly, then she made me swear to give her a decent burial."

Chrysothemis shuddered as she related these details. "After all that, she sent her women for the high priestess, so she could drink poppy juice and hemlock, and kill herself so Orestes wouldn't have to stain his hands with her blood. I think she would have done it, too, but Aegisthus heard all the noise and came in, and he talked her out of it."

Had Clytaemnestra only committed suicide like a decent woman, Orestes would not be suffering now. "Did you bury her?" I asked.

"She didn't want to lie with Aegisthus," Chrysothemis answered. "She said that to me once. I forget when. I buried her with Father and Iphigenia. Aegisthus and Aletes were buried with their followers in a ditch near the Chavos ravine."

Erigone returned. I gave her the swan's feather and watched her eyes brim with gratitude. "Are the crumbs gone already?" I laughed. "Then let's leave those fat swans alone before they burst, and find some flowers for your hair."

In the evenings, we gathered in my sitting room to sew Erigone's new clothes, and with six of us working we soon finished a linen shift, a dress, and a flounced skirt and bodice for special occasions. Sometimes Helen visited bearing small gifts, but her coolness intimidated the other women, and she gave me the impression that she came solely because my father had ordered her to be solicitous.

Chrysothemis waited until my mother left to voice her observations. "Helen's perfect, just as they say. Aren't you worried that your suitors will all stare at her?"

True as it was, why did my cousin have to be so tactless? "No," I said tightly. Even the old veterans stared at my mother, and they had wives at home.

Let them gawk. While they were ogling Helen, the real marriage prize would be slipping from their grasp. My mother had had her day.

SOTERA BROUGHT IN A LETTER bearing Apollo's sacred seal. Delphi! I set my shuttle down and broke the wax to unfold the papyrus, but did not recognize the handwriting. I skimmed over the salutations to identify the sender, the priest who had been assigned to attend Orestes.

"Princess," the man wrote, "forgive me for not answering your query sooner, but the priesthood did not wish to distress you with troubling news. We all hoped that your cousin would have recovered his health and spirits during the winter months, yet there has been little progress.

"Prince Orestes spent his first fortnight with us neither speaking nor moving, his gaze fixed upon empty space. We forced nourishment into him, and kept him clean and comfortable, but the Daughters of Night entered the sanctuary and roused him from his catatonic state to torment him. It stirred our sympathy to see him so afflicted, thrashing and beating his head. I assure you that we restrained the prince from doing further harm to himself, and did our utmost to soothe his spirits through the grim winter months."

Pressing the papyrus to my lips, I held back a sob. Aethiolas had assured me that Orestes was not a raving, gibbering madman, but what could he know? He had not been to Delphi.

Sotera came over to me. "Mistress, what's wrong?"

I shook my head, while struggling to get my emotions under control and finish the letter. "To ease his suffering, we have given him Queen Helen's medicine. Its effects are truly remarkable, calming his fits and allowing him to remain somewhat lucid, but it also shortens his breath if we give it to him too often. We are gradually lessening the dose, and pray that by weaning him away from the nepenthe and applying other treatments he will be able to stand trial without losing his mind."

Then it had worked. I had done something meaningful for him. And yet it did not feel like enough.

A final paragraph remained. "Perhaps you have heard rumors that our pilgrims clamor for a glimpse of the man who murdered his mother to avenge his father, and that they debate his case as a philosophical exercise. I would not trouble your ears with such unpleasantness, except to assure you that whatever you may hear, your kinsman is being treated with the utmost respect and consideration. He is being lodged far from any curiosity seekers, and he remains ignorant of these matters."

The priest need not have elaborated, as the situation was no different here. Men congregated around the great court to weigh the question of mercy versus justice, and the father's right over the mother's. Listening to those graybeards deliberate day after day turned my stomach. Orestes was not some hypothetical criminal, an academic exercise for them to mull over, but a flesh and blood man tormented with unbearable guilt for a crime he had never meant to commit.

I folded the letter, stowed it in my sewing basket, and tried to resume weaving, yet my heart remained heavy. Orestes was no longer the outgoing adolescent I remembered, but a madman, a matricide, a freak, and not even my mother's nepenthe could erase that horrible reality.

CHAPTER FIFTEEN

A WARM SPRING BREEZE SNAPPED the colorful banners on their poles and stirred the horsetail crests of the sentries standing at attention along the ramparts. Garlands draped the terraces, the scent of the fresh flowers competing with the fragrances the court ladies wore, and sunlight sparkled against gold and jewels, and gleaming bronze armor.

Only a king's visit could warrant such pageantry, or persuade my mother to don a queen's regalia and leave her apartment. Her bodice and flounces were edged with gold work, and the queen's glittering gold diadem covered her coiffed ringlets. I stood beside her, also richly dressed but flustered after days of overseeing the preparations for Nestor's arrival. What would the king of Pylos and his sons think when they compared me to my perfect mother?

Stop that! I thought crossly. *They're not coming to see her.*

Cheers from the town below alerted us that the royal procession was on its way. I counted my breaths. Then Menelaus's snow-white team trotted through the gate, a dozen more painted chariots and matched teams following in succession. Up on the walls, the sentries saluted my father's distinguished guests by drumming their spears against the stones. Grooms wove among the vehicles to secure the horses, while porters descended upon the baggage carts bringing up the rear.

Menelaus stepped down from his chariot's platform and crossed over to his chief guest. I glimpsed my brothers among the retainers, each one having been assigned as a companion to one of Nestor's sons. From what I could see, the Pylian princes were all tall and dark-haired, graceful and good-looking, but it was going to take much more than physical attractiveness to impress me.

At length, my father climbed the stairs leading to the portico with an elegant old gentleman who expressed his delight at everything he saw. "What a marvelous situation you have here in Sparta! Rich fields and vines, groves and high mountains all around for your protection. You couldn't ask the gods for better." King Nestor was well on his way to proving those rumors about his garrulousness true. "And look, here's the foremost ornament in your palace! I swear she still looks as fresh as she did when Tyndareus gave her to you."

Helen inclined her head in polite welcome.

Nestor gave her rouged cheek an old man's smacking kiss. "With each passing day, you remind us ever more of your sweet mother. Have I ever told you about the first time I ever set eyes on Leda?" He did not wait upon an answer before plunging into his narrative. "I was just a young man then, hadn't even gone to sea with Jason. And there she was, the queen of Sparta, shining like the morning dew with her long black hair, walking into the megaron on your father's arm. Tyndareus was a fortunate man, wasn't he?"

I caught my father's tolerant smile.

Menelaus cleared his throat meaningfully. "King Nestor, this is our daughter, Hermione."

Nestor descended on me to bestow a grandfatherly peck upon my cheek. "It's true what they say about Spartan girls. How do you sleep at night, Menelaus, with such beautiful women under your roof?"

Then Nestor called his sons forward in order to introduce them. "Echephron is a swift runner and archer, and all man under those dandified Cretan lovelocks. Stratichus is an excellent wrestler and sailor. Peisistratus is our youngest boy, just twenty-two, but he commands his own chariot corps."

Each man was handsome and courteous, but none attracted my particular interest. It would depend on how they behaved and what they said once they opened their mouths; even men who knew they were being scrutinized, who rehearsed every speech and action, often let slip clues revealing their true quality.

I had arranged for my grandfather's vacant apartment to be freshly plastered and painted for the occasion, and furnished with cots heaped with linens and snowy fleeces.

An elegant bathroom adjoined the apartment. Water birds and leaping fish graced walls painted soft blue. Bath slaves awaited us in the dressing room; the princes grinned their appreciation as the comeliest girls descended upon them to remove their clothes. Nestor affectionately rumbled at them to behave. "You're not at home, boys."

I withdrew to allow the men to undress, and consulted with the Pylian servants unpacking a large chest in the bedchamber. One man gave me clean garments for the king and his sons, and took the discarded clothes, while another oiled the men's leather sandals.

Feminine giggles and husky masculine laughter issuing from next door lured me back to the bathroom. Some male guests could not keep their hands off the bath slaves; the girls later complained about the men's lewd demands, yet these handsome young princes seemed to be restricting their flirting to good-natured ogling and jests, and the women were not complaining.

I could see why. All three men were delectable, with broad shoulders tapering down to narrow waists and hard buttocks. Seeing the oil gleaming on their naked skin brought a burning flush to my cheeks.

A subtle change in the atmosphere drew the youngest prince's attention to the doorway. Peisistratus. Was that his name? He gave a start when he saw me standing there, and nudged his brothers. An awkward silence descended upon the bathroom.

Nestor, who was enjoying a soak in the terracotta tub, regarded the scene with good humor. "Where are your manners, boys? Or has Helen's daughter got your tongues?"

Inclining my head, I withdrew again, my embarrassment now

tempered with annoyance. Helen's daughter. Did he not remember my name? It was not that difficult to remember. If Nestor and his sons had come seeking a younger version of my mother, then they were going to be very disappointed.

IPHINOUS HAD OBTAINED RECIPES for Nestor's favorite dishes. Carts had brought mussels and fresh fish swimming in jars of salt water all the way from Helas. Succulent beef and lamb turned on the spit. We would feast every night during the Pylian king's visit.

Echephron and Stratichus made little effort to court me; their eyes kept wandering to my mother or lingering on my half-brothers. But Peisistratus took immediate interest, and addressed me without hesitation. "I hope we weren't too forward with your women this afternoon."

"Why would you say that?" I asked.

Peisistratus tucked into the almond cake on his plate. "You seemed upset when you left."

So someone had noticed. "Not at all," I lied. "It seemed the women were quite enjoying themselves."

"As long as Father is there, we'll be keeping our hands to ourselves," he replied, chewing. "He's very strict about respecting the laws of hospitality."

Nestor was a wise man, though in this instance his strictness would confound my efforts to observe Peisistratus and his brothers in their natural element. I wanted to know how they behaved every day, not just when they were on their best behavior. Perhaps, as the days wore on, they could be lulled into complacency.

On my left, Chrysothemis caught my arm and pulled me toward her to whisper, "Peisistratus likes you. I think it's those little freckles on your arms. He's wondering whether you have them all over." I could smell the retsina on her breath. "Oh, look! He's turning his head this way. He's probably wondering whether you're a redhead down there, too."

Exasperated, I reached for her cup to whisk it away. "I think you've had quite enough to drink."

"Oh, don't be so serious!" Chrysothemis snatched the cup back. "No one ever lets me have any fun. I heard you watched them take a bath this afternoon. I bet they look good all oiled and naked."

Antimachus performed on his lyre. It was late. Menelaus rose to pour the fourth libation to Zeus Xenios, then invited his guest of honor to regale us with stories, boast about his exploits, or make a toast as he pleased. Nestor had spent all evening reminiscing about the war and dispensing long-winded advice to all the young men, while my father drank and my mother perfected her look of polite boredom.

Nestor turned out to be an excellent storyteller, weaving a tale about his youthful adventures with Jason and the Argonauts. "*Argo* was a black pentekonter with a scarlet griffin on her sail. Nowadays, you can't go anywhere without meeting some old man who claims to have sailed with Jason. I have two doddering fools on my council who boast about being on that first voyage, and then pretend to be senile whenever I remind them that I *was* there and don't remember them!"

Menelaus laughed heartily. Nestor winked at me and my brothers. "*Argo* made more than one trip to the Euxine Sea," he explained. "Jason took men on for a season or however long they chose to stay, and made his living raiding.

"The locals used to spike fleeces into the riverbeds to catch gold dust. I forget who invented that tale about the dragon, but whenever we went ashore to plunder the fleeces, the local women came at us alongside their men. You should have seen them! They were so unkempt they looked more like animals than women, and they fell on us howling like maenads, brandishing clubs and spears, and then their bare fists and teeth and fingernails. A six-headed serpent would have been a gift from the gods after that!"

"Is that how Jason met the beautiful Medea?" Menelaus asked gamely.

Nestor grimaced. "That horrid woman! She was cursed with a pitted horse face and flaming red hair to match her savage temper, and she was always muttering in her barbarian's tongue. Never learned a single civilized word. Whenever she looked at you, it was enough to make your blood freeze, because you knew you had done something to offend her. Gods only knew what. Perhaps you ate too much garlic or pissed where she could see you, or scratched your balls once too often. It didn't matter. She would shriek like a harpy and hurl herself at you to try to claw your eyes out, or she would twist the head off a pigeon and spray you with the blood." He shuddered for emphasis. "Jason took it the worst. She was fixated on him. Never let him from her sight. He tried to abandon her, but he could never get her drunk enough to move her, and the one time he did leave her behind she found her way back! It's no wonder Jason took to wine and left her for that Theban girl. Herakles liked to boast about encountering Amazons in the Euxine Sea. Hah! Medea would have made him piss his loincloth."

"You met Herakles?" Megapenthes gazed admiringly at him.

Nestor moistened his throat with a draught of mead. "That arrogant old bugger joined us for the first voyage. Couldn't pull an oar worth shit, or avoid trouble for more than a few hours. I suppose your grandfather told you otherwise." He flashed my half-brothers a mischievous grin. "He must have told you about the lion skin Herakles always wore. I've *been* to Nemea, and the real Nemean Lion was a sad old beast the priests kept in the temple. That stinking, flea-ridden pelt Herakles wore came off some half-starved creature he cornered in Arcadia."

Tyndareus would have been scandalized to hear his hero denigrated like this, but Nestor had a grudge to repay. When Herakles had sacked Pylos sixty years ago, he had slain Nestor's brothers and cousins, and seized several royal women. Nestor could not clash spears with the dead hero, but he could wage war on the man's reputation.

"Those twelve Labors the bards sing about are complete rubbish fabricated by the Herakleidai and their Dorian allies," he continued. "I once rode up to Elis before the war to settle some border dispute and asked King Agasthenes to show me his father's famous Augean Stables. Imagine my surprise to find a rickety shack leaning over a trickling stream! The only horse stabled there was an old nag that looked like she'd been there since Prometheus stole fire from Olympus. I swear, her ears pricked up and she snorted when she heard me mention Herakles. Turns out the fool used to idle about in the hills, rustling cattle and harassing the local women and boys to avoid finishing the real task Augeas gave him, breaking up stones in the quarry to refortify the citadel wall."

Laughter rippled through the megaron. Menelaus absorbed the tale with a wink and nod; he knew exactly what his guest was doing. There was no love lost between the Herakleidai and Atreidai, either. Since my grandfather's death, my father had forbidden Antimachus to sing about Herakles's deeds.

Then Nestor turned to me. "Young lady, should a hero ever come to claim your hand, gather up your skirts and run away from him quick as you can. Heroes are either madmen or liars, and oftentimes both. It's better to marry a brave, sensible man who's content to stay at home."

After the feast, my mother accompanied me upstairs, where she dismissed my handmaidens to attend me herself. "Nestor is dispensing advice again," she observed.

"Yes, I noticed." Helen was not sentimental enough to linger over me like this unless she had some specific purpose in mind. What did she want?"

She came around behind me to unfasten my necklace. "Do Nestor's sons appeal to you?"

So she sought my opinion, so she could whisper it in my father's ear. "It's been but a single day, Mother," I said.

"I saw you talking earlier to Peisistratus." Helen deposited the necklace on my dressing table. "Did he have anything interesting to say?"

Was she really going to make me recite the entire conversation by rote? "A few courtesies, nothing more." I drew the golden hoops from my ears.

"I also noticed that Echephron and Stratichus weren't looking at you as much as they should have."

It was very late, and her observations jarred my nerves. "Why would they, when they can stare at the world's most beautiful woman instead?" I caught the bitterness in my voice, but it was too late to take back the scathing remark.

"Foolish child. They only stare because they want to gawk at the woman who 'started' the war." Helen moved around to unlace my girdle. "If I were anyone else, they would see only an aging woman and not give her a second glance. Look here." She laid a finger against the corner of her right eye, tracing a fine network of crow's feet visible even through her paint. "You see? I'm not perfect. It's just that no one ever looks closely enough." Then she sighed. "Sometimes I think only your father sees me as I truly am."

ATHLETIC CONTESTS, HUNTING, and feasting marked the royal visit. More noblemen arrived, straining the palace's ability to accommodate them. Iphinous helped me divert them to temporary pavilions erected near the parade ground below the citadel. Harried stewards strove to maintain order while scrub maids and stable hands kept the premises as spotless as possible.

Iphinous took on as much of the work as possible, but managing lodging, food, and diversion for several hundred visitors wore me out, leaving me unable to enjoy the spectacle as much as our guests did.

Aethiolas staged games for the noblemen and visiting princes, while my father doled out prizes for footraces, archery contests, wrestling and boxing matches, javelin and discus throws, and chariot races. I awarded the victory crowns.

As Aethiolas claimed his myrtle chaplet for the discus, he affectionately chided my lack of enthusiasm. "Put a smile on your face and try not to look like you've eaten bad figs. Echephron's limbering up for the sixty meter race. He'll win with those long legs of his."

"Then maybe we should have Nikostratos crown him." Earlier, I had noticed the prince throwing fond looks at my younger half-brother.

Echephron presented a bland countenance during his crowning, a marked contrast to his youngest brother, who won the chariot race. A dusty, sweaty Peisistratus sauntered up to the platform like a conquering hero. "It's a shame you couldn't accompany me, the way Pelops had Hippodamia with him for his fateful race," he said.

"So my father could chase you to the Isthmus and nail your severed head to his door?" I lifted both eyebrows, but kept my tone light. At least the compliment was original. "Or were you planning to replace his linchpins with wax?"

Peisistratus gave me a sheepish smile. He had not thought it through. "It seems love was more dangerous in those days," he replied.

*****

NESTOR WANTED TO PAY HIS RESPECTS to Tyndareus and Leda, so we went down from the citadel bearing garlands, leading a sacrificial calf, and carrying the wine and mixing bowls. Nestor performed the blood sacrifice before the tomb, then seized the opportunity to turn the traditional drink offering into a long-winded speech. I tried not to show my boredom, even attempted to follow the old king's rambling conversation with the dead, but at last gave up the effort. At least it was a pleasant day. We were standing in the shade, and were about to enjoy a picnic by the river.

I sat with my mother and the other women on blankets under the trees. Servants brought roast veal from the carcass, and additional food and wine from the palace. I picked flowers and wove garlands with the young women, listened to their gossip and endured their questions about the handsome princes, who, with the other young men of the court, raced and wrestled in the grass.

Late in the afternoon, Peisistratus escorted me back to the palace. He presented me with a perfect swan's feather he had untangled from the reeds, and tucked it behind my ear among the flowers Erigone had woven for my hair, using the gesture as an excuse to brush his fingers against my cheek.

I blushed. "Would you like to wear my daisy chain?"

"Your flowers look lovelier on you than they would on me." Peisistratus twined his arm in mine. Stratichus walked with Chrysothemis, while Echephron carried on an animated conversation with my half-brothers. A forlorn Erigone wrestled with tears until Aethiolas gallantly came to the rescue.

Peisistratus acknowledged the mishap. "I'm afraid Echephron is a bit thickheaded when it comes to women. All he cares about is athletics. Father will have a word with him."

Had I not observed the man's athletic obsession firsthand, I would have assumed that Peisistratus was trying to disparage a rival suitor. Not that he had to try very hard. I remembered what Nestor had said about his son that first day. *He's all man under those dandified Cretan lovelocks.*

Echephron's manliness fell short when it came to women, though. Stratichus tried harder, paying me trite compliments, but I found his company painfully dull. Peisistratus alone managed to be engaging.

The late afternoon sun washed the valley with gold and tinted the growing shadows blue and violet. A gentle breeze blew at our backs. I was enjoying the walk, and leaned into my escort. "I like your father and his stories."

He laughed. "That's because you haven't heard them six dozen times."

"Have you ever traveled or been on any adventures like him?" I asked. As we started to ascend the mount, the sentries saluted us from above.

"Not much," he admitted. "Whenever Father has to send one of us to handle a border dispute or greet an ambassador, it's always Thrasymedes or Aretus he chooses. Don't misunderstand, I love them very much, but it's difficult being the youngest."

In the lower court, the party began to disperse, with the young men headed toward the palaestra to while away the hour before supper. Peisistratus looked torn.

"You should go," I said.

Locking eyes with me, he took my hand and raised it to his lips. Only one man had ever done that, yet while an uncertain shiver passed through me at the intimate gesture, it felt nice.

Impatient shouts from his brothers and mine threatened the moment. Groaning, Peisistratus waved them on. "I pity the women they marry," he muttered, then swiftly banished his displeasure to resume his wooing. "Will you sit beside me tonight when Antimachus plays?"

A furious blush crept from my cheeks to my breasts. Glancing aside, I noticed our fathers standing on the stairs beneath the portico, observing and conferring with each other. I turned back to Peisistratus and, realizing to my dismay that my voice was quavering, answered, "You know that isn't allowed, but I can bring you honeyed wine before the third libation."

Peisistratus gave me a wry smile. "Then it will be like ambrosia from the gods."

Nestor's youngest son was pouring on the charm. "Perhaps you should release me now." I indicated Menelaus and Nestor watching from above.

Acknowledging them, he let go my hand, yet when he took his leave, he forsook the palaestra to climb the stairs and pay his respects to the two kings. I should have left then, retired with my women to bathe and dress for supper. Instead, I lingered below to watch the three men interact. Peisistratus spoke in low tones, while our fathers nodded and looked pleased with his answers.

Stunned, I realized what was happening. *No, not like this!* I had always assumed it would be a solemn occasion with libations and bride-gifts, with me, my mother, and a priestess present to witness the marriage negotiations, not this casual conversation in the courtyard!

Menelaus gave Peisistratus an amiable thump on the shoulder. Nestor looked on like a sage old priest, smiling his congratulations. I felt sick. They had done it, they had just decided my marriage, without even consulting me.

IT DID NOT GET BETTER. That night, raucous guests soused on honey mead, retsina, and the festive occasion banged their fists on the tables to demonstrate their impatience. Good-natured catcalls rang out.

"Do it properly, young man!"

"Give her your tongue!"

First, the negotiations had been a sham, and now the betrothal announcement was a drunken disaster. Menelaus and Nestor had waited too late, until most of the guests were drunk and ready to hurl all decorum out the window. My mother wore a long-suffering look, while my inebriated father gestured for me and my new fiancé to oblige the guests.

Peisistratus took me in his arms for the betrothal kiss. I tasted too much honey mead on his mouth. He lingered over the kiss, giving me his tongue, to thunderous applause. It did not feel right. A Spartan princess's betrothal ought to be a sacred occasion, not some voyeur's cheap entertainment!

When we sat down again, I found it difficult to tolerate my fiancé's presence. He should have been sober and respectful; he had no right to drink so or strut about, for he had not won anything. Menelaus had liked his breeding and initiative, and simply handed me to him.

Peisistratus noticed my sour mood. "Is something wrong?" he asked.

Confessing the truth would be pointless. "Everyone is drunk."

"Of course!" he exclaimed. "It's a celebration."

When the time came to retire, he caught my hand and kissed it. "We should have had the wedding tonight." What a transparent seducer! "Six weeks is an unbearable time to wait."

I withdrew my hand. "I'm sure you will survive it."

Chrysothemis trailed me all the way back to my bedchamber. Her hangdog look alerted me that she was going to brood all night unless someone cheered her up. For once, why could she not find someone else to pester with her problems? "What's wrong?" I asked.

A little sob escaped her. "I'm not drunk." Her slurred words gave evidence to her lie. "I simply thought maybe one of the other princes..."

I dismissed the maids and sat down on the edge of the bed to console her. "You truly want to get married, don't you?"

"More than anything." As she clung to me, her heavy scent twitched my nostrils. "I don't want to end up the old spinster aunt everybody pities and shoves into a corner."

I sympathized, but lacked the patience to cosset her all night. "I thought you liked Prince Stratichus."

Chrysothemis made a sulky face. "He's as dull as clay, and his older brother is worse, always mooning over Nikostratos." She sniffled, then wiped her knuckles across her nose, ruining her paint. "Surely there must be someone for me to marry! He doesn't have to be a prince, just suitable."

I found a linen cloth on the dressing table and retrieved it for her, while repressing the urge to shake her and snap at her to stop being such a goose. "Perhaps you should ask my mother to ask my father." Chrysothemis blew her nose. "There might be an eligible bachelor or two at the wedding feast." Of course, she would also need a proper dowry to sweeten the offer, but she was a pretty and biddable noblewoman, the daughter of the late High King, and surely it would be nothing for my father to dower her with an estate and some treasures.

Two days later, Nestor and his sons departed. Peisistratus kissed me again in the courtyard as our kinsmen said their farewells. Although I had had time to adjust to the idea of marrying him, and to accept that our fathers were acting in our best interests, I remained uncomfortable with him. His slick manners seemed less genuine and more a younger prince's calculated ploy to become Sparta's next king.

I forced a smile as he climbed into his chariot. My father and grandfather had been fortune seekers, too. Why should Peisistratus be any different?

My mother whisked me away to the storerooms that very morning to select the fabric for my wedding costume. We had a mere six weeks to sew and cut new clothes; prepare an apartment, stables, and storerooms for my husband and all his possessions; invite guests and ready their accommodations; organize the bridal feast; and observe all the rituals.

I selected a fine, light blue wool, and gave it to the weavers to saturate the fabric with virgin olive oil to make it shine. Once it was rinsed out and dried, my maids fitted me for a bride's traditional open bodice, pinned the cloth, and cut it. Helen traced leaves and curling vines onto pale green bands with a charcoal stick, then chose skeins of thread in various shades of cream, green, and soft yellow.

From her chests, she brought out the sheer linen veil spangled with golden starbursts and spread it across my lap where it lay like a shroud. "Mother," I said, sighing, "I don't know..."

"Would you prefer something else?" Throughout, she had remained oblivious to my misgivings.

"It isn't the veil." I crushed the linen between my hands in my frustration. "It's everything."

She rescued the delicate fabric and draped it across a chair before sitting down again with the unfinished bodice. "I thought you liked Peisistratus."

"No one asked me." Articulating my emotions proved a challenge. "Father and Nestor just stood there in the courtyard and decided. I saw them, and they saw me, and they never once called me over to ask what I thought."

Helen's harsh laugh deflated me. "Foolish girl! Listen to you, complaining about the arrangement when you have no idea how fortunate you are. Perhaps you would rather have been outraged and thrown into a chariot like your aunt, or subjected to a spectacle like I was? Peisistratus is handsome and courteous, with a sensible head on his shoulders. He can read and write, and commands a chariot corps. You should be grateful, and thank your father for his consideration.

Her words stung, all the more so because she was right. "I know." I twisted my fingers in my lap. "But I am not looking forward to it."

"You're thinking about the wedding night." Helen rolled the bodice's raw edges under and pinned them. "That's how it is when your first time is rape. It doesn't make any difference how considerate the second man is. All the old terrors come back. I had to drink retsina on my wedding night."

How I wished I had brought my wool basket. I felt naked sitting there with nothing to do. "Peisistratus will notice that I'm not a virgin."

"It isn't always easy for a man to tell." She held up the basted bodice to gauge the seams. Next, she would want me to strip down and try on the garment. "Give him enough alcohol to befuddle his wits on his wedding night and he won't notice a thing." She was so cold and calculating, weaving her webs like the spider she was. "Rub oil between your thighs beforehand to moisten the way, drink some honeyed wine to calm your nerves, and just let him do whatever he wants." Helen stood and motioned me to my feet. "Here, let's see how this fits."

Stripping to my waist, I tried on the bodice. "What was it like for you?" I winced at the myriad pins pricking my bare skin.

"It was exactly what you would expect when a fourteen-year old girl lies with a man twice her age. Hold out your arms." She wrapped one of her own girdles around my waist to secure the bodice. "I drank strong wine and rubbed myself with oil as the priestesses advised, and your father tried his best to make me comfortable, but... Hmm, yes, I think that will do."

I massaged the pinpricks while readjusting my clothing. "Do you love him?"

"There is more than one kind of love."

"You know what I mean."

Helen sat down again and selected pale blue thread from her sewing basket. "We are comfortable together. He's a considerate and good-hearted man who's never struck me, never abused me or flaunted his concubines in my face. He's a loving father and an excellent ruler. A woman could not ask for a better husband." Rare emotion choked her voice, forcing her to pause and collect herself. "It may seem strange to you, but a woman can like a man and be content with him without knowing passionate love. Sometimes it's better that way."

Chapter Sixteen

Peisistratus would surely make a good husband. I accepted my lot as a fortunate one, and began to take pride in organizing our home together: supervising the plastering and painting of his rooms, making certain the cooks knew his favorite recipes, and preparing a place in the stables for his horses and chariot.

In the evenings, my mother's maids sewed my bridal clothes while she worked the intricate embroidery. Chrysothemis glowed at the prospect of finding a husband at the wedding feast, now that my father had agreed to dower her. Erigone quietly sighed over the young men at court.

The nerves twisting in my belly gave me no peace. Polycaste assured me that all brides were anxious before the wedding, and that I should enjoy my nuptials. Aphrodite assumed a prominent place on my altar. I began to visit her small cult house in the afternoons.

When I arrived, a few slaves and charioteers lazed around the deserted agora while their masters were conducting some last-minute business by the stalls. Several saluted me, though I recognized none. I left my escort outside, for Aphrodite's priestesses forbade men from entering the sacred precinct, and took only Sotera inside with me.

The cult house was dim and cool, and reeked of the myrrh burning in ceramic braziers near the altar. I wanted to revere Aphrodite, to receive her blessings, but her gifts were dangerous and terrifying.

Polycaste had told me that the goddess liked flowers and rich things. I had brought white lilies to arrange around the idol's feet. "Great goddess of desire, accept this gift." I started to untie the bouquet. "Look with favor upon me, and be with me when—"

Strong arms suddenly seized me from behind, jerking me back from the altar; lilies went flying everywhere. A rough gag stifled my cry. Panicked, I twisted and flailed against my unseen assailant. I saw Sotera open her mouth to scream. A second man's fist smashed her to the altar steps, where she lay crumpled in an unmoving heap among the lilies.

An unfamiliar voice grunted in my ear. "Stop struggling, Princess." What did these men want? They were not going to rape me here! I dug in my heels to keep from being dragged from the altar, until the second man suddenly grabbed me around the waist, hoisted me over his shoulder like a bale of fleece, and carried me out the door.

I fumbled with the gag, spitting it out as we emerged into the agora. "Help me!"

Blood spreading across the steps marked where my guards had fallen. Chariots crowded the empty agora, but after a few frantic moments it became apparent that the armed men rushing forward were not there to rescue me.

"Shut her up!" the first man shouted.

The second man dumped me onto the floor of the nearest chariot and attempted to replace my gag. I fought him, kicking and shrieking, scratching at his bearded face when he grabbed my wrists to bind them to the chariot guardrail. Why was no one coming to help me? Rough fingers tangled in my hair, pulled at my scalp to wrench my head back and stuff the gag into my mouth again. I turned my face away to prevent the last from happening. "No! Let me go!"

"Eumaeus!" Again, the first man.

His name still rang in my ears as his massive hand struck me across the face—once, twice, snapping my head back. Pain swelled my left cheek. Eumaeus shoved the gag back into my mouth. I was a princess of Sparta. How dare he!

Both men crammed into the chariot alongside me, shoving me onto the plaited leather floor between them. A whip lashed the air and we lurched forward. I hung and twisted by my bound hands. Each rut we jolted over sent vibrations juddering through my body. My straining arms felt like they were being wrenched from their sockets, and the ropes chafed painful welts into my wrists.

When we rolled to a halt, First Man dragged me upright. I swayed between my captors, faint from my ordeal and the realization that we were in the open countryside. Therapne must be miles behind us. "Hold onto the rail." First Man. He did nothing more to assist me.

Eumaeus snapped the reins and we started moving again. As the platform lurched under me, I tried to grip the chariot's guardrail as First Man advised, but my blood-starved fingers refused to obey. First Man shouted reassurance over the creaking wheels and frame. "You'll be all right once we get there!"

But where were we going? I could not cry out past the gag to ask. Seagulls circled high above. Groves and fields had given way to marshland. A salty breeze assailed my nostrils. My fevered brain worked to piece together these clues. South, we were headed south toward the coast.

At long last, after what might have hours, a town came into view. I saw whitewashed buildings. Helas. Eumaeus slowed the chariot to navigate the narrow streets, bellowing at pedestrians to clear the way, till we emerged onto a broad pebble beach crowded with three pentekonters.

Eumaeus brought the chariot to a halt. Men raced forward to take the reins and unyoke the horses. First Man's knife sawed through the rope lashing me to the guardrail, yet left my hands bound. Eumaeus hauled me from the platform and hauled me stumbling across the beach to the nearest pentekonter. Charioteers began stripping harnesses and disassembling vehicles.

I was being abducted. Just like my mother. It did not take a learned man to realize what was happening. I balked and twisted in my captor's grasp. It did no good. Eumaeus slung me onto his shoulder and ran up the gangplank to hand me over to the ship's crew.

Armed men thronged the rowing benches. "Myrmidons." First Man stood at my elbow, finally giving me a good look at his face. He was young and tall, with long yellow hair bound into a tight ponytail. I lifted my bound hands to loosen my gag. He grasped my wrist to stop me, shaking his head. "Not yet."

First Man found me a place to sit on a rough plank near the stern, and directed someone to stand guard. I fought to collect my racing thoughts. Myrmidons. Achilles led the Myrmidons. But Achilles was dead.

I scanned the beach, searching for my father's chariots or any other hint of deliverance. He could not be that far behind. I clung to that hope, but as the minutes passed without any sign, my growing disbelief tightened my chest. Where was he? I fought to breathe, to hold back my frightened tears. He had to come for me, he had to! Who else was going to rescue me?

I realized then how late it was. Hours had passed since the abduction in Aphrodite's domain. The westering afternoon light dappled the water with shadows. Once the sun set, we would crash into the rocks, but the men remained oblivious, continuing to load chariot frames. I whimpered through my gag, wishing I had the courage to defy the hulking Myrmidon guard and remove it myself. It was not bad enough that these savages had seized me from a holy cult house and thrown me into a chariot like a common slave woman, but now they were going to drown me, too!

As the last chariot frame came aboard, all the men except First Man and the steersman leapt ashore to heave at the hull, shoving it toward the water. Pebbles crunched under the keel, and the vessel shuddered. Then the crew returned, scrabbling over the ship's side, crammed onto the rowing benches and unlocked the oars from their thwarts.

Terror gripped me anew as the oars splashed into the water. A last glance toward the town showed me the horses, which must have been hired from local stables, running wild on the beach. No rescuers. No one was coming. Other crewmen raised the mast, and the square sail began to fill. A tailwind. Lady Artemis, that treacherous goddess, was smiling on my abductors.

I was overwhelmed with a fierce urge to jump over the side, even though it probably meant drowning. Why had I never learned how to swim? At least I would drown in Spartan waters, and escape these brutes.

But I had no courage. Fear paralyzed my limbs. I huddled on my plank like a snared animal.

First Man drew his dagger and sliced through the ropes binding my wrists, then removed the gag. Painful spasms curled my fingers as the circulation slowly returned. First Man sheathed the dagger, then took my left hand between his to massage it. "I trust you not to do anything stupid, like throw yourself over the side."

I licked numb, dry lips. "Who are you?"

"Neoptolemus, son of Achilles." He worked my knuckles, rubbing life back into them. "I'm sorry we handled you so roughly. It won't happen again."

A brown-haired woman with a rich dark cloak slung over one shoulder suddenly appeared. I focused on her in an attempt to regain my equilibrium. The son of Achilles. Myrmidons. "Where are you taking me?" I asked. "I'm to be married in two weeks. You can't just—"

Neoptolemus switched to my right hand. "I'm taking you to Epirus. And yes, you're still going to be married. To me." He turned to acknowledge the woman. "Here, give me that and sit with her. She's a bit rattled from the trip."

I ignored the soft, midnight blue cloak he draped around my shoulders. "I'm betrothed to someone else."

"But you were promised to me first." Neoptolemus fastened the golden clasp below my throat. "You don't know, do you? When Agamemnon quarreled with my father at Troy, he sent a peace offering promising land and treasures and a royal princess, if only Father would fight again. Father refused, so then Menelaus came to him in secret with another offer, a marriage alliance between children." I did not believe him. My father never would have compromised Atreid ambitions and broken my betrothal to Orestes. Agamemnon would not have stood for it.

Neoptolemus took my silence as his cue to continue. "I meant to visit your father this summer and ask for your hand, but then I heard he had given you to Nestor's son. I had no choice but to act."

"You could have gone to him like a civilized man." Anger thickened my voice. "You seized me from an altar! Your man hit me!"

Still, he defended his actions. "Your father left me no choice."

Frothing waves churning around the hull sent spume flying into my face. The swiftly fading light reduced the escorting pentekonters to flanking shadows. "I don't want to marry you."

"You have no choice." Neoptolemus stood, then extended his hand. I refused to budge. "Don't be stubborn," he said sharply. "You can't sleep here on the deck."

Go with him into the ship's narrow cabin, and who knew what he would do to me? "Leave me alone."

"I *said*, you have no choice." His voice dropped to a menacing growl. "I don't want to have to have someone carry you." When the woman interjected with a meaningful cough, his demeanor changed entirely. He straightened, cleared his throat, and held out his hand again. "I apologize again for my rough manners, Princess. I thought you might want to rest and relieve yourself in private. Briseis is here to attend you."

When I continued to hesitate, he wagged his fingers at me. "Come, it's getting dark out."

Briseis helped me stand, then lent me her support when my knees buckled. I needed her assistance to wobble across the deck. The cabin was warm and close inside, pungent with goat-smell. I fumbled in the near-darkness, banging my head on the low ceiling until Neoptolemus brought a clay lantern to illuminate the space. A curtain partitioned the goats tethered to the deck from a small area where fleeces had been heaped into a makeshift pallet.

"It's as comfortable as it can be," he explained ruefully.

He was insane, insulting a goddess by violating her altar, abducting me, and risking war with both Sparta and Pylos. Did he think a few kind words would win me over? "My father will never agree to this," I said.

"Don't expect him to muster his host over this. I'm your promised husband, and he knows that." Neoptolemus stood aside to let me sit on the fleeces. "Menelaus is a second-rate warrior who hasn't got his big brother to fight his battles for him anymore. What makes you think he's going to lead an assault on Epirus when he couldn't even defeat Paris in single combat? I will send him a message and suitable presents, and that'll be the end of it."

Bile soured my throat. "King Nestor won't stand for this, either."

"Do you think that arthritic old graybeard is going to go to war over you when all he did at Troy was sit around drinking Agamemnon's wine and talking? Or maybe you think the dashing Peisistratus is going to come to your rescue?" Sarcasm impregnated his every word. "I am the son of Achilles. I was born to fight. I spent my childhood training for war. I went to Troy when I was fourteen. I killed Priam with my own bare hands. And what has Peisistratus done?" Neoptolemus snorted his contempt. "I heard he commands a chariot corps. How splendid. I command the Myrmidons. I've spent these last eight years helping my grandfather fight the Dorians and carving out a kingdom. Menelaus and Nestor won't do anything because they know there's no better man to marry the daughter of Helen than the son of Achilles."

He was not just delusional, but a petulant braggart, too. I stumbled to my feet, gasping and nauseous. Either I got some fresh air, or I was going to be violently ill. "You have no claim on me."

Eyes blazing with violence, Neoptolemus wrenched me forward into a savage kiss. I struggled against him, tried to twist my face away from his, until he clamped a firm hand on the back of my head and forced me to endure his mouth. "I have you in my possession," he growled, breaking off the kiss. "I could take you right now, right here, and that would be enough."

He spun on his heel and ducked out, leaving the lantern. I tasted him on my lips. *I could take you right now, right here.* Pressing a hand over my mouth, I stumbled to the chamber pot I had noticed standing beside the pallet and spewed my breakfast. Briseis remained with me through the subsequent dry heaves.

"Lie down, Princess." She removed my shoes and tucked me among the soft fleeces, arranging the blue cloak over me. "Rest a while."

The taste of vomit soured my mouth, and the cabin stank even after she took the vessel outside to empty over the side. I shivered under the cloak. Briseis brought back a soothing ointment to rub into my wrists, and encouraged me to eat some fresh bread and figs, but I lacked the will to do anything more than lie very, very still and let my sullen tears roll down my cheeks. What else *could* I do? I had no weapon or training in its use, and no hope of taking on all the Myrmidons at once. I could not swim. I was but a woman, alone and vulnerable.

What would a woman like Clytaemnestra or Elektra have done? Even Clytaemnestra had been overpowered by armed men, treated like so much baggage by Agamemnon, and after worse treatment than mine. And I had seen for myself how Elektra had fared struggling with the strong men who had dragged her from the citadel just before Agamemnon's funeral. A sober realization. They had had no more power than I did.

"I will leave the curtain open to catch some air." Briseis wiped her fingers on a clean cloth before extinguishing the lantern. I did not answer her. What could I have said? Unless my father's ships managed to intercept us, Neoptolemus was going to take me to his pigsty palace in his backwater kingdom, and there do to me what Alaksandu had done to my mother.

I did my best, though, dozing fitfully in the cramped, stale cabin, stirring before dawn. Pain throbbed throughout my entire body, from my cheek where Eumaeus had struck me right down to my chafed wrists and aching calves.

When I woke, Briseis helped me up to use the chamber pot and wash with water from a jug. She gave me herbs mixed in sour wine to settle my stomach, and tried once again to get me to eat the bread. "You won't have it again for many days." She had an accent I could not place, until she told me that she had come from Anatolia.

It was not that I did not want to eat, for I knew I ought to keep up my strength, only that the twinges of seasickness, mingled with my present circumstances, killed my appetite.

After sunrise, Neoptolemus came in to check on me. "It looks like we'll have good sailing conditions today." He bent down to turn my face this way and that in the growing light, examining my swollen cheek. "It looks better. Tonight we'll sleep ashore. You can join us as long as you behave." When I failed to respond, he added, "Don't even think about trying to escape. You have nowhere to run."

I jerked my head away. Neoptolemus gripped my chin to force my head back. "Don't be difficult, Hermione." Releasing me, he shoved the untouched bread at me. "Eat something. I expect to bring home a queen, not a sickly waif. I want everyone who looks at you to know you're Helen's daughter."

"Stop calling me that."

Neoptolemus knelt down across from me and braced a hand on the rocking deck. "Anyone who knows who you are will call you that, whether you like it or not. Do you think it's any different for the son of Achilles?" I shredded the bread into smaller and smaller pieces to avoid looking at him, until he stopped my hand. "Eat your bread, and I'll take you on deck for some exercise and fresh air."

With him looking on, I choked down enough food to satisfy him. He kept his promise afterward and escorted me outside.

"Look there." Neoptolemus directed my gaze to the dolphins leaping through the ship's churning wake. "It's a good omen."

Disheartened, I turned away to hunker down in the stern sheets.

He sat down beside me. "Did you like him, Nestor's son?"

"Does it matter to you?"

He sucked an aggravated breath between his teeth. "I am trying to be kind! You're not making it easy."

"Why should it be?" I challenged him with a direct look. "You seized me from the goddess's altar, dragged me away from my family and my betrothed. You manhandled me like some common slave girl, and now you expect me to *like* you?"

Neoptolemus reached out to caress my cheek. I flinched away from his touch. "Have it as you will, then," he said. "After a while you will learn to like me."

He sounded so confident, as though he believed the salacious tales about my mother going from one husband to the next with dry eyes and wet thighs, and now expected the daughter to do the same. "You don't know me at all," I said.

Neoptolemus frowned. "I don't need to know you, except in the ways that matter."

When he left, Briseis joined me so we could sit together and watch the Laconian coastline and the dolphins frolicking in the spume. We said nothing to each other. Whatever she was, servant woman or Neoptolemus's bed-slave, I did not entirely trust her.

Around mid-afternoon, we caught a second tailwind that carried us around Cape Tainaron.

Sunset brought us to a secluded inlet with a freshwater spring. The Myrmidons beached the three pentekonters and went ashore to replenish their waterskins and build a driftwood bonfire. A slaughtered goat roasted on a spit, while several men erected an ox-hide tent and piled fleeces on the ground for me. Briseis heated water in a cauldron so we could share a sponge bath, then she gave me a clean dress and fresh loincloth to put on.

I managed to eat a little, now that we were on land, and later I let her plait my hair. "He should have simply gone to my father and asked for my hand like a proper suitor." That much, at least, I could express in her presence. "Did he think he would refuse?"

"You heard what he said last night." Briseis ran the comb through my hair to part it into sections. "Once he heard about Prince Peisistratus, there was no more time to negotiate, or any reason to think Menelaus would jeopardize an important alliance with Pylos. So he had to act."

"He acted foolishly." I winced as she tugged my scalp with each plait. "My father will never agree to this."

"It's too late to go back," she answered quietly. "Neoptolemus left a messenger behind to explain everything to Menelaus, and he will send rich presents to compensate him for any insult." Briseis secured the braid with a ribbon. "There, now! You have lovely hair. We don't see that color very often in Anatolia."

I snatched the mirror from her and hurled it at the tent wall; it landed in the soft sand. Childish of me, something Elektra would have done, but at the moment I could scarcely help it. "You're not listening to me!"

"No," she corrected, "you're the one who isn't listening. Neoptolemus is trying very hard to be courteous and considerate, which is certainly more than he does with his first wife."

Her remark went straight over my head at first, then struck me hard.

"You mean he's already married?" Briseis tried to shush me. I shoved her hands away. "Does he expect me to be his concubine?"

"Princess, please..." She cast an apprehensive glance toward the tent flap. Did she think I cared whether Neoptolemus heard the commotion? Let him stick his head in and ask what was wrong! "She's not his legal wife, but his concubine. Prince Hector's widow."

How dare he insult me like this! "You said she was his wife."

Briseis clearly regretted having opened her mouth. "It is easy to forget sometimes. She's the mother of his children, and he's had no other women for some time, so..."

"And what does he plan to do with her now?" I demanded.

She shrugged. "I honestly don't know. They despise each other, but he enjoys keeping her captive and getting sons on her as an insult to Hector's ghost. She's a princess and his prize, his spear-bride. You will have to be very careful how you deal with her."

Bad enough that Neoptolemus had wrenched me away from my family and betrothed, and had threatened to rape me, but now he expected me to share his dominion and bed with a rival, too? Was there no end to this outrage? I knotted my hands into fists, wondering when this sordid nightmare would end.

CHAPTER SEVENTEEN

"WEAR THIS." Neoptolemus fastened a strand of lapis and gold beads around my neck. "It matches your gown."

Briseis had dressed me in deep blue edged with golden embroidery over an azure shift, and draped a matching veil of the sheerest linen over my curling red hair. When she held up the polished bronze mirror, I had to admit that I looked like a queen.

After a ten-day voyage, we had disembarked on Epirote shores to rest for two days in the governor's residence while Neoptolemus sent a messenger inland to Ephyri with instructions to prepare the palace for our arrival. I eagerly bathed away the grime and goat-stink, luxuriated in the comfort of a feather bed, and tried to avoid brooding over the fact that my father's ships had not intercepted us.

The ships would come, of course they would. I was the sacred heiress of Sparta. They had to come.

Neoptolemus bent to kiss my rouged cheek. "You look lovely today."

My bruises had healed, but my seething contempt for him remained. It did not matter how courteous he was, or how well he cleaned up. All the courtly manners and scented oil in the world could not hide the fact that he was still a hot-headed young ruffian.

A painted scarlet and gold chariot drawn by white geldings awaited us in the courtyard, along with a Myrmidon escort. Neoptolemus extended his hand to help me onto the platform. Briseis rode in another chariot with Eumaeus.

People crowded the streets and rooftops of the port town to watch the procession, cheering as we passed. Neoptolemus must have announced far and wide that he was marrying the daughter of Menelaus and Helen, because the people called out my name as they flung posies into the chariot. They ran after us, beyond the walls into the pastures and fields, shouting blessings.

We headed northeast across open country, following a broad, swift-flowing river past dusty vineyards and fields green with ripening wheat. In the distance, a formidable range of snowy mountains presented a bulwark along the eastern horizon. Peasants abandoned their labors in their dozens when they heard our jingling harnesses and saw the sunlight glinting off bronze spears and gold jewelry; they flocked by the roadside to watch the procession. Neoptolemus drew my attention to them. "Hear how they welcome you!"

Along the way, he pointed out landmarks he thought might interest me, and promised he would send for swans to stock the rivers if I desired it. For all I cared, he could jump into the water with them.

At length, we arrived at his seat of power, a small citadel crowning a limestone hill overlooking a middling lower town. Here, too, crowds waited to welcome us, cheering us along the route from the circuit walls to the citadel gates. Our escort led the way into the outer courtyard. On the supporting terraces above were bright awnings shading the lords and ladies of the court.

Our driver brought the chariot to a rolling halt. Neoptolemus stepped down first, then held out his hand to help me. Together, we ascended the steps so he could present me to his courtiers. It was a monotonous affair, a seemingly endless parade of elegant Epirote noblemen and their stylish wives. There were even rough Molossian chieftains wearing shaggy animal-skin cloaks.

Then, we came to a dark-haired woman whose Anatolian silver headdress and spangled veil framed an oval face bearing a guarded expression. Servant women stood behind her holding three young children. She must be the Trojan concubine. Hector's widow.

Neoptolemus introduced us. "Princess, this is Andromache." I shifted my gaze from his face to hers just in time to catch her slitting her eyes at him. "And these three handsome lads are my sons."

One was a mere babe, but the other two eagerly called out and reached for their father. Neoptolemus greeted each one with enthusiasm, yet he forgot to introduce them to me.

The older, dark-haired man standing beside Andromache aroused my curiosity. Something about his hawkish features and Anatolian dress recalled vague memories of the fateful Trojan delegation. He reminded me somewhat of Prince Alaksandu.

Returning his youngest child to the maids, Neoptolemus presented the strange man. "This is Helenus, the last of Priam's sons."

Golden crescents swung in the man's ears as Priam's son nodded graciously toward me. Helenus. It did not sound like an Anatolian name.

Neoptolemus escorted me into the palace. As we passed through the great court and up the stairwell leading to the private apartments, he pointed out rich frescoes and any other details he thought might interest me. He was trying much too hard to impress upon me that his backwater palace was just as splendid as the one from which he had taken me.

Fortunately, he withdrew as soon as we reached my designated apartment. "I will leave you to rest." Taking my hand, he raised it to his lips. "We feast tonight with the court."

I explored my surroundings under the anxious gazes of the three young girls who had been appointed to serve me. An empty loom stood flush against the far wall, and beside it a basket containing copper needles, a spindle, and snowy fleece. A terracotta tub stood in the bathroom, and in the bedchamber Briseis opened chests and jewel caskets to let me inspect their contents. My prospective bridegroom had prepared everything for my arrival.

After the maids undressed me, I dismissed them and ducked into the bathroom to change my menstrual linen; I had started bleeding aboard the ship, and was in the heaviest day of my flow. Cramp bark tea and an hour's rest would be just the thing to restore my energy, yet at the same time I chafed at my ongoing confinement. "Is there a garden or inner court where we can walk?" I asked Briseis.

"Yes," she replied, "but you will need permission."

This was intolerable! "All I want is to walk inside the walls!" I realized I was being irrational, but Mother Dia had chosen a terrible time to send my moon blood.

"Try to be patient," Briseis urged. "I'm sure you will be able to go wherever you please after the wedding."

I seized a cushion from the bed and hurled it at the wall. Sitting down at the dressing table, I sank my head into both hands.

Then she was there behind me, massaging my shoulders with a firm touch. "Lie down and rest," she advised. "Later, we'll dress you for the feast, and you can send for Lord Helenus and Lady Andromache."

I stared at the elaborate pyxis on the table before me. Had Neoptolemus chosen all these things, the clothes and furnishings and jewels, or had it been a woman, perhaps even Briseis herself? "Why would I send for them? I don't need to see them, to humiliate them."

"Helenus could make a valuable ally," Briseis argued, "and you must establish to Andromache that she is not the mistress here. She might no longer be a princess, but she has her dignity, and will do whatever she can to protect her sons."

I could care less about her dignity or her sons, or who ruled as queen. Frowning, squeezing my eyes shut, I tried to think more rationally. Of course it mattered. "Helenus. Andromache. Those are not Anatolian names, are they?"

"No," she admitted. "Helenus's real name is Hantili, but his captors thought it amusing to name him after your mother."

It was a slight, then. That did not surprise me. "Should I call him by his real name?"

"He will not mind, but she will," Briseis told me. Her mouth tightened. "You must tell no one, but Neoptolemus called her Andromache because she fought him so hard when he first took her. You would be showing her great respect by using her real name. Ashakumila."

I mouthed the harsh, unfamiliar syllables. "Do you also...?" I knew Briseis was Anatolian, perhaps also a Trojan captive, perhaps even a bed-slave, but did not want to offend her by assuming she was a concubine. I tried again. "Does he keep you as he does her?"

"No," Briseis said. If my question bothered her, she did not let it show. "I belonged to his father. Achilles set me free just before his death, but I had no home to return to. Neoptolemus took me under his protection after the war."

So *she* was the Anatolian princess that Achilles and Agamemnon had quarreled over. That Briseis. She was a winsome woman, past thirty-five, with dimpled cheeks and almond-shaped gray eyes, but no great beauty. "If I may ask, what was Achilles like?" I asked.

I observed the pink blush suffusing her cheeks. Her enigmatic smile made her seem twenty years younger. So she had liked the hero. Considering what Nestor had said about heroes, that they were either madmen or liars, her reaction surprised me.

"Achilles was god-touched, like no other man." Her dreaming look evaporated, and she peered intently at me. "If you're asking whether his son is anything like him, then no, not at all. Neoptolemus is no more Achilles than you are Helen."

The servants were lighting the lamps in the bedchamber when I rose to greet my visitors. "Thank you for coming. Will you join me for a cup of wine before we go down?"

Helenus raised an eyebrow, but accepted the invitation, claiming the chair beside me. Andromache hesitated, then accepted the other chair. Helenus took the vessel, mixed the wine and water together, and uttered the libation prayer in his native tongue. Afterward, he set the vessel down without having drunk.

Awkwardness thickened the air. Taking a deep breath to steady my nerves, I addressed Andromache first. "You have beautiful sons, Lady Ashakumila. What are their names?"

Her nostrils flared. "Are you asking so you can curse them?"

The mere suggestion blindsided me. "I had no such intention."

Helenus addressed Andromache in a foreign tongue. Whatever he said, she defiantly set her jaw and glanced away. He spoke again, more sharply this time, and it did not require a translator to tell me that he was a kinsman commanding a recalcitrant woman's obedience.

Finally, she relented, forcing out each name in grating tones. "Molossus, Pielus, and Pergamos." Disdain flashed in her dark eyes. "You do not look like her at all."

Like my mother, she meant. Perhaps I could turn that difference to my advantage. "I have little in common with her. I get my red hair from my father."

That did not work, either. Andromache spat her contempt. "Menelaus is a weakling, to let his wife and now his daughter be stolen."

Andromache spoke with the thickest accent and most stilted diction I had ever heard. I let the insult slide, while trying to ease the tension by stating the obvious. "I am not here because I wish to be. Neoptolemus abducted me."

She hooded her eyes. "So now a thousand ships will storm Epirus to recover Helen's daughter?"

Simple courtesy would not win over this woman. Andromache's hostility called for a firmer hand. "I will say this once, Lady Ashakumila: I have no desire to be your queen or make trouble for you or your sons." I lifted my right hand. "I swear by holy Hera and Athena that I will not harm you or your children. Let them witness this oath. In return, you must swear to give me the same consideration."

Andromache pursed her lips together. Tension coiled through her tall frame. Her fingers clawed at the armrests.

Helenus barked at her in their native tongue. Slowly, her fingers uncurled, and she spoke, grinding out the words. "I swear by Tarhunt the Storm God not to trouble or intrigue against you. Let him hear this oath."

She left then, exiting the sitting room in a resentful swirl of dark skirts, leaving Helenus behind. He waited several minutes, until she was truly gone, to address me. "Ashakumila will not trouble you. I will make certain of it," he stated. "I cautioned Neoptolemus to meet with your father and conduct a civilized negotiation, but he does not always heed my advice. I apologize for any rough treatment or distress he might have caused you."

"Sparta won't stand for this."

Helenus nodded. "I expect your father will send ships very shortly, but do not expect an armed host. When Alaksandu took your mother, Menelaus tried diplomacy first. It did not work then, and I doubt it will work now."

"Then there will be war," I said hotly.

"Not this time," he replied. "Menelaus does not have Agamemnon's resources, and under these circumstances his Pylian and Arcadian allies will not supply ships or fighting men." Helenus's thick brows knitted together. "I am afraid this is what your people refer to as a legitimate abduction."

Legitimate abduction. Authorized rape. However one labeled it, the phrases tasted sour. "There was nothing legitimate about it. I was never betrothed to Neoptolemus."

Helenus did not try to argue. "I will do my best to advise and assist you, but you must understand that you have very little choice in the matter. You must be prepared to accept your fate as queen of Epirus."

I would do no such thing. Neoptolemus had no valid claim on me. None. "Is that what my mother did, accept her fate?" I asked bitterly.

Helenus's face remained impassive except for the faint twitch of his eyebrows. "Your mother kept her true feelings hidden." A pause. "You are nothing at all like her."

A SPARTAN AMBASSADOR ARRIVED a fortnight later. Carts containing my belongings rolled into the outer court. Monime and Thebe hunkered among the baggage. Seeing them overwhelmed me with crushing disbelief. My father could not have capitulated that easily! Where were the demands for my release, the warships, the threats of retaliation?

Porters under the direction of a rotund household steward awaited my command. I ignored them while the driver helped my handmaidens down from the mule cart. My face burned with humiliation and rage. "Is this it?"

But neither handmaid understood my meaning. "These are all your goods and furnishings, Mistress," Monime said.

I had no patience, and it was all I could do not to slap her. "And my father just sent them?" Disbelieving tears filled my eyes. "He just said yes?" Monime and Thebe froze at my outburst. "He wasn't even angry?"

"Yes, yes, he was," Thebe stammered. "He executed the stable master who supplied the horses, and throttled the man who brought him the letter. Only the queen could talk to him. She ordered us to pack up your belongings and told us we were going to Epirus."

I had recovered some of my composure while she spoke, and was already regretting my outburst. "Where is Sotera?"

"Mistress, she..." Thebe glanced aside. She must be dead. "Whoever attacked her struck her too hard."

Several feet away, the steward discreetly coughed to remind me that the porters were waiting. I gave him my instructions, and then vacated the courtyard with my women in tow.

Upstairs, I balled my hands into fists. Sotera's death rankled as much as Menalaus's capitulation. How dare Neoptolemus treat me like this! How dare his men kill my servants with impunity and my father do nothing! I seized the spindle from the chair and hurled it against the wall.

Briseis brought more unfortunate news. "Neoptolemus wishes to dine with you tonight."

His was the absolute last face I wanted to see, right next to my father's. "Tell him to go hang himself."

"I doubt he will oblige." Briseis indicated the slave girls who were on their way to the bathroom carrying steaming water jugs. "I ordered you a bath."

By the time I had finished bathing, chests and bundles crammed the apartment. Having helped my mother pack, my handmaidens knew where everything was. First, we took out my gods, which my mother had packed in soft fleece to protect them during the voyage. We carefully arranged the deities on my altar and gave them food to help them settle into their new home.

Servants arrived to prepare the sitting room for supper, shifting the baggage to one side so they could set up a small table and linens. Neoptolemus arrived just as the lamps were being lit. "Hermione, I have letters for you from your family." Shaking his head, he sat down across from me. "Your father is furious with me over the abduction. When you write back to him, assure him that you weren't harmed."

He could do that himself. A servant mixed and poured the wine, while another laid out the first course: a salad of cucumbers, radishes, and sliced olives drizzled with seasoned olive oil and vinegar. I had no appetite. "Did Nestor say anything?"

"Nestor can't argue over a pre-contract. I hear Peisistratus is taking it as well as one can expect from a boy who clings to his father's greaves. I'll send him a splendid chariot and matched team. We breed fine horses here in Epirus." Neoptolemus tucked into his salad. "Your father's ambassador is here for the wedding. A week ought to be enough time to arrange a feast and invite the guests. Helenus will see to everything." Chewing, he nodded toward my plate. "You're not eating?"

A mere three days. "I'm more interested in what you're saying."

He called me on the fib. "And I'm more interested in presenting a glowing bride to the guests. Eat your salad, or you'll have to wait to read the letters."

Like a father telling his daughter to eat her vegetables, just as he had done aboard the ship. I smarted at his reprimand, but ate enough to satisfy him. Over the last course of sweet figs, he rewarded me with a thick packet. "Go ahead and look at them. If you want to write back, give your messages to Helenus and he'll give them to the ambassador."

Monime brought over a lamp while the servants unobtrusively cleared away the dishes. I broke the seal on my father's letter first.

Menelaus confirmed the tale Neoptolemus had told me that first evening at sea, but went on to explain further: "Neoptolemus and I met a few times, but the conversation always turned to his late father. We never discussed a marriage alliance. I have no idea who told him there was a binding contract. It was an informal and private arrangement between Achilles and me, which was never seen through. We never offered a blood sacrifice or swore before any gods to seal the alliance. And I considered the matter completely void after he died.

"I realize this isn't what you want to hear, Daughter, but what's done is done. Neoptolemus might have handled you a bit more roughly than he meant to, and insulted your pride, but he assures me that you haven't been harmed and will be treated with all the respect due your station. I know him well enough to believe him." If he believed that, then he obviously did not know his prospective son-in-law at all. Or maybe manhandling a princess during a "legitimate" abduction did not count. "I have made certain arrangements regarding his place in the Spartan succession, but this is a delicate matter, and my ambassador will discuss it with him when the time comes.

"Nestor is gnashing his teeth at the moment, but he understands and will explain the matter to Peisistratus. Life is filled with many unexpected changes in fortune, and many disappointments, and sometimes we have to accept them as best we can. A war now would be ruinous."

Bitterness soured my throat. My father had given up on me, just like that. The Spartan ambassador was not even going to demand my return.

Neoptolemus stretched out his long legs and munched on a fig. "From the look on your face, it seems like your father isn't pleased."

As though my father's opinion was the only one that mattered. "No, not at all."

Helen's letter offered more practical advice: "You have no choice in the matter. Accept Neoptolemus as your husband and remember that your situation could have been much worse. I sent you nepenthe for the wedding night. Use it along with a liberal amount of olive oil."

Another mother would have wrung her hands and wept over a daughter's abduction. Helen the spider advised me to weave webs and submit to my captor bridegroom. I read on. "Your father and I have discussed the succession, and have decided that Neoptolemus should not become king of Sparta after your father dies."

A chill passed through me, reading and rereading that passage. My parents were disinheriting me, through no fault of my own. "This has nothing to do with you," Helen wrote, "and everything to do with your bridegroom's inexperience and immaturity. No doubt he's boasted to you that he rules a kingdom while your former betrothed still clings to his father's greaves. Did he also tell you that he let the Dorians overrun Phthia while he played at war with the Molossians? He will not have the same chance to ruin Sparta."

My gaze darted to the prospective bridegroom in question, snacking on figs and relaxing, oblivious to the arrangements being made behind his back; he would not have been so nonchalant had he known Sparta was not going to become an Epirote vassal after my father's death.

I returned to the letter. "Your grandfather would have used this incident to make Aethiolas sole heir, but the Spartan assembly balks at the thought of overturning the old sacred traditions overnight. They want a queen of ancient royal blood. Chrysothemis is your cousin through the maternal line, and in the same degree. The assembly will accept her as heiress, and Aethiolas as her consort. She is woefully ignorant and empty-headed, but she will simply have to do."

Chrysothemis would jump at the chance to marry my personable, good-looking brother, but what were my parents thinking? She would have to act as a high priestess and manage the royal household. She could scarcely read or write, or add a column of figures, and now she was going to inherit my station?

What Helen said next came as a complete surprise: "I have enclosed a letter from Orestes. He is much more lucid now, but still quite unwell, as you will see. He doesn't know that you have been abducted, so say nothing. Also, don't send a reply directly to Delphi. Orestes may question why you are writing from Epirus. Neoptolemus may also object to your correspondence with him, however innocent it might be. Send your reply to me instead, and I will forward it."

Tucked into her letter I found a smaller packet bearing a broken seal; my mother had pried into its contents. *Send your reply to me instead.* Could she have been more obvious? She meant to censor our letters to each other.

Across from me, Neoptolemus kept daydreaming and munching on dates. Why could he not just go away? It was not as though he was interested in interacting with me.

My mother said Orestes was lucid. If he was strong enough to write his own letters, then that might mean he was ready to stand trial.

I unfolded the papyrus. The Delphic priest's crabbed handwriting met my eyes; he explained that he was taking dictation from his patient. And he was no pedagogue; he had copied exactly what he heard, right down to Orestes' disjointed grammar.

"My dearest Hermione, forgive me for having someone else write for me. I can't hold my hands steady, can't even focus to make this a proper letter. Whoever else reads this will think me crazy. I am. All torn up inside, splintered into so many pieces I can't even begin to find myself, because whenever I reach for one piece all the others slip away and I have nothing again.

"They give me drugs to sleep, drugs to wake me up, and drugs to stop me from dreaming. I wish you were here next to me. Then it wouldn't matter how my letter sounds, because then you could see me lying here and hold my hand, and feel it shaking. I would like to have someone special sit with me for a while."

I swallowed to hold back my tears. Reading his letter in front of Neoptolemus was a mistake, but I could not help myself.

"I love the blue cloak you sent. Its color is so soft, it feels so soft, it soothes me. I smell your scent in it, and remember how lovely you always look in blue. I know I shouldn't be talking like a love struck boy. Didymus is sitting right here next to me shaking his head, asking do I really want to say all this. Yes, yes, I do. I heard you were to be married soon. Nestor's son. I hope he's a kind man. Aegisthus said things when I went to kill him, things that made me snap inside and smash him into pieces, but I don't want to think about them. There have been so many lies and betrayals it's hard to know what's true anymore."

I had to stop and wipe away the tears before reading the rest.

"Once I'm well enough to face judgment, they'll tell me what I must do in order to cleanse this pollution. Perhaps the priests will sacrifice me. It's all right. I will go willingly, because it's what the gods have decided, and because spilling my blood might cleanse all that's rotten and part of the curse. Don't cry if you hear that they led me to the altar, because I will have consented. It will be all right. With all my love, Orestes."

Letting the papyrus sheet slide into my lap, I wept into both hands. A foolish thing to do in front of Neoptolemus, I knew, but I could not hold back.

"What's wrong?" I peered out between my fingers to see Neoptolemus leaning forward across the table. "Bad news?"

"It's my cousin. He's very ill."

"Orestes, isn't it?" Neoptolemus mused. "I don't see why you're crying about him, or why he's so tormented over the whole business. It was absolutely right, what he did. That bitch deserved to die."

"That bitch was his mother." Neoptolemus was as dense as he was insensitive. "Would you please excuse me?" I managed a polite smile when I yearned to point an angry finger at the door and scream at him to get out. "This has all been very upsetting."

I submitted to his solicitous kiss on the cheek before withdrawing to lie down in my bedchamber. A lamp burned on the dressing table, casting eerie shadows onto its enameled surface. Next door, the servants began clearing the table. I heard Monime murmuring to someone. A dog barked in the distance. It might have been an evening back home, except it was not.

Briseis entered the room. She crossed over to the bed, then the mattress shifted and she was sitting beside me. "You're brooding too much, Lady. It's not healthy for you."

I had not asked for her opinion, and did not want it. "Leave me alone."

"Learn to accept your lot, Hermione." Briseis sounded like my mother, saying that. "Believe me, it's the best thing you can do." She paused. "I was married once, before Achilles sacked Lyrnessos and claimed me. I loathed the husband my family chose for me, but crying about it only made it worse."

A bad man was still bad whether one smiled or cried, I reflected grimly. "I have other cares," I said. "My cousin Orestes has been polluted with madness. They're going to kill him for his sins. He consents to the sacrifice, but it isn't right. He had no choice but to do what he did."

"I know what it feels like to be so helpless when those you love are suffering." Briseis filled the space above and before me like a benevolent mother goddess. "I remember lying in Achilles' hut after he died, as you're lying here now, listening to the warriors holding the funeral games in the distance." A scent of wildflowers wafted from her skin when she moved to stroke my hair. "It was wrong, how he died. He wanted to die in battle, covered in glory, not convulsing and crying in agony from a poisoned arrow."

She was not comforting me at all. "Why are you telling me this?" I mumbled.

"Because fate is cruel, and you are not its only victim." Briseis withdrew her hand. "Now dry your eyes. Write back to Orestes and tell him all the things on your mind, while you still can."

Thebe and Monime came in to attend me, to remove my clothes and cosmetics, and dress me for bed. I felt shaky and wrung out as I headed back into the sitting room.

Briseis had laid out writing materials for me: a stylus, clay tablets, and a finger bowl of water. I had not used clay since my childhood lessons, but I knew that in many places in Hellas the scribes and priests did not use papyrus.

I picked up the stylus and scored horizontal lines across the clay. Tomorrow I would have to send the tablets to the kiln, but was determined that neither Helenus nor anyone else handle my letters. I would give them to the Spartan ambassador myself.

My mother would read the contents, maybe even show the letter to my father before sending it on to Orestes. Let her. She knew how I felt.

"My dear Orestes, I am so very glad to hear from you again. Please forgive my sending a clay tablet. I had nothing else to write on when I received your letter, but this will last forever.

"I wish with all my heart that I could sit beside you, and stroke your hair and hold your hand when the nightmares come. All I can do is send you my love and hope that it's enough to sustain you. Forget all this grim talk about curses and sacrifices. All who know and love you know that you are a good and pious man. Should the worst happen, do not go to your death believing in your guilt, or thinking that no one will care. Pythian Apollo and Mother Dia receive my daily prayers for your deliverance. Your dearest and most loving cousin, Hermione."

Chapter Eighteen

Helenus arranged a splendid wedding feast, consulting with me over the details. "I know there are certain traditional rites Spartan royal brides observe," he said, his tone hinting at deeper knowledge.

So he knew about the ritual bath and the pomegranate seeds, but those rites were for presumptive king-consorts, and Neoptolemus would never rule as king in Sparta. "This is not a Spartan wedding," I answered firmly. "The local customs will suffice."

Sudden doubt seized me. I had no idea whether Neoptolemus had met with my father's ambassador and learned the truth. "Has he asked about Spartan wedding customs?"

"He left the arrangements to me." A faint, enigmatic smile twitched the corners of Helenus's mouth. On a small clay tablet, he marked my preferences in the wedge-shaped cuneiform his people used. "Now, if there are any particular Spartan dishes you would like served, tell me now so the cooks can do their shopping."

I stared at the jewels spilled across the dressing table, the rich garments scattered spread over the bed, unable to decide what to eat or drink any more than I could choose what to wear.

Helenus laid the tablet and stylus on the table's edge, then bent down to me. "I have arranged for you to spend tomorrow night in the temple of Artemis. The custom here is the same as in Sparta." A pregnant pause. "Is there anything else I can do?"

"No, thank you, Hantili." I had taken to using his real name because it seemed like the correct thing to do.

Later, I called for Briseis and gestured to the mess. "Choose something for me. Thebe, did Mother pack my doll?"

Briseis stood her ground. "Stop moping and get involved. Making what decisions you can will help you feel less powerless."

Perhaps, but I could not decide. "I don't know. Your taste is far better than mine," I said. "You know what he likes."

Thebe brought me the doll. Its cloth body was attached to a painted terracotta head with rooted yarn hair. Leda had given it to me. She had helped me clothe it. I touched my finger to the well-worn, faded pink dress with its childish stitches, not wanting to dedicate this childhood treasure in this foreign place, among these strangers.

Virgin brides spent their wedding eve with Artemis. Again, I found myself prostrate before a goddess who had never protected me.

After I made the customary reverences, the high priestess snipped a lock of my hair to burn before the altar. Then she directed me to the offering table where I would place the doll.

Artemis might as well have been a foreign goddess for all the reassurance she extended to me. I held out the doll, relic of a much happier time, while yearning to snatch it back and flee the sanctuary. Why had I not substituted a lesser doll? I wondered. Because Artemis would have known the difference and directed her wrath toward any future children, as she had punished Agamemnon's hubris through Iphigenia's innocence.

A knot formed in my throat when it came time to utter the dedicatory prayer. "Protectress of children, be with me on this last night of maidenhood." It was a lie! I was not even a maiden. Yet I said the words because they were mandatory. "Receive this precious gift of my girlhood."

My handmaidens joined me for the sacred songs and dances, and we tried to make merry as the sun set on my final day as an unmarried woman. But the harder we tried, the sharper my grief became. At last, I broke down. The priestesses assumed my weeping was the natural response of an anxious bride, and I did nothing to disabuse anyone of that notion. Nonetheless, I strove to dry my tears, smile faintly, and project a queenly demeanor, so that the women in the sanctuary should not speak ill of me, or claim that my incessant crying was a portent of evil things to come.

I did not sleep very well that night. Artemis's sanctuary seemed to me like a place of danger. I avoided glancing over at the goddess on her plinth, illuminated by sacred fire. There was subtle menace in her gaze. I had dared proclaim myself a virgin when we both knew the truth.

Morning brought Briseis with the priestesses of Hera into the sanctuary to array me in my wedding raiment. Briseis truly had wonderful taste, having selected a royal purple bodice cinched with a golden girdle, a flounced skirt glittering with amethyst beads and golden roundels, and a sheer lilac linen veil spangled with glittering gold rosettes.

"Mistress, you look beautiful." Monime stepped back among the other women once the final flounce was adjusted, the last ribbon tied, and the linen veil arranged in place over my coiffed ringlets.

Beautiful. It was just a word. I had not felt beautiful when Aegisthus used to corner me to steal a caress, or when he had forced himself on me. And I did not feel beautiful now, standing in the coolness of the shrine with my naked breasts thrusting out from the open bodice. Neoptolemus would be getting a marble bride, a doll such as the one I had left on the altar.

Shouts from outside distracted me. "Come out, daughter of Menelaus!" Male voices. "Let us see your beauty!" Neoptolemus and his friends had arrived for the ritual abduction.

Briseis turned to me. "It's time."

Neoptolemus let me exit the sanctuary so as not to offend the goddess, but the moment my feet left sacred ground he clasped me around the middle and swung me into his chariot. Briseis and the maids raised the alarm, their initial cries ritual protests, then genuine squeals as the bridegroom's friends snatched them into their garlanded chariots for the ride back to the palace.

"You're a ravishing morsel." Neoptolemus kept one arm around my waist as he drove. "Much more beautiful than your mother."

I stared straight ahead. "Watch where you're going."

Neoptolemus steered into the palace's outer court, tossed the reins to a groom, and carried me across the megaron's threshold. He had had an ivory chair placed for me upon on the dais, and took immense pride in presenting me to his guests as his new queen.

"Behold our bride: Hermione, daughter of King Menelaus Atreides and Queen Helen, descendant of the great royal houses of Sparta and Mycenae!" Neoptolemus grasped my hand. "She comes to us heiress to the rich fields and pastures of Laconia. She is a fit mate for the heir of glorious Achilles."

So the Spartan ambassador had not yet informed him that he would not be claiming those rich Laconian fields and pastures once my father died. I was not anticipating that moment with any relish.

Hera's high priestess conducted the ritual, binding our hands and directing us to circle the hearth three times. Then we sat down on our thrones as king and queen of Epirus.

Epirote nobles and Molossian chieftains formed a queue to congratulate us and to present their gifts. Her face half-hidden under a spangled Anatolian veil, Andromache hung back among the maidservants and scribes. When her turn came, she dropped an anonymous present at the pile's edge. I had Thebe bring back the necklace with its silver pendants to inspect it for strange markings that might be a curse, but upon close examination it seemed innocuous.

At noon, servants set up the trestle tables for the wedding banquet, and brought out steaming platters of roast sirloin, mutton dripping with crackling fat, lamb seasoned in coriander, and tender venison in milk. Neoptolemus and I shared a bridal cup, a painted kylix once owned by Achilles, which the king's server kept filled with a potent cocktail of mead, beer, and retsina.

"Paris once told a story that Aphrodite had promised him the most beautiful woman in the world." Neoptolemus focused on the female acrobats gyrating by the hearth as he related this anecdote. "It began with a wedding very much like this," he said.

"What's that?" I had not been paying attention.

He gazed sidelong at me. "Paris, dear. When Agamemnon's envoys questioned his right to keep Helen, Paris fabricated some nonsense about the gods. They were invited to a mortal wedding, you see, all but the goddess of discord. So Eris took a golden apple and inscribed it with the words 'for the fairest,' and rolled it into the megaron. Athena, Hera, and Aphrodite all laid claim to it."

"And where did you hear this?" I asked.

"Helenus told me." Neoptolemus nodded toward his advisor, sitting beside the Spartan ambassador. "Of course, the gods all had Anatolian names, but I understood what he meant."

I stifled a yawn. "Ah, yes, I see." My not sleeping well the night before was catching up to me.

Oblivious to my boredom, he continued, "Zeus knew better than to judge the matter, so he chose a handsome young goatherd grazing his flock on Mount Ida. Paris told the envoys he had been raised as a peasant after a terrible prophecy inspired his parents to abandon him on the mountainside. Hah! Paris did only one thing with goats, and it wasn't drive them to pasture."

I hoped Neoptolemus was not as bad a lover as he was a storyteller. If I had to suffer him in my bed, I at least wanted him to be a considerate mate. "Go on," I urged, feigning interest.

"All three goddesses promised him fabulous rewards," he answered, "but then Aphrodite whispered hot in his ear that if he gave her the apple he could have the most beautiful woman in the world. So how do you think that peasant decided? With his cock."

My head was starting to ache. "That's a ridiculous story."

"So it is." Neoptolemus clamped a hand on my wrist as I reached for the kylix. "You're getting tipsy. I think it might be time for you to retire."

Nervous anticipation cut through my stupor. "It's not even sunset." Was he that randy already?

He kissed my fingers. "But summer nights are so short."

Raucous catcalls and applause attended me as the ladies of the court escorted me from the megaron. Upstairs, ladies crammed into my bedchamber, jostling aside my maids for the honor of sponging away my cosmetics, and removing my jewels and clothes. Briseis attempted to keep order, but as a foreigner she exercised no authority over the Epirote noblewomen; it was all she could do to rescue the discarded garments and trinkets from the floor.

All the arguing and chaos further chafed my nerves. "Stop your bickering!" I shouted. A stunned silence overtook the chamber. Ladies and maids alike gaped at me. "Let us be sensible about this. Out, all of you. I am going to lie down to wait for the bridegroom. Let my maids clean up."

At least they obeyed me. I smothered an unladylike yawn behind my hand and climbed between the linen sheets, ignoring admonitions not to fall asleep. I must have dozed a little, because the sudden clashing cymbals, trilling pipes, and boisterous male laughter outside my apartment gave me a start. The bridegroom's party sounded like a troupe of satyrs.

Furniture shifted and fell over in the next room as the gentlemen entered the apartment. I heard the women nearest the bedchamber door laughing and calling out. Startled, I sat up just as the curtain parted, and the bridegroom appeared with his retainers. The ladies who followed them in fell like honeybees upon a laughing Neoptolemus to undress him, while his attendants burst again into drunken song. My head ached.

As Neoptolemus winked at me, instinct prompted me to clutch the bed sheet to my breasts. Did he intend to take me in front of his entire court? Determined not to endure that indignity, I prepared myself to speak up.

Yet my intervention proved unnecessary. "All right!" the bridegroom called, hustling men and women alike out the door. "Leave us to it."

Briseis left last, closing the outer door as she withdrew.

Now we were alone. Neoptolemus finished undressing, removing his loincloth and tossing it aside. He had a handsome physique, long and lean, and dusted all over with fine golden hairs. Moreover, the conceited fool knew it, crooking a confident smile as he sauntered over to the bed and sat down beside me to pull at the sheet. "Why are you so shy, Hermione? I've already seen your breasts, remember?"

I let him expose me because he was now my husband, but could not help but shiver as his hand ghosted over my left breast. It was happening, he was touching me, and in a short while he would be atop me, inside me.

I shut my eyes. The sheets rustled and I felt him move even closer, until we were close to share each other's breath; he exuded an odor of drunkenness. As I made that observation, his bracing arm went around my back. I knew he was about to kiss me.

His lips touched mine, gentle at first, giving me space to reciprocate, then more demanding as he slipped his tongue into my mouth.

I willed myself to relax as he stretched out on the bed beside me. I tried hard to remind myself that this was my wedding night, and everything would be all right. Neoptolemus was my husband, he was supposed to be doing this, and I told myself over and over how nice it felt and how gentle he was being.

But his hand sliding down my belly revived old terrors. He was going to touch my thighs, then he was going to pin me to the mattress and mount me, and it would be Aegisthus all over again. I was not melting with desire for him, and with the ladies causing such chaos I had not been able to go into the bathroom to rub oil inside me. It would hurt.

He kept kissing me, while his hand rubbed circles up my inner thigh. I tried to relax, but it was no use, and soon enough he noticed. "It's all right," he murmured into my ear. "I'm not going to hurt you."

I forced myself to smile. "I know."

Then his probing finger sank inside me. The intrusion burned. Now it was coming, he would mount me, he would notice, and...

Withdrawing his finger, he glared down at me. "You have no maidenhead." Mingled fear and shame kept me from responding. "You're not a maiden at all, are you?" Anger blazed in his eyes. "Did you spread your legs for Nestor's son, or did you let some stranger enjoy you during one of those orgies you Spartan women like so much?"

That did it. I might have been ashamed on account of his discovering my maidenhead was gone, but he was not going to insult my honor as a Spartan princess. "How dare you! It was rape. *Rape!*" Furious tears slid down my cheeks. "I never wanted to be taken, never!" Gathering the sheet to my breasts again, I turned onto my side, away from him, and curled into a tight ball.

Neoptolemus cursed under his breath, then bent over me and asked, "Who was it?"

"Leave me alone."

Instead, he stroked my upper arm. A kiss landed on my shoulder. "Who was it? Tell me. I will kill him for you."

"He's dead." Saying Aegisthus's name would have been inviting his shade into the bridal chamber.

That answer satisfied him, and he had other concerns at the moment. As he nibbled my ear, he spooned against my back, where his erection prodded my buttocks. "It's all right. It's still our wedding night, after all." He reached around to squeeze my breast. "I won't hurt you."

I sobbed into his kisses as he rolled me onto my back and resumed caressing my inner thighs; he was going to have me tonight no matter what. When he took me, each thrust stretched and burned me inside, and he never seemed to notice. Even when he finished and withdrew, when he kissed my mouth and rubbed his thumb over my sticky cheeks to try to soothe me, he pretended everything was all right when even a fool could have seen it was not.

Afterward, Neoptolemus dropped into a sated sleep beside me. I stared at the painted spirals whirling across the ceiling, trying to ignore the raw and pulsing void between my thighs. Silent sobs wracked my body. So this was what it was like to be married.

CHAPTER NINETEEN

I TOOK A MOMENT TO STUDY Priam's last surviving son. Helenus's full lips were the only generous feature in a lean face graven with deep furrows. Crow's feet radiated from his dark, almond-shaped eyes. Gray streaked his braided ponytail. He favored Anatolian clothing: a fringed wrap over a long woolen tunic and red leather shoes with upturned points.

"All these men are competent and trustworthy scribes." He handed me a tablet to study in the sunlight spilling through the sitting room window. "I recommend Kephalon. Perhaps you will allow me to arrange an interview?"

Palace administration should have been foremost on my mind, but I found it hard to throw myself into the role of dutiful wife. Instead, my attention kept wandering to the frescoes splashed across the wall, the loom behind Helenus, the flies buzzing in through the window—anything to avoid the task at hand.

For some strange reason I could not fathom, Helenus also seemed distracted. Though it took me long enough to notice, at last I did. "Is something wrong?" I asked.

"Not at all, my lady."

"You seem like you would rather be elsewhere."

Helenus indicated the tablet lying forgotten in my hand. "So do you."

Chastened, I tried harder to focus on the names before me, a task which should not have been so overwhelming to a woman who already knew how to manage a large household. "You choose," I said at last, glancing away.

"My lady," he said quietly, "I know you are not happy with him."

That was an understatement. I hated everything about my husband—his boorish manners, his immaturity, and his inconsiderate lovemaking, but discussing such intimate details with a male servant, even a high-ranking one, was something a queen simply did not do. And Helenus was not just any servant, but a Trojan prince, and brother of the man who had abducted and raped my mother. I forced a smile onto my face. "Marriage is a woman's lot. It's something I have to accept and endure."

"That sounds like something your mother might say." Helenus's chair creaked as he leaned forward. "Hermione, look at me."

He should not have called me by my name. It was too personal, too familiar, and summoned forth emotions a queen ought to keep private. "I really shouldn't complain," I said.

"I am well-acquainted with women who are dissatisfied with him."

"That doesn't reassure me."

"You are not your mother." His mouth crinkled in a wry smile. "She hid behind walls and veils. That does not seem to be your nature."

I turned toward the window. There was not much of a view. "Did you know her well?"

"I knew her well enough to like her," he replied evenly. "I felt sorry for her, seeing how Alaksandu treated her, and how people blamed her for the fighting when she had nothing to do with it. I even asked to marry her, after Alaksandu died."

Startled, I looked back at him. "You loved her?"

"No, no, it was not like that." Helenus laced his fingers together, tightening and loosening them; the question seemed to have struck a nerve with him. "We Anatolians practice the custom of levirate marriage, which means that an unmarried man takes his brother's widow so she is provided for, and his sons with her are his brother's sons. I asked for your mother because the omens said she must be returned to your father.

I meant to restore her to Menelaus." His chest swelled with a deep sigh. "My father saw right through me, and gave your mother to my older brother. I suppose my intentions were too obvious."

Clearing his throat, he assumed his businesslike demeanor. "Let me send Kephalon to you," he said. "I think you will find him competent and pleasant to work with."

But his willingness to interact presented a welcome diversion from my own dour circumstances. I seized upon it, preferring to leave dry household expenditures and talk of scribes and storerooms for later. "Do you have any family left?" I asked.

"A few half-siblings who fled to Assyria or Hatti, but the others..." Helenus's voice trailed away. "All my immediate family is dead except for me."

"You were spared, though." As he went ashen, I regretted uttering those words. "Forgive me for being so thoughtless."

Helenus slowly waved aside my apology. "You would not be the first person to comment on it. Agamemnon would have cut my throat, except for one thing." With an elegant, deliberate finger he tapped his temple. "I am a seer. Tarhunt, the Storm God of Hatti, speaks through me. As such, my person remains sacred, even though I was technically an enemy. So I was allowed to live."

Shame at having wounded him like this outweighed my surprise at his revelation. "I seem to be saying and doing all the wrong things today." I extended my hand to him, but he did not take it.

Instead, Helenus turned his head toward the door. "I will send Kephalon to you tomorrow."

PLEADING SEVERE MENSTRUAL DISCOMFORT, I tried to avoid the summons, but when my husband's young manservant returned he advised me that Neoptolemus was in a foul temper and that it was best not to gainsay him.

"And you told him about my condition?" I asked. The hot leather pad pressed against my womb was just starting to work, but the cramp bark tea had not yet taken effect.

Keos looked uncomfortable, as most men did when having to deal with female complaints. Myrmidons were no exception. "Yes, my lady." A flush crept across his cheeks.

In the end, my husband left me no choice but to attend him. Surely he could not be stupid enough to expect conjugal relations tonight. But no, Keos had said he was angry.

I loathed visiting Neoptolemus's bedchamber; he had made it a shrine to his deceased father. Neoptolemus's inlaid bed sat underneath a fresco depicting Achilles dragging Hector's bleeding corpse behind his chariot, while his father's childhood shield and spear hung on the wall opposite the door. The wedding kylix sat beside a yellowing boar tusk helmet displayed on a wooden stand. Ghosts haunted that room. I had learned more in the last six weeks about Achilles than Neoptolemus, and found myself having to bite back the urge to complain about the wrongness of it all.

I found my husband drinking strong wine, which did nothing to improve his temper. He was in an outright snit, red-faced and slurring his words. "The Spartan ambassador tells me your cousin just married your brother." Neoptolemus screwed his mouth into a tight line. "And do you know what else Myron told me? He told me your father gave away your dower lands, your entire inheritance! Agamemnon's empty-headed daughter is going to be the next queen of Sparta, and Aethiolas..." He slammed his fist down on the inlaid table, rattling his cup and the pitcher. "Damn Menelaus! First he insults me by withholding your hand, and now this."

So the blow had fallen at last. Not wanting to further rouse his anger, I said nothing.

He swept the table clear. The ceramic cup shattered as it hit the wall, and the pitcher landed on its side. Rich dark wine spattered across the trajectory, and started pooling on the painted stucco. "Did you know about this?"

But he did not give me a chance to answer. Neoptolemus surged from his chair and seized me around the waist. "You bitch! I am your lord and master. You and everything you own belongs to me. *Me!*"

"Let me go!" I twisted my head away from my husband's savage kisses, but he did not release me or acknowledge my revulsion. He squeezed my sensitive breast, making me wince.

Neoptolemus hauled me toward the bed, just as he had dragged me away from Aphrodite's altar, and tore open my dress; the thin linen ripped as easily as onionskin between his strong hands. *Gods, no. Please, no, not this.* "Stop! I'm bleeding." I continued to struggle. "Stop!"

Another rough kiss stifled my scream before he shoved me back onto the bed. "You're hurting me!" I wrenched myself free enough to scrabble away from him, but there was nowhere to go; he had me trapped. Clutching my torn gown closed, I curled into a little ball against the wall. "Don't touch me!"

Neoptolemus grabbed my wrist and jerked me forward. Then, switching hands, he slapped me across the face—once, twice—striking both cheeks and each time he struck me, his profanity turned the physical blow into something even more reprehensible.

"Your lands are mine!" Merciless fingers twisted my right nipple. I screamed. "Just like your tits and cunt. Mine!"

When he shoved me away from him, I slumped bawling and hiccupping to the mattress, with one hand clasped over my throbbing breast. Even then there was no reprieve. Clutching my hair in his viselike grip, he dragged me forward, over the mattress edge. "Since you're not going to spread your legs like a dutiful wife, then get off my bed."

I seized the opportunity to scramble away from him to the washbasin. My face and breasts felt swollen, and I was shaking so violently I had to grab onto the sideboard just to stay upright long enough to splash water onto my burning cheeks. To get away from him was my only thought. Get far, far away before he changed his mind and raped me, menstrual blood and all. I held the ragged ends from my dress together. Let the sentries and servants stare at me, let them whisper about how my husband had treated me, as long as...

"Where do you think you're going?"

It took all my nerve to turn and look at him. Neoptolemus jabbed a finger at the chair he had vacated. "Go sit down." He waited for me to obey before snapping at me again. "And stop acting like I forced you. I'll send you a new dress."

As though that would take away his actions. Anger rushed through me. "You bastard!" I shrieked. "I had nothing to do with my father's decision."

Neoptolemus leapt from the bed, seized the washcloth, and thrust it at me. "I am your husband, and entitled to rule over your lands." When I did not take the dripping cloth, he shoved it into my chest. "Gods above, women get worked up over such nonsense."

I took the washcloth, just to have something to hide behind. "Send my father a letter, if it upsets you so."

"Oh, he'll hear about it." His fingers clamped down on my shoulder, as though trying to convince me through his physical strength that he was Menelaus's equal. "Come back to bed. You can't leave like this, crying and with your dress hanging open. You'll set tongues wagging."

At that moment, I did not care who saw me disheveled and distraught. I loathed the prospect of lingering with him and pretending intimacy where none existed. "No, I hate that fresco over your bed." There, I had said it. "Achilles has taken over this room. I might as well be married to him."

A sharply indrawn breath indicated his displeasure. His face clenched, and he knotted his large hands into fists. But he did not strike. His expression betrayed a struggle against the urge to hit me. For a moment, I feared he would, but he somehow managed to master his anger. "You foolish woman. You have no idea what you're saying. Now shut your mouth and come with me." So saying, he took my arm and marched me back to the bed.

I climbed onto the bed and curled up facing the wall, but Neoptolemus failed to take the hint. It was as though the last hour had not happened. He nuzzled against my back, wrapping his arm around my waist. "Yes, Achilles dwells in this room, in me. How could he not?"

Neoptolemus exhaled a moist sigh against my temple. "You don't understand. It's not enough to be a hero's son. I have to *be* Achilles, and be better than him, too. You never feel that way about your mother? I would think you'd have to compete with her."

"Never. I am my own woman." I did not want to look at him. Even his apologetic tone nauseated me. "You can't be Achilles. He was god-touched, born for war, and there are no more wars to fight."

"That's not true. Heroes forge their own glory. That's why they're heroes," he said.

Heroes were also their own men, and he did not have that in him. "You shouldn't have lost your temper with me," I said. "I have no control over what happens to my dower lands."

"Of course not." But I did not believe in his apology, because I knew he did not see that he had done anything wrong. Although my dread had receded with the lowering of his voice, my revulsion remained.

"I'm not feeling well tonight," I murmured. "Keos must have told you about my impurity. I should sleep in my own bed until it passes."

Mentioning my moon blood sufficed this time. Neoptolemus released me, grunting his permission; now that his anger was spent, the wine was making him sleepy. "When you feel better, write to your father. Sweet-talk him as women do when they want something, and get him to change his mind." He swallowed a yawn. "Tell him I would make a good king."

I crawled from the bed, while searching the room for something I could use to sash my torn gown. Neoptolemus started to snore. I was not going to try to wheedle concessions from my father, or do anything else on my boorish husband's behalf. Let him be a man and make his complaints through the Spartan ambassador.

MY FRAGILE COMPOSURE DISSOLVED the moment I entered my darkened apartment and crept on silent feet into the bathroom. There, I fell to my knees on the stucco floor and sobbed soundlessly into my hands. I was not his slave woman to be knocked about and humiliated, but his queen, a daughter of the royal houses of Sparta and Mycenae. How could he dare treat me thus, and then expect me to speak favorably of him to my father?

Tremors shook my body. Had I not been bleeding, he would have forced me. I knew he would next time, for he was coarse and clueless, and of course there would be a next time. I bit down hard on my knuckles to suppress my sobs, not wanting my women to hear me, to come running and see me in such a state.

As the thought formed in my mind, a presence filled the doorway. Alarmed, I clutched my arms over my breasts.

Briseis wore a knowing look on her face. "I was waiting up for you." On bare feet, she moved closer. "I will order you a hot bath. I know you need one."

I dragged the back of my hand across one sticky cheek, then the other. "It's not necessary. He didn't..."

"But you still feel unclean," she said. "I can see it." She placed her lamp on the floor and let herself down onto the low stone ledge beside the privy. "Marriage can be a very unpleasant business. I used to spend many nights lying where you are now, hating my husband and my lot in life."

I did not want to commiserate with her, not yet, when I could not even face the goddesses upon my altar. "Calling for hot water at this hour will be too much trouble."

"You will not be able to sleep all wound in knots like this," she said. "As for making trouble, you are the queen. You have but to give the command and it will be done."

By now, my handmaidens had awakened and congregated in the doorway with their lamps. Briseis hustled them back to bed. "I will attend your mistress tonight."

It was less trouble than I had thought to have steaming water brought up from the kitchens, and soon the slave girls were pouring their jugs into the terracotta tubs. Briseis made me surrender the torn shift and step into the bath where she washed my hair and massaged scented oil into my skin. "You should not be doing this," I said. "You are not a maidservant."

"I do these things because I choose to," she answered. Her hands worked hard and deep, loosening knotted muscles. "There are letters for you. Keos delivered them after you left."

Afterward, she dressed me in a clean shift. Chamomile tea awaited me in the sitting room. Briseis had left the letters on my chair. I had no desire to read them. Apathy surged through me.

I knew it was the wrong thing to do. Moping would accomplish nothing but to send me deeper into a morass of frustration and dread. Neoptolemus would violate me again in his anger and drunkenness, exercising a husband's right over his wife. I either had to find some way to dissuade him, or to accept my lot and lie submissively under him.

I glanced down on the first letter with its familiar seal. Menelaus. I had no wish to suffer through his feeble solicitudes and excuses, and flipped the sealed letter against the wall. The second letter bore my mother's seal. I should have tossed that one against the wall, too, but even from a distance my mother somehow commanded my attention. I broke the scarlet wax with my fingernail.

Helen showered me with recipes, spells, and remedies to help me conceive. "I pray that by the time you receive this letter, you will not need these measures," she said, "but if you are not already with child, do as your mother says and undo all the knots in your bedchamber. Rub mandrake root on your kourotrophoi, avoid sage and mint, as these will expel the seed from your womb, and remember to offer Eleuthia and Artemis the prayers I am sending with this letter."

There was more, much more, but she could not have chosen a worse time to send me her recipes and incantations. Any maternal aspirations I might have had after the wedding night now stained the menstrual linen between my thighs.

I set the letter aside. Maybe a night's rest would let me think more clearly about matters.

Apollo's sacred seal on the next letter gave me a start. So did seeing my cousin's steady and articulate hand.

"My dearest Hermione, I am well enough to sit down and write my own letters, although Didymus cautions me not to overexert my strength. I dispatched messages to Pylades and your father this afternoon. You are the only other person in this world to whom I want to write.

"I heard about your abduction and marriage. I find it impossible to believe that Nestor's son did not value you enough to pursue you. Believe me, I would have gone to the very end of the world to get you back." I raised my hand to my mouth. Cruel fate that Orestes had not been there! "Menelaus assures me that your husband treats you well. Neoptolemus had better love and honor you, because if he mistreats you I will either haunt him as a shade or land a Mycenaean host on his shore and kill him myself."

In the next line, he apologized for his brusqueness. "Forgive me for sounding like such an insolent brute. I am about to stand trial, and am terribly anxious, or I would never snap at you like this. And since this may be the very last time I ever write to you or anyone else, there are things I do not want to leave unsaid."

Briseis noticed my growing distress from her place nearby, the footstool where she sat spinning wool. "Do not tax yourself, whatever it is. It can wait until later."

Except that later would be too late.

I resumed reading to discover that Orestes had changed the subject. "I will have to meet the Erinyes where they dwell, deep under the earth. Not everyone survives that ordeal, because when a guilty man has truly offended the gods, then the Erinyes devour his substance and cast his shade down into Tartarus. If that is to be my fate, then let the double curses on our house go with me. I will go consenting. I have already made my funeral arrangements. Pylades will rule as king at Mycenae. It is the least I can do for him after dragging him down with me.

"I am prepared for this, and will accept whatever the outcome may be. And you will be with me, just as you have always been with me, watching over me every moment since we last saw each other. I am yours, until the waters of Lethe steal away my memories of you. Orestes."

Orestes did not have to tell me what he was about to face, for any woman who had ever entered a sacred cave understood. Now the man who slew his mother must return to the womb to confront the primordial female powers he had so offended, and those remorseless goddesses would either absolve or devour him. I held out little hope that it would be the former. Men knew better than to intrude in those places. Few ever emerged whole.

"Briseis, I need writing materials."

She stopped the spindle in her hands. "You need to rest."

I vehemently shook my head. "No, I need writing materials. Orestes cannot wait."

Briseis brought me the papyrus and cuttlefish ink the Spartan ambassador had brought as gifts. Waiting for her to gather the materials gave me space to think. This letter would go straight to Delphi. Let others say what they would. Orestes was my kinsman. I should not need permission to send him a farewell message.

"Dearest Orestes," I wrote, "let swift Hermes deliver this in time for you to read it. I am not unhappy here in Epirus." I hesitated over writing such a boldfaced lie, but then swallowed my misgivings; it was for his own good. "Right now, my only tears are for you. I am very glad you are ready to face your trial. It will mean an end to your torment, and I have no doubt that you will meet the Erinyes with all the courage and conviction you have shown these many long years.

"Other men would have fled abroad or denied their crime, but not you, because there is neither falsehood nor cowardice in you." Each word cost me heartache, and my hand started shaking. The Erinyes would devour Orestes. I had to set down the stylus and pull a shuddering breath.

"Hermione," Briseis began.

"Not yet." I had to finish, no matter what. Taking a deep breath, I reached for more ink. "I wish with all my heart I could be with you, and hold your hand and go with you into the darkness. Should I hear that the Erinyes refused to absolve you, I will weep bitter tears because my heart is breaking." And those were not simply words. My heart truly *was* breaking. "I am always your loving cousin, Hermione."

CHAPTER TWENTY

"THIS IS FOR YOU, MY LADY." Neoptolemus's herald held out a black woolen cloth upon which a splendid silver necklace and earrings nestled. "From the king."

Another meaningless present. I despised my husband's gifts, even these jewels with their stunning silver and amber pendants, and loathed them even more when the herald added his rehearsed little speech, "These jewels are for the beautiful Queen Hermione, Helen's daughter, to help her forget unpleasant things."

So Neoptolemus thought he could barter for my affection, but was not even man enough to make his own apologies. "Tell the king..." I did not know quite what message to send except that he could choke on his baubles. "Tell him the jewels are very lovely." At least that was true.

Once the herald departed, I ignored my handmaidens' inquisitive glances, took the jewels into my bedchamber, and shoved them deep, down into my clothes chest where I could forget about them. Then I shut the lid and went back to my spinning.

An hour later, Andromache barged into my sitting room, her jangling amulets and trinkets mirroring her agitation. "Why are you lying to him?" she demanded.

I looked up from my spinning, stunned by the naked accusation. "Lying to who about what?"

"You have told the king that I bewitched you so you cannot have sons."

I could not believe my ears. Her obsession with curses, amulets, and spells was all-consuming, as was her belief in my rancor. "I never said any such thing to him, Ashakumila," I replied. "Monime, Thebe, leave us."

Andromache claimed one of the chairs my handmaidens had vacated, Her eyes kept darting around the room, seeking out daggers, curse tablets—whatever horror she believed awaited her in my apartment. "Now tell me what this is all about," I urged. "Start from the beginning."

She straightened like a rearing cobra, hissing out her explanation. "This morning, he came in a rage and demanded to know whether I had bewitched you to keep you from conceiving. I told him no, but he would not believe me."

Had Neoptolemus not complained about my menses and my failure to conceive right away, her story would have rung false. Andromache was an eccentric, inscrutable and hostile, and there was no guarantee that she was not trying to foment further discord between me and my husband through her visit. "So you think I accused you from spite?" I asked.

"I have no idea what you are talking about," she answered contemptuously.

Her haughtiness and ongoing disdain strained my nerves. "And you are spouting nonsense," I retorted. "I swore a sacred oath to leave you alone, and have held to it."

Andromache regarded me with slitted eyes. Her right hand went to the winged goddess hanging between her breasts. On the handful of occasions when we met, I had not given her trinkets a second glance. "Why do you wear so many amulets?" I asked. "Is one not enough?"

Her nostrils flared. "You should hold your tongue. A woman in a strange land such as this is easy prey without her patron goddesses."

"I, too, have a patron goddess," I said. "Her name is Dia."

Andromache held out her amulet on its silver chain; the goddess had a woman's body but the spread wings and clawed feet of a bird. "Kamrusepa heals sickness and guards against the Evil Eye. I keep her with me. I hang her images in the nursery to watch over my sons."

"You have handsome children," I said. Yet her eyes narrowed again, as though she believed I meant her sons harm. Perhaps the best thing to do, since she was making no effort to leave, was to change the subject again and find a topic that we could both discuss. "I've noticed that Hantili is a man of great talent."

She tilted her chin proudly. "His prophecies brought us here. Pyrrhus knows how to lead men into battle, but nothing else. Hantili knows how to *rule*." A peculiar softness suffused her face to match the admiration in her voice. Once the bitterness slid away, she was a strikingly lovely woman.

"Why do you call the king Pyrrhus?" I asked.

"Because that was the name his mother gave him." Andromache uttered a savage laugh. "He despises it!"

I could not help the smile curving my mouth. "I see."

But she interpreted it wrongly, as she did everything else. "Go, run to him like a scheming first wife and tell him how I mock him." Resurgent contempt obliterated all hint of her natural beauty, and she goaded me with yet more scornful laughter. "It is no secret. I spit on him and on his father's ghost!"

What would it take to make her understand that I was not her enemy, that I hated Neoptolemus, too? "Ashakumila," I said softly. "I'm not going to tell him anything."

Andromache stroked the goddess at her breast. "We will see."

KEPHALON WAS A PLUMP, pretentious old man who never stopped talking as he led me through the palace's stifling storerooms. "As you can see, my queen, we have ample room set aside for the harvest." Upstairs, he showed me the empty threshing floors and even escorted me out to the yard where slave children were patting wet clay into tablets for the tallies.

"Will I be able to go out and bless the harvest?" I had not enjoyed the slightest breath of freedom since my arrival, even though there were certain duties a queen must leave the citadel to fulfill; the blessing of the sheaves was the most significant of these.

Kephalon demurred, revealing more through his hesitancy than his words did. "That I do not know, my lady." Yes he did. Neoptolemus's distrust, or hypervigilance—whatever he chose to call it—forced me to draw up lists for necessities requiring his approval, and to summon merchants and priestesses to the palace rather than venture down into the agora as I ought.

It was infuriating. I was the queen, not a slave woman or spear-bride like Andromache.

"Then ask him," I said hotly. "I must perform my duties if the kingdom is to prosper."

The scribe took his leave with a halfhearted promise that told me not to expect results. I would have to approach Neoptolemus myself. Another woman might have relished the challenge. She might have lingered over her dressing table plotting how to seduce him and wheedle concessions from him, but it was not in my nature to meddle with a man, especially when he revolted me so.

I returned upstairs to my apartment to bathe my perspiring face with a cool cloth and seek solace among the deities. Even after six weeks of marriage, Neoptolemus refused to let me visit the cult house as a queen and high priestess. Still, he failed to grasp that Eleuthia controlled my fertility. My quickening would not happen according to his will, but hers.

Perverse satisfaction coursed through me, knowing there would be no children and it would be his sin, yet my glee lasted only as long as it took me to realize the goddesses would punish his impiety through me. I wanted babies, not for his or the kingdom's sake, but to quench my own longing. I was twenty-seven years old, half a lifetime older than when most women started their childbearing, and I craved some precious seed to nurture and love.

Queen I might be, but that was merely a title. I was not a queen in any meaningful way. Neoptolemus trotted me out for feasts, decked like a trophy in my jewels and rich garments. He paid me regular conjugal visits. Sometimes he deigned to talk to me. That was all he ever did.

I could not continue to live like this, cloistered and sullen, and slowly morphing into my mother.

"Great goddesses, let my husband see reason." I clasped my hands over my breasts. "Persuade him to let me honor you as a true queen."

Silence. Sometimes I wondered whether my gods were still back in Sparta, wondering where their votaries had gone, and angry and confused over my sudden disappearance.

Neoptolemus later interrupted my evening devotions, creeping behind me to squeeze my right breast and drop a lascivious comment into my ear along with a hot tongue. "You know your prayers will do no good without my sword inside you, don't you?"

Another, more pious man might have prayed with me. "Can it not wait until I finish?" I asked irritably.

His pinching fingers found my nipple and rubbed it through my thin linen dress. Disgust filled me at the prospect of his rough lovemaking. "But I won't be seeing you again for the next fortnight," he murmured huskily. "I'm taking the men out."

Was he leaving? Thank the gods. "Out where?"

"Where do you think? It's been a while since the Myrmidons and I have had a good time."

"So you're taking them on a raid?"

Masculine laughter accompanied his kisses. "Harvest is an excellent time to do it."

Harvest. "Are you going to let me go out and bless the sheaves?" I asked. "It's important." His hand kept wandering, squeezing and pinching. "Would you stop fondling me for just a moment and listen?" Exasperated, I turned in his embrace to confront him. "I am a queen. I shouldn't have to plead to be able to perform my goddess-given duties."

His lustiness subsided while he demurred. "I don't want my queen participating in wild revels."

"Harvest is the time for reaping, not sowing, and you know that." Or did he? Skyros, his childhood home, was said to be a backward place. "You never let me out. How am I supposed to conceive a child or act as a proper queen, when you keep me prisoner like this?"

"I won't have some randy Molossian chieftain abducting you while I'm gone." With one finger, Neoptolemus he traced the line of my jaw.

"They look at you, you know, and they've heard the stories about your mother. I can't risk the loss of my prestige."

Helen. It always came back to my mother. "So you're going to keep me imprisoned here until I'm old and ugly?" And what nonsense was that about his prestige? Was that all I meant to him?

He silenced my protests with his mouth before hustling me into the bedchamber; it was no answer at all. Wet linen had been tacked across the windows, but there was no breeze to disseminate the coolness through the room. Perspiration filmed our naked bodies, and we stuck together the moment he pressed himself against me. I spread my legs for him, and let him heave and thrust into me while sending my thoughts elsewhere. It was easier that way.

Afterward, I wanted a cool bath and solitude, while he preferred to stretch out beside me and linger. "You never answered my question," I said into the growing darkness. "Do you plan to keep me a prisoner here forever?"

Neoptolemus insulted me with a hearty yawn. "I've already let you and your women clean out the storerooms to receive the harvest. You have a personal scribe, and Helenus keeps you informed of everything that goes on. You have an inner court to exercise in, and I let you sup with me in the megaron. You have everything you could possibly need."

How ignorant he was! "Do you know nothing?" I retorted. "The queen must serve as a high priestess the way a king must serve as a captain when he leads his men into battle." I drew on the one analogy he was likely to understand. "Acting as high priestess means going outside, placing my hands upon the warm earth, gathering the sheaves, and communing with the goddesses. They do not see me here, locked up like this. For all they know, I am still in Sparta. How will they know where to find me to plant a child inside me?"

A long, uneasy silence passed between us, till he spoke. "Hmm, a baby might change your father's mind about restoring your inheritance." I heard the air swell in his lungs, then a deep sigh. To my utter surprise, he then relented. "Very well, Hermione. Go out and touch the earth. Receive the sheaves. Nothing else, though, and you must return to the citadel before dark."

At least it was something. "Yes, that will do."

"I will be leaving half the Myrmidons behind to guard you and the children." I felt his damp thigh pressed close to mine, and smelled his sweat. Pyrrhus. I recalled the hated childhood name Andromache had divulged to me, tasting it as the delicious secret it was.

"Why do you never mention your spear-bride when you talk about your sons?" I asked.

"What's that? My spear-bride? Andromache? And why do you ask?" Amusement undercut his query. "Are you jealous?"

He would have loved that, too. I was not going to give him the satisfaction. "I was simply curious."

"Because I hate her. The Molossians can take her, the spiteful bitch, with my thanks." Neoptolemus snorted his contempt. "I use her whenever she needs to be reminded who her lord and master is, but she means nothing to me. I should have cut her throat at Father's tomb and taken the princess he ordered me to sacrifice instead."

I shifted a little so our limbs were not touching. Sweat dampened my breasts and the skin under my arms. I would have to have my handmaidens change the linens before I retired. If the gods were benevolent, Neoptolemus would not stay all night. "I thought Achilles was already dead when you got to Troy."

"He was," Neoptolemus answered glumly, "but just before the lots were to be cast for Polyxena, he visited me in a dream to demand her blood be spilled on his tomb. And he came again the next night, and the night after that, always with the same demand." A growl rose from deep in his throat. "I had to make the sacrifice myself. What a waste. I apologized to the girl at the altar and cut her throat quickly, so she wouldn't suffer."

Iphigenia entered my thoughts. I banished her ghost. "That was kind," I said. Neoptolemus could be courteous when he wished it, only that it was not often enough.

CHAPTER TWENTY-ONE

THREE DAYS LATER, I accompanied my husband into the cool dawn to set his boar tusk helmet with its flowing blue crest upon his head, and kiss him farewell before the entire court.

Neoptolemus lingered over the kiss. "Tell me that you will miss me."

The lie sprang easily to my lips, along with a disingenuous smile. "Of course."

After his chariot rolled out the gate and he left Ephyri, I waited two more days before deciding to test my freedom. That was easier said than accomplished. A fierce Myrmidon bodyguard named Phylakes dogged me like a foul odor, and curtailed any expeditions to the agora or the sanctuaries below the citadel mount. "You will wait for the harvest, lady," he grumbled.

"Are the Epirote sanctuaries dangerous places, then?" I challenged.

"I have my orders." Phylakes loomed inches above me, all corded muscles and bullish neck. A diagonal scar beginning above his right eyebrow slashed across his nose to his left cheek. "Not until the harvest."

I flashed him a beguiling, poisonous smile that Clytaemnestra would have applauded. "Suppose the king doesn't come home for a while?"

Phylakes threw me a contemptuous look. "Return to your chamber."

Ignoring his command, I ventured downstairs to visit Helenus in his office. "Are the Myrmidons always so thickheaded?" I asked.

"I take it you object to your bodyguard?" Helenus acknowledged my minder with a curt nod. Grunting, Phylakes folded his arms across his chest and assumed his station at the door. "Single-mindedness can be an asset sometimes."

"He's not going into battle." I accepted a chair nearest the window. Helenus maintained his office above the outer court, where he could watch petitioners and supply wagons going in and out. I found it an intriguing chamber, in which Anatolian textiles, Cretan pottery, and furnishings crafted by local carpenters attested to his eclectic tastes. "Neoptolemus seems to think some lascivious Molossian chieftain will abduct me the moment I step outside the citadel."

Helenus broke the seal on a wine jar to offer me a drink. "And you believe his concerns are foolish?" He mixed the rich dark liquid with cool water before pouring it into a ceramic cup and handing it across to me. "Do you think he keeps you shut up for spite?"

Either he knew how to read me, or someone had told him about my grievance. Briseis, most likely. "I have no idea what to think." I sipped at the wine. "You know him far better than I."

"Yes," he admitted, "and his concerns are legitimate ones. Not all the Molossian tribes owe him their allegiance. Even those chieftains beholden to him stare at you. You are a very beautiful woman." Helenus marked my ponderous sigh. "Think twice before you defy him by venturing outside the citadel. Neoptolemus knows this region and its dangers far better than you do. If he cannot trust you, he will tighten his grasp even more. Be wise and patient. Obey him, even though it means swallowing your pride. One day, you will prevail."

Sensible as it was, nonetheless it was not the answer I wanted to hear. "I might have to wait decades, and be old and used up by the time he grants me any freedom."

"I doubt that," Helenus said mildly.

I drank a second, longer draught. It was an excellent vintage, the wine. "How is it that you have his ear? Without you, the kingdom couldn't run." Neoptolemus might lead the Myrmidons and impose his brute strength on the native tribes, but kingship was as much about effective administration as courage in battle. Helenus regulated tithes and taxes, maintained the peace, and let my husband take all the credit.

At that, his mouth twitched into an ironic smile, but when he answered his tone was somber. "How do you know he does not still call me a Trojan dog sometimes?"

HARVEST'S FIRST DAY ARRIVED with clear blue skies and Phylakes blocking the door. "You're not to go out, lady. Molossian raiders have been seen in the area."

"Then you should be out there fighting them," I said mock-sweetly, "and not oppressing a harmless woman and her maidservants."

He glowered at me. "I have my orders."

Plans frustrated, I spent the morning attending to the deities on my altar and praying to Apollo to watch over Orestes. It had been almost a month since my cousin's last letter. In the summer months, twenty-four days was certainly sufficient time for a message to reach Delphi and a reply to have come back.

Something must have gone wrong. Orestes must be dead, and no one wanted to tell me. "Great Apollo," I whispered, "Orestes acted only as the laws and his dying father ordered. Persuade the Erinyes to let him live."

I spent another half-hour praying and burning myrrh. As an afterthought, I made an offering to Poseidon to safeguard my husband, wherever he and the Myrmidons had gone. Ithaca, most likely. Odysseus's ongoing absence had left his kingdom without a strong leader to protect the coastal towns against pirates.

Briseis had no such restrictions placed upon her movements, and could come and go from the citadel as she pleased. Earlier, I had sent her to apologize to the priestesses on my behalf. In the afternoon, she brought back unexpected news. "There was a skirmish just north of here this morning. Corythus has them on the run." She named a Molossian chieftain I had often seen at the king's table.

I dabbed a cool cloth against my neck. "Then there truly was a threat?"

She accepted wine from my maids. "There is always a threat at harvest time. The wild Molossians come down from the mountains to seize the new-mown grain and the women harvesters, and rustle cattle. Lord Amyntor has doubled the guard on the fields, and is having the sheaves brought inside the walls tonight." Briseis wiped her mouth with the back of her hand. A touch of sunburn reddened her face. "You won't have to go out to the fields, after all. The women are being allowed to bring the sheaves to you tonight."

That left me sufficient time to rest and bathe, eat a light supper, and dress. Monime mixed the white clay and eggs for the moon-mask and smoothed it across my face, letting it dry before she painted on the sacred dots representing the sun and the phases of the moon, and daubed scarlet ocher mixed with fat onto my lips. Briseis laced me into the leather girdle that cinched my waist in the fashion of the ancient Cretan priestesses. My bare breasts, too, were painted white and my nipples enhanced with ocher. Thebe dressed my hair in oiled snake-like ringlets.

Briseis had ordered the servants to erect a fringed awning above the outer court where I would stand as goddess-on-earth and receive the women and their gifts. People had begun to gather; guards at the gate inspected them to make certain they were not Molossian raiders in disguise. I saw Myrmidons everywhere. Servants went around lighting torches as the sun sank.

Flutes and singing voices carried the women's procession from the lower town to the citadel mount; I had heard that the women, too, were subject to inspection, and watched carefully. Did the Myrmidons think the great, hairy Molossian warriors could successfully disguise themselves as women and hide among the ranks? Even their women were rough and unlovely.

A triton call pierced the twilight as the sentries opened the gates to admit the revelers. Head held high and palms raised in the ancient ritual manner, I patiently awaited them under the canopy. Clytaemnestra had long ago taught me the tricks priestesses employed in order to comfortably maintain the goddess's rigid posture through the many long hours a ritual might last. I could shift my weight on the balls of my feet to circulate the blood, flex my back and shoulders ever so subtly, all without appearing to move.

The sacred sheaves were infant bundles plaited from wheat ears and colored ribbons, dolls for me to rock and nurse at my breast. I loved this ritual more than any other because it was filled with such life-affirming joy. It linked me with the women chanting and clapping their hands below. I accepted the sheaves the local priestesses placed in my arms, and kissed and nursed each one before handing it back. "Mother Gaia!" I cried at the end, calling on the goddess by the name she used in the north. "Bless the children of the earth." I cupped my naked breasts with both hands and squeezed. "Bless the mothers and the fruit of their wombs."

Half a hundred women ululated in exultation. Linking arms, they started to undulate in the intricate spirals of the Serpent Dance. Those ancient rhythms called to me. I had been restricted for months, amputated from the sacred life of the land, and wanted so very much to descend into the women's circle.

Phylakes thrust out a restraining arm as I started to descend. "You will stay where it's safe, lady."

Not now! "Stand aside. I am the goddess-on-earth."

Phylakes remained immovable. "You will obey."

His insistence on obeying his orders to the absolute letter reduced me to a forlorn spectator. I remained under the awning, footsore, my joy sapped along with my energy.

At long last, the gathering dispersed and my duties were done. After sponging away the moon-mask and removing my priestess garb, I took my handmaidens onto the palace roof to watch the blazing bonfires scattered like stars across the dark landscape. Somewhere in the night, in a black oak grove, the priestesses were sacrificing a straw man to send the year-king to sleep. Or perhaps they still shed human blood here, some unfortunate slave chosen by lot, drugged, and bound to the altar.

"It's superstitious garbage," Phylakes muttered. For a guard, he certainly had no qualms about voicing his opinion.

I turned to him. "Do you not believe?"

"Myrmidons have nothing to do with sacred dolls and dancing

women." Lantern light cast threatening shadows across his scarred face. "We thrive on the blood and the fear of our enemies."

His hubris astounded me. Even kings knew better than to spite the Great Mother Goddess.

Beginning at dawn, Kephalon sent me tallies as carts bearing wheat, barley, and lentils came into the citadel. Later, he followed me to the rear court where slaves winnowed the grain in flat baskets. Dusty chaff drifted away to settle on the hillside below. At least I had the tallies to attend to, and the threshing, and the making of the sacred goddess cakes.

In the Hellene lands, it was the queen who ground the first flour to shape and sanctify the cakes. Even here in backwater Epirus, the women kept the ancient rites, because on the third day the court ladies exchanged their dresses and jewels for linen smocks to join me on the threshing floor. A slave girl piped a lively melody as we worked. And work we did, flailing the stalks, winnowing outside where the dust would not bother us so much, and working the millstones to grind the flour till our arms and backs ached.

Andromache joined us after the threshing and milling, shooing aside curious spit boys and assistant cooks to commandeer us a large kitchen table where we could sift the new-ground flour, mix it with salt and water, and shape the dough.

"We made goddess cakes in Wilusa, too." Her fist pounded salty dough against the sturdy oak. Yet she had not come earlier, and had not been present for the blessings of the sheaves. She avoided the Epirote women, who whispered warnings in my ear to beware her foreign curses. Briseis told me that Andromache was not uttering curses at all, but simply saying the prayers in her native tongue.

Andromache brought out her sons to watch over them, although some of the ladies balked at letting male children near the sacred rites, and instructed them to play with their toys in the kitchen yard and not disturb the women.

Helenus came while the first cakes were baking. He observed the customs, and did not venture into the kitchen where the goddess was being honored, but remained in the yard with the boys. Waving aside the nurse, he crouched down on his haunches to amuse baby Pergamos with a wooden horse before drawing Molossus and Pielus close to show them how to make signs in the dirt. In the heat of the afternoon, he had exchanged his fringed robe for a short-sleeved tunic, baring arms slashed with livid scar tissue. I nudged Briseis and asked, whispering, "Did he get those in battle?"

Briseis drew in a sharp breath. "Odysseus tortured him. Ask no more about them."

Helenus did not seem self-conscious about his scars, but wore them as easily as the leather belt around his waist. A broad smile creased his mouth as Pergamos banged the horse against his shin. "He likes the boys," I observed.

Andromache overheard me. "Of course he does!" Vivid scarlet flushed her cheeks under the smears of flour dust. "A good man looks after his brother's widow." But I had said nothing about her, only her sons. "Who else is going to teach the boys how to read and write?"

I noticed how she was setting aside dough to shape into ordinary round cakes, for only women were allowed to eat the goddess cakes. When they were ready, she brushed honey onto them, placed them on a cloth, and carried them into the yard along with a jug of spring water. Helenus gazed up at her, with her mussed hair and flour-stained hands and apron, and took the cakes as though accepting a gift from a goddess.

I observed how Andromache fussed over each of her sons before returning to the kitchen. Helenus watched her go with a thoughtful, longing look which lasted as long as it took him to burn his fingers on a cake. Molossus and Pielus hung at his knees, eager for their treat. Still blowing on his fingers, he urged patience while the cakes cooled.

Andromache resumed her station across from me. "I think he likes you," I commented.

But she did not take the compliment in the intended spirit, and in alarm glanced around at the other women while urging me to be still. "Do not say such things!" she hissed.

I folded over the dough and pounded it. Helenus seemed to be doing as much longing for as looking after. Sitting there with the boys, blowing on his burnt fingers, and casting fond but surreptitious glances toward the kitchen revealed an aspect to him that I had never seen before.

It should not have surprised me. According to their Anatolian custom, Helenus ought to have married Andromache a long time ago. The language of their bodies told me much about their feelings in this respect, however circumspect they were otherwise. Did Neoptolemus know about the custom of levirate marriage, or did he even care? No matter. He was not going to hear about it from me.

A few sweet hours dozing in the predawn coolness ended with a familiar dull ache in my womb. A trip to the privy confirmed the worst; those scarlet stains dashed my maternal hopes once more. I blew out the lamp, hunkered down on the cool stucco floor, and stared forlornly at the floor.

How I wanted a child! A baby son or daughter to rock in my arms like the sacred sheaf. Someone to love, someone who would look after me when I grew old, who would bury me and remember to make the offerings after I was gone. Just one child, so I would not be alone, and so people would not shake their heads and mutter that the goddesses were punishing me.

Awakened by my small movements, my handmaidens comforted me, and sent to the kitchen for cramp bark tea and a hot leather pad. As dawn broke, they laid out fresh figs and warm bread, and dressed me. This was no day to huddle in bed. I was still the queen, the high priestess, and Ephyri's barren women were relying upon me to receive them this morning.

Polycaste had taught me how to empty myself during rituals, to thrust away all that was Hermione, and become a vessel for Mother Dia. It was hard, though, so hard when the goddess of fertility was mocking me. Menstrual blood was unclean, it was a sloughing of impurities, a sign of barrenness. It had not mattered before my marriage, because a maiden priestess had nothing to do with childbearing, even if she was not a virgin in truth. Yet all that was changed now. I should not have been handing out the goddess cakes or laying my hands upon hopeful or pregnant mothers in my state, as it would pass to them and curdle their milk.

Helenus appeared late in the morning, as the last female supplicants exited the megaron. "You seem unwell."

Menstrual cramps gnawed my belly. "It's the heat."

Despite acknowledging my answer with a polite nod, a knowing glint in his eyes told me that he saw past the lie. "I see you sent your maid for cramp bark tea."

Half a morning spent holding in my emotions in the close heat of the megaron had left me in a peevish mood. "I started bleeding this morning," I said tartly. "I'm not with child. Are you satisfied?"

"It troubles you too much," Helenus answered. "I have seen you holding in your arms a child, a son with your red hair."

I folded my arms over my naked breasts. Discussing women's intimate matters with this reserved, hawkish foreigner unsettled me. "And can you tell me when I should expect this miracle?"

"Do not snap at me," he said sternly. "A seer sees only what the gods show him, not what others what him to see. I thought the knowledge might comfort you."

But it was an answer that was no answer, typical prophetic nonsense. I felt like shoving him. "It does not."

Chapter Twenty-Two

Briseis roused me from a fitful morning doze. "Helenus sends word for you to come down to the megaron." I refused, started to push her away, but she kept tugging me, adding, "He says at once." My handmaidens rustled around her as they started to open the jewel casket and cosmetic box. Briseis shooed them aside. "Bring ribbons for her hair and a comb, and a simple dress. There's no time for anything else."

I stirred reluctantly. Cramps and heavy bleeding made venturing downstairs an unpleasant prospect. "Did Helenus tell you why?"

"An important message has come." Briseis helped me change into a fresh linen gown and comb my hair. Had word come from Neoptolemus, wherever he was? Let it not be from Delphi. Something about the summons felt amiss, a foreboding implicit in its haste and Helenus's unwillingness to specify.

Passing through an empty great court into the megaron reinforced my uneasiness. Neoptolemus's regents should have been hearing petitions, but the stone benches lining the frescoed walls were deserted. Helenus stood below the dais, a grim sentinel with his arms folded in his voluminous Anatolian sleeves. The Molossian chieftain Corythus and my husband's Thesprotian regents, Echelaos and Amyntor, sat nearby.

"Shut the doors," Helenus said.

When the guards pulled the oaken doors closed, it seemed like they were shutting us inside a tomb. As Helenus conducted me to the queen's chair beside the empty throne, my gaze went to the man slumped on a stool beside the hearth. A young Myrmidon, bruised and bloodied, his arm tucked into a sling. "What is this?" I asked.

"Aglaos will tell you."

In faltering fits and starts, the youth spilled forth a horrifying account. Neoptolemus had landed on Phocian shores and led his Myrmidons on a quick march thirty miles inland to Delphi. Not kingless Ithaca at all, as I had suspected, but sacred Delphi.

"M'lady, I thought we were going to pay homage to Apollo, like all the other pilgrims, but when we got there the king went straight for the nearest altar and smashed the god's image." Aglaos trembled as Helenus administered strong wine to keep him going. "Guards and pilgrims fell on us from all directions, shouting for us to stop, but he ordered us to cut them down, to avenge Achilles."

A chill shuddered through me. Sacrilege. Briseis brought me a cup of the same potent wine. I gulped it down. Sacrilege. Neoptolemus had violated a holy sanctuary. No wonder I had started bleeding. Eleuthia had terminated whatever seed I might have been carrying.

Helenus urged the young man on. "Tell the queen the rest."

A wilting Aglaos fought unconsciousness long enough to finish. "There were too many of them, with stones and walking sticks, hoes, and shovels, bludgeoning us all, and we couldn't break free to fight our way to him. We..." Aglaos's eyes rolled back in his head, and he crumpled from the stool to the floor.

Helenus knelt down beside him. "They were not able to recover the king's body," he finished. His gaze moved to Phylakes, who maintained his position beside my chair. "Take Aglaos to the physician."

But the bull-headed man refused to budge. "I stay with the queen."

"You will do as you are told."

Phylakes spat, "I don't take orders from Trojan slaves."

Imminent confrontation roiled in the smothering air. I surged to my feet, shoving back the chair so violently it almost tipped over.

Neoptolemus's sacrilege affected me, too, unless I made reparations to the gods. "Do as you're told!" I thrust a finger at the unconscious young man. "Take him to the physician, and don't you *ever* disobey or insult Lord Helenus again!"

Phylakes folded his arms across his chest with an exasperated look that said he did not have to listen to a petulant, overwrought woman.

Corythus came to my defense. "Queen Hermione gave you an order, you thick-headed Myrmidon dog!" The Molossian's fierce bellow shook the rafters. "Now get out!" He remained standing, smacking his meaty fist into his palm as Phylakes and another guard grudgingly obeyed, lifting Aglaos between them and dragging him from the megaron. "Savages."

"Blasphemers," Amyntor muttered, shaking his head.

Briseis helped me sit down again, where I had little else to do but listen to the lords speak.

Echelaos addressed Helenus. "I know Neoptolemus consulted you for an oracle before he set out. Did you foresee his death?"

"Are you asking whether I knew what he intended to do?" Helenus resumed his old stance, arms tucked into his sleeves, and an inscrutable tightness in his features. "I doubt even he knew exactly what he intended to do until he got there"

"Speak clearly," Corythus rumbled. "No prophetic double-talk."

Helenus regarded him impassively. "I have explained to you before how my gift works. I saw darkness hanging over him whenever he talked about avenging his father, and nothing more. I warned him to tread with care in whatever he meant to do, but you know that he did not always heed the advice of others."

The Molossian shook his head, his breath stirring his thick red moustache as he muttered his displeasure. "Foolishness."

Amyntor turned to me. "My lady, do you wish to retire?"

So they wanted me gone in order to discuss men's business. Amyntor was courteous and well-meaning, though, and right to ask. Queen though I was, I had relatively little to contribute to the conversation. "Apollo must be appeased," I stated. "You must remember that."

Echelaos and Amyntor responded simultaneously, "Of course, my queen." Corythus grunted agreement.

Helenus acknowledged me with a curt nod. "It will be done. Go rest now, my lady. I will come later and bring you news."

Briseis escorted me out via a side door and hustled me upstairs, away from the crowd beginning to gather in the great court. My handmaidens greeted my bloodshot, puffy eyes and sticky cheeks with concern as Briseis gave them the news.

They felt obliged to offer their condolences. "Mistress, we're so—"

"Leave me alone." I cut Monime short with a brusque gesture, removed my own sandals and dress, and lay down in the stifling room. Tension crackled through the hot air like the electric charge before a thunderstorm.

On the surface, it might have been any other drowsy late summer morning. A Molossian mastiff barked in the distance, sandaled feet slapped along the pavement below, an irritated taskmaster shouted orders to lazy servants. Baking bread and the mingled fragrances of thyme and sage from the kitchen garden competed with the smell of sweat and the incense smoking on my altar. Everyday sounds and smells to deceive the senses, though not mine. I could not lie there and pretend nothing had happened. People must already know that the king was dead, might even have heard rumors about the sacrilege. My mind visualized servants and courtiers stopping each other in the cool passageways to ask after the latest news, and then their jaws sagging in horrified disbelief.

Numbness had begun to creep over me. Neoptolemus was dead, his body lay battered and broken in the sanctuary he had defiled, and I did not care; what horror I nursed was not for him. I floated above the concerns of the great lords debating the matter downstairs, the surviving Myrmidons now without a leader, and the common people who wanted nothing to do with such madness. I was an outsider, a captive bride, and as the morning became afternoon a curious thought entered my mind, that this was how my mother must have reacted when Alaksandu died.

I must have dozed, for it was growing late when the servant girls filed through the curtain with the bath water. Briseis had remained in my apartment all afternoon, and as my maids washed my hair and sponged my sweaty limbs, she told me that the word had gone around. "People refuse to believe what they are hearing, and are gathering below the gate and in the agora to wait for more news."

Violence might yet come when the truth was confirmed. I saw the fear reflected in my handmaidens' eyes.

Evening brought the acrid tang of wood smoke and roasting animal flesh. Priests must be conducting sacrifices to appease Apollo, as I had urged. A second thought occurred to me, a thought which had lain dormant all these hours, and which frightened me enough to send me to the altar to pour out a libation and burn incense before Apollo's image.

Orestes. Suppose he had not yet undergone his trial when my late husband barged into the sanctuary. Angry gods did not distinguish the righteous from the blasphemers, a fact which the pilgrims who had killed Neoptolemus knew all too well. Apollo must not withdraw his protection from my kinsman as a result, but must be persuaded to continue to watch over him.

Determination to see it done spurred me to rouse my women from their domestic tasks and force them to join me at the altar. "Pythian Apollo, look kindly upon your supplicants and keep us safe from harm." As I knelt, I raised my right hand, palm facing outward, to my forehead to salute the deity. "Forgive us our transgressions. We revile the crimes of the son of Achilles. We had no knowledge of his intentions."

Helenus found us congregating on the floor around the altar; he waited for me to stand before addressing me. "King Strophius is outraged over the incident," he said. "It falls to the council to try to repair relations with the Phocians, while the priests try to placate the god." He regarded the idol wreathed by our offerings. "I fear it will take a human life to appease his anger."

Orestes. "Has he not already claimed a life?" *Do not think such a thing. Have hope.* So I shoved the thought from my head.

"A consecrated slave will go to the altar." He answered. "You need not attend the sacrifice." But his gaze was stern, and when he spoke again, he advised me, "When you finish your bleeding, you should receive special purification to remove any taint by association."

My skin crawled. Two more days seemed far too long to wait. "Is there anything else I must do?"

"The priestesses will tell you." Helenus's wandering gaze seemed to reproach my poor manners. I realized then I was not being a good hostess. Abashed, I dispatched Monime to fetch cool water and wine, and offered my guest a seat by the window.

When he was comfortable, I sat down across from him. "I blessed the sheaves four days ago. Now the grain will be infested with mice and weevils." Despite myself, I started wringing my hands in my lap. "Young animals and babies will die from my impurity."

"I would have foreseen that," he said."

"And yet you did not foresee the king's death."

Helenus acknowledged the mixing bowl and wine my maid set before him. "You were not listening earlier," he answered reprovingly. "Only he who inscribes the tablets of Fate can read the future whole. I saw a blackness gathering about Neoptolemus when he told me he meant to demand restitution from the gods for his father's death. I urged him not to give offense, but the choice was his." Pausing, he poured the wine and water into the bowl to mix it. "Remember, Aglaos said the Myrmidons did not know what he was going to do. I do not think even he knew until the moment came."

That was true. "Is Aglaos going to be all right?"

"He has taken a fever from his wounds." Helenus made the libation, then poured wine into a cup and drained a long draught. "I do not know yet whether he will mend."

All I knew for certain was that my husband was dead and I was not carrying his child. "What will happen now?"

"If you are referring to the kingdom, then it is to be partitioned," he replied. "I have nothing to do with that. Amyntor has asked me to stay on as an advisor, but I have served long enough." Helenus crooked a wry smile. "Neoptolemus granted me an estate near Buthrotum. I will take Ashakumila and the children, and retire there. She will not want to remain here. As for the Myrmidons, I do not care where they go."

I shared his smile. "Neither do I."

He grunted. "Perhaps you should return to Sparta."

"Does the council wish me to leave?"

Thebe came forward with a tray of cold sweetmeats. Helenus waited for her to withdraw again before answering, "No, but I assumed you would want to go home." He pored over the selection, chose a nut pastry. "No one expects you to decide while you are in mourning."

"No one" meant him, and him alone, it seemed. Amyntor sent a scribe the next morning to help me arrange my passage home. So the council had decided to banish me, to expunge the tainted woman from the kingdom. Actually, Amyntor and the other councilors sent their deepest condolences, and placed porters, ships, and an armed escort at my disposal. And I would have chosen to go home, anyway, so I should not have taken offense. Rather, it was their condescending manners, their preemptory dismissal that set my teeth grating.

I did not fare any better with the priests or priestesses who came to examine and purify me. Far from respecting my status as a queen and high priestess, they treated me as a weak and sinful woman, and took sanctimonious pleasure in making me purge and fast. I came away feeling filthier than ever, and eager to be gone from this backward land.

Although I had not expected to mourn, a peculiar heaviness hampered my efforts to arrange my departure. I moved through my days as though through viscous honey, unable to function beyond the most simple things. As with my wedding and the post-nuptial adjustment period, making decisions overwhelmed me. Briseis did what she could to alleviate the strain by consulting with the scribes and ordering my women. She walked with me in the cool mornings, and told me about her childhood in Anatolia, but even she could not pierce the gray veil swathing my spirits.

I wanted to go home, to surround myself with comfortable and familiar things, and forget this misadventure, and yet I dreaded the homecoming. Chrysothemis would resent my return, and view my presence as a threat. And I did certainly not want to see my father, who had thrown up his hands and surrendered me to my abductor without a struggle. Second-rate warrior, Neoptolemus had called him. A man who no longer had Agamemnon to fight his battles for him. I was ashamed to look at him.

Helenus visited me whenever he could. "Briseis tells me you are unwell."

"Briseis should stop acting as a spy," I said hotly.

"She worries about you." Helenus took in the clutter of boxes and chests with an approving eye. "If it consoles you, Ashakumila is wading through the same mess. She is very happy to be leaving."

While my horizons seemed to have dimmed and shrunk in, theirs were bursting forth like the exuberance of spring now that their jailor was dead. I could not hold it against them. "And the boys?" I asked. How I wished I had gotten to know them!

"It is an adventure for them," he replied. "They know their father is gone, but nothing else." Then his expression grew thoughtful. "I am going to take them to the necropolis to perform the rites. Perhaps you should join us."

"You want me to come with you?" Here was my chance to escape my prison, to breathe some fresh air and see the Epirote countryside, and all I could do was balk!

Helenus saw it, too. "You have spent far too long pent up here. It would do you much good to get out."

I would have preferred to visit the riverbank, or walk through the dusty vineyards and sample the ripening fruits. A mournful air clung to the hill of the necropolis where Hades and Persephone dwelt in their cult house, a squat building set amid cypresses and juniper, where not even the birds dared sing. Even the flies, that perpetual nuisance around altars, avoided the area.

Anyone venturing into the presence of the Lord of the Dead and his dread queen wore black, and brought black sheep for the offering. Andromache's dark clothes and sober demeanor, however, could not quite conceal the ebullience sparkling in her eyes. She accepted Helenus's arm when he offered to escort her to the sanctuary door, and relaxed her vigilance just enough to let me interact with her sons.

Six-year old Molossus was a polite, dignified young gentleman who appeared to understand far more than the adults realized. On his own, he poured out the libations of milk, wine, and honey, but hesitated when it was time for the blood offering. The high priest was a kindly man, though, and knelt down on rickety joints to show him how to slap his hands against the bare earth to summon the god.

Pielus was a sweet, inquisitive child too young to comprehend the rituals. He wanted to pet the ewe and explore the antechambers: the high priest let him stroke the sacrificial animal's curling fleece before Andromache and his nurse took him and baby Pergamos outside.

I did not want to linger in that funereal sanctuary, and so followed the boys out into the bright afternoon. Pielus was a chasing a bee through the greenish gray lavender, around the weed-tangled grave markers of the long-neglected dead. Sunlight flashed against his mother's jewelry, and in her somber robe with her myriad amulets she might have been a priestess of the place.

A boy's muffled sobbing filtered down to us. Andromache turned her head back toward the sanctuary, where Molossus had remained with the priest and Helenus. "Death is a hard lesson to learn," she said quietly."

She had left me alone during the mourning period, as she had avoided me before, so it came as a complete surprise when she visited my apartment the very next day. "Is there anything of his that you want?" she asked. "I am setting a few things aside for the boys."

I shook my head. "Let them keep everything."

She reached out to grasp my hand. "Oh, I am not letting them keep *everything*." Andromache had elegant white fingers, too slight for the chunky silver rings she wore, but hard as marble under the soft skin. "Come, I will show you."

Boxes and chests littered the floor in the king's vacant apartment. Neoptolemus's favorite dog, an enormous Molossian mastiff who liked to nap across the threshold, was gone. "Where is Konon?" I asked.

"Molossus has him." She crossed the room to step onto a linen drop cloth. "I see the plaster is almost dry."

Andromache said it so casually it took me a moment to realize what she had done. I started in astonishment. That dreadful fresco depicting Achilles dragging dead Hector's corpse behind his chariot had been erased, obliterated under several coats of whitewash. "You—?"

She walked over to a chest, removed an object, and undid the fleece wrapping to reveal the wedding kylix. I knew what she was going to do, but not how. She carried it to the window, and from there let it drop three stories to the court below. I heard the ceramic shatter against the paving stones, and clapped my hand over my mouth to stifle the shock.

Andromache turned to me, wearing a slyly innocent look. "What an unfortunate accident!"

I sputtered with amazed, delighted laughter. "Have you left anything for me?"

She indicated the mess the plasterers had left. "I have a task for you."

Among the discarded scrapers and trowels was a pot of leftover lime plaster, not yet dried out. Andromache dragged out the weathered ox-hide shield that had belonged to the dead hero. "It is so worn and ugly," she said. "You will find water in that jug."

I sloshed the water and lime in the pot, then flicked my wrist to let the mixture fly. Great gobs of whitewash spattered the shield and dripped down.

Andromache and I shared a conspiratorial smile as she approved my handiwork. "Such clumsy slaves," she drawled. "One cannot trust them with anything." I set down the plaster pot while she tossed the ruined shield aside. "I feared I might be an arthritic old woman before that fool died, but he blessed us all with his stupidity. Hah! Just like his father, rushing to get himself killed." Then she held out her hand to me. "Come, I have saved you some other treasures."

Andromache led me into the bathroom, which the porters and plasterers had not yet touched. Vessels still stood on the shelves near the terracotta tub. Scented oils spattered and dribbled down the walls as we took turns smashing the jars. Soon, the room was awash in perfume, a great mess of unguent congealing together, and we howled our laughter. "There will be no oil of lilies or saffron for you now, Pyrrhus!" Andromache threw back her head and cackled. "Pyrrhus, Pyrrhus, Pyrrhus!" She fashioned it into a song, finding half a hundred ways to chant that hated name, to utter what had been forbidden. She became drunk on her glee, crazed from having held it in so long.

But she was not yet done. With her, it was one insult after another, and she left the greatest for last. In her hand she held his favorite bracelet, twirled round and round with it like a maenad, and then dropped it down the privy. She lifted her skirts like the rustling of crow's wings, sat down on the stone seat, and voided her bladder. "They will smell my woman's blood upon him in the nether world and laugh!" she cried.

Caught up in her exultation, I crowed my delight.

We left the king's apartment once we regained our poise. Andromache halted me at my door. "Come to my apartment tonight, and bring Briseis. I am hosting a funeral supper."

Her invitation was unexpected, given what had just come before. "For him?"

A grim smile hovered on her lips. "You will see."

That night, she received me as an Anatolian princess, having thrown off the black of her captivity like a chrysalis and become resplendent in embroidered scarlet and dark blue, with golden fringes and spangled felt shoes. Amber and silver pendants hung from her headdress. Such was the vision who clucked her tongue at my black-edged widow's veil before whisking it from my head, snagging my hair as she did so. "You do not need that here."

Pins hung askew from my mussed curls. "You said it was a funeral supper."

"So it is." Escorting Briseis and me into the sitting room, Andromache gestured to the table where Helenus was already seated. Savory aromas made my mouth water. My stomach growled at the platters of grilled lamb spiced with cumin, coriander, and diced onions, sourdough flat bread, cucumbers and fried chickpeas, boiled millet, and Egyptian beer.

Briseis gave a start when she saw the Anatolian dishes. "Oh, but he hated our food. He will starve in the afterlife."

"Let him." Andromache bestowed a deceptively sweet smile upon us. "I never said this supper was for him. These were Hector's favorite dishes. We feast in his honor tonight."

I wished she had told me beforehand, to let me dress appropriately. "Are you sure you want me to join you?" I asked. "I did not know Hector, and my father and uncle were..."

Helenus moved a silver mixing bowl between his hands. "Hector befriended your mother during her time in Wilusa. She attended his pyre as one of the chief mourners. Come and sit down, so we may have the libation."

Once everyone was seated, he lifted the bowl in both hands. "Iyarri, Lord of the Bow, receive this drink offering and safeguard us from your anger." Droplets splashed into the alabaster libation bowl before him. "Apaliunas, Mouse God and Plague Bringer, receive this drink offering and watch over your servants." Raising the bowl heavenward, he repeated the prayer in his tongue before passing the vessel to me. "Speak to your god Apollo for us."

I lifted the bowl between my hands as he had done. "Apollo, receive this drink offering and look kindly upon your supplicants. Watch over us and our loved ones."

Helenus also offered a libation for the shade of his deceased brother. "Lelwani, goddess of the dead, receive this drink offering and continue to watch over Harunta, firstborn son of Piyamaradu. Let him rest content in the nether world."

As Helenus poured the wine into cups, Andromache passed an amulet across the table. "You must wear Kamrusepa on your way home," she told me. "She will safeguard you from plague and seasickness."

Kamrusepa felt heavy and strange in my hand, and I did not know how Dia would take to having her high priestess wear so foreign a goddess around her neck. "Hector has great fame among our people," I said. Having heard it but once, I did not feel confident enough about the pronunciation to attempt his Anatolian name. "I know he was a warrior and breaker of horses, but nothing else.

Andromache made a commiserating little noise in her throat. "So it always is," she commented. "Singers remember nothing but how the great men strode across the battlefield in their gleaming bronze, who they slew, and how they in turn were slain. I knew a man who was more than his victories or defeats, more than the chariot or bow." She spoke like a bard who had nursed her song in her heart for a very long time. "Your singers will tell you that Hector broke horses, but they will not sing about his gentleness. Hector was not a man for brute force, with horses or with women." Sweet reminiscence brought a glow to her face. "He could whisper in a horse's ear, as though the gods had granted him the speech of animals, and no matter how wild, a horse would do as he said. He loved leading them out, and seeing how their ears would prick up and their tails would dance. When the war came, it tore up the plain below the city, and the horses were slaughtered, for food or for spite. Sometimes it seemed to me that Hector wept more for the horses than the men."

"Did he not speak out against the war?" I spooned onions and a morsel of lamb onto a piece of bread.

"Many times," Helenus said. "But Alaksandu had a silver tongue."

Andromache's face grew hard. "Indeed. He knew how to loosen the old men's ears as well as a pretty woman's robe, and he told them what they wanted to hear. He made them believe that your leaders despised Agamemnon and would rebel, that your warriors would grow tired of the fighting and suffering and go home, and that Wilusa's walls would never fall."

"I heard them say it in Lyrnessos, too," Briseis added. "Agamemnon would go home within a season, and Menelaus would take a new wife and forget Helen."

All the while, I wrestled with the question growing in my mind. "Did Alaksandu kill my young brother?" I finally asked. Although I believed my mother, in the end she had not known for certain.

Briseis did not know the story, and looked bewildered. Andromache showed no reaction. It was Helenus who drew a deep breath and leaned back in his chair. "Hector confronted him with the crime, but he always denied it, even swore in the name of the Storm God that he had shed no blood."

"Pleisthenes was smothered with a pillow," I retorted.

"I know how he died," Helenus said sharply. "I saw his body laid out. But Alaksandu never told the truth to anyone about anything. He should have given the boy back to your father."

"Lelwani will torment him forever for the lies he told and the deaths he caused." Andromache nodded her solemn certainty.

"Let us speak of other things." Helenus reached for his wine.

He told me about his travels before the war. In his youth, he had journeyed with Hector as far east as Hattusas, the great Hittite capital on its mountainous plateau, as far south as Ugarit and Carchemish, and as far west as Lesbos. As he talked, the servants brought dessert: candied figs and apricots, nut pastries, and sweet cakes with more wine.

Helenus offered the third libation to Zeus and Hera, as was proper, though he gave them Anatolian names.

Andromache chose for me a cake stuffed with dates and almond paste. "I made this once for Pyrrhus." Oh, how she delighted in calling his ghost that! "When he took me, he told me he expected me to do his laundry and cook for him, like an obedient wife should. After he tried this, someone else did the cooking. Hah! Was it my fault he had no taste for good food? Hector liked my pastries."

One bite explained why my late husband had not liked the pastry; it was far too rich.

After we finished dessert, we dedicated the fourth libation, and readied ourselves to depart. Andromache started to escort Briseis and me to the door, only to change her mind at the last minute and invite us into her bedchamber.

She went to her dressing table, rummaged among the trinkets scattered there, and returned bearing an amulet. "Hantili says you will one day conceive," she told me, "but Shauskha may help the day come sooner."

Another winged goddess, this one with full breasts, incised into an ivory wafer. "You are also wearing her," I observed.

Her hand went to the amulet hanging between her breasts. "Yes," she admitted quietly. "I hope to conceive again soon."

Briseis gave her a congratulatory kiss on the cheek. "Hantili is a good man."

"How soon will you marry?" I asked.

"Once we are settled in Buthrotum."

It would have been nice to attend. "Send word when you have the wedding. I want to send gifts."

"Send gifts for a baby." Andromache bade us wait again, and returned to the dressing table as if searching for another amulet, yet the thing she brought back was neither ivory nor silver nor gold, but a scrap of fabric nestled in a black wool cloth. It was threadbare, unraveling at the edges where it had been torn from a larger piece, and yellowed with old stains.

Andromache nursed the rag like the finest linen, petting it with soft fingertips as she held it out to share. "I wove this for my firstborn son. He was wearing the tunic the night Odysseus tore him from my arms to hurl from the walls. When I reached for him, this little piece ripped away in my hands."

Briseis made a sympathetic noise and brushed the relic with a reverent finger. I wanted to do the same, to acknowledge the honor Andromache did me by showing me her treasure, but remained uncertain. Perhaps I had become too accustomed to the repressed and suspicious Andromache. "I am sorry, Ashakumila."

"Do not be." She brought the torn fabric to nuzzle against her cheek, turning her head to seek out her child's scent within the fibers, although it must have worn away a long time ago. A smile curved her mouth, a brittle crescent set in her white face. "They slew my son to extinguish Hector's seed, but the gods have tilted the scales, and they will send him back to me."

CHAPTER TWENTY-THREE

AETHIOLAS'S DISTINCTIVE RED-GOLD HAIR stood out among the swarthier men awaiting me on the beach. Abandoning etiquette, I waved to him.

"Princess," the captain warned, "we're going aground."

I forced myself away from the rail and urged my handmaidens to a vacant bench. Behind me, the coxswain was shouting orders, and the rowers banked the oars to let the pentekonter's momentum ground the keel. I braced myself against the wooden bench as a shudder raced through the hull. As it subsided, oarsmen deserted the rowing benches, and leapt into the shallow surf while others tossed down cables. Inch by straining inch, forty-five men heaved the great pentekonter above the tidemark.

As I disembarked onto dry land, Aethiolas offered his steadying arm; the gaunt steersman and the first mate assisted my maids. Two other pentekonters were beaching some twenty yards away. Porters scurried back and forth unloading my chests, vessels, and furnishings to pile into mule carts for the trip home.

Aethiolas swept me up into a crushing hug. "It's good to see you!" he said. "I hope the voyage was mild."

"I spent most of it seasick."

He chuckled to hear that. "Poseidon doesn't favor you."

The Epirote ambassador hiked up the beach toward us on a seaman's legs, and extended a weathered hand to my brother. Aethiolas greeted him, thanked him for the generous escort, and offered him Sparta's royal hospitality.

Aethiolas had arranged lodgings in the governor's residence. I bathed and rested a few hours before joining the men downstairs in the megaron. As the only noblewoman present, I tried to feign interest in the conversation, while wishing the ambassador and governor would retire to let me have some time alone with my brother.

All I managed were a few minutes when he escorted me upstairs to my apartment. "It's been hours and you have not yet said anything about your wife," I chided gently.

Aethiolas drew a heavy breath. "She is well." I caught his atypical gloominess, and was about to inquire when he bestowed a kiss on my cheek and dismissed me. "Go to bed, Hermione. We rise early tomorrow."

Autumn had brought the first blazing leaf-fall to the Laconian countryside, and snow blanketed the mountain peaks. As I breathed in the clear fresh air, I recalled how much I had missed being outdoors during those stifling summer months in Epirus.

My mother met us in the lower court. Helen said little to me, but gave brisk commands to the servant girls awaiting her pleasure. Upstairs in a guest apartment, she ordered me a hot bath and meal, though I did not want either, and laid out the rest of my day. I balked. Attending her in her apartment and dining with the court were among the very last things I wished to do on my first day home. "Mother," I said, "I just want to lie down."

She arched her eyebrows. "Are you unwell?"

"I feel terrible." Let her think it was seasickness.

Helen laid her hand against my forehead. "You are not feverish. Very well, then. Lie down if you wish, but you will be up and about starting tomorrow. There's no need to dwell on this unfortunate business. It's finished."

Trust my mother to dismiss my troubles, and attempt to smother them behind a veil.

I submitted to the hot bath. As my mother's women dried my hair by the brazier, my father appeared. Menelaus dismissed Helen's hissing admonishment to let me rest, then wrapped me in his embrace. "Thank the gods I have my little girl back safe and sound." He stroked my still-damp hair while I stood numb. "It hasn't been the same around here without you."

He had abandoned me without a fight. Had he been anyone else I would have flung that fact back in his face. I forced a hollow smile to my lips instead. "I am glad to be home."

"That's good." Gazing down at me, then at my mother and maids, he cleared his throat. "Well..." Another nervous cough. "I suppose I should leave you ladies alone now."

Menelaus withdrew wearing an awkward look. My mother waited until he was safely gone to comment. "He missed you very much."

I did not want to have this conversation right now. "I suppose."

"Do you doubt it?"

She was going to press the matter. "Mother, I am very tired."

Helen brushed her fingertips over my hair, testing a few strands. "I think it's dry enough." She took the comb from Adreste and teased out the tangles. "Tomorrow you can begin unpacking."

Unpacking all my belongings took three long days, after which I became a recluse, spinning and sewing in my apartment, taking long walks along the ramparts, and sitting idle in the inner court. What was the matter with me? I ought to have been helping with the winemaking, dyeing, and making winter preserves. Olives were ripening in the groves this year. I should have visited the sanctuaries and agora, though my father refused to let me venture outside the citadel without half a dozen guards dogging my steps.

I resented the not-so-subtle reference to my abduction, yet he remained obstinate on that point, stating, "A princess needs a suitable escort."

"I see no need for so many men." I decided to call him on his blatant fib. "Why would anyone bother to abduct me now?"

"That's not..." Menelaus tried a second time. "No one is going to abduct you, because then they *will* have a war on their hands." But his halfhearted attempt at levity fell flat, and he abandoned the effort. "Now don't sulk young lady. I have some very good news to share with you." His shaggy eyebrows twitched upward, and a broad grin split his face. "Your cousin Orestes is on his way back to Mycenae."

Orestes. I needed a moment to make certain I had heard him correctly. "He's alive?" A rush of excitement banished my gloom.

Menelaus nodded, beaming. "Alive and well."

Orestes had survived his trial and been exonerated. Profound relief washed over me. I had not heard anything so wonderful since... I honestly could not remember when.

"I thought you'd like to know." My father held out his arms for a hug. "Ah, that's more like the little girl I know!" He squeezed me tight. "No more brooding. You're safe at home now, and we will find you someone worthy."

But I did not want to think dwell on that now. Orestes! Once Menelaus left, I knelt before my altar. "Thank you!" Joy set my heart fluttering as I raised my palm to my forehead to salute Apollo and the goddesses arranged around him. "Thank you for letting him live."

I went to bed that night wearing a smile, and woke more cheerful and refreshed than I had been in months.

My euphoria was short-lived. Chrysothemis threatened my celebratory mood to pester me with her troubles. "This morning when Aethiolas was eating, I suggested we go down to the river to feed the swans," she complained, as we spun wool in my sitting room. "Do you know what he did?"

Aethiolas did not have time to toss crumbs to swans; an astute wife would have realized that. "No. What did he do?"

"He told me he had business in Amyklai and would not be back for three days." She threw up her hands. "What's wrong with me? I do my best to be agreeable and obedient, but he's always so cold. Half the time he isn't even home."

"Aethiolas has important work to do." Anyone who observed them together could see what the problem was. My brother found his new wife empty-headed and boring, and she was too dense to realize it. "Have you ever asked him about his duties?"

Chrysothemis made a face. “He never wants to talk.”

“Then let him be.” I twisted raw wool between my fingers.

But Chrysothemis could not let anything be, and slumped brooding in her chair. “How does he expect me to get pregnant when he won’t even lie with me. He always makes some excuse.”

So she wanted advice on how to bewitch a man, did she? I flicked the spindle whorl between my thumb and forefinger. Did she think I knew any better than she? “Ask Polycaste what to do.”

“Has she even been married?”

“Yes.”

Chrysothemis continued to dither, driving me to distraction. “I thought marriage would be different. I thought he would love me, and there would be babies, but it isn’t that way at all.” I did not want to hear her complaints, to be reminded of what I had left behind with Neoptolemus. “It’s painful and embarrassing.”

It was time to change the subject, before I lost my patience with her altogether. “Father says Orestes is on his way back to Mycenae to claim the kingship.”

As she grasped the words, her eyes went wide. “He is? You mean he’s alive?” So no one had told her.

I sensed a thousand questions coming. “Yes,” I said, “but I know nothing else. Orestes wrote to Father. I didn’t see the letter.”

“He’ll surely write to us soon!” she exclaimed. “I have so much to tell him. Little Orestes, king of Mycenae! Oh, but he isn’t so little anymore, is he?” She laid aside her spindle, kicked off her shoes, and pulled her knees up to her chest. “He’s a great big man now.” I resigned myself to her enthusiastic chatter, hoping she did not spoil it by mentioning the murders or trial. “How splendid he’ll look sitting on the throne! Do you think he’ll wear purple, Hermione? I think he ought to wear purple. It’s such a marvelous color on him.”

SOME EVENINGS, I abandoned my women’s work, wrapped myself in a fur-lined robe, and huddled near the brazier to brood.

Coming home should have felt different, liberating and comfortable, yet it did not. Helen, who now managed the household, did not seem to need me. As the acknowledged heiress, Chrysothemis was now responsible for carrying out all the ritual duties. Between them, they made me feel redundant.

Dreary weather bred grim thoughts.

Footfalls outside my door and the turning of the latch drew my attention. I had not been expecting anyone at this late hour.

Helen dismissed my women with a curt gesture, banishing them to the bedchamber. In her hand she held a letter. "This arrived for you this afternoon. It was tucked among all the other correspondence, and your father's secretary with his weak eyes didn't notice until after supper." She handed it to me. "It's from Nemea."

I knew no one in Nemea. Even the seal was unfamiliar; it depicted a lion resting before a mountain flanked by olive trees. "Do you know who this is from?" I asked.

"Iphinous tells me that is King Orestes' new seal." Helen claimed Thebe's seat. "Why do you think I brought it to you myself?"

Did she mean to watch me read the letter, or to peruse it afterward? Orestes! Hearing her use his title drove home the reality that he was no longer a pariah or exiled prince. King Orestes Agamemnonides of Mycenae. It sounded so regal. Like Chrysothemis, I wondered what he would look like seated upon Agamemnon's throne, cloaked in purple and gold, and grasping the royal scepter in his hand.

I slid a fingernail under the wax to break the seal and unfold the papyrus.

"Dearest Hermione," he wrote, "please accept my condolences on your recent bereavement. How strange it is, writing to console you, when it has always been you lending me your comfort! I would have left you alone, to mourn and find consolation among your family and friends, but I did not wish you to be troubled by any lingering concerns about my trial, or any scabrous rumors you might hear."

Orestes sounded as though his dead pedagogue was once again standing over his shoulder dictating how a proper prince should write.

"I will spare you the details about the trial, except to say it was a difficult ordeal, and that the double curses on our house are now broken. We are all free." Bless him! I kissed the words on the papyrus. "I left Delphi a month ago. Since then, I have discovered that some rather vicious rumors have been circulating with regard to your late husband's last hours there."

Why did he have to spoil my joy by mentioning the matter? "You may have heard talk that Neoptolemus and I encountered each other at the god's altar, that we quarreled over you, and that I killed him because he stole you from me." My mouth fell open. I stared at the papyrus, poring over that passage two more times. Until that moment, it had never even occurred to me that Orestes and Neoptolemus might have met at Delphi.

"I assure you, the rumor is quite false. Neoptolemus and his Myrmidons arrived the very day of my trial. I did not witness the attack, or hear about the altercation until several days after. I cannot be certain, but I believe the rumor may have started in part because my Phocian guards left their posts and joined the mob in bludgeoning the intruders."

Helen's expectant gaze crawled over me. I did my best to shut out her presence, to smooth over my distress and keep reading. "These rumors have traveled with troubling haste. King Strophius has asked about the incident, as have others. Just this very evening, the lord of Nemea showed his tactlessness in asking whether you had prevailed upon me to kill Neoptolemus."

Again, I had to pause and reread his words before continuing. "I can understand why others would slander me—I have become quite accustomed to their vile accusations and whispers—but there is no excuse for them to do likewise to you. You are blameless," he wrote. "I defended your good name, but the sad truth is that people prefer to believe sordid falsehoods over dull facts."

No wonder no one wanted to marry me. They all thought me a coldblooded Spartan whore, a murderous bitch, painting me in lurid strokes as another Clytaemnestra, another Helen.

"What's wrong?" Helen asked.

"It's nothing," I answered unsteadily.

"Don't lie to me, young lady. Your hands are shaking. Something he said upset you."

I did not want to talk to her about it. "It is nothing." Why could she not go away? "Let me finish reading."

Turning back to the letter, I found my place. "I know the last thing you want is to revisit your husband's death, and I apologize for upsetting you. That was not my intention," Orestes said. "Your words comforted me in the darkness during my trial. I held them against my heart when the Erinyes came to judge me, and it was as though you were there beside me." So he had gotten my letter in time for the trial. Thank the gods! I read down to his final lines. "For that, I shall always be your servant. Yours, as long as life endures. Orestes."

"Orestes always seems to have this effect on you." Helen observed.

"What do you want me to say?" I thrust the papyrus at her. "Here! Go ahead and read what the Nemeans are saying, how I wrote to my lunatic lover and begged him to murder my husband!" Enraged as much by her prying and unflappable calm as by the calumnies themselves, I crumpled the letter into a ball and hurled it at her. "Go ahead and show Father! Let him get it through his head that no one wants to marry me now!"

Indignant, Helen straightened in her chair. "Is that true, what they're saying about you?"

"Pick it up and read it for yourself!"

She did just that, bending down to retrieve the wadded letter, smoothing it out over her knee. As she read, her mouth pursed into an ugly line. "Well, is it true, young lady?"

"Of course not!" How could she believe that rumor, when she had in her hand a letter from Orestes explicitly stating it was a lie? "What sort of conniving bitch do you think I am? I would never do such a thing."

Slowly, Helen set the letter aside. "Now you know what it feels like to be slandered."

"Is that all you can say?" I shouted. "Why should I be despised and slandered? What ill have I ever done to deserve that?"

Helen rose and crossed over to me. She grasped my chin between pincer fingers and forced me to look at her. "You have no choice," she rebuked. "The world is what it is, and we mortals are nothing but the playthings of the gods. It's obvious you've been sitting idle too long, because your delusions have gone to your head." Releasing me, she left.

I nursed my resentment as my maids ventured back into the room. Just this once, why could she not have comforted me and lied to me, and told me that everything would be all right, the way a normal mother would have done? But she was a stranger, a cipher, and she understood nothing at all about me.

In the bedchamber, I huddled near the brazier to undress. Thebe lowered a linen nightgown over my head. Then I climbed into bed, sliding between the sheets while Monime blew out the lamp.

I contemplated the coals glowing in the brazier, seeking some semblance of peace without much success. Doubts swirled around me like the wind gusting through the leaves outside. I closed my eyes and tried to focus on the positive things Orestes had said, only to realize my mother had taken the letter with her.

MENELAUS CAME TO SEE ME early the next morning. "That's enough of that." He dragged the widow's veil from my head and tossed the black linen to the floor. "You were married to that blasphemer for less than three months, and he didn't deserve you."

So my mother had run straight to him after last night's argument. "You didn't object when he abducted me."

"What else was there to do?" he replied gruffly. "There's nothing wrong with a man stealing a woman when it's a legitimate abduction and there's no harm done. Neoptolemus had a kingdom he won through his own prowess, an honorable name, and the wherewithal to defend what he stole." My father huffed. "I had no idea he'd turn out to be such a colossal fool."

"*No harm?*" I heard myself raising my voice. "He snatched me from a sacred altar! I had no idea who he was, or what he was going to do with me. I thought he was going to rape me."

I should have shut my mouth, but now that the dam had broken I could not seem to stop; this outburst had been months in coming. "Stop lying to me. There aren't going to be any more suitors. Or did you make some other arrangement that you forgot to tell me about? Did you negotiate with Odysseus over the latrine trench to marry me to Telemachus? Or did you—?"

"That's enough!" Menelaus's barrel chest heaved. When he opened his mouth to speak again, he made several abortive starts before he found the right words. "I had no idea he rough-handled you like that. He gave me his solemn word you were safe."

"Bruised and terrified obviously doesn't count," I answered sullenly.

"I did what was best then," he grumbled, "and will do what is best now." He wagged a finger at me. "There will be no more moping and mourning. Take your ladies and go down to the agora. Buy whatever you fancy. Ruin me. Forget this nonsense about abductions and slanders. You are my daughter, Hermione, and the daughter of Menelaus doesn't hide behind walls or veils on account of a few rumors. She holds up her head like a queen."

"YOU MUST PRESIDE over the midwinter rites." Aethiolas claimed a seat near the brazier, waving aside the mulled wine my maids brought. "You're the only one who can do it."

Aethiolas had always made a point not to pry into women's business, so this was not something he would have said on his own. "Did Mother send you to talk to me?" I asked skeptically.

"She might have said something, yes."

"Then let her lead the rites," I retorted. "Is she not the queen?"

"And one day *you* will be queen!" Aethiolas rubbed his bearded jaw in frustration. "Chrysothemis is no good. More often than that, she forgets her place, and then the ritual has to start all over again."

I twisted fleece between my fingers, pausing only to flick the spindle whorl. "I am a childless widow whose husband committed an unspeakable sacrilege. My being his wife has tainted me. I have no business blessing anyone."

"Stop this self-pity!" he snapped. "Neoptolemus got what he deserved for his presumption. You knew nothing about it. You were miles away when it happened, fulfilling your duties to the gods."

Distance and innocence were no assurance against the wrath of the gods. Iphigenia was proof enough of that. But Aethiolas would never understand my deep-rooted fears; he was not a woman, he had not known Iphigenia, and he not been at Mycenae when she was sacrificed. "Father never even came after me."

Aethiolas hissed an expletive under his breath. "Is that it? You're sore because Father didn't start a war over you?" Eyes blazing, he leaned toward me, bracing a hand on his thigh. "Leave it in the past where it belongs. You're home now. People want their high priestess back. They want you."

Although the local women had flocked to me the other day in the agora, wanting to kiss my hands and receive my blessings, it had felt more like simple courtesy than a burning need to have me as their high priestess again. Sighing, I stopped the spindle's rotation. "A true queen has to be a mother. I bled in Epirus. My womb could not nourish my husband's seed."

"Would you rather still be in Epirus, stuffed with that man's seed? Thank the gods you weren't cursed with bearing his sons!" Aethiolas shook his head, then he smiled. He saw my barrenness as a blessing? I had not considered that point of view before.

When he spoke again, his tone had softened. "I know a dozen excellent Spartan gentlemen who would die for the chance to court you."

I wanted to throw my arms around him and kiss him, and push him away and cry, all at the same time. "You're just saying that to be kind."

He snorted in mock indignation. "Are you calling me a liar? They're coming to Megapenthes' wedding, and it isn't simply to wish him well. Just think, we could have an old fashioned marriage contest."

Aethiolas left me with a glow that lasted as long as it took my sister-in-law to drag her heels into my sitting room. "Aethiolas is giving up the kingship." Her bottom lip quivered uncontrollably. "He's giving up the kingship so you can be queen!" She broke down then, and bawled out the rest. "I tried, but everyone hates me, everyone hates me as priestess, and..."

I set aside my spinning to gather her into my arms, rocking her while trying to sort out my confusion. After my earlier conversation with Aethiolas, I believed he had done exactly as Chrysothemis said, but how could he have? What man in his right mind would refuse power and prestige for a woman's sake?

Chrysothemis's sobbing distracted me. "It's not your fault." I stroked her tumbled hair.

"Yes, it is!" she blubbered. "People don't want me as a priestess. Aethiolas says I embarrass him!"

"That's not true." Had he truly said that? I waved my maids to the bathroom to bring water and fresh linens. "Hush, don't cry."

"I have every right to cry!" she wailed. "He hates me!"

Lying to her would accomplish nothing, but telling her the truth would be no easy task, either. "Chrysothemis, listen to me," I began carefully. "Aethiolas wants you to be a silent, proper wife, and not bother him with your chatter."

"*He makes me nervous!*" As I feared, she struck a hysteric note, her face burning scarlet and screwed up with frustration. "I try to be quiet, but then it's *too* quiet. I try going to his athletic contests and taking an interest in his work, but he just shoos me away like a child." She blew her nose into the linen Thebe handed her. "Isn't there a spell or love potion or something to make him like me?"

"Ask Polycaste," I answered.

"She hates me, too! I can't ever do anything right in the sanctuary."

Right now, my sister-in-law was making *me* hate her, too. Aethiolas had left me contemplating a return to the cult house, but Chrysothemis's hysterics cinched the decision. Sparta had to have better than this empty-headed goose.

CHRYSOTHEMIS LOVED TAKING PART in the women's rites, and naturally felt excluded when she was not invited to the cult house for my re-investiture, even when my mother explained the situation. "You will not like watching Hermione take back her estate as sacred heiress."

Her tactless explanation sent my sister-in-law into hysterics again. Helen let her bawl. Perhaps she thought Chrysothemis would outgrow her childishness, if no one indulged her. If so, then my mother was wasting her time. Clytaemnestra had already tried toughening up her middle daughter. At twenty-six, Chrysothemis was far too set in her ways to change.

So I asked Erigone to sit with her that night, while reassuring her that they were both invited to the midwinter rites.

Consecrating a sacred heiress began with a ritual bath. I shivered despite the five braziers exuding their warmth through the small lustral chamber and the heated water the novice priestesses poured over my head and shoulders.

"Great Mother Goddess!" she cried. "Receive as high priestess and heiress this royal daughter of Sparta: Hermione, daughter of Helen, daughter of Leda. Let her keep the altars and the feast-days. Let her bless the sheaves in the fields and the grapes upon the vine. Let her bless the young and make the women fruitful. Let her do all these things in your service."

For this part of the ritual, I had to walk naked to the altar and kneel shivering on the bare floor, my hair hanging limp and damp down my back. My mother stepped forward to sponsor me. She was dressed like a high priestess, wearing the moon-mask under her round headdress and coiling black ringlets, and her women had painted scarlet suns upon her cheeks.

"Great Mother Goddess!" she cried. "I am your servant Helen, daughter of Leda. I am the sacred queen of Sparta. Receive my daughter Hermione back into your service." I shivered, as much from the cold as from the goddess's awesome presence and the power my mother was channeling into her invocation. "Let her bless the sheaves in the fields and the grapes upon the vine. Let her bless the young and make the women fruitful. Let her do all these things to serve you."

I clenched my jaw to try to suppress my chattering teeth, and stood up when Polycaste gave me the signal. I raised my arms to salute the goddess, keeping them aloft as another priestess smeared my breasts and belly with consecrated oil.

"Let Mother Dia breathe life upon her." Helen wafted myrrh smoke from a clay incense burner over me. I choked back the impulse to cough. "Let her be filled with the holy essence."

She replaced the incense with ochre paste, and began to mark the places the other priestess had already anointed. "Let her nipples give milk to nourish many children." She ventured lower, to my navel. "Let her womb become a fertile field." I dared not breathe as her fingers touched my skin, for it was not merely pigment mixed with cold goose fat she was painting onto my nipples and womb, but the goddess's own blood which permeated my skin and made me glow from within.

As Helen anointed me, the priestesses began clapping their hands and chanting in unison.

Look upon her breasts!
They are white as cream.
Round with blessings for the people.
Look upon her nipples!
They are holy pomegranate seeds.
Sweet and fit for a king.
Look upon her womb!
She is the fertile earth, the sacred cave.
Life comes from her!
Life comes, with the Great Goddess's blessing!

My arms started trembling from the strain of maintaining the votary's stance. "Great Mother Goddess," I called out, "I am Hermione, daughter of Helen, daughter of Leda. Let me bless the sheaves in the fields and the grapes upon the vine. Let me bless the young and make the women fruitful. Let me do all these things your service."

Afterward, my handmaidens dressed me in a woolen gown and robe. A novice brought mulled wine to warm me.

Helen stayed close. "Did you feel the goddess's touch during the ritual?"

"When you were painting the sacred signs on me," I said.

She nodded slowly. "Then you know that returning to her service was the right thing to do. The goddess always lets her servants know when she approves."

A WEEK LATER, we returned to the cult house to celebrate the winter solstice. Noblewomen came with their daughters to celebrate with the queen and sacred heiress, while elsewhere in the town the common women doused their hearths, swept away the old ashes, and started new fires from brands lit here in the sanctuary. I helped bake and distribute goddess cakes and stayed near the hearth with my mother to bless the fire with my presence.

Once the last woman left with her brand, we shut the doors. Polycaste clapped her hands and marshaled us into line for the procession into the inner court. We carried torches as we went, and our shoes crunched over the gravel the novices had laid down so we would not slip on the frosty ground.

Stars glittered like silver spangles against the night sky. I glimpsed my breath turning to smoke. Once we reached our destination, a navel stone in the court's very center, we gave our torches and wrappings to the novices, and linked hands to form a circle around the omphalos.

Polycaste started the chant. It was old Cretan. I knew but a few sacred words, and fragments of songs and spells, for it was no longer taught as it had been in the sanctuaries of the great Labyrinth of Knossos. Serpents understood the tongue, though, and the sacred bulls used in the bull-leaping. Sometimes I thought about what would happen when the women could no longer sing to the house snake hibernating under the omphalos to remind her that spring was coming, or urge her to carry our messages to the gods.

I remembered my promise to Chrysothemis. But Polycaste was not so eager to accommodate her. "You should concentrate on bearing your own children," she told me, after we had danced the Serpent Dance and come back indoors.

"You say that as though I can simply go out, choose a man, and lie with him." I let my gaze wander to the Cretan-style fresco splashed across the wall behind her; it depicted rows of brown-skinned young men with serpentine lovelocks and waspish waists adoring a priestess. It belonged to another time, when ordinary men could approach the goddess-on-earth and receive her favors.

Perhaps I should revive the old ways. Perhaps I should step down from my seat during the next revels, select the comeliest man, and let him serve me while the goddess inhabited my skin. Let my father fume and my mother tsk-tsk me for the impropriety. I was a high priestess, a sacred heiress, and descended from a long line of priestess-queens who had taken consorts and borne holy children as they pleased.

Yielding to a stranger of my choosing, a man sent by the gods, could not be any worse than submitting to a husband I had despised. "Sparta needs daughters to continue the bloodline," I said.

"And you're hoping Chrysothemis will bear them?"

I dared not confide my rebellious thoughts to her; she would only shake her head and urge me to wait for a true king. "Chrysothemis needs to get my brother into her bed first." I felt self-conscious having this conversation with my sister-in-law standing less than twenty feet away, but it had to be done. "I know there are things you can do to help her attract him and conceive."

"Yes," Polycaste admitted, "but she has to be bright enough to use the gifts she's given, or nothing will happen."

I omitted that caustic remark when telling my sister-in-law that the high priestess had agreed to help. I also accompanied her to the cult house, to ease her apprehensions.

Polycaste met us on the portico. Mellow lamplight beckoned to us through the open doors. "Princess Chrysothemis," she announced, "you are entering Dia's sacred domain. The Great Mother Goddess is all things to all women. She is the fertile womb from which men spring, and the tomb to which they return. Enter here, and you *will* do her bidding."

Her ritual greeting sounded too much like a reprimand. Chrysothemis hung her head. I had to urge her forward.

"Let me enter," Chrysothemis said. "Let Mother Dia help me please my husband and bear him a child."

Standing a step above, Polycaste loomed over her like the goddess on her plinth. "And will you submit to her in mind and body?" she asked sternly.

"I will do anything you ask."

I empathized with my sister-in-law and cousin, a demoted high priestess and heiress, and a barren, unloved wife forced to grovel in the freezing cold. Just coming here took immense courage on her part. I climbed another step to stand beside her. "I, Hermione, daughter of Helen, sponsor this woman Chrysothemis. She is sincere in her desire to become a good wife and mother. Let her enter the sanctuary and receive the blessings of Mother Dia."

Polycaste's women whisked Chrysothemis into the lustral chamber to purify her. A novice brought mulled wine to banish the chill while I waited with my handmaidens in the inner sanctuary.

Chrysothemis returned naked and shivering, her wet hair wrapped in a cloth. An older priestess urged her toward a cot covered in sheepskins laid out before the altar. To her credit, she did not complain about the cold. She did not even resist as the priestesses began crowding in around her like vultures. Her white limbs vanished amid their bodies as they began to draw sacred signs on her womb.

When they finished, they covered her and told her lie to quiet while the design set, but she drew aside the blanket to show me what they had done. I was astonished, having never seen the like. A tree of life spread its limbs across her womb, and a serpent coiled where the tree's roots met her shaven vulva; it was an amulet painted with henna into the skin itself.

"What do you think?" Chrysothemis asked, uncertain.

"Aethiolas won't be able to ignore you now," I said.

Mortified, she pulled the covers over her. "He'll be aghast." She flung an arm over her eyes. "He'll laugh. What have I done?"

"Stop being such a worrywart!" I exclaimed. Maybe it was time to get her drunk and let Dionysus remove her inhibitions. "Aethiolas isn't going to laugh, not when you show him the sacred signs and let him know you mean it."

*****

NOT LONG AFTER, Helen returned the crumpled letter to me. "I took this with me by mistake. Have you written to him yet?"

Her query piqued my suspicions. "No," I answered. "Why do you ask?"

"Phaidon is leaving shortly." She named Sparta's new ambassador to Mycenae. "Your father suggested that Orestes might like to hear from you. Your cousin is a king now, and it is not polite to ignore a king's letter."

Helen's explanation rang hollow, but with so little time left to compose a reply, mulling over her duplicity would have to wait. Once she withdrew, I called for writing materials and sat down by lamplight to try to find something suitable to say to a king.

"To Orestes Agamemnonides, king of Mycenae. Thank you for your letter and good wishes. I am relieved to hear that you have been acquitted and reclaimed your rightful station." A groan escaped me, rereading my stilted words. "Thank you also for dispelling any rumors surrounding the death of my late husband. No such tales have yet reached Sparta, but hearing them from you first softens the blow." Nothing could have alleviated my dismay. "It never occurred to me that you might have been involved.

"I hope you find joy in your homecoming, and that Elektra has not completely taken over the palace. Chrysothemis and Erigone are both doing well. Chrysothemis longs for a child. Erigone has made a few friends, and sometimes we catch her casting glances at the handsome young men around court. I have become very fond of her."

By now, the words felt like empty courtesies, and it simply would not do. After all this time, I had to be straightforward with him. "You must forgive me for curtailing the family gossip, but my heart is not in it, and writing to a king is not like writing to a dear cousin." As I caught my self-control starting to unravel, I discovered a strange solace in the correctness of my grammar. "I do not wish to burden you with my troubles, not only because you have so many more cares now, but also because you have already endured enough suffering. I do not think you would understand a woman's concerns, or worse, it would embarrass you, and you would shake your head at the impropriety.

"Spring cannot come quickly enough for me. I have never liked winter. I feel the cold creeping into my bones, and the gray winter skies reflect what I feel inside. When it rains, it seems the gods are weeping with me."

Had I gone mad? I wished I had taken the time to inscribe a wax draft, to be able to erase that last paragraph. Curse my mother for having waited until the last minute to remind me to write! Now it was too late to begin again. "Do not mistake my tone for a widow's mourning. I grieve because there are no children, and perhaps never will be. I should have liked at least one child to love, a son or daughter to look after me in my old age, and to remember me after I die.

"You must forgive me for spilling my thoughts like this." I had gone too far. "Send me news to brighten my days. Let me hear all about your nieces and nephews. I want to hear about the servants we knew, and how they are doing. Always, your loving cousin, Hermione."

I blew on the ink to help it dry faster, folded the letter, and sealed it. Perhaps it was a mistake, confiding such thoughts in him like when he had no time for my troubles. All I knew was what my heart told me to write.

THE EARLY SPRING DELUGE battering against my shutters could not dampen my sister-in-law's effervescence as she danced into the sitting room.

Chrysothemis flung her arms around my neck and kissed my cheek. She should have been lying down, sick as she had been the last few days. "Hermione! I have to tell you the good news. I think I might be—you know!" She squealed with girlish delight.

Monime and Thebe beamed congratulatory smiles at her. So she was with child. I felt a sharp stab of jealousy. "Does Aethiolas know?" I asked.

"I'm going to go tell him right now." Flashing me a naughty smile, Chrysothemis bent to my ear and whispered. "Did you know he was so excited when he saw me shaven and painted down there that he couldn't keep his hands off me?"

She kissed me again and darted away, leaving me numb and bereft. I should have been elated. Instead, I bit down on my knuckles to stifle the grief of an uncontrollable mother-hunger.

I wrestled with my tears, but they fell, anyway, splotching the new wool cloth stretched across my loom. This would not do, not at all. It must be the gray weather working on my spirits. After all, I was still young enough to marry and bear children, and this news was a blessing. A child would bring my brother and his wife together. Eleuthia had granted Chrysothemis a precious gift. There was no reason to think the goddess might not also be smiling upon me, to let me share in it.

CHAPTER TWENTY-FOUR

I SPENT THE MORNING in the pressing shed supervising the women and boys carrying in baskets of washed olives. Men worked the press, turning the millstones, crushing the fruits into a paste which would sit for an hour to extract the virgin oil. Olive pulp and oil smeared the floor. Sand sprinkled across the packed earth kept the workers from slipping.

Startled silence filled the shed at the queen's arrival. A coiffed and bejeweled Helen filled the doorway, holding her flounced hem above the mess. Dressed for the megaron, she did not belong here.

"Your father wishes to see you," she announced.

I wiped my oily hands on my apron, wondering why she had come herself rather than send a messenger. "Is something wrong?"

"An important visitor has arrived." Waving the slaves back to work, my mother scrutinized my rough gown, right down to my hair tied back in a kerchief. "You're not going to meet him dressed like that."

Helen hustled me back to my apartment and straight into a hot, scented bath. She examined the contents of my jewel casket and clothes chest, holding up this necklace or that skirt, selecting my raiment without asking my opinion.

"Mother, what are you doing?" I asked.

"Making you look like a princess." Royal purple embroidered with gilded blue and green bands joined a blue linen shift across my bed. Amethyst beads and a collar studded with gold drops clattered onto my dressing table. Matching gold and amethyst earrings joined the baubles.

All this must have something to do with my half-brother's wedding. Perhaps the bride's family had arrived. Lord Alector was the governor of Asopos, on the southeast coast near Cape Maleas, but we were not expecting him till tomorrow. Had he come early? "Are you going to tell me who all this fuss is for?"

Helen held up a hammered gold diadem. "You'll see soon enough. Forget the crimping pins, Thebe. There's no time."

Everything felt rushed, unnatural. I wanted to shout and make everything stop long enough to have some answers. Megapenthes' wedding meant nothing to my mother but extra work; she certainly would not have come in her jewels and paint to fetch me for visitors who could wait until evening. "It's a suitor, isn't it?" I recalled the names from my father's list of a year ago. "Father wants me to meet some lame old nobleman with a dozen children and two dozen grandchildren, doesn't he?"

She remained infuriatingly noncommittal. "Would you refuse?"

I lifted my arms for the blue shift. "Is he repulsive?"

"He's not too disagreeable," she replied. "Monime, galena for the eyes, and hand me the earrings. Wipe the scowl off your face, Hermione. Your father worked very hard to make this arrangement."

Robed and jeweled, my hair still drying under the diadem, I followed my mother downstairs and across the great court into the megaron. Fresh pine logs blazed upon the hearth. Asphalion stood at attention near the dais. Someone occupied the seat of honor to the right of the throne, probably the arthritic nobleman my father had chosen for me, but when Menelaus rose to greet me with outstretched arms, his bulk obscured my view.

I saw movement as the guest of honor rose to acknowledge my mother and me. Menelaus released me from his embrace and stepped aside, and I suddenly found myself staring not at a crook-backed graybeard but a hulking young man with short, reddish-gold hair.

Then I heard my father speaking in my ear, introducing the stranger. "Orestes Agamemnonides, king of Mycenae."

Was this my Orestes, then? The fussy little toddler who had picked his nose the first time I met him? The frightened adolescent who had escaped from Mycenae spattered with his father's blood? It could not be. This Orestes was a giant, a square-jawed, handsome man, not at all the boy I remembered. "Is it you?" It came out as an unbecoming squeak.

When he smiled his familiar lopsided smile, I melted. "Yes, it is," he answered. *He's here, he's really here.* My mind went completely blank. All I could do was gaze at him and blush.

Menelaus cleared his throat meaningfully, but it was my mother who interjected. "Perhaps we should all sit down?"

Inlaid ivory chairs awaited us. Asphalion brought cups filled with wine, and my father offered a libation in the stone channel beside his throne. "King Orestes and I have been talking while you ladies were fussing upstairs, but we won't bore you with politics. Let me show you the gift he brought me."

I tried to focus on what my father was saying, and forget about the flush burning my face and creeping down my breasts. *Orestes is here. He came.* Sitting no more than six feet from him, I felt his rapt gaze on me. I dared not look back at him.

Menelaus passed the gift to my mother, who then gave it to me. The last time I had held Agamemnon's golden seal, it had been stained with his blood. I turned the ring in my hands, and made a show of examining it before returning it.

"I have my own seal now," Orestes told my father. He spoke with a deep voice commensurate with his giant frame; the messengers had been right in their descriptions. "It was only right that you should have a memento."

Menelaus tucked the ring into his tunic. "Orestes, you are our honored kinsman as well as our guest, and as such you are entitled to the gifts due a king. Foremost among those is my daughter, the chief jewel in my house." Rising, he turned to me and extended his hand. Anticipation rolled over me, even as my mother urged me to get up.

This moment could not be happening; it must be a dream. I rose, gave my father my hand, and let him lead me to this stranger bearing my cousin's name. "I severed your betrothal due to conditions which no longer apply," Menelaus told Orestes. "I see no reason now why you should not have my daughter's hand in marriage, if you still wish it and she is willing."

Orestes towered inches above me. All I heard was my own heartbeat, impossibly loud, his breathing and mine, and my father finishing his announcement. "Megapenthes celebrates his wedding in three days. Let us celebrate two weddings on that day."

Reality did not find me until later, upstairs in my apartment as my maids began undressing me. My fiancé was the king of Mycenae, my cousin, my Orestes. Then it seized me all at once. I sagged breathlessly to my knees.

"Monime," my mother ordered, "loosen her girdle and then fetch a cool cloth for her face."

"Mistress, what's the matter?" Thebe chafed my hands. My handmaidens had not accompanied me into the megaron; they did not even know that a Mycenaean royal delegation had arrived. "Are you ill?"

"She's going to be married," my mother explained calmly.

Thebe looked torn between congratulating me and offering her condolences. I drew a deep, steadying breath. "King Orestes is here."

Helen interrupted with a crisp order to lie down and rest, and stern words for my maids. "No one is to disturb her."

To reinforce her point, she moved into my sitting room—maids, sewing basket, and all. I closed my eyes and tried to doze, yet the excitement racing through my veins made it impossible. Orestes was here! I kept his image before my eyes. How handsome he had grown! And my father had given his consent. We were going to be married!

My mother woke me in the late afternoon to prepare me for the betrothal feast. "You're still in shock, I see."

I swung my legs over the edge of the mattress to wiggle my toes in the sheepskin rug. "Did Orestes decide to come to Sparta on his own, or did you suggest that Father invite him?" Something must have prompted this sudden change, and my mother's propensity for spinning webs came immediately to mind.

Helen let her fingers play over the jewelry scattered across my dressing table to draw out the suspense and torment me. "Your father does as he pleases." She found my ivory comb and lingered over it, removing strands of coppery red hair one at a time. "Though I admit, someone may have dropped a tiny hint in his ear."

AN EMBROIDERED PURPLE CLOAK pinned over one shoulder, and his narrow waist belted with hammered gold medallions, Orestes cut a regal figure that evening as he entered the megaron alongside Menelaus. All eyes were drawn toward him, especially the women's. Every conversation ceased as my father presented him to the court as the king of Mycenae, and bestowed upon him the seat of honor. Orestes honored his host by partaking in the first libation. He behaved with the utmost dignity and courtesy, even though some of the guests, who had heard about his crime and ordeal, were not yet certain about him.

Once the feast began, he greeted his sister and her good news by seizing her in a crushing hug, and swinging her around with a mighty laugh. Chrysothemis squealed and protested like a little girl, while shoving at his broad chest. "Stop! You'll crush the baby!" She could be so stupid sometimes; she was not even showing, and my mother and Polycaste had already explained to her about the rudiments of childbearing.

Orestes released her to her husband with a kiss, and joined me at the high table. I still could not quite believe we were sitting together talking like this, that this was real and we were about to be married. Just the sound of his voice brought fire to my cheeks. I pictured myself fainting away in his arms the moment he kissed me.

Kissing was all right, I thought, but then he would want to do other things with me. I blinked hard to banish the thought. Orestes was not like those other men. "They never told me," I said. "Right up until the last moment, Mother let me think some decrepit old veteran had come to ask for my hand."

"I had no idea, either," he confessed.

"But you came, anyway."

His eyes twinkled with merriment. "Lord Ambassador Phaidon hinted that your father might make such an offer. I didn't know for certain, but would have asked regardless. I certainly didn't come all this way for your bastard half-brother's wedding." Orestes craned his gaze to the left, where my parents sat together. "Anyone who says your mother is the most beautiful woman in the world hasn't seen you."

His platitude elicited a groan. "When did you become such a flatterer of women?"

"Do you prefer the boy to the man?" he asked playfully.

He was not going to seduce me that easily. "I don't know the man very well." Then I relented with a heavy sigh. Playing the coquette was not something I did. "I prefer whichever causes me the least worry, and you the greatest joy."

Orestes shared the hero's portion with me, while the dancers and acrobats performed in the empty space around the hearth. I teased him a bit about the bare-breasted girl dancers, and we talked. Although this sudden change left me rattled, his good humor and solicitude made it easier to relax.

After the dessert course, Menelaus rose from his chair to make the betrothal announcement. "Esteemed guests," he began, "in two days, we celebrate the marriage rites of our natural son Megapenthes to the daughter of Alector, lord of Asopos. But on that day, we say that we shall celebrate not one wedding but two, as our kinsman and most honored guest, Orestes Agamemnonides, king of Mycenae, takes our daughter Hermione as his bride and queen."

There was a moment's hesitation, for the assembled lords and ladies had not been expecting this, then polite applause rippled around the megaron. I wondered how truly glad the Spartan court was to learn that, through me, another Atreid would someday rule over them.

When it was quiet once more, my father continued, "Now, let's allow King Orestes to say a few words."

Standing, Orestes inclined his head toward his host and raised his cup. "Thank you, King Menelaus. We are most honored to accept your daughter's hand in marriage. She is, indeed, the most beautiful woman in

Sparta." My blush deepened at the compliment. "If you will indulge us, we have brought a betrothal gift for our lovely bride."

Orestes put down his cup, opened the box his manservant brought forward, and withdrew a glittering object. Firelight burnished the golden daisy chain hanging from his hands to a glimmering sheen. "As a little boy," he explained, "we used to bring the princess wildflowers from the fields around Mycenae." I caught my lower lip between my teeth, realizing he was going to tell them about the wilted daisies. "More often than not, they were dead by the time she got them, but with her good grace she always accepted."

Amid laughter and, this time, genuine applause, he crowned me with the daisy chain. "At last," he exclaimed, "we have found flowers even we cannot kill!"

I touched my fingers to the hammered gold flowers, my cheeks burning even more furiously. Not having known that he meant to give me a betrothal gift at tonight's feast, I felt like a fool, and whispered urgently, "Why didn't you say something?"

Orestes sat down. "I wanted it to be a surprise."

Antimachus the bard assumed his seat beside the hearth and sang about the hero Orion. Afterward, it was customary to ask for a shorter song, or to invite the guest of honor to recount his own exploits.

Heroic boasting was an art few men mastered. It was one thing to achieve a brave deed, but quite another to spin it into a yarn without sounding like a hot-winded braggart. Neoptolemus had always banished me from the megaron before the songs of the heroes were sung, but at times he and his men had been so rambunctious that I could hear their bluster from afar. How like a vain child my late husband had been, playacting at being a hero whenever he recounted how he—yes, he with his own hands—had slain old King Priam.

Orestes took his time to moisten his throat with wine, and pay his respects to my father and the great Spartan lords who were his audience.

"I was there at Mycenae the day my father was slain," he began, dropping the royal plural. "I was twelve years old then, and had not seen him for many years."

An uncomfortable collective murmur moved through the hall. I held my breath. Surely he was not going to tell them the same story he had told me that night almost nine years ago, with all its gory details.

Gods, yes—yes he was! "You see, my sisters and I had not been told he was coming that day, yet there I was, sneaking into the ritual bath wondering why the water and customary sacrifice had been set out a day early when suddenly I heard him enter, call out to my mother, and reprimand her for her shameful behavior. For all I knew, he intended to murder her right there in the megaron. His anger made me too afraid to venture out to greet him but there was nowhere else to go, so I hid in the privy adjacent to the bath, and peered out through the curtain. Thus it was that I saw my mighty father cut down before my very eyes, trapped beneath a fisherman's net in his purifying bath." Hearing Orestes tell the tale now, many years later in an adult's calm voice, stood in stark contrast to his original garbled account.

"I crouched helpless behind the curtain, clutching my dagger, holding my breath for fear the murderers would hear," he said. "And sure enough, Aegisthus, that foul spawn of incest, did hear me. He turned his head toward the curtain, and frowned, but just when he would have discovered my hiding place, my mother laid her hand on his arm and told him it was nothing but a mouse."

Orestes had never before shared all these little details with me. I was hearing them for the first time along with everyone else.

It both was and was not the story everyone wanted to hear. Menelaus sat stone-faced, while Helen was impassive. Chrysothemis blanched and leaned into Aethiolas. How it shocked them all to hear Orestes acknowledge that Clytaemnestra had shown some vestige of mother's love during the slaughter.

Now followed the details I already knew, the things that he had told me that very night, and in his letters. "I heard screams and dying groans from next door, as Aegisthus's men slew the companions and turned my father's megaron into a charnel house. But afterward, once the murderers left the field of slaughter, the gods gave me the courage to crawl forth on my hands and knees and take my father's battered hand, and hear his last whispered words as he died." Orestes gave a pause, as I knew he would have to. No matter how many times he had told this story before—and it was obvious that he had rehearsed it—he was not so dead inside that he could not feel the pathos behind his own words.

He concealed his distress with a draught of wine. "I went behind the curtain again and remained there while the slaves came and went with their scrub buckets, and removed my father's corpse." I heard a long, low groan to my left. Menelaus wept openly into his hands. Orestes paused to show his respect; my father waved him on. "Day and night were indistinguishable in that windowless room, but I knew that it must have been very late when the last slaves left. I found enough courage to crawl out, and then found my faithful old pedagogue in his cubicle, and told him everything."

His omitting my role bothered me not at all. People would have whispered about it: a twelve-year-old boy alone in his older cousin's bedchamber, lying on her fragrant bed as she dried his tears and tried to comfort him.

"Loyal guards helped us escape through the postern gate," Orestes said, "and from there we fled into the night and the rugged wilderness. Aegisthus had his men watching the southern roads, so we took the most unlikely course, north toward Phocis, where my father's sister was wife to King Strophius. I wish I could tell you that our journey was uneventful, but alas, no." What a liar! Orestes relished recounting his adventures.

"Aegisthus, that foul usurper, sent his ruffians to track us down and do away with us. Most were thickheaded men with brawn but no brains, and we lost them easily, but two were skilled hunters. I, however, had a brave companion..."

Chrysothemis chose that moment to lean in and whisper, "Please! Timon was a grouchy old bore."

Trust her to ruin a good hero tale. I hushed her to keep from missing anything.

Orestes continued, oblivious to her side comment. "Timon was unaccustomed to rough living or long-winded treks through the mountains. I steadied his resolve through my steadfast example, even at my tender age." Now he had begun boasting, although it was not such an exaggeration to those who had known him as a child, when he used to drag his pedagogue around with him on his excursions. "I hunted and found shelter for us. He kept me company, comforting me like a father during those difficult days.

"Together, we ambushed the remaining trackers. From a ledge overlooking a narrow goat path, we loosed a hail of stones upon the first man, pitching him into a deep gorge. It was no easy feat, for we had to climb twenty feet up the rock face to reach the ledge. I was light on my feet, though, and knew how to find hand and footholds. I encouraged Timon, helping him when his strength began to waver."

"You should've let him fall!" cried a drunken man in the audience. "Useless!"

Irritated hushes silenced the catcalls. Orestes waited a space to resume speaking. "Timon might have been old, but he was far from useless. He helped me collect rocks to rain down on our pursuer, and it was he who bravely offered himself as bait to catch the second tracker, and afterward it was he who saved my life.

"I wrestled the man in the open," Orestes said proudly. "I fell upon him as he lifted his axe to sever my brave companion's head. We traded blows back and forth, cutting, slashing, and bruising each other." I doubted the struggle had been quite as glorious he claimed, but more squalid and vicious.

"I took a wound upon my thigh grappling with him," he continued, "and as the blood flowed he knocked the blade from my hand and laid me flat out on the ground. I had no other followers, and it seemed as though the villain would cut my throat, yet at that very moment my father's ghost whispered in my ear what to do. So as that vile tracker pressed his dagger against my throat, I grasped around in the dirt for a stone and with it, bashed in his skull until his brains leaked from his ears."

I saw my father's mouth hanging open. Not a single soul moved or made a sound, not even old Lord Peukestas, who hacked on his own phlegm from morning till night.

"I did not come away from that battle a conquering hero," Orestes admitted. "I was gravely injured, and could go no farther. Now, I had learned from a tender age how to suture a gash, but we had neither needle nor sinew, and my companion lacked the stomach for the task. So I cauterized the wound myself, with my own dagger. To this day, I bear a scar where the modest ladies of the court would blush to look."

Titters rose from the court ladies, who had been ogling and flirting with him throughout the evening. Obviously my father had not yet told Orestes that the court matrons would get a good look at his scars and all his other assets during the ritual wedding bath.

"A shepherd's dog found our hiding place. His master was a kind-hearted man who sheltered us and nursed me through the fever that followed. It was four weeks before we could travel again, and cover the remaining distance to Phocis, where, in my uncle's stronghold at Krisa, I revealed myself to the queen and showed her my father's seal. Anaxibia, that most gracious lady, took me under her protection, and introduced me to my uncle the king, noble Strophius, and to my cousin and dearest friend, the valiant Pylades."

"Tell us more!" An inebriated graybeard pounded his fist on the table, interrupting Orestes with slurring catcalls. I recognized Paios as one of the many councilors who had sat around the great court debating Orestes' dilemma as a philosophical exercise. "Give us how you slew Aegisthus and that scheming, husband-murdering bitch!" Other fists banged the table; the men were getting too deep into their cups.

Orestes shot him a furious look. "Enough!" His bellow gave me a start. "Old man, do you dare insult the mother who bore me?"

Paios sat bolt upright. Menelaus, not about to let a royal guest suffer embarrassment in his hall, slammed down his cup and started to his feet. "Apologize!"

Orestes had the situation under control, though. Paios was not about to further cross a man who could rip his head from his shoulders, but sent his silver bracelets to the high table as a peace offering. Orestes drank once again from his cup, using the interval to let the man squirm a bit before giving his answer. "So you all wish to hear about Aegisthus, do you?"

Menelaus interjected, "King Orestes, you are our honored guest. You need not tell that tale."

"No, let them hear how Aegisthus died. I should be glad to tell that story." Orestes saluted the courtiers with his cup. "On that day, brave Pylades and I entered Mycenae's lower citadel disguised as workmen. I remembered Aegisthus's habits well, and knew that in the mornings he liked to go down to the workshops.

"Now some say we caught him in the men's sanctuary, and cut him down while he prayed. It was not so. Aegisthus always made his offerings in the evenings, to thank the gods for having granted him yet another day to enjoy his ill-gotten gains. No, we took him in the morning, the day after the harvest festival, when the guards were still thickheaded from too much drink and celebration.

"I climbed to the head of the great ramp leading up to the palace, and there awaited my enemy. And when he at last appeared, I stepped across his path and called him out—wife-stealer, murderer, usurper, vile spawn of incest!"

With each epithet, Orestes stabbed an accusing finger toward an imaginary foe at the hearth. "Yet rather than face me with a man's courage, he cried out for help, help, because Orestes, Agamemnon's son, had come to murder him." He characterized Aegisthus with a shrill falsetto that made my skin crawl. "How many men do you think rushed to his aid? There was no one," he shouted, "for treachery and evil deeds beget no friends!

"We fought to the death upon the great ramp, first with sharp bronze, and then with our bare fists. Evil words spewed like curses from his mouth. I shattered his teeth with my knuckles, then took off his head with a single cut to the neck." Orestes pantomimed a sword's sweeping arc. He relished the details as any warrior might, but visualizing his homicidal rage made me queasy. "As Aegisthus's trunk slumped to the ground, it spewed gobbets of black blood. I tossed the severed head down the ramp, where it tumbled like a stone, spitting out blood and gore all the way to the Lion Gate.

"As for what came next..." Orestes directed his menacing gaze toward an ashen Paios and anyone else who might challenge him. "We respect the laws of gods and men, and the womb of the mother who bore us. It is a matter never to be discussed in our presence."

An anxious silence fell over the megaron; one could hear the logs crackling and spitting on the hearth. Then Menelaus stood, embraced his guest of honor, and proclaimed the tale well told. "The hour grows late." His awkwardness showed in his voice. "Let's have more wine, and a final libation. Join us, King Orestes."

After performing his ritual duties, Orestes rejoined me at the high table. He was glowering. "I meant only to tell about my adventure with Timon, but..." His chest heaved with a mighty sigh.

"I wouldn't have asked you to tell that story," I said.

"That's because you don't regard me as a curiosity, a freak of nature." Orestes managed a slight smile. "It might surprise you, but my life as king is quite ordinary. There are petitions to be heard, advisors to consult, and tallies to be taken. Alas, I fear our life together will be rather unremarkable."

I laughed softly. Elsewhere in the hall, several ladies and graybeards were taking their leave; the feast had concluded with the last libation. Soon, I would have to bid my fiancé goodnight. "I don't mind at all. In fact, King Nestor once advised me to flee if a hero ever came for my hand."

Orestes grinned sheepishly, his sour mood forgotten. "I thought women adored heroes."

Now he was just teasing me. "Speaking of heroic exploits, you never told me you were injured during your flight to Phocis. Was it true what you said, that you were wounded and had to cauterize the gash yourself?" I had no doubt that he bore a scar; he would not be so foolish as to lie about it when he knew others would look for the evidence.

A nod. "We had no sinew or needles, and I was almost unconscious from blood loss. And Timon didn't know how to suture a wound, anyway. It was either a red-hot dagger or bleed to death."

I felt a twinge of sympathy for the frightened twelve-year-old boy bleeding to death in the wilderness, but then remembered what else he had said when he had flirted with the ladies of the court. "Is it truly in an unmentionable place?"

Orestes threw me a playfully lascivious wink. He was enjoying this far too much! "You'll have to wait for the wedding night to find out."

CHAPTER TWENTY-FIVE

I STARED BLEARY-EYED at the hazy morning light streaming through the window, and tried to clear my head. I had drunk too much the night before. It took me a moment to recall that Orestes was here in Sparta, that the king of Mycenae had come for me. Our reunion and the betrothal feast that followed still felt unreal, more like a daydream conjured by a lovesick girl than the result of my mother's machinations and my father's compliance.

Monime entered carrying a basin of steaming water. "Mistress," she said softly, "the queen says you must hurry. You are going to see your betrothed this morning." Thebe came in with the breakfast tray, and behind her five servant girls bearing jugs filed into the bathroom. I heard water splashing into the tub.

So the daydream was real. "How soon?" I asked, yawning.

"An hour." Monime handed me my dressing gown. Thebe took a fingerbowl of goose fat from the breakfast tray and began blending it with red ochre from my cosmetic box to paint my lips.

I had no appetite, only a fierce longing to see Orestes again. "What do you think I should wear?" Since when had I cared so much about impressing a man? But Orestes liked me in blues and greens. "Did my mother say it was to be a formal meeting? Do I have to dress for the megaron?"

"No, Mistress." I caught Monime exchanging smiles with Thebe. How like Chrysothemis I sounded! "The queen says you will have an hour to visit this morning. She is also coming this afternoon to help you choose your wedding clothes."

I forced down my bread and honey. After my bath, the maids dressed my hair, and chose my gown and jewels. Thebe was still arranging my curls across my forehead when my chaperone, a dour court matron, arrived to escort me. "We will be going to the ramparts, Princess," she informed me. "You and the young king may talk and take your exercise together, but there will be no kissing, no lewd behavior."

With her, that meant no handholding or laughing, either. Hebe was my mother's creature through and through. I decided to confront her now, to make my position clear, before she embarrassed me. "I am a widow with an impeccable reputation, and King Orestes is my kinsman."

Hebe remained unperturbed. "He's also a lusty young man and your betrothed."

Let her grouse and gnash her teeth all she liked. I was a grown woman who knew how to behave in public with a man.

It was a crisp, beautiful morning, and everyone seemed delighted to greet the new day. I felt like dancing. Scrub maids exchanged smiles with me. Sentries saluted my passing. I must be the happiest woman in all Sparta.

Orestes met me on the circuit wall overlooking the Eurotas. Ignoring Hebe, I let my betrothed take my hands and kiss me on both cheeks, where the soft touch of his lips ignited a blush that traveled all the way down to my breasts.

At first, we accomplished nothing beyond holding hands and staring speechlessly into each other's eyes. It was one thing to look at someone indoors, by firelight, but quite another to see them under the bright sun. Orestes still owned the most brilliant blue eyes I had ever seen. He wore his red-gold hair cropped unnaturally short; he had told me last night that the Delphic priests had shorn it for his ordeal, and it had not yet grown out again.

He spoke first. "You look beautiful."

"You used to say that to me all the time as a boy." Hearing him say it again in a grown man's deep voice set my heart fluttering. "I'm amazed your friends didn't tease you about it."

"They teased me all the time, but none of them could boast about being betrothed to such a beautiful princess." Orestes laughed heartily. "Look at you! You're blushing bright red."

Here I was, a widow, flushed and excited like a virgin girl. "So you boasted?"

Orestes slipped an arm around my waist, despite a disapproving cough from my chaperone, and drew me closer. "Oh, I boasted about many things. My prowess in boxing and wrestling, my lovely betrothed, and the fine Trojan shield my father sent me."

Having him hold me, even in this light embrace, threatened to scatter my wits. "As I recall, your mother had that nailed to the wall where you couldn't get at it."

It was the wrong thing to say. I had not been thinking. Releasing me, he braced his hands against the ledge and stared out over the countryside. At last, he growled out, "It's still there. She left it for me."

"Orestes..." I did not remember his moods ever having been this changeable. "Forgive me." I set a hand on his broad shoulder. He was all solid muscle, under the rich dyed wool of his clothes.

Blinking, he shook his head trying to clear it. "It's not your fault. I have to stop brooding whenever someone mentions her." Then he forced a smile and turned toward me. "Let me tell you about all the changes at Mycenae. I had the entire palace renovated."

Now there was a subject we could discuss. "All of it?" I asked.

"Every last inch," he assured me. "Of course, Elektra fussed over the noise and mess. So I let her decorate the women's quarters, and choose the furnishings. She has good taste." Orestes gave me a genuine smile. "I hope you like your apartment. I told the artists you were to have blue and green, and whatever birds or flowers the Spartan ladies have on their walls."

I laughed, "Were you so certain my father would give you my hand?"

There was a sight, the king of Mycenae abashed and blushing like a little boy! "I wouldn't have left without asking for you." Orestes lifted his hand to touch my cheek. Hebe rattled her throat again. "You're the only woman I want as my queen."

Heat radiated from his body. I trembled at his light touch. "Has my father told you about all the rituals?" I asked.

"The bath and the pomegranates?" he replied. "It seems my comment about not showing the ladies my scar was rather premature, wasn't it?"

I noticed his gaze starting to stray, until he was staring at something behind me. "What is it?" Had someone come?

Then he smiled and focused on me once again. "I was looking at that peak with the five fingers. Is that Mount Taygete?"

I swatted him playfully. "Shame on you! You're not going climbing until after the wedding."

Laughing, Orestes hooked his arm through mine and escorted me back inside where it was warmer. There, in the corridor, we took our leave. I attended to my household tasks, while he, like any visiting king, discussed politics with the councilors and noblemen in the megaron.

That day, my father set guards upon the megaron's vestibule and galleries, prohibiting the court ladies and other, uninvolved parties from observing the meeting of the Spartan assembly. Yet the men's voices carried into the great court and the corridors beyond the galleries, and soon the palace was awash with talk of objection to the betrothal. Menelaus had violated his kingly duties by neglecting to inform the assembly beforehand. Moreover, Sparta's lords did not want an absentee king, which they would get with Orestes of Mycenae, and they would not tolerate losing its queen and her blessings to some other land.

Curse those old dotards! At last, Orestes had come to make me his wife, and the Spartan assembly threatened to undo it all.

Helen sent for me at once, ordered me to take the footstool beside her and sort through colored threads while she laid out the situation. "You're not to fret about anything. This is nothing more than the assembly exercising its right to gripe and grumble. You and Orestes will wed, and that's an end to the matter."

"They could deny Orestes the scepter," I said.

"Listen to you! Your father and I aren't going anywhere for a long, long time." Moons and suns blazed from the pale blue linen stretched taut across my mother's embroidery frame. "When the time comes,

Orestes will appoint a deputy to administer Sparta. He hasn't yet named one, but I expect it will be Aethiolas."

When I saw them later, Orestes and my father assured me that I would be wed in two days, no matter what threatened. "Though I may have to abduct you to do it." Orestes crooked a playful smile. "Would you mind, my dear?"

"Will you be gentle?" I could not let him see how much the mere mention of abduction and forced marriage bothered me.

Taking my hand, Orestes kissed it. "I shall dote upon you the whole way."

"Nonsense!" Menelaus huffed. "I have chosen the best man and given my consent before witnesses. The Spartan assembly will come to heel, whether they like it or not."

Orestes and I feasted again that night with the court. As more noblemen and their wives arrived for my half-brother's nuptials, they were delighted to hear their king had chosen a worthy man to wed his daughter; the assembly apparently did not speak for everyone, and there was, I learned, friction among its own ranks.

Aethiolas brought around several prominent councilors who expressed admiration for the respect and interest in local affairs that Orestes had shown during the afternoon's council. "Ignore the naysayers," the senior among them urged my betrothed. "You have a strong arm and Spartan blood, and will learn much under King Menelaus. Hold to that, and Mother Dia and Zeus Thunderer will smile upon your investiture when the day comes."

That speech and the others which followed heartened me. Orestes was courteous, though cautious and noncommittal; he did not trust strangers easily. "Those lords are men of their word, and they think you show great promise," I assured him. "Aethiolas wouldn't waste your time introducing them, otherwise."

"Aethiolas and I will get along well together. As for your other brothers—" Orestes nodded toward the table where my half-brothers sat surrounded by their companions. "Is Megapenthes always so sour?"

"Yes, but he's also jealous of you," I answered. At that moment, my younger half-brother caught Orestes staring; he offered an apologetic smile. "Let him sulk a bit. You'll fare better with Nikostratos."

Orestes dedicated the next morning to socializing with the young noblemen in the palaestra. Iphinous reported that they talked politics and war, and tested their mettle through wrestling and boxing. "Alas, my lady," the steward said, "your father the king took it into his head to spar with your intended."

"Is he injured?"

Iphinous shook his head. "No, it was his pride that suffered more than anything else."

When I attended my parents in the king's apartment, I found my father complaining to my mother about his aches and pains. "Good gods! Remind me to sit next time out." Menelaus winced, hissed under his breath as he rotated a bruised shoulder. "He throws like a Cretan bull!"

Helen wore a tolerant look as she rubbed hot oil into his sore muscles. "I warned you not to play with him."

Grimacing, Menelaus mumbled something unintelligible.

On that night, the wedding eve, there was no feast in the megaron. I spent my last hours as a widow in Mother Dia's sanctuary, where the priestesses arranged a bed for me before the altar, under the goddess's benevolent gaze. Young noblewomen arrived with honeyed wine and cakes to celebrate. Monime brought her four-stringed phorminx, but all the music we needed we supplied with our voices, clapping hands, and stomping feet. Even Polycaste took off her shoes to dance with us. "Rejoice with the goddess!" she cried. "Mother Dia loves your joy!"

MY MOTHER WOKE ME just before dawn. I yawned over my breakfast while my maids laid out my clothes. Therapne was celebrating a double royal wedding today, and once the day with its many ceremonies began, we would all be far too busy and excited to rest.

I knelt before the altar to dedicate my widow's veil and receive Hera's blessing. Polycaste placed a grandmotherly kiss on my cheek. "Don't be afraid," she whispered. "He loves you, and you love him. Tonight will be wonderful."

Dawn tinted the east with streamers of soft rose and lavender as we returned to the palace. Smoke from the open-air altars curled against the lightening sky, and the smell of roasting meat hung in the air as the bridegrooms and fathers performed the sacrifices.

Chrysothemis languished in bed, stricken with morning sickness; she would not be accompanying me to the king's ritual bath. I hoped she felt well enough to join the wedding procession.

A Spartan king-consort had to be without defect, and it fell to the queen mother and the court matrons to examine him for deformities before letting the bride anoint him. Menelaus escorted his prospective son-in-law to the door, as Tyndareus must have done with him on his wedding day, blessed the endeavor with a hearty chuckle and slap on the shoulder, and left Orestes to the women's mercy.

Orestes blushed to his very roots as the bare-breasted matrons swarmed in around him to disrobe and examine him. They took turns feeling his bulging biceps, and running appreciative hands over his broad chest and flat stomach; they even touched the shaft dangling between his muscled thighs.

"What a specimen!"

"He's built like an oak."

"Ah, but does he have a stout limb or a green twig?"

Orestes shot me a questioning look; he did not know whether to be flattered or downright embarrassed. I smiled back, both to reassure him and conceal my irritation with the matrons, who were enjoying themselves far too much for my pleasure.

Helen clapped her hands to marshal the women to the corners. She was dressed as a high priestess, in a leather bodice and seven-tiered flounced skirt, her long ringlets spilling from her high headdress; she seemed to have emerged from a Cretan fresco, where the artists always depicted their goddesses half again as large as their supplicants.

Once the matrons had their turn, Helen carried out her own inspection, touching, squeezing, and scrutinizing her prospective son-in-law. She took his manhood in hand, measuring him. I cringed. Orestes did not enjoy her attention, but stood there anxious and uncomfortable.

At last, she called out, "The king is without imperfection!" I exhaled a sigh of relief. Of course, the scar tissue running along his thigh was no impediment to his kingship—because he had gotten it in battle, it was a badge of honor—but one could never be sure where a priest or priestess might find an ill omen. "Now let his queen come forward with the scented oil and anoint him."

A matron handed me a stirrup jar of oil. Another brought the sand and strigil. Orestes sat down on the footstool in the middle of the bathroom to allow me to work sand and oil into his shoulders; his skin was still rosy and warm from the real bath he had taken after performing the blood sacrifices at dawn. I wanted to be alone with him, free to explore his muscles bunched under his freckled skin, and to delight in the feel of his bare skin, but my mother's presence turned my nerves to dust and my hands to clay.

"The queen chooses her bridegroom!" Helen began to rotate her hips and snap her fingers. "She smothers his skin in consecrated oil!" The glittering amulets sewn to her skirt tinkled with her movements, and her bare feet drummed a rhythm upon the stucco floor. "She blesses his sacred rod!" Her snaky ringlets swayed with her movements. "She moistens the way!"

There was much about Helen that was ancient and inscrutable; her kharis radiated through her skin. It was not often that she chose to lift the veil and become the goddess-on-earth, but when she did she outshone women half her age. Orestes sat up straighter, and followed her every move, where he had not noticed her before.

I concentrated on working the strigil across my betrothed's naked skin to scrape away the oily sand, as he reached behind him to take my hand and squeeze my fingers, an intimate little gesture to tell me he loved me. Helen finished her dance, though the spell she cast lingered. Orestes released my hand, allowing me to take a cloth and blot away the excess oil.

Sparta's new king had been anointed. Now we dressed Orestes in his wedding finery. I fastened his pale blue cloak with an enormous gold and amethyst brooch, and set his gold circlet upon his brow. He slid thick gold bands around his wrists, and then, garbed as a king and bridegroom, took me in his arms to kiss me full on the mouth. All the matrons mock-scolded him, laughing. I started to twine my arms around his neck, when a word from my mother jolted me back to reality.

Orestes left to join my father in the megaron. It was now time for the matrons to attend to my toilette. A steaming bath awaited me in my apartment. My mother's handmaidens washed my hair and rubbed me down with fragrant oil, after which my women dried me with soft linens, and oiled and rolled my hair into wooden curling pins.

A shaky Chrysothemis appeared in time to watch Thebe apply my cosmetics. Erigone came with her. She looked lovely in blue, but was very pale and frightened. Helen had at last impressed on her the fact that she was a young noblewoman who was expected to make an appearance no matter how sick, scared, or miserable she was.

I held out my arm. Alcippe slid golden bangles over my wrist. "Erigone, you mustn't be afraid when you meet Orestes. He's not here to harm you."

Erigone shook her head. "He's a monster," she whispered.

"I know what you saw that day, but that wasn't him. Those were the Erinyes raging inside him." I reached for my jewel casket and started rummaging through it. Erigone mewled in protest, "No trinkets."

"This isn't a trinket." I searched through necklaces, bangles, and earrings for Aegialia's amulet, at last finding it tucked into a corner near the bottom. "This is Mother Dia," I said. "Someone gave her to me long ago when I was hurt and afraid. Now you can let her watch over you."

Erigone took the goddess in both hands. "Thank you."

I kissed her cheek as she bent down to let me loop the chain around her neck. "Go over to the altar and ask Dia to watch over you."

Then it was time to get dressed. Like a vapid girl, I had agonized two entire days over my costume, and even now questioned my choice. Should I wear the open bodice my mother had embroidered but which had gone unworn for my first wedding? Would a seven-tiered skirt look more becoming than chevron flounces?

I was being ridiculous. Only virgin brides showed their breasts on their wedding day, and my chosen skirt was fit for a queen. Thebe lowered a fine linen shift over my head and secured the ties at my shoulders. Adreste helped me into the azure bodice edged with golden scallops, and Monime fastened the skirt, which was brand-new, sewn with golden roundels along its banded azure and turquoise hems. Alcippe cinched the golden leather girdle stitched with freshwater pearls tight around my waist.

Phylo tied gold and lapis beads around my neck, and hung matching drops from my ears. Maybe more pearls, or perhaps some rare turquoise along with the lapis would better compliment the skirt... Would that be too much? Gods, I had to stop fretting over small details!

Adreste unfastened the curling pins and twisted my ringlets down my back with blue ribbons, leaving my head bare for the daisy diadem.

"You look beautiful!" Chrysothemis exclaimed.

Briseis had said that, too, on the day I married Neoptolemus, but this time I truly felt it. I was beautiful and radiant, desirable and regal—and wanting very much for my bridegroom to set eyes on me in my wedding finery.

I scrutinized my bodice and skirt for imaginary wrinkles, felt my earlobes to make sure the lapis drops hung properly, and restrained the urge to touch my hair, for too much fussing would ruin the curls.

With the ladies of the court in their jewels and colorful robes attending me, we wound our way down the stairwell like a garland of bright blooms, and crossed the great court. The doors to the megaron stood open. As the herald announced the queen and the princess of Sparta, the men congregating by the hearth ceased their talk and respectfully shuffled to their places.

I saw my father and Orestes waiting together by the dais; they exchanged nods of approval, and smiled at us. Polycaste was there, also, amid a knot of priestesses. She wore the moon-mask above a scarlet bodice. A mottled snakeskin fastened her girdle.

I was not permitted to stand beside my betrothed until the wedding rites began. Oh, let it be soon!

Moments later, laughter and girlish squeals from outside announced the less-dignified arrival of the second wedding party. Megapenthes and his friends were flush with excitement from the ritual abduction, and he carried his young bride across the threshold to present her to our father. I knew he resented having to share a wedding day and our father's attention with Orestes, but thus far he was managing to conceal his bitterness.

Panope was a pretty fifteen-year-old girl who seemed content with her handsome bridegroom. Alector handed her to Megapenthes to signify he approved the abduction. Polycaste bound their hands with a scarlet ribbon, and thus joined together they made a circuit of the hearth before taking their seats to the left of the dais.

Then it was my turn. Helen and the court ladies led me back outside, and sang the bridal paean as Orestes hooked one arm around my waist, the other behind my knees, and lifted me over the threshold; as my husband and the future king of Sparta, this would one day be his house, too. I clung to his neck, smelling his skin and the scented oil rubbed into his short hair, and did not want the moment to end.

Orestes set me down before the hearth. Menelaus came over to me, kissed both my cheeks, then took my hand and gave me to my bridegroom. "Orestes, son of Agamemnon, take our daughter Hermione with our blessing. Make her your lawful wife and queen."

Polycaste bound our hands with the scarlet ribbon. "Great Mother Goddess, Queen of Heaven, you who are called Hera, protectress of marriage, witness these wedding rites! Bless Orestes, son of Agamemnon, as he leads Hermione, daughter of Helen, from her house of mourning and makes her a joyful and fruitful wife."

Helen carried the queen's ritual pomegranate around the hearth. A sacrificial dagger flashed in Polycaste's hand, and she sliced and broke the fruit open to reveal the arils nestled like rubies inside. "Great Mother Goddess," she intoned, "you who are known as Hera, most holy protectress of marriage, bear witness as the sacred queen of Sparta, your mortal servant on earth, sanctifies her sacred king."

I fed my bridegroom the three holy pomegranate seeds that would bind his blood, bone, and spirit to Sparta as dread Hades had bound Koré to the underworld. A hot flush passed through me with the offering of each aril, as Orestes found in the ritual an excuse to suckle my fingertips. "Orestes, son of Agamemnon, be my husband." My voice shook with desire and the gravity of the moment. "Rule Sparta with me as my sacred king."

Gazing deep into my eyes, he covered my hands with his, and said, "I, Orestes, son of Agamemnon, will be your husband and rule by your side as your sacred king."

And then, to my complete surprise, he gently took the pomegranate half from me, and his thick fingers plucked loose a seed to brush against my lips. "Hermione, daughter of Helen, be my wife. Rule Mycenae with me as my sacred queen."

Murmurs passed through the crowd at his unorthodox amendment to the rite. I let him press the seed into my mouth, and savored the tart juice as my teeth broke the tender skin. Now I was shaking all over, about to cry. "I, Hermione, will be your wife and rule Mycenae by your side as your sacred queen."

Orestes and I sat down to receive the traditional accolades. Megapenthes wore an ill-concealed glower when he observed the gifts the guests bestowed on my new husband and me. Having a second wedding thrust upon them at the last second meant that many were at a loss to produce enough suitable gifts, with the result that the future king of Sparta invariably took precedence over bastard Prince Megapenthes.

His roiling jealousy pricked me throughout the ceremony, souring what should have been a wonderful episode. I pitied his young bride. Panope sensed his changing mood, and within a few hours she went from radiant to subdued. For her sake, I hoped his temper improved by tonight.

In the afternoon, we sat down to a splendid feast. Mouth-watering aromas had permeated the air all day, and I had eaten very little that morning, so my belly growled anticipating the succulent roast meats, grilled fish and vegetables, stuffed breads and pastries about to be brought in.

First, Menelaus offered the libation. "Zeus Thunderer who watches over us, receive this drink offering to honor the marriage of our daughter Hermione to Orestes, son of Agamemnon, and king of Mycenae." Droplets of wine splashed upon the hearth. And again, he offered the libation for Megapenthes and his bride.

Servants carried in the first course: olives stuffed with goat cheese, oysters in seasoned olive oil, and fried bread. Others mixed wine and water in large kraters to pour into serving jugs.

Orestes insisted on feeding me from his own plate. "You're picking at your meat like a sick child," he said. "I thought you were hungry."

"I *am* hungry." It was hard to concentrate on eating among all the noblemen and their wives ingratiating themselves into our company trying to win my husband's favor. "There are simply so many well-wishers."

"They are rather bothersome, aren't they?" Orestes popped a morsel of fish into his mouth.

The whole scene with its dancers and tumbling acrobats, gossiping ladies in their sparkling jewels, rich food, and music took on a peculiar dreamlike quality, as though any moment now I would wake to find myself alone in my bed, with Orestes still far, far away.

On my right, Chrysothemis gave me a sudden pinch. "Smile!"

I realized to my dismay that I had been brooding. "My mind is a hundred miles away."

"Cheer up and don't drink too much. At least Orestes *wants* to do it with you." Chrysothemis indicated Panope sitting with Megapenthes and her parents farther down the high table. Alcohol only served to draw out my half-brother's gloominess. "How grateful I am not to be her, losing my maidenhead to that sourpuss."

She always dwelled on the most unpleasant things, and her words reminded me that there was still the wedding night to come. Would loving Orestes and wanting him suffice to make me enjoy our first time together, or would I lie frigid and apprehensive, as I had with Neoptolemus? I did not want anything to spoil our intimacy, and yet, he was not my first man, or even my second, and I still did not know how to take pleasure in sex.

Sunset came and went, spilling its ruddy brilliance across the hall's wide threshold. As twilight fell, the servants lit more lamps. Antimachus performed a song about Eros and Psyche, the mortal girl whom the young god had loved so much that he defied his own mother to rescue her from death. I choked back tears when Psyche held up a lamp and found not a monster but a beautiful young man lying beside her. And later, when Eros, having abandoned her in anger, kissed her cold lips to revive her, and took her to Olympus to make her his immortal bride.

Orestes let me lean against him throughout the performance. "Women cry even when the song ends happily." he observed good-naturedly. Chrysothemis was sniffling into a linen cloth on my other side. "Should I forbid my bard from ever performing that song?"

"Don't you dare!" I said, playfully shoving his arm. "I have to have something sweet, sad, and romantic to enjoy while you men boast about your deeds."

Orestes planted a soft kiss on my temple. "Not to worry. Elektra won't have it, either."

Antimachus received the audience's applause, and normal conversation resumed. Soon, it would be time to bed the brides. My stomach fluttered with tremulous anticipation.

"Welcome, my honored guests!" My father's sudden exclamation drew my attention to a dark-haired young stranger receiving a princely reception farther down the table. "Join the feast!"

Whoever he was, the young stranger must be an important visitor, yet it was his companion who brought me up short. Oh, no! It could not be! What in the world was Nestor's youngest son doing here on my wedding day?

Peisistratus was congenial, paying his respects as if he had never been a suitor for my hand, and inclined his head toward my husband. "I have heard much about you, King Orestes," he said, shaking Orestes' hand. Orestes received Peisistratus graciously, though, sensing my discomfort, he kept a protective hand on my shoulder.

"How did you know to come?" I affected a casual tone. "Orestes and I were betrothed only three days ago. Are your father's messengers so blessed by Hermes nowadays that they travel on wings?"

Peisistratus's eyebrows crept up an inch. "Our presence is a fortunate coincidence, my lady." He, too, was cool and calm. "Prince Telemachus and I have come on another errand."

So the handsome young stranger was Odysseus's son. Orestes received him with great enthusiasm, reaching across the table to clasp his hand. "Then we are kinsmen, Telemachus."

We made room for the two men at our table, and sent for additional food and wine. Telemachus thanked us for the courtesy. "Forgive me for marring your wedding with my troubles, but King Nestor told me that Menelaus was among the last people who saw my father. I have been praying for some fortunate news to carry home." He heaved a dramatic sigh. "If not, then at least let me find someone who knows how my father met his end and where his bones are buried so I can retrieve them."

Orestes served Telemachus from the hero's portion. As the young man tucked into the roast sirloin, they discussed the suitors plaguing Odysseus's household. Orestes wasted no time in dispensing advice. "Don't waste time trying to negotiate with them. You must either kill them, or drive them out. Start with the two ringleaders."

"Believe me, I would have killed them long ago. Cut their throats and cleansed my father's house of their lawlessness." Telemachus narrowed his eyes. "But there are simply too many of them."

"If your servants are still loyal, there's much you can do." I smothered a chuckle as Orestes relished the chance to expound on a subject he knew so well. "I killed all the brutes Aegisthus sent to murder me, because I learned to be more cunning than they." This could go all evening, or until someone reminded the bridegroom that it was his wedding night.

Peisistratus cleared his throat to get my attention. "I must apologize for not pursuing the matter after Neoptolemus seized you." He hunched his shoulders. "When my father heard about the possible pre-contract, he judged it best to avoid a quarrel with Epirus."

Orestes would have come, regardless. "I see," I said.

As he started to reply, perhaps to argue his case further, the conversation ceased. My father rose to make the evening's penultimate announcement. "Helios has driven his shining chariot over the horizon, and now the sun has set. It's time for love play." Menelaus never waxed this poetic unless he was deep in his cups. And he was slurring his words. "Ladies, attend to the brides. Their eager young husbands are getting impatient listening to the old men talk!"

Raucous cheers and fists banging on tables greeted his remarks. I blushed as furiously as the virgin bride sitting at the end of the table.

Helen led the ladies who clamored around my chair to hustle me upstairs. I resisted them long enough to drop a few last words in my bridegroom's ear. "Telemachus will be here in the morning, love."

*****

AT LAST, WE WERE ALONE TOGETHER. I lay naked between lavender-scented sheets as my mother and the matrons had left me moments ago, and watched my bridegroom undress in the lamplight.

I wanted him to take me in his arms and fasten his mouth on mine, yet at the same time I wanted to withdraw, to be left alone and self-contained. For I had never been naked and intimate with a man by my own choice, and did not know what to expect with Orestes. It would not hurt this time. He was no Aegisthus, to be sure, but would he be like my first husband, young, rough and impatient, pushing me into accommodating his desire, or would he be considerate and gentle, taking his time? Was consideration and gentleness in bed a thing of myth? Polycaste seemed to believe so, but I was not so certain.

"You were having a marvelous time with Telemachus." Surely he could hear my heart racing. "I wasn't sure you would ever come to bed."

A mischievous twinkle danced in his eyes as he removed his loincloth and slid under the sheets beside me. "Your mother wouldn't let me forget." Orestes touched a hand to my cheek, brushing his thumb over my lips. I knew what was coming, and closed my eyes.

Kissing him felt good and natural. When his arms went around me, it felt so right, as though the gods had meant us to be together from the very beginning, yet it was not so passionate that my reason was entirely stripped away, as in the salacious stories women told around the well curb. I could think, and reflect, and realize that even the pleasure of our coming together could not quite banish old demons.

I ended the kiss before he did. "Orestes..."

"Hmm, what's wrong?" he asked. "Am I hurting you?"

"It's not your fault." This was so hard. "Forgive me." I felt the tears coming, when tonight should have been glorious; the wound surprised me with how raw it still was. With Neoptolemus it would not have been an issue; he was not linked with that incident. But Orestes... "I'm ashamed."

His callused fingers pressed against my lips to silence me. "There's nothing to forgive," he murmured.

This was a mistake. I could not bear to look at him. I should have remained silent, accepted his kiss, and let him take his pleasure. Now it was too late. "I'm sorry. A man wouldn't understand."

"Are you afraid you won't be able to please me?" I shook my head morosely, hating this whole ask-and-evade situation. "Then what is it?" Answering him, explaining my dilemma, would take only three words, but I could not get them out. Orestes expelled a wearisome sigh. "Is this about your first husband? Did he mistreat you?"

An Atreid woman was expected to be a lioness, not a cringing shadow. "This is not about him, but something that happened before, after your father died." I was starting to ramble, to cushion the blow with extraneous words. "I did not want it, it was forced on me, but—"

"Hermione, look at me," he said sternly, sliding his fingers under my chin to tilt my face toward his. "I told you there was nothing to forgive. I've known about Aegisthus for years."

He knew? Relieved, I leaned into his chest, sobbing like a foolish girl, yet somehow not at all sorry. A secret shared was a burden lifted. Those tears were a welcome release. "I never meant to spoil the occasion like this, but when the moment came..."

"Let's not talk about it again." I felt his lips move over my scalp, and his arms tighten around me. "I'm your husband now, and I say there'll no more tears on our wedding night."

It was some time, however, before we could begin again. I would have been content to lie snug in his arms until dawn, and make love some other night, but he was a man, with a man's hungers; it was remarkable that he held back as long as he did.

I closed my eyes and focused on the hot salt taste of his mouth on mine, the sensation of his muscular arms enfolding me, and the slow and sensuous way he caressed my breasts and belly.

Aphrodite did not visit me with fierce sexual hunger, or enable me to achieve passionate release when Orestes entered me and started to thrust his hips. Making love with him was safe and comfortable, without shame or frustration, but it was not the mindless passion engendered by Eros's darts. Orestes achieved climax without me.

Time might heal my inhibitions, or perhaps not. I remembered what my mother had said about married love, how gradual and contemplative it was. I nuzzled Orestes against my breast, stroked his sweat-damp hair and shoulders, and was content with what the gods had granted me.

I could hear my husband's heart pulsing through his skin, a soothing rhythm urging sleep. My eyelids grew heavy. I drank in his clean masculine smell, like new-mown straw, horse, and oiled leather, and the juxtaposition of his hard muscles sheathed in smooth flesh, so different from a woman's yielding curves.

After a short interval, Orestes stirred to fetch a towel. He returned to bed with two cups of wine, and mumbling a sheepish apology for not being able to manage a second round.

Orestes did not yet know me well enough to realize that I did not want to rush headlong into sex, no matter how much I liked him. Perhaps he was accustomed to sharing his bed with willing women, but for me it was somewhat disconcerting to go from sleeping chaste and alone to lying unclothed beside a man. I would have our intimacy grow naturally, to encompass more than just his body atop mine, and his manhood inside me. "It's all right. All this—" I made a sweeping gesture that took in the bed, and us, naked and drinking wine by firelight. "This is new to me."

"Did your first husband not enjoy your company afterward?" he asked.

I wished he would not ask about Neoptolemus. Next, he would want me to draw a comparison between them as lovers and men, and say that he was better. So I kept my answer neutral. "He liked to sleep."

Orestes tucked his arms behind his head, and stretched out atop the coverlet with the sensual languor of a man who knew full well what a magnificent physique he had. "Ah! He was a typical man, then." Chuckling, he grinned at me, coaxing a laugh from me. I had not expected him to make jokes on our wedding night. "Well, I have to warn you that I sometimes do the same."

"I don't mind." Lying there, with a smile on his face and the firelight playing over the hard contours of his body, he invited a woman's touch. I set aside my wine to snuggle against his warmth. "As long as it's with you, and no one else."

CHAPTER TWENTY-SIX

THE WEDDING FESTIVITIES LASTED SEVEN DAYS.

I spent each morning under an awning with my mother and the ladies of the court, watching the men compete. My husband cut an impressive figure among the boxers and wrestlers, fearlessly challenging the more seasoned competitors and giving as good as he got. Orestes had always been an aggressive athlete. In his letters, he had boasted about his victories, and judging from the way he strutted and flexed to impress me, he meant to do the same here.

"A typical man," my mother observed dryly.

"Megapenthes is doing likewise." I indicated my half-brother, limbering up for the footraces. Dressed in a scarlet kilt which displayed his broad chest and shapely legs, he made the unmarried ladies sigh, while his bride looked miserable at her mother's side. Although Megapenthes treated Panope with utmost courtesy in public, there was not the slightest hint of affection between them.

Helen snorted disdainfully at the spectacle of my half-brother preening for the ladies. "At least Orestes plays only to you." She leaned toward me and lowered her voice. "I see his charms are working. You're blushing like a virgin girl."

Next, she would want me to describe for her the wedding night in detail. I looked away. "Mother..."

Polite applause rippled along the stands, calling my attention back to the match. Orestes had slammed Ctesippus, a local favorite, onto his stomach, and now they were grappling on the sand. Orestes tried to lock Ctesippus into submission, as the man kept moving, squirming to keep my husband from pinning him. I heard grunts and slapping flesh.

Ctesippus's scarred cheeks and intimidating silences were enough to cow most opponents, but Orestes was a stubborn challenger, tackling his foe with single-minded determination until his tenacity began wearing the man down.

Wrestling was a sport that held little appeal for me. I had better things to do than watch half-naked grown men throw each other onto the sand and grapple like little boys, but all that changed with my beloved competing. I restrained an unladylike urge to shout encouragement.

Ctesippus refused to tap out, even for the king of Mycenae. Minutes dragged by. Orestes stumbled back when Ctesippus wriggled from his grasp and knocked him away. I gritted my teeth, knowing how deep Atreid stubbornness could run. Orestes was not some local youth who could gamely submit and then go home happy with having lasted this long against a fearsome champion, but a young king and warrior with something to prove.

My mother shook her head. "Neither one is going to yield."

An air of seriousness moved among the crowd as they realized the combatants were going to continue wrestling until someone fell down. Already, the two men were stumbling and lumbering on the sand like drugged bulls. I tore my gaze from my panting husband to gauge my father's reaction. Would he let them grapple to the end, or stop the contest before things got out of hand?

A horn sounded. Menelaus stood up to signal an end to the match. Even so, a man had to go onto the sand to separate the two men.

My father waited until both wrestlers regained their feet and were facing him. "Valiant Orestes! Fierce Ctesippus!" He toasted them both. "This has been a bout to be celebrated in feast and song! The honors shall be divided equally among you."

Neither Orestes nor Ctesippus liked having their match curtailed, and each morosely accepted his share of the winner's portion, which included bronze cauldrons and women skilled in weaving and other handiwork. I grimaced. Orestes could collect all the cauldrons and tripods he pleased, but any women he won had better remain out of my sight.

My mother observed the scene with aplomb. "Men are never happy unless they can pound each other black and blue. Castor and Polydeukes could never let two days pass without squabbling."

Watching my husband's attendants swarm around him prompted me to get up. "Excuse me, Mother."

Helen gave me a disapproving look. "Fussing over him will only encourage him further."

I found Orestes grousing to his retainers. "Just a little longer and I would have taken him." A murmured comment from his manservant drew his attention to me, and all at once the men observed a reverent silence. Orestes straightened his back, lifted his chin, and squared his shoulders like a conquering hero. "I fought like a bull."

"You're black and blue all over," I said reprovingly.

Orestes inspected his bruises with a shameless grin, and wore them like trophies as we returned to the palace. Claiming victory, he flaunted for the servant girls pouring his bath.

I dismissed the women, along with his retainers. "It's bad enough you won that Euboean slut, but now you're ogling the bath girls, too?" I gathered his clothes as he stepped into the bath. "You're too much."

"It's nothing, my love." Orestes sluiced hot water into his face. "I never laid a hand on the attendants. As for the Euboean, she's not half as lovely as you, and I can already see she's dull-witted. Elektra will know what to do with her."

I could not remain cross with him for very long. "You stubborn man." Having discarded his sweat-stained clothes, I returned with a sea sponge. "You would have kept at it out there until you dropped."

"Nonsense!" he cried. "Had your father given me but another moment, I would have pinned Ctesippus."

"Only because you would have collapsed on top of him." I threw the sponge at him; it bounced into the water. "Any more such foolishness and we'll have to bear you home on a litter. You won't be able to make love for a month."

Orestes laughed. "I foresee no such difficulty." Seizing me around the waist, he dragged me squealing across the naked lap to kiss me. Hot water sloshed from the tub and soaked through my gown. Neoptolemus had never been so affectionately playful. "These bruises are nothing. I've had worse."

His competitive spirit persisted. Later, he arm-wrestled my brothers and their retainers on the aithousa, demonstrated his strength in the palaestra, and sparred with my father, who once again ignored my mother's advice and sprained his shoulder.

Peisistratus and Telemachus stayed for the wedding festivities, even competing in a few events. Telemachus was an excellent runner and boxer, but a poor charioteer. He graciously refused my father's gift of a chariot and matched team, saying, "Ithaca has no meadows for horses to run about in. It's pasture land for goats."

Menelaus liked his forthrightness and good breeding, while snubbing my former fiancé insofar as the laws of hospitality allowed. For his part, Peisistratus remained unobtrusive and deferential.

Orestes owned impeccable manners, and said nothing to antagonize my father's guest, yet on those rare occasions when Peisistratus came too close to me, he assumed a possessive stance.

Peisistratus was in no position to offer a challenge even had he been inclined to do so. I breathed a sigh of relief when he and Telemachus departed, laden with gifts but no news about Odysseus.

Once the festivities ended, and the guests had gone home, Orestes settled down to the business of learning Spartan administration from my father. I often found him discussing legal matters and trade with my father's councilors, and on three separate occasions he heard petitions in the megaron. Menelaus declared himself well pleased with what he saw.

As the spring days lengthened and grew warmer, Orestes went hunting in the Taygetus Mountains with my brothers. Menelaus escorted him on a casual tour through Sparta to show him the fields and groves and marble quarries, and introduce him to his future subjects. I slept alone on those nights when he was away, and thought constantly of him.

As king of Mycenae, Orestes also had to attend to matters from home. Pylades kept him updated. In the evenings before we retired, he pored over petitions and tallies, and took particular interest in the Argive king's failing health. Cyanippus had not attended Orestes' coronation last autumn, but had made repeated requests—Orestes disparagingly referred to them as demands—that the new king of Mycenae visit him in Argos. I did not see what was so wrong in an elderly king wishing to extend hospitality to his neighbor when he himself could not travel, but Orestes clearly considered it a nuisance—no, a threat to his autonomy.

I had no idea he bore the Argive assembly such malice, but now he educated me on the subject of his grievances. Argos had done nothing to defend Agamemnon's followers from Aegisthus's depredations, and had asked the exiled young Orestes for concessions while promising nothing but air. Alas, their hands were tied! What a pity it was that they had no jurisdiction to arbitrate Mycenaean affairs! Yet at the same time, they claimed the authority to select Mycenae's kings. Argos could not have it both ways.

So I understood and sympathized with my husband's position, and even agreed to some extent with his ambitions. That did not, however, mean I wished to spend our newlywed evenings together talking about war when his tenderness and charm had begun to unlock the goddess inside me. Just to be near him made my pulse race and my thighs moisten. I wanted him to put aside his accounts, his grudges, and give me his undivided attention.

Enough was enough. I bundled my needlework into my sewing basket, crossed over to him, and, leaning over his shoulder, snatched the papyrus sheet from his hand. "There'll be no more of that tonight."

"Hermione..."

Holding the document behind my back, I bent down to kiss him. "This can wait until tomorrow."

He returned the kiss, albeit briefly. "By the way, did I tell you that your father's coming back to Mycenae with us? He wants to make an offering at my father's tomb and see all the changes I have made."

We could discuss it later. "It's late. Come to bed."

"I'm not tired yet."

Men could be so thickheaded sometimes. "I said nothing about sleeping, dear." Still withholding the document, I claimed another kiss, drawing it out, even using my tongue until he grasped my meaning. "Come to bed."

"Hmm," he hummed, turning in his chair to wrap an arm around my waist. "Don't ever do that in the megaron." He drew me closer. "You'll make the graybeards burn with jealousy."

Orestes managed to find the papyrus and loosen it from my grasp, but then let it fall to the floor before leading me to the bed.

He had done as he swore he would do and sent the Euboean woman to his sister, but that incident and the way the ladies of the court ogled him set a question burning in my mind. A few nights later, as we lay entwined in each other's arms, I asked, "I have been wondering. Do you keep any concubines?"

"I have one," he admitted. "Pylades gave her to me a few months ago."

"Is she pretty?"

A hearty laugh shook his frame. "Are you jealous? Chione works the loom, and minds her own business. Elektra makes certain my women cause no trouble."

Elektra. My kinswoman was far greater potential thorn in my side than a mere concubine. "I hope your sister doesn't intend to rule the household."

Orestes laughed again and kissed me. "You'll be mistress of the house, never fear. Elektra has always liked you." Then, he exhaled a ponderous sigh that told me all was not well with his sister. "She hasn't been the same since..." A pause. "Did you know she wrote a note to congratulate us?"

I nudged his ribs. "You said nothing."

"Because she's such a poor letter-writer," he answered. "You should have seen how she rode me when your father's ambassador arrived with his invitation. She said I had better ask for your hand, because she wouldn't tolerate any other woman as my queen." Orestes nodded. "I think it'll do her much good to have you there. She's been very lonely."

FIVE WEEKS AFTER THE WEDDING, an Ithacan messenger arrived bearing a letter for my father. I knew this because Menelaus greeted the message with a roar so alarming that all the sentries within earshot dashed with their spears and shields into the megaron believing the king was under attack, and the lords and ladies of the court came by their dozens to see what trouble or madness had afflicted him. Helen led her maids and mine downstairs, where we forced our way through an aisle the guards hastily cleared for us.

"Husband, what is the matter?" My mother wasted no time in approaching the dais, where my red-faced father stood hurling questions at the messenger, a young man wearing a harried look on his face. It must have been bad news.

Behind me, the crowd jostled and grumbled, and opened again to disgorge my husband and brothers.

"What is going on here?" Orestes' hand strayed toward his dagger. "King Menelaus, has someone done you harm?"

My father thrust the tablet toward him. "Read for yourself what that old dog has to say." I wondered who had written to him to elicit such a reaction. Had some disaster befallen Telemachus? Perhaps the suitors had succeeded in murdering him and forcing his mother into marriage.

Orestes sheathed the sword, took the message, and stepped to one side where a sunbeam slanting through a clerestory window offered sufficient reading light. Helen hastened to my father's side, where she admonished him in low tones to calm down lest he have a seizure. An irritable Menelaus, intent on his son-in-law's reaction, waved her away; she did not oblige.

Orestes chuckled over the letter.

"What is it?" Nikostratos asked. Murmurs in the crowd echoed his query. Telemachus and Penelope must be safe, then, and the news good, if it elicited such a reaction from Orestes.

"Husband, what is going on?" My mother's patience was visibly fraying.

"Odysseus, that's what!" he roared, shoving away her hands and getting to his feet "That thieving rascal who cost us seven years in Egypt decided to show his face once again in Ithaca." He heaved a mighty breath before continuing. "After ten years freebooting around the Aegean, he came home to slaughter his wife's suitors. Locked them all in the megaron, and butchered them with swords and spears and his great bow until he and Telemachus waded ankle-deep in blood." Grunting, he sought out the messenger, who, fearing my father's prodigious temper, had moved several paces back. "How many men does Odysseus claim to have slain again?"

"A hundred and eight, my lord," the young man stammered.

"So the old dog thinks he's Herakles, does he?" Menelaus turned to my mother and gestured. "Attend to this young man. Tonight we'll hear the entire story."

That evening, everyone who could manage it crammed into the megaron or loitered in the vestibule to listen to the Ithacan messenger relate his master's adventures. Despite his relative youth, the man possessed the poetic gift, for the tale he spun was an honest-to-goodness hero story replete with battles with monstrous creatures, strange lands, and buxom seductresses.

"I myself," he stated, "have seen a Cyclops skull tumble from the rocky Ithacan earth. Its single eye socket is large enough for a hero to thrust his fist into. Thank the gods that man-eating beast perished long ago, and that he and his ilk no longer trouble honest Hellenes, but such was brave-hearted Odysseus's misfortune that Poseidon's wrath led him to an island where these giants still dwell."

I leaned toward my husband, and whispered, "Do you believe him?" Odysseus was said to be a shameless liar.

"Some of it, yes," Orestes murmured back. "I've also seen the bones of monsters come out of the earth."

Whether or not the poet-messenger related the entire truth, it was an excellent tale, and all who heard it had a splendid time. Menelaus, mellowed by honey wine and the song of Odysseus, and rewarded the envoy with gifts. "When you return to Ithaca, young man, tell your king that we forgive him that unfortunate business in Egypt. His silver tongue and yours have once again saved his hide."

DISJOINTED DREAMS CHASED ME through the paths of sleep. I saw myself as a black crone stuffing sacred herbs into Orestes' mouth before sending him clambering up a stack of giant clay tablets to confront my mother, a bird-faced creature who had turned my father and the entire court into a menagerie of wild animals. Watching her try her wiles on my husband turned my stomach. Seeing him plunge a sharpened stake through her one eye intensified my nausea, until, crawling back toward consciousness, it dawned on me that the pain was real.

My diaphragm heaved a warning. Clapping my hand over my mouth, I stumbled from bed and through the bathroom curtain just in time to spew last night's supper down the privy.

Bare feet slapping across the floor brought my maids. Monime knelt down and wrapped an arm around me to support me through wracking dry heaves. Thebe wrung out a wet cloth to wipe my brow with, and then helped me rinse out my mouth once the heaving subsided. "Mistress," she asked, "do you want me to call a physician?"

A chill sweat filmed my body through my thin woolen shift. Maybe it was just nerves. I was not looking forward to the sea voyage, or leaving my Spartan home.

Or it could be something else. I tried to count back to my last menses. Almost seven weeks ago. What a fool I had been, not to have noticed something amiss! "Bring my mother," I said. "She'll know what to do."

Helen arrived wrapped in her dressing gown with unguents still smeared across her face. Once she saw my trouble, she sent for a midwife, a hook-nosed grandmother who subjected me to a thorough and embarrassing examination.

"You're soft," the crone said, feeling between my thighs. "It's just the right softness for a baby to take root in. Are your nipples getting darker?" She pinched them hard enough to elicit a cry, and grinned. "Ah, yes. A baby-seed is growing inside you."

I wished someone would send her away, with her probing wrinkly fingers and musty odor, but she was a servant of the goddess who had delivered many babies. My mother saw to it she had wine and meat and cloth for payment, and she withdrew. I lowered my shift and crawled back into bed.

Helen sent a maid for tea to soothe my nausea. "Eleuthia laughs over the troubles of mortal women," she commented wryly. "Children might be a blessing, but they're also an agonizing and embarrassing business. Learn to bear it. It is the goddess moving inside your mortal skin."

I ran a hand over my womb, although there was nothing to feel except the soft linen shift and my skin that warmed it. So I was not a barren field. A seed was gestating inside me, a sprout that would one day bear fruit. "I will be sick again tomorrow, like Chrysothemis," I said.

"Not every child sits so in the womb," Helen told me. "It's not good for your health to worry over a little morning sickness. Believe me, the aches and strains will come soon enough." She drew a fleece over me. "You will not work today, but lie here and think good thoughts."

Chrysothemis heard the news, and burst into my apartment radiating good cheer. "Oh, I know! It's dreadful now, not being able to keep anything down, but it goes away after a few months. Thank Mother Dia for that!" She smoothed her dress taut over her four-month belly. "Aethiolas calls it a little pimple."

I was going to miss her silliness. I was going to miss Erigone, and my mother's handmaidens, the ladies of the court, and Polycaste. Mycenae's high priestess was a dour old crone, and its cult house a foreboding place haunted by ghosts. There would be no more excursions to the riverbank to feed the swans, and no more afternoons spinning with my mother, or helping her distill scented oils or medicinal herbs. Elektra promised to be a imperfect substitute for all I was leaving behind.

Polycaste undertook a second examination under my mother's watchful gaze, but this time it was for show, to honor Dia. The high priestess rubbed my nipples and peered between my legs, but did not probe me there. "You are exalted in the goddess's eyes," she said. Her joints protested as she got up from the bedside chair. I rose with her, to let her gather my hands in hers and kiss them. "Eleuthia has blessed the sacred heiress's womb."

Chrysothemis and several court matrons joined us in anointing the kourotrophoi upon my altar, and giving thanks. Polycaste chanted over me. "This is the season for tilling the earth, for sowing the man-seed. Remember Mother Dia. Honor her as Eleuthia, and she shall make you fruitful. Honor her as Artemis, and she will watch over your children."

Orestes returned from the hunt late that afternoon. It did not take long for the news to reach his ears. Ecstatic, he burst into my bedchamber, swept me into his arms, and planted a kiss on my mouth. "Is it true?"

I flung both arms around his neck. "He will be born at midwinter."

Despite my mother's objections, he kissed me again, drinking me in for longer this time. "I brought back some venison."

Just thinking about food turned my stomach. That night, my mother ordered for me small portions of soft bread, whipped eggs, and gruel from the kitchen, and shoved away the veal my husband tried to press on me.

"Stop fussing, Mother," I groaned. At least it was a private supper, without the entire court watching this farce. "I'm not an invalid."

"You need to keep up your strength," she said.

"Then stop feeding her slops." Orestes proffered the meat skewered on his knife.

"Ugh!" Chrysothemis wrinkled her nose. "Orestes, don't be foolish. Hermione doesn't want meat when she'll be sick again in the morning. Just give her a little mulled wine or some tea."

"She's my wife." Orestes gesticulated with the knife, shaking it and the veal at his sister. "I know what's best for her."

"Settle down," Menelaus said lightly. "It's always better when men leave these matters to the women."

Orestes subsided, sourly chewing the meat off his dagger while I choked down my gruel. That night in bed, he restrained his passion for fear he would hurt me or the baby. Having him make a scene at supper was one thing. This was quite another, and I did not like it. "Are you going to tiptoe around me for the next eight months?" I asked. "Women have babies all the time."

He turned his face from me. "I fear something will happen. The gods can be so cruel, playing games with us mortals, giving us what we most desire, then snatching it away again."

I flung my arms around him. "Here I am, blessed by the goddess after fearing I was barren, and all you can do is mope."

Orestes gave a deep sigh. "I have a great talent for that."

Sliding my hand under his chin, I urged him to look at me again. And when he did, I kissed him. "Let us choose a name for our son."

ORESTES LEFT MY BED in the gray and silent hours before dawn, so he was not there when the morning sickness resurged and sent me stumbling through the curtain to reach the privy. I spent the next several hours lying miserable in my chamber, leaving all the household and ritual duties to my mother.

A message came from my father, forbidding me to exert myself beyond what was absolutely necessary. When my mother came with her maids to supervise the packing of my belongings, she banished me to her apartment so the noise would not disturb me. I chafed at the treatment. A pregnant woman was not an invalid.

I felt well enough by early afternoon to return to my apartment, which was now a cluttered field of boxes and chests. It saddened me to see my rooms slowly stripped bare.

My family treated me like a delicate eggshell cup. My mother brought Polycaste for one last visit, rather than letting me visit the cult house, while my father curtailed the festivities celebrating my departure. "You can't be awake all night when you need your rest for tomorrow," he said.

I spent that last night unable to sleep but for two or three stolen hours. At first light, my mother came with her women to rouse me and make me ready for my journey. She watched me pick over my porridge and eggs, and pressed on me an herbal remedy she had discovered in Egypt. "It's very strong, so use it only when you absolutely must." She handed me a small wooden box. "I also made a list of herbs and foods for you to avoid."

These were to be our last intimate moments together. Fighting back tears, I leaned against her. "I wish you were coming with me."

Helen stroked my hair. "You speak as though we will never see each other again. Mycenae is not as far away as all that. I'm sure Orestes will bring you back to visit."

I wanted to stay like this, to freeze the moment forever to avoid having to let go. "It won't be the same."

"But nothing ever remains the same." Helen slowly drew back from the embrace. She wiped away her tears with delicate fingers, though she was smiling. "You will see. One day, you, too, will have to say goodbye to a daughter."

CHAPTER TWENTY-SEVEN

MY FATHER INSISTED I LIE DOWN in the covered mule cart during the five hour trip to Helas. "You need your rest, young lady."

"I feel fine, Father." I also knew that trying to close my eyes in the cart would increase my nausea. "Mother gave me one of her herbal remedies. I feel much better."

Menelaus relented and left me. Moments later, Orestes peered into the cart to raise the same argument. "Are you certain you don't want to lie down?"

I wanted to swat him. "I'm going to spend the next five days seasick. Go away, and let me enjoy the view."

Thebe tied back the goatskin flap to let me observe the green Laconian countryside. The air was cool, heavy with the scent of turned earth and cattle dung. Seeing our caravan amble past, farmers left their orchards and olive groves and tilled fields to acknowledge their king and the royal kinsmen. I waved to those who called out to me, while holding back sentimental tears.

As we entered the Eurotas estuary, the salty ocean breeze ruffled my hair. Seabirds circled above the marshes. In Helas, we rested the night in the governor's residence while the ships were loaded.

Just before sunset, Orestes accompanied me on an invigorating walk along the circuit walls. "Look there." He indicated the pentekonters down below; his four ships rested like beached whales above the tidemark. "And those five pentekonters next to them belong to your father. And beside them, where the men are loading the chests? You'll be traveling in the most comfortable merchant vessel the Peloponnese has to offer."

I nudged him affectionately. "That's not saying much."

Neither he nor my father told the sailors I was with child, on account of some ancient superstition about pregnant women at sea.

Late spring was excellent sailing weather, but sudden squalls always remained a threat. I feared being shipwrecked or attacked by pirates, even though Orestes assured me that the sailors were highly skilled, and that few pirates would dare engage nine pentekonters at once.

At night, the sailors grounded the vessels and built driftwood fires on the beach. Orestes made me sit near the fire and tried to press some skewered goat meat on me. All I could manage were a few figs.

"You're wasting away to nothing," he complained.

I did feel a bit weak and worn-out, but my mother's herbs were helping quell the seasickness and the morning nausea. "I'll feel better once we arrive."

Orestes had me sleep with him in his tent every night. Wrapping me in fleeces, he held me close, with his sword and shield at the ready should any brigands be foolish enough to attempt a night raid on our camp.

On the sixth afternoon, we entered Argive waters. Having sighted our ships, the warden of Tiryns sent a delegation to meet us on the beach and conduct us to the citadel. Orestes saw to my comfort before sending a message on ahead to Mycenae to inform Pylades that we had arrived.

I luxuriated in a terracotta tub, enjoying my first real bath in a week, and rested in a guest apartment overlooking the harbor. Aegialia was no longer there; she had been confined to a remote estate by her brother-in-law the Argive king, and had not been heard from in six years. I wondered whether she was dead. In her place, I was compelled to endure the warden's aging wife, who mothered me like a sick child once she learned about my condition.

"Thank the gods we're leaving tomorrow," I told my husband, irritably crossing my arms over my breasts, "or I would have to box that woman's ears. I'm not made of eggshells."

"Your father wants you to ride in a litter," he said.

Litters were for indolent court ladies and fat lords, and I would have none of it. "Tell him I mean to ride with him in his chariot like a proper queen."

"You could always ride with me," Orestes suggested.

I uncrossed my arms, my annoyance melting away under my husband's fond gaze. "Let him escort me. I think he would like that."

In the morning, I had my maids dress me in the lilac and royal purple costume I had worn for my first wedding, and arrange my hair in elaborate serpentine curls to fall down my back. The warden's wife fussed over imaginary wrinkles and dust, and tried my patience within a hair's breadth. I breathed an audible sigh of relief when Orestes came to my door to escort me downstairs.

He must have conveyed my wishes to my father, because Menelaus had already dismissed his charioteer when I climbed into his vehicle. "Since you insist," he said affectionately, "I'm taking over the reins and driving you myself." He had brought with him his favorite splendid scarlet and gold chariot, and had the stable hands attach a fringed canopy to shield me from the sun.

As we traveled the northward road, we attracted the notice of peasants working the fields and groves. Drawn like moths to the gleaming bronze and gold, the painted chariots with their royal occupants, and jingling bells, they gathered in droves by the dusty roadside to salute their young king and admire the elegant lady riding beside the great Menelaus.

Mycenae's high-walled citadel, sprawled like a golden lioness upon the knees of Mount Charvati, awaited in the distance. I gripped the chariot's guardrail to steady myself as the wheels jostled over a paved bridge. My back and thighs ached from maintaining the proper flexed-knee stance.

Fields and groves gave way to Mycenae's lower town. On the left, we passed Atreus's monumental tomb, its plastered beehive dome gleaming against the blue sky. Pylades had sent word down from the citadel, so people thronged the thoroughfare to welcome us. Women and little girls chanted my name, reached out their hands for my blessing, and tossed crocuses and daisies and cornflowers into the chariot. I heard the veterans and old men, who remembered my father from his youth, call out to him, but most of the cheers were for the handsome young king, son of Agamemnon.

Our passage through the lower town progressed in a chaotic rush of faces and bodies, cheering, and posies striking my skirts to land in the chariot, so it was with considerable relief that we approached the citadel where the welcome was more orderly. Sentries stationed along the ramparts fronting the Lion Gate drummed their spears upon their shields and shouted their allegiance to Orestes. Palace officials in their bright robes crowded the terraces.

Menelaus brought his chariot to a halt before the great ramp. Grooms rushed forward to take the reins. Great knots had formed in my back and shoulders, my knees wobbled, and my father had to brush aside all the flowers with his sandaled foot before I could step down. I took his proffered arm to let him escort me. Orestes walked with us on my right.

Yet more flowers spilled across our path as we ascended to the great court where Pylades and Elektra awaited us amid a throng of visiting Argive nobles and their wives. Elektra drew my immediate gaze. How could she not? Motherhood and time had transformed a strapping girl into a regal and formidable lady.

Menelaus greeted her first, taking her large hands and kissing them. "Young lady," he said, "it seems you've grown quite a bit since we last met."

Misty-eyed, she welcomed him.

Pylades was a tall, handsome man with black beard and vivid blue eyes. Three children also awaited us on the aithousa. The two boys, Strophius and Medon, were dark like their father, while the girl, Antiklea, was a darling, dainty five-year-old with copper-red hair; she cried a little when Menelaus, who was a complete stranger, admired and dandled her. Elektra handed her over to her nurse to hush.

"Our two youngest are still in the nursery," Pylades explained. Recalling Aethiolas's comment, I found that Elektra's husband truly did possess a very thick Phocian accent.

The Argive nobles and their wives followed us into the megaron. Fragrant pine logs burned upon the hearth. I held my breath against oppressive memories and slowly exhaled as I realized this was no longer the same megaron where the murders had taken place. Colorful new rosettes and checkered squares bordered the doorways, and a new lion hunt fresco had replaced the old one depicting warriors besieging a walled town. Reposing lionesses flanked the dais alongside the traditional goddess-sacred griffins.

Pylades performed his last act as regent, welcoming his king home with a silver rhyton for the customary thanksgiving libation. "Honor the gods for us, King Orestes."

To my surprise, Orestes stood aside, offering the rhyton to my father. "King Menelaus, as our elder and father-in-law, as a royal son of Mycenae, and our most distinguished guest, you take precedence over us."

People approved the correctness of his gesture. Menelaus raised the vessel in both hands to salute the gods. A trickle of wine splashed onto the hearthstones. "Poseidon, Father of the Sea, Artemis, Mistress of the Winds, and Zeus Thunderer, receive this libation of rich dark wine in gratitude for a safe voyage and a peaceful homecoming."

Once Orestes made his libation, he turned again to my father. "King Menelaus," he inquired, "who is this woman adorned with gold whom you bring into our house?"

Menelaus grasped my hand and led me to my husband. "King Orestes," he answered, "this is Hermione, our only daughter and the most precious jewel of our household. Will you accept her as your wife and queen?"

Orestes took my hand with a radiant smile. "We shall accept this woman with your blessing, and make her our wife and queen in this house."

Elektra brought the queen's crown, a hammered gold diadem radiating seven wafer-thin spokes, an heirloom of the house I had seen Clytaemnestra wear. Orestes fastened it around my head, and presented me thus to the people. "Behold Queen Hermione, the daughter of King Menelaus and Queen Helen of Sparta, and our beloved wife. Revere her as high priestess. Obey her as the mistress of the house!" he announced.

Then he handed me the rhyton. "My lady, we surrender into your keeping the cult house and hearth-gods of Mycenae. Honor them for us."

I stood where Clytaemnestra had once stood, and performed the rites as she had taught me. "Mother Dia, you who are honored here as Hestia, gentle Mistress of the Hearth, as Hera, Queen of Heaven, and as Athena, Mistress of Battles, receive now this drink offering." I tipped the rhyton to splash wine into the channel running among the hearthstones. "Let the wheat and barley ripen in the fields, the grapes burst forth upon the vine, and the olives bear fruit. Let the flocks multiply in the pastures. And let the mothers under your holy protection bear healthy children."

Orestes led me to the dais, and we sat down together as king and queen, with my father in the seat of honor. Orestes and Pylades had overturned the old Mycenaean nobility, executing or banishing those who had overthrown Agamemnon, with the result that there were many new faces among the courtiers.

After the nobles paid their respects, Orestes dismissed the court and closed the megaron. Elektra led me and my women upstairs to the queen's apartment. I held my breath in anticipation, remembering the vivid blood scarlet Clytaemnestra had loved, and also recalling my husband's comment that the apartment had been redecorated.

"Is it beautiful?" I asked.

"It's not as it was." Elektra opened the door. "Come and see."

Orestes had kept his promise. Soft greens and blues tinted walls decorated with lilies and darting swallows. I drank it all in. Clytaemnestra might never have been here.

In the bedchamber, a handsome inlaid bed covered with snowy fleeces and a pale blue woolen coverlet beckoned to me. The porters had already brought in my boxes and chests to let me unpack, but that could wait until tomorrow.

Elektra observed me in guarded silence. She was no longer the headstrong brat who used to strain her mother's patience, but a respectable matron wearing a subdued demeanor that seemed contrary to her nature. When Orestes had warned that me she had changed after the killings, I had not realized how profound the change would be.

"Are you all right?" I asked.

As she folded her arms over her ample bosom, her bangles clanked against her necklaces. "Fine."

I sat down at the dressing table to let Thebe untie the ponderous diadem. "What's wrong?"

Elektra set her jaw and bunched her mouth, but could not keep her bottom lip from quivering. I was thunderstruck. My stalwart sister-in-law was going to cry.

I swiftly dismissed my maids to the sitting room to await my pleasure, then snatched a linen cloth and went to wrap my arms around Elektra as the first sobs shook her stolid frame. "Oh, there's no reason to cry."

Elektra bawled on my shoulder, her weight dragging at my torso and leaving me unable to do much more than murmur reassurances in her hair. I could not fathom what had brought on this storm, only wait for it to pass.

She left my fine linen shift a sodden, paint-streaked mess. I handed her the cloth, which she blew into. "Forgive me," she mumbled. "I never meant to blubber like this."

"But what's wrong?" I pressed.

Elektra dabbed at her nose. "I was afraid you would shun me. Sometimes, they say I, too, am a matricide, for helping Orestes. They're afraid of me down in the sanctuaries and agora." She made no sense, and with her hair mussed and cosmetics smeared and smudged, she looked like a madwoman.

"Why would you think such a thing?" I exclaimed. "Why would I turn from you?"

"Chrysothemis wanted nothing to do with me, and my in-laws, and Pylades refuses to talk to me!" she spat. "*He's* the one who swore to stand by Orestes and then left him, but he calls *me* mad." She blew her nose. "Most people here in Mycenae expect me to burst into flame, like Medea. The rest call me the true daughter of Agamemnon, the faithful sister of Orestes, and I'm not sure that's a compliment."

What did she expect me to say, having laid her troubles in my lap so soon? "When we arrived, the people in the town and countryside cheered loudest for Orestes."

"Well, he's a man, that's different." Elektra's mouth twitched, and then she uttered a harshly ironic laugh. "I am glad it was you, and not some pretty but empty-headed maid barely out of her mother's womb." A tremulous smile played across her lips. "Orestes sent a message yesterday that you're with child."

Babies were a cheerful subject to talk about. "I have only known for two weeks."

"Then you're due at midwinter?" Elektra seemed more composed now that she had relieved her burden somewhat. She blotted her nose, noticing then how the linen crumpled in her hand was soaked and stained. "There must be water in the bathroom. I ordered the women to set it out for you."

We went into the cool chamber, and found water set out in an alabaster basin. "Did you bring things for the baby?" Elektra discarded the soiled cloth, then plunged both hands into the water and sluiced her face. "I have a cradle you can use, and good linen diapers."

Amid all the chaos, it had not even occurred to me to start collecting furnishings and clothes for the baby. Thank the gods my sister-in-law was a mother five times over, and knew what to do, and that there was ample time to make everything ready.

Elektra's troubles were a greater concern. I found a fresh cloth and handed it to her. "Are you truly all right?" I asked.

"I am as well as can be expected for a woman whose husband refuses to talk to her."

"Elektra..."

"It's nothing. Pylades is always a cold fish." Elektra patted her cheeks dry with the linen. Her entire face would have to be repainted, and her disheveled curls dressed again. A sigh escaped her. "At least now I have a woman to talk to who understands things."

NIGHTFALL REVIVED THE CITADEL'S SLUMBERING GHOSTS. Pylades and Elektra had arranged a sumptuous feast which filled the megaron with light and joyful music, but after the last libation was poured, the final toast made, and the guests began to withdraw, I sensed the darkness closing in. Suddenly, I dreaded going upstairs and lying down to sleep where so many unhappy Atreid queens had lain before me.

Whether Orestes noticed my apprehension, I did not know. More pleasant thoughts may have been meandering through his mind when he reached for my hand. "Let me escort you upstairs. You haven't yet seen the king's apartment."

I noted the familiar glint in his eyes. "Can't it wait until tomorrow?" I asked teasingly.

Orestes laughed, "Ah, but my bedchamber is best seen after dark."

Playing the coquette restored my spirits somewhat. "I thought you wanted to show me the entire apartment, not just your bedchamber."

He twined his arm through mine as we rose from the high table to leave the megaron. "You know, I've been waiting all these weeks to show you my seven-foot bed."

As we ascended the stairwell, I kept teasing him. "Is your seven-foot bed sturdy?"

"Quite!" he exclaimed.

"And how do you know for certain," I asked him playfully, "unless you've already put it to the test?"

Orestes hemmed and hawed a bit, which told me he had done exactly that, and with whom; I had yet to meet his concubine, Chione. Not surprisingly, his answer was evasive. "Then we shall have to test it ourselves, won't we?"

Turning the corner, we approached the royal apartments, and at that moment my mirth suddenly deserted me. I had never been in the king's apartments but once, on the day my aunt wrecked it to create a memorial for dead Iphigenia, yet it had been refurbished and occupied since Agamemnon's murder, and knowing by whom gave me pause.

"Orestes..." I hung back on the threshold as he opened the door.

His grin started to evaporate when he saw the look upon my face. "What is wrong?"

I chose my words carefully to avoid saying the dreaded name. "*He* used to sleep there, after you left." My chest felt constricted, my breath labored. "Does anything of him remain?"

Orestes grasped my meaning without further explanation. Taking the lamp from his manservant, he banished the young man and my women. "Hermione," he said softly, persuasively, "this apartment is mine, and mine alone." He extended his hand. "Come, let me show you."

I let him lead me inside. The darkness yielded the mustiness of old incense and the fresh masculine odors of oiled leather, cedar, and coriander. Flickering lamplight played against the sitting room walls, illuminating part of a fresco depicting supplicants bearing laurel branches and paying homage to a seated goddess whose arms were wreathed with serpents. An image better suited to a woman's sanctuary within the cult house than a king's apartment.

Orestes lit a second lamp on an inlaid cedar wood table, so I saw the gods arranged upon his altar. And there, with his enigmatic smile and serpentine lovelocks, was the kouros, the young god Apollo with sacred serpents twining up his arms.

A black and white shepherd dog looked up from a fleece spread out on the floor; with a great yawn, he rose and, wagging his tail, ambled over to smell me. He was an old dog, I could tell, but an amiable one. "This is Hermes," Orestes said. "I told you about him, remember?"

Hermes had discovered Orestes lying feverish and wounded after his near-lethal encounter with Aegisthus's tracker, and led his master to him. "The old shepherd and his wife didn't live long enough for me to repay their kindness," he told me, "and the shepherd's heir mistreated his dog, so I lifted Hermes into my chariot and made him a royal companion." Orestes scratched the shepherd dog behind the ears. "Go back to sleep, boy."

Orestes gave me the second lamp to carry into the bedchamber. Lamplight washed across a boar hunt fresco dominating the wall above the bed, which was as huge as he had claimed, and heaped with richly woven coverlets and snowy fleeces; its headboard was inlaid with carved ivory and ebony. A waisted shield hung upon the far wall, a pair of spears leaning beside it.

Taking both lamps, Orestes set them down on a table, then turned to me again and laid his large hands upon my shoulders. "Stay with me tonight."

After all this time, he did not need to ask. "Yes," I whispered.

Gently, he began unlacing my golden girdle. I trembled with desire as he untied my skirt to let it pool around my ankles. Stepping free from the flounces, I unfastened my own bodice and removed my shift while he undressed.

Orestes hooked an arm behind my knees and swept me to his great bed, laying me down among the fleeces and embroidered wool. I clung to his neck when he bent down to claim my mouth, and parted my thighs to welcome him. As we joined together, it was as though the gods had granted us a second wedding night, to make amends for the first.

Afterward, we drowsed in the darkness, the lamps having guttered out hours ago, and listened to the night sounds of the citadel. "You never told me about your trial." I knew he was still awake.

Orestes smothered a heavy yawn. "I did not think you wanted to know the details."

"Tell me about it."

"You may regret having asked," he said. "I had to purge myself and fast the day before. At dawn, the priests led me into a sacred cave. It was steep going, and cold and damp. I was allowed to wear a cloak for the descent, but nothing else underneath, and no shoes, even though the path was very rough. It seemed like the priests were leading me to my execution.

"The entrance passage was so narrow I had to suck in my belly to squeeze through, but then the tunnel widened. I knew we had entered a cavern from the way the darkness swallowed up the torchlight, and the way the air moved through the space. I saw stalagmites dripping down the walls like melting wax." Orestes tightened his embrace as the memories flooded in. "Faces and hideous beasts seemed to jump out at me from the rock, and there was an altar carved from the living rock, with broken bones and potsherds scattered around.

"I was told the priestesses carried out their rites there." Orestes exhaled a shuddering breath. "I knew the priests were going to leave me to face divine judgment, but now, seeing the altar and the bones, I was afraid the judgment would be the sacrificial knife."

"And the priests said nothing?" I asked. "Did they let you think your throat would be cut?"

"No. Knowing would have made no difference, though," he replied. "It was the entrance to the nether world. You could smell the age and decay in that cave. It had been there since before men, before the gods.

"The priests left me lying on a sheepskin near the altar, with my ankle tethered to a ring in the floor to keep me from wandering in the dark and injuring myself. They left me in total darkness, naked and cold, waiting for the earth to open up and swallow me.

"As I lay there listening to the air moving through the cavern, I heard voices, and then those voices began whispering, accusing me. I began to imagine horrors in the dark, demons and vengeful shades crowding around me. I smelled the decay seeping through the walls.

"I called out, trying to drown the whispers with my own voice, but the darkness devoured my echoes. I felt small and weak, like one of the tribute children left to die in Minos's Labyrinth. At last, I broke down sobbing. I admit, it wasn't heroic at all, but great men are nothing next to those ancient goddesses." I rubbed my cheek against his chest, and kissed him there to comfort him. "All I could do was submit and admit my guilt. I begged forgiveness, but made no excuses for my actions. I knew there was no absolution for matricide. I curled into a tight little ball and waited for the goddesses to devour me, but then they were suddenly gone, and the torment ceased. I didn't know what to think. Had I been forgiven? I didn't know how long the priests meant to leave me down there, or even how much time had passed. There's neither night nor day under the earth, and time loses all shape.

"I gathered my wits enough to wrap myself in the sheepskins to try to stay warm. Maybe I even slept a little. Then the priests were there to lead me from the cave. I remember how the torchlight made my eyes burn, and how the priests kept telling me to keep my eyes open and walk, but not much else. All I wanted to do was sleep."

"How long were you down there?" I asked.

"An entire day and night," he answered. "Then I slept for another day and night, until they woke me and made me eat something, because I hadn't eaten in almost four days. A scribe recorded what I had seen and heard in the cave, but he couldn't tell me anything. I had to wait two more days before the high priest sent for me."

An owl hooted outside. I was growing sleepy, despite my best effort to remain awake and listen. "Why did you have to wait so long?"

"Priests always dither when they have to interpret signs. The high priest told me my willingness to atone meant that the curses on our house had been broken. I could be purified and come home, although..."

His hesitant note banished my growing lassitude. "What is it?" I raised my head from his chest.

"She was *old!*" he groaned. "I murdered an old woman!" Orestes rolled over then, away from me, and broke down. Great sobs shuddered through his body.

I heard a dog's panting breath. Hermes, drawn by his master's distress, crossed the floor with soft footpads, then lay down again with a snuffling sigh.

"Orestes..." I hugged his back, pressing my lips to his skin, gently stroking his hair. "You had no choice."

He moved again, throwing his arms around my waist, and clasping me to him. "I did! I swore to let her take her own life, to avoid all this, but it was too late." Each agonized word was a hot exhalation against my skin. "I killed Aegisthus first. I was covered in his blood and raging with blood-madness. It was too late."

"You're not a monster."

"Never leave me, Hermione," he whispered. "My world would be nothing without you."

"Orestes..." I found his mouth in the darkness, but paused before kissing him. "I'm not going anywhere."

CHAPTER TWENTY-EIGHT

At daybreak, Elektra took me down to the cult house so I could begin my duties as queen. "You'll find everything in order," she said. "It's spotless inside."

My sister-in-law sounded so uncertain and anxious to please, even striding on ahead to open the door. She had been like that last night, too, worrying over every detail so she was unable to enjoy the feast.

Pylades had much to do with her skittishness, I surmised. At the table, he had behaved with perfect courtesy, deferring to my husband and father, engaging them in conversation, and solicitously inquiring after my health after Orestes announced my pregnancy to the court, all while scarcely acknowledging his wife. King's son and royal kinsman he might have been, but I thought him a colossal ass.

Orestes seemed not to notice his sister's discontent. Or rather, I thought, he expected her gloom to vanish now that she had my company. Perhaps I ought to say something to him, but not yet. I would not meddle until I was certain it was the correct thing to do.

Elektra described the fresh paint and frescoes, new vessels and offering tables, rambling on and driving me to distraction till I could bear it no longer. "Enough!" I cried. "You're starting to sound like Chrysothemis."

At that, she started, turning wan with hurt. "Hermione..." Moisture glistened in her eyes.

Her reaction astounded me. The Elektra I knew was not this sensitive. She ought to have scowled, and snapped, and boxed my ear like the lioness she could be, not shrunk back like a kicked dog.

"I'm sure everything is beautiful," I reassured her. "Let's go inside."

Elektra led me to the main altar, where she began to arrange the painted offering table before the deities. Our maids assumed their place against the wall with the offerings.

I arranged the votaries on the altar, lingering over my favorite, a hook-nosed old woman who absorbed our sins, and whose face we always kept turned toward the wall; I liked her because she reminded me of the loud-mouthed vendor women typical of the agora.

Then I noticed the sprigs of birthwort tucked into Eleuthia's votive slots. "Who placed these here?" I asked.

"I did," Elektra admitted, "after we got the message about the baby."

Taking the offerings from the maids, we poured out the libations of honey and wine. A new house snake dwelled under the navel stone in the rear court. Once we set down the milk, Elektra told me, "I found her sunning herself on the omphalos the very day Orestes went free. It was a good omen."

The lower citadel was alive with activity when we left the cult house. I heard the whir and clack of shuttles in the weaving house nearby, and suddenly found myself wondering what Elektra had done with the Euboean woman Orestes had won.

"Her?" Elektra snorted her disdain when I asked. "She had skilled hands when she cared to use them, but I never met such a clumsy, lazy slut. I sent her to the slave market in Tiryns. Got four head of cattle for her."

"And Orestes doesn't mind?"

"Orestes won't take a concubine unless I inspect her first," she replied. "He expects them to behave at all times and earn their keep." As she spoke, a hint of uncertainty once more crept into her voice. "I've always overseen them, but if you'd rather..."

I shook my head vigorously. "I want nothing to do with his women."

"He has but one at the moment," she said, "and she knows her place." A cart lumbered past on its way to the potter's workshop; the driver saluted us. Elektra urged me toward the great ramp. "But come, there's something I want to show you."

Upstairs in the nursery, we found her daughters playing dolls with their old Phocian nurse. I had not visited this room since Orestes was six years old.

A treasure stood in the corner: a cedar cradle inlaid with ivory and gold. Bullion glittered on the purple blankets, and the linens had come from Egypt. "Anaxibia gave it to us when young Strophius was born." Elektra ran a wistful finger over the headboard. "It seems a shame to waste it."

"It's beautiful," I agreed.

"I have something else for you, too." Elektra cooed at her playing daughters on her way to a chest, where she removed a stack of linens. I hesitated, for although the diapers were clean, they looked used, and not at all suitable for a king's firstborn son.

Elektra caught my reaction. "New mothers always want brand-new linens, but after you have three or four babies, clean and serviceable is all that matters. Children grow faster than they can wear out their clothes."

As she explained, two servant girls entered carrying water for the toddlers' bath. Elektra stopped them to dip her fingers into both jugs. "I said hot, you slut!" Her palm cracked across the nearest girl's cheek; water splashed onto the floor as the girl almost lost her balance. "Now, get out!"

I watched the girls retreat. "You can still be a harpy when you want to be."

"Not around my husband." Elektra bent and lifted little Anaxo in her arms, nodding to the nurse, who withdrew to give us privacy. "When Pylades was regent, you would have thought he was king. So strict and cold. He's always been that way, of course, but this time it was different." Her mouth twitched with the effort it took to let the words flow. "I tried to talk to him, but he kept ignoring me until I could no longer bear it. So I shouted at him, right there in the great court." Her arms reflexively tightened around her daughter. Sensing her mother's agitation, Anaxo started to fuss. "Do you know what he did then? He locked me in my chamber for four days, with only bread and water to eat, and he refused to let me out till I agreed to behave like a proper wife."

I watched her rock her daughter to calm her, and bury her face for a moment in the child's tousled curls. What did the children think, seeing the discord between their parents? "Should I say something to Orestes?"

Elektra's eyes went wide. "Gods, no!"

"Are you certain?" I asked. "Pylades will listen to him."

"And he expects everything to be all right, now that you're here." Elektra's voice grew thick with emotion. "I told you, Pylades has always been that way. He never wanted to marry me, but then, marriage isn't really for love, anyway."

"Oh, don't say that!" I exclaimed, even though I knew better.

"It's true." Anaxo began to whine in her mother's arms. Elektra set her down beside her sisters on the sheepskin rug. "I haven't been the best wife, either."

I started to speak, but the little girls, having watched us with growing curiosity, decided at that moment to interrupt. "Mama," five-year-old Antiklea said, "the pretty lady has red hair, too."

"She's your Aunt Hermione," Elektra replied.

"What lovely girls you all are!" I took the nurse's vacant chair, sat down, and held out my arms. "Why don't you come here and show me your dolls while we wait for your bath?"

Antiklea crinkled her nose in disgust. "No bath!"

"Princesses have to take baths so they can make themselves pretty," I told her.

Meanwhile, three-year old Charis had come over to show me her well-worn rag doll. "See my dolly!"

I smoothed the doll's chewed, tangled yarn hair and admired it. I, too, had had a rag doll at that age, receiving the one with a ceramic head only when my grandmother saw I was responsible enough to properly look after it. "She's a very pretty doll." And dirty, and threadbare. "Maybe we should put a little perfume on her and paint her lips so she can be even prettier."

"I should have the stuffing pulled from that thing and have it thoroughly washed," Elektra commented, "but she refuses to be parted from it."

Charis hugged my knees as the chastised servant girls reappeared with the water jugs. "No bath!"

Elektra tested the water a second time, and then sent the women into the bathroom. Both little girls whined to hear the bathwater splashing into the tub. "I want to play some more!" Antiklea whined.

"You do as you're told, young lady," Elektra said firmly.

"Come here, sweetheart." Antiklea shuffled over wearing a hangdog look. I hugged both girls close. I adored them already. "You take a bath as your mother says, then once you're all clean and fresh, you can play at my dressing table. My women will paint your lips, and you can try on my jewels."

Charis beamed up at me. "We can play dolls?"

I stroked her red-gold curls. "Yes. We can play dolls, too."

ORESTES AND PYLADES TOOK my father boar hunting in the hills northwest of the citadel. As I did not follow hounds, I remained behind to manage the servants and prepare the night's feast.

To no one's surprise, Elektra joined the hunt, driving her own chariot. I heard she carried extra spears, and accompanied the hunters on foot into the brush. Pylades and Orestes shook their heads at her recklessness, though to my bewilderment, neither one forbade her to stalk the boar, or cast her spear when the moment came. Perhaps they feared her ritual power as a high priestess, or the darker impulses she had inherited from Clytaemnestra.

It amazed me that she, a woman, would presume to wield anything more than the sacred labrys and sacrificial dagger, but Menelaus found her high courage admirable. "A true granddaughter of Atreus!" he exclaimed.

While they hunted, Menelaus and Orestes plotted to undermine the Argive assembly. Even after many weeks, I still thought the elderly Argive king's persistent requests to receive my husband in Argos were perfectly reasonable, as his ailing health made it difficult for him to travel, but Orestes maintained his rigid view that going to Argos was a sign of his submission.

At last, he could delay no longer. Although Orestes traveled to Argos two days after the boar hunt, he did so strictly on his terms. He waited until the last possible moment to send Cyanippus word of his intent to visit, then, to further strengthen his position, he unexpectedly brought my father along as his elder kinsman, and arrived early. Clever. Foolish. I heard later that the Argive assembly had had to swallow its collective dismay at the united Mycenaean-Spartan front that Orestes and Menelaus represented.

Orestes returned confident in his authority. Menelaus was elated to have exercised influence in Argolis once more. Despite my misgivings over how they had antagonized the Argives, I had never seen my father as lively as he was during those two weeks.

Then the time came for him to leave. How I wished he could stay longer, at least until the child was born, but that was a daughter's selfish wish. Menelaus had a kingdom to rule. Orestes needed to stand on his own feet as king. I had to let go for his sake and that of our child.

Before he left, my father gathered me in a tight embrace. "Remember to write," he said. "Let us all know how the little mite is faring."

Thus far, the mite in question was punishing his mother with renewed bouts of morning sickness. Elektra made me comfortable upstairs while taking over my duties downstairs. From among the palace scribes, she recommended a competent personal secretary, but always double-checked the ledgers after I finished.

Did she think I was new at managing a household? I asserted my authority the third time she did this. Once was an honest mistake, twice an irritation, and thrice a habit I would not tolerate. "I know my figures," I said sharply.

"Of course you do," Elektra answered, ignoring my flash of temper. "But you haven't been to the kitchen lately. You remember Mykale? Well, she's grown absentminded. Constantly orders items she already has, and is too stubborn to hear it from her assistants. A shame Orestes likes her cooking so much, or she would be retired."

As long as she did not dictate to me, I let her manage the household stores and servants. She was efficient, and the regular work kept her spirits high. Nonetheless, I would not let her assume my duties in the cult house. Propitiating the gods was the queen's responsibility, and given to me alone.

I interviewed the new high priestess of the town, a sickly, middle-aged woman who held her title due to her rank, and began receiving the ladies of the court in the afternoons, something which Clytaemnestra had never done. I understood why. Mycenae's noblewomen were ambitious, preening birds who brimmed with inane gossip and dropped constant hints about spouses and sons seeking royal favor.

Orestes neither needed nor wanted a woman's interference in his affairs. I listened to the ladies over my spinning, smiled and nodded at their courtesies, and gave bland, noncommittal answers.

Elektra, on the other hand, bared her claws whenever she thought a petitioning noblewoman went too far.

"Astyoche!" She singled out a woman who had spent the last half-hour singing her son's praises. "Diokles is old enough to petition the king on his own behalf. So stop encouraging him to cling to your skirts, and let him be a man."

Wincing at her bluntness, I did my best to undo the damage without coddling the noblewoman. "Lady Astyoche, forgive Princess Elektra for speaking her mind. I realize you love your son, but he is grown, and perhaps it would be wise to let him handle his own affairs. The king will grant him a fair hearing."

Astyoche was not the only woman at court who despised my sister-in-law; they all did, and it had little to do with her perceived crimes. Like her mother, Elektra typically avoided her own sex, preferring instead the company of men, but her brother, husband, and their followers did not want to hear her views. So she inflicted them on the women, who were not accustomed to her bluntness.

No wonder she had been so lonely.

LETTER AND GIFTS ARRIVED FROM HOMe. My mother sent recipes, prayers, advice on selecting a good wet nurse, and new linen diapers. Chrysothemis wrote to me, too, her excitement bubbling through as her time neared.

She was fretting over everything. I imagined some poor Spartan scribe shaking his head as he took her dictation.

Elektra groaned as she commented, "I thought you said she wasn't such a goose anymore."

I folded the letter and stowed it in my wool basket. "No, I said she and Aethiolas were getting along better. She's still a goose."

"She needs someone to tie her down. All this fussing won't help her." Elektra held two red skeins up to the light, trying to decide which one to use. "I pity your brother."

A moment later, she laid aside both skeins. "I almost forgot to tell you. There's another baby on the way. Chione is with child."

I encountered my husband's concubine only once. Chione was young, fifteen years old, with a winsome face and nimble fingers on the loom. Moreover, she remained invisible, making no demands and affecting no airs. I liked her despite myself, but did not believe for one moment that my sister-in-law had forgotten to tell me about her condition. "How far along is she?" I asked.

"She will deliver early next spring."

That meant Orestes had gone into her since our return. I swallowed hard, biting back my hurt. All kings had concubines and bastards. I stared out the window. Had Orestes not taken slave women for his pleasure, people would have mocked him as uxorious, or worse, as a pederast.

Chione's pregnancy upset me more than it should have. Marking my distress, Elektra offered a blunt, business-like solution. "I can have her take the medicine and lose it."

But Chione did not belong to me, so it was not for me to decide. Orestes might already know about her condition and, exulting in his sexual prowess and glowing with paternal pride, want her have the baby. "Do nothing to her."

"Are you sure?" Elektra asked.

I propped an elbow on the armrest and leaned into my hand, a hair's breadth from bursting into tears. This irrational weeping would not do! "Did Orestes sire any bastards back in Phocis?"

"No. I made certain of it." Elektra found a linen cloth among her threads, and handed it across. "Here, I used to cry all the time when I was pregnant." Just staring at the linen threatened my resolve. "Go ahead and cry," she urged. "then dry your eyes, and tell Orestes he's going to be a father twice over. Let him give the girl some cheap beads or a new dress. Her child isn't the one that matters."

Orestes absorbed the news with obvious pleasure. "Make certain Chione has enough to eat," he said, "and that she rests if she's ill or gets too tired."

"The girl's a slave, not a wife," Elektra said sharply.

Orestes glared at her. "Do you object?" He brooked no challenge to his authority, not even from behind closed doors from his own sister. Elektra had no choice but to see his will done.

After she withdrew, he asked me to remain, which I did not necessarily want to do, even when he solicitously took my hand. "I knew about the child. Chione told me a few days ago," he confessed, " but I preferred not to trouble you with it."

So when had he intended to tell me, his wife? When the girl's belly started showing, or when her labor pains began?

Orestes noticed my distress, as his sister had. He rose and came around behind my chair to wrap his arms around me. "Her child is nothing next to yours," he murmured into my hair. "You know that."

"I know." I forced back tears. Orestes had announced my pregnancy to the people. He escorted me every month to the altars of Eleuthia and Artemis in the lower town, and made certain that I enjoyed every comfort; he had not done that with his concubine, and never would. "It's the baby that does this to me. I have no quarrel with Chione."

"When her child is born," he said, "I will give her glass beads. You shall have bright gold."

Chapter Twenty-Nine

Summer's heat parched the scrub clinging to the citadel mount, and in the white-hot furnace of the afternoon not even the insects stirred. Orestes limited the petitioners he received each morning, and closed the megaron early. At night, the servants slept on the rooftops to catch what cool breeze blew in from the south.

Orestes liked nothing better than to lie naked beside me in the warm evenings and contemplate my swelling belly, stroking and nuzzling my navel as though he could reach through my flesh to the baby quickening in my womb.

While the midwife assured him that I could receive him as long as I did not find lovemaking uncomfortable, Orestes would not risk injuring me. He continued to lie with Chione, though that arrangement could not last much longer. Elektra urged me to focus solely on my child, and not to concern myself with my husband's pleasure; she would find him suitable bedmates.

Men could be so ruthless and violent among themselves yet completely dumbstruck when it came to a woman's natural cycles. Imagine, the king of Mycenae, reduced to uncertainty, even awe, over a single baby! How his enemies would have laughed to see him behaving like an overprotective nurse, admonishing me to eat the correct foods, and giving me his arm to escort me down the stairs each evening!

"Our son will be a mighty warrior and hunter." Orestes kissed my belly. "He'll take his first lion at twelve and go to his first games at fourteen like his father, and all his enemies will tremble in fear when he steps on the sands."

His stubble tickled me. "Stop it!" I cried, laughing. "You went to your first games at sixteen!"

"Don't tell Kretheus." Orestes moved up to my breasts. Pregnancy made my nipples even more sensitive, and he knew that. "He hates having to change his songs."

I hissed in a breath. "What else have you been exaggerating?" Sometimes he brought my name into his boasts, which I did not like at all.

Orestes glanced at me over my breasts, his mischievous look betraying him. "Sometimes the truth doesn't make a very good song."

His exploits had become popular among the Mycenaeans and Argives. I sat beside him while the bard chanted the songs of the heroes, for Orestes never received important guests without introducing me to them. "Here she is, my lords," he relished telling them. "Queen Hermione, daughter of Menelaus and fair Helen. Is she not the most beautiful woman in Hellas?"

When mortal men boasted so, it made the gods jealous, and invited disaster. "You mustn't say such a thing!" I whispered sharply.

"It's the truth," he said, taking his seat again.

I sighed. "How can you know, when you haven't even seen all the women in Hellas to judge them."

Orestes raised his cup to his lips. "Any woman more splendid than you would have to be an immortal goddess."

I had come to realize that Orestes *needed* to boast, to salt his tales with heroic exaggerations and half-truths so they became grand enough to live inside, a refuge from the ghosts dogging his quiet moments. His mother's death troubled him enough that he fasted and sat vigil in the hot sun on the second anniversary of her death. Perhaps the gods ordered him to do so, as he claimed, or, just as likely, what he heard was the voice of his own guilt.

He found solace in his work, in poring over petitions and correspondence, and in supervising building projects that bolstered his vision of a grand new Mycenae. I woke each dawn to the echoing clink of hammers and chisels as masons shored up Atreus's old fortifications, or labored at a new site outside the northeast circuit wall, where a gang under a Hittite master builder was tunneling into the citadel mount to construct a massive new cistern.

I knew he anticipated conflict with Nemea and Corinth, which had broken away from Mycenaean rule after Agamemnon's death, and whose obedience and tribute Orestes meant to reclaim. He began taking his men out on grueling night marches to prepare them for the kind of stealth raids Atreus had specialized in. I had no doubt he meant to seize Nemea in just such a fashion, after its lord had refused to send tribute. Orestes would not let that insult stand.

I also knew that sooner or later he intended to consolidate his Mycenaean and Spartan territories by taking Argos. To be king of Mycenae and Sparta would not suffice. Orestes meant to become nothing less than a High King like his forefathers.

Such ambitions required equally ambitious measures. I held my tongue like an obedient wife over his proposed military campaigns, but did not shrink from asking my husband outright how he intended to pay for his various building projects. All those stonemasons, carpenters, and plasterers expected payment, the raw materials cost, and our treasuries and storerooms were not bottomless. "I thought Aegisthus spent everything," I said.

"Much Trojan gold remains," Orestes told me. "Mother oversaw the stores, and you know how frugal she was."

While he enjoyed the logistical challenges his projects presented, he also found time to encourage his nephews in their adventures. Strophius and Medon adored their uncle. I watched them together, reflecting that one day soon Orestes would be wrestling and boxing with our son, and teaching him all the things Agamemnon should have taught Orestes.

Autumn came, bringing cooler weather, but no relief for my changing body. After the grape harvest and the feast of the vines, my swelling belly strained my back and pulled at my gowns; my women loosened the latter, but could do nothing for the former. No matter how much Orestes tried to reassure me, I felt cumbersome and ugly, like a beached pentekonter or swollen pithos. Never mind that he considered pentekonters beautiful ships, or pithoi lovely vessels, I did not share his sentiments, and continuously had to remind myself that the baby moving inside me was a miraculous thing.

Elektra prepared everything for the birth. She moved the local midwife into the citadel, and even selected a competent new mother among the servant girls to act as the infant's wet nurse until my own milk came. Moreover, my sister-in-law offered reassurance and good advice. "I know it's hard now, and you're swearing to yourself that you'll never, ever do it again," she said, "but once the baby is born, you'll be so besotted with him that your pains will seem as nothing to you."

I prayed that was so. It was becoming increasingly difficult to move about, and when my ankles swelled, impossible to leave the palace to attend my duties in the cult house. Orestes forbade me to set up a bed there, citing the fact that the lower citadel was noisier and the air more unwholesome. That left Elektra to act as high priestess, which not only rankled, and left me feeling like a secondary wife, but the religious implications concerned me. A queen's conduct affected her people. Should I falter in my duties, I risked inciting divine wrath. Mother Dia might blight next year's crops. Eleuthia and Artemis might punish me in childbirth.

Elektra considered my misgivings premature and unfounded. "You send me to the cult house every day with new offerings," she said, "and there isn't a woman in all Argolis with a better-tended altar than yours."

"It isn't the same."

"You're certainly not the first queen of Mycenae to have this trouble," Elektra told me. "I remember Mother couldn't leave the palace at all in her last three months when she was carrying Orestes, and he turned out healthy. Now stop worrying about everything and relax, or you'll become as bad as Chrysothemis."

A month ago, a Spartan messenger had arrived with word that Chrysothemis had borne a daughter called Thalaia. It delighted me to hear that Sparta had a new princess. Aethiolas offered further details in his letter. Chrysothemis took motherhood so seriously that she badgered the wet nurse, and was so thoroughly useless in the nursery that everyone breathed a sigh of relief when my mother took over.

"I will never become such a terror," I vowed.

"No," Elektra agreed, "because I won't let you." She thoughtfully stroked the silver and amber pendant between her breasts. A gift from Pylades, who, she told me, almost never gave her presents. Her relations with him seemed less strained now. I suspected Orestes had had a hand in that.

My nieces wanted to see and touch my belly, and feel the baby kicking. "Do you have a girl in there?" Antiklea asked.

"When can she play dolls?" Charis wanted to know.

"I think it might be a boy," I told her.

Charis refused to accept that. She wanted another playmate. "Did it tell you it was a boy?"

I did not feel like explaining Helenus's oracle to a precocious three-year-old, even had I known what to say to make her understand. "I don't know what it will be, dear. That's for Mother Dia and Eleuthia to decide."

As autumn turned toward winter, the baby started to descend in my womb; it kicked me day and night now, and that constant back pain made it almost impossible for me to find a comfortable position. Add to that a persistent need to urinate which forced me to maneuver my bulk from the bed and hobble to the bathroom several times a night. I wept in exhausted frustration.

My women tucked feather pillows against my spine to relieve my backache, and spread soft fleeces over me. Lying idle when there was so much to do grated on my nerves, for at the very least I should have been working at my loom. Instead, I dozed away the afternoons with one hand clasped protectively over my womb, and listened to the wind knocking against the shutters.

I remembered my mother had lain just so in her chamber when she was pregnant with Pleisthenes. She had been sick before and after the birth, as she had been with me. My nurse had told me how my mother had labored for two days to bring me forth, and was so weak by the end that everyone had feared for her life. How I wish she had never told me! I did not want to die giving birth to my first child, after having waited so long for it.

Orestes offered to send for Helen, so she could be with me when the time came, but it was too late in the year for her to make the journey. And besides, Chrysothemis needed her far more than I did. Bearing babies was a natural thing, I told myself. The gods had made women to bear children. I was strong and healthy. I had skilled women to help me. There was nothing to fear.

That was far easier to say than to believe. As high priestess in Sparta, I had seen women die in childbirth. Sometimes they asked for me, to give them my blessings, but though I held their hands, wiped the sweat from their brows, and said the prayers, they died, anyway.

Opening my eyes, I gazed at the kourotrophos standing on the table nearest the bed. She was very old, crafted in an outmoded Cretan style, and her scarlet and black paint was fading. She had faithfully watched over the confinements of my foremothers for eleven generations. Not a single laboring woman had died under her benevolent gaze. Let that be so now!

AN INFANT'S MEWLING CRY WOKE ME.

Winter rain sleeted against the shutters. A minty fragrance wafted past my nostrils; someone had tossed herbs into the brazier to fumigate the chamber. Kourotrophoi and amulets occupied every available space, cramming my dressing table and the little table beside my bed, silent guardians against any malevolent forces which might seek to harm me or my child. Foremost among them was the Cretan idol, which someone had anointed with a sheen of fresh oil and decorated with red ribbons.

Drowsiness suffused my entire body, tempting me back to sleep even as my tentative movements roused sore muscles. I felt a dull ache between my thighs.

Just as I closed my eyes again, I heard an infant whimpering and gurgling next door—my son with the wet nurse! A fierce mother-hunger flooded through me, a physical ache to have my child beside me, to kiss and dandle him, and clasp him to my breast. Only my exhaustion was stronger, preventing me from rising and going into the next room to claim him.

But he was safe with the nurse, I reminded myself, and my milk was not yet flowing. I lay snugly under the fleeces, listened to the hypnotic rhythm of the rain beating down, and browsed through recent memories. I remembered the midwife showing me my newborn baby, then laying him upon my breast. Orestes, jubilant at the birth of a son, had come in and seen the child before his sister and the other women shooed him out.

I strove to forget the labor: the contractions, the hours of waiting, and the agonized straining as my women supported me on the birthing stool. Delivering a child was like being turned inside out and beaten like a rug! Sweet Mother Dia, I had not realized women possessed the fortitude to endure such an obscene amount of pain and blood. The birth seemed impossible, until, strained to the limit of my mortal strength, and with a last, exhausted push and prayer to the goddess, my son left the cocoon of his mother's aching womb and entered the world.

Soft footfalls alerted me that someone had entered the bedchamber. I cracked an eyelid. Monime carried a tray with steaming broth and tea, for which I had no appetite. "I want to see him." My voice was weak and hoarse, and my throat sore from screaming during the birth.

Monime withdrew. I heard murmuring voices in the next room, then the curtain parted to admit Elektra, bearing a swaddled bundle which she laid down beside me. "He's sleeping now," she whispered.

Tisamenus. It meant Great Retribution. Orestes had chosen the name months ago, on a humid summer night when Zeus's thunder had rolled across the hills. He claimed divine inspiration, after rejecting all the other possibilities as unsuitable. Tisamenus. I knew only that it was a terribly large and ominous name for such a small child to fill.

Our firstborn son was red and wrinkled from the birth, with a moist rosebud mouth and downy wisps of reddish-gold hair that clung to his scalp.

His name notwithstanding, he was so small, and warm, and wonderful! I traced a fingertip along his butter-soft skin, drinking in his scent.

Elektra forced me to drink the nourishing broth and tea. Thank Eleuthia and blessed Artemis for her presence! She had been with me since my labor began, and had taken charge of the birth.

After I finished, she called my women in to help me relieve myself. I found I could hobble to the privy on my own, despite my exhaustion and soreness, but needed their assistance to change my padding.

Sleeping through the night, I woke with the dawn, and ate and washed again. This time, I felt strong enough to don a dressing gown and venture into the sitting room, where the young wet nurse had just laid Tisamenus down for a nap in the lavishly decorated cradle Elektra had given me, and was now suckling her own infant. Elektra and the midwives had promised that my milk would start flowing soon, but for now, I envied the wet nurse the simple intimacy she enjoyed with her child.

At my altar, I honored Eleuthia and Artemis with libations of wine and honey, and promises of greater offerings in the cult house. It had all been arranged before the birth: lengths of purple and scarlet cloth, perfumed unguents, gold bangles, rings, and necklaces.

Thebe plucked a soft melody on her four-stringed phorminx while Tisamenus contentedly dozed in his cradle. Monime fetched my spindle and wool basket, that I could sit beside the brazier and work.

Outside, it had stopped raining. I scented wood smoke in the air, and heard the distant lowing of cattle and the monotonous chanting of the high priest carrying across the citadel mount. Orestes must be making the thanksgiving sacrifices, driving the animals through the Lion Gate to the altar. Anticipating the birth, he had sent to his estates for the best animals in his herd more than a week ago, and had instructed the priests to keep the sacrificial labrys and knife in readiness.

I spun wool and listened to Thebe's playing, while frequently pausing to watch my son sleep; he was the most beautiful thing in the whole world. For this magical moment, we were removed from the life of the citadel, quiet and secure in the snug cocoon that was the queen's apartment. Aside from the naming day ritual and the mother's usual thanksgiving offerings, there were no pressing matters requiring my attention. Elektra leapt at the chance to take charge, and had already reassured me that she would manage the household until I had recovered from the birth.

Just before noon, Orestes arrived smelling of the precious unguents his bath servants had rubbed into his skin, and wearing a richly embroidered tunic and a broad grin. Seeing him again made my heart race. I set down my spindle and raised my face to receive his kiss. At a brusque gesture from him, my women and the wet nurse respectfully took their leave.

Orestes bent over the cradle, and lifted his swaddled son onto his shoulder. Tisamenus mewled, whimpered at the strange man holding him, and then subsided as his father began rubbing his back with practiced ease. "Are you well?" he asked.

"I'm still a bit tired," I admitted, "but much better than before."

"I want you to rest, Hermione," he said earnestly. "Elektra made all the offerings last night and this morning, and she's already agreed to oversee the preparations for the naming day feast. You don't have to do anything." An avid gleam of pleasure lit Orestes' eyes. I knew that look; he was planning something. "We're going to have a splendid celebration. There must be at least seven days of games, feasting, and sacrifices."

Did he have no head for figures? "It'll ruin us."

"Our son is worth it." Claiming the vacant chair beside me, Orestes kissed the fuzz on Tisamenus's head. It was hard to believe that one day Tisamenus would grow into a big man like his father, or that Orestes himself had ever been so small. "He's a blessing from the gods, after all our troubles."

Never had Orestes been more endearing, sitting there with his newborn son in his arms. Never had I loved him so much.

Then I heard Thebe softly plucking the lyre in the next room. One day, there would be a song about us, a king and queen who had endured many sorrows and long separation, but whose love had banished a curse and set the old ghosts of Mycenae to rest. A bard would choose this singular moment, a man and wife together with their newborn son, to close his composition.

But we were more than just a song, more than the son of Agamemnon and the daughter of Helen. We were Orestes and Hermione. Creatures of flesh and blood. We were the sum of our memories, convictions, and longings, and where the bard made his ending, we made our beginning.

Author's Note

Hermione, the daughter of Menelaus and Helen, was betrothed to her younger cousin Orestes when they were both children, and was sent to live with her aunt Clytaemnestra at Mycenae while her father and uncle fought at Troy. Ancient sources make Hermione nine years old at the time of her mother's abduction, and seven years older than Orestes, meaning he would have been twelve and she nineteen when the Trojan War ended.

After the war, Hermione was either abducted by or given in marriage to Neoptolemus, son of Achilles, with whom she had a short but disastrous union. Neoptolemus was killed by the priests of Apollo for committing sacrilege; in another version of the story, he was killed by Orestes, from whom he had stolen Hermione. I have tried to remain faithful to both versions while creating my own narrative.

Hermione's reputation has not fared well over this incident. From Euripides to the Anglo-Saxon theologian Aldhelm to French playwright Jean Racine, she has been branded by her mother's infamy, and portrayed as a wanton vixen who plots intrigue and murder during her time in

Epirus. If she existed, the real-life Mycenaean Hermione may have been a very different woman.

I have taken some liberties when filling in the blanks of Hermione's life. It is not inconceivable that Aegisthus, given his personal history, could have raped Hermione as a way of escalating his blood feud with Menelaus and Orestes. Nor is it implausible that Menelaus might have looked to the royal dynasty of Pylos to secure a suitable husband for his daughter. In *The Odyssey*, Peisistratus accompanies Telemachus to Sparta, and seems to know Menelaus, so perhaps he had been there before.

Hermione and Orestes were married, and she bore him a son, Tisamenus, who inherited the united kingdoms of Mycenae and Sparta. There is no mention of other children, nor do we know how or when Hermione died. She might not have outlived Orestes, who, according to tradition, lived to be seventy.

The details about Helen's birth, early life, and her abductions by Theseus and Paris come from *The Cypria*, which also mentions that she took her young son Pleisthenes with her when she left Sparta. Dictys Cretensis mentions Helen's three sons by Paris, and their early deaths due to a roof collapse. Megapenthes, known from *The Odyssey*, was Menelaus's son by a concubine, but Nikostratos may have been his son by Helen. Aethiolas is more obscure, as is another son, Maraphius, who does not appear in my story.

Neither archaeology nor the Linear B tablets offer any evidence that kingship in the Mycenaean world was matrilineal, although I chose to play with the idea and have Tyndareus rework the Spartan royal genealogy as a nod to the long-standing theory.

With regard to the correspondence between Hermione and Orestes, there is no concrete evidence that the Mycenaeans used Linear B for anything other than record keeping, or that aristocrats were literate. It is worth bearing in mind, however, that the clay tablets which do survive did so through the fortunate accident of being exposed to palace conflagrations, and that those archives may have contained additional documents inscribed on wax, wood, or papyrus. Given that the Mycenaeans had contact with other, literate civilizations throughout the eastern Mediterranean and Near East, it is certainly plausible that a shrewd and enterprising ruler like Atreus or Agamemnon might have recognized the advantages in having his children educated.

Despite New Age claims to the contrary, there is no definitive evidence that the Mycenaeans or Minoans worshipped a single Mother Goddess figure. The names of certain gods and goddesses appear on Linear B clay tablets, but their worship did not survive into later, Classical times, so we know very little to nothing about them. One such deity was Diwia, or Dia, a female counterpart of Zeus.

Helas, not Gytheum, was the port of Sparta in Mycenaean times, and the point from which Paris would have abducted Helen. Nowadays, Helas is landlocked due to the silting up of the Evrotas estuary, but in the Late Bronze Age it had a quarry and was an export center for green Laconian marble.

Delphi has been inhabited since Neolithic times, and Mycenaean artifacts have been discovered there. Apollo was known to the Mycenaeans, as his epithet, Pa-wa-jo-ne, or Paian, has been found on Linear B tablets.

ABOUT THE AUTHOR

LAURA GILL has a passion for Mycenaean and Minoan culture. She has a Master's Degree in English Literature from California State University, Northridge, and has worked as a secondary school teacher and florist. She is also the author of The Orestes Trilogy and *Knossos*.

Excerpt From

Knossos

Available now on Kindle

ONE
THE FOUNDER

6300 B.C.

KNOS THE MARINER had three talents: navigating, haggling, and seducing other men's wives. Those first two talents, which were his livelihood, kept him from being stoned for the third.

He worked his mischief in foreign ports, where he had been able to wheedle his way out of most of his troubles. When his tongue did not smooth the way, his fists and his loyal crew won him the argument. But this particular dilemma? Knos gritted his teeth. By Potidnu's balls, it figured the gods would find some way to reverse his fortunes.

How was he to guess that the garishly painted woman who had toyed with him behind the waterfront and then taken him home for an hour of vigorous lovemaking was in fact a daughter of one powerful chieftain and the recent bride of another? "You must be mistaken," he told the men of the Dolphin Clan who came around at sunset the following day to question him about what he had done with their kinswoman. "That girl was a whore if I ever saw one. Why, *she* seduced *me!*" The moment the words left his lips, Knos realized that was the wrong thing to say. "Easy, friends, easy!" He put up his hands to forestall any violence. "A chieftain's daughter? No, there must be a mistake. I don't believe it! No respectable chieftain's daughter would know tricks like that."

But those five men, who included the woman's eldest brother, did not look amused. Divos folded his brawny arms across his chest and glowered. Knos's three wives, meanwhile, regarded him from their corner like a trio of she-demons from whom he would surely suffer an earful later.

"She swears it was you," Divos insisted.

Knos did not have to feign surprise. "Me? Your sister's but a child. I like my women older, more experienced, as my wives will tell you." He jerked his thumb backward.

An older man of the Dolphin Clan shook his head. "Sinopi named *you*." Nurbas thrust a finger into Knos's chest. "And everybody knows your reputation in the ports."

Did Nurbas have to say that in front of the women? Knos cleared his throat. "Friends, you know that's a grievous exaggeration, and must you say it in front of my dear wives. I'm always on my best behavior. Why should I stray, when I'm happily married?" He felt three icy stares at his back. "You'd better go home and ask Sinopi again. She's probably named me to avoid naming her real lover—that is, *if* she's committed adultery. I don't know anything about that." He shrugged nonchalantly before wiping the perspiration from the back of his neck. Gods, the late afternoon was hot. "The woman I had was painted and must have been above twenty-five."

Divos narrowed his eyes, but the older men with him looked bewildered, uncertain of their own judgment. Even Knos was puzzled. Sinopi was a slip of a girl. Pretty enough, too, but not his type. "Go home," he urged. "There must be some mistake."

Once the men of the Dolphin Clan left, Knos's wives descended on him with a vengeance, pinching, slapping, and reviling him. "What in the hells were you doing with a slut from the waterfront?" Hariana, the youngest of his wives, fetched him a blow to the temple hard enough to set his ears ringing.

Urope kicked his shin with her sandaled foot. "Sinopi's barely old enough to have tits!"

"Ladies, ladies!" Knos shielded his head with both arms. "What could I do? The woman threw herself at me!" Seeing his second wife about to strike, he grasped Fidra's wrists. "Would I ever betray you with some other man's wife?" he implored. "Don't I always provide for you and our children, and bring you gifts when I return?"

"Don't lie, Knos." Urope, his first wife, braced her fists on her ample hips. "Your eyes are always wandering."

"Of course they are! Sea habits are hard to break," Knos exclaimed, still holding onto Fidra. "What sort of captain relaxes his vigil? Only the gods know when danger threatens." His spirits flagged. All three wives remained stone-faced. He could see he was going to have to work for their forgiveness. "Oh, come! Don't be angry. The woman was shameless. I enjoyed none of it."

Hariana snorted unbecomingly. "Nobody forced you to thrust your pole inside her."

Knos released Fidra in frustration. "She beguiled me! You should have seen how many love amulets she was wearing. Why, even the soles of her feet were painted scarlet. But it wasn't Sinopi. I swear on Potnidu's balls that it wasn't."

"Then why do her kinsmen say otherwise?" Urope challenged. "And don't play us for fools."

Knos became aware of a burning odor. Turning, he noticed the gray smoke issuing from the hearth at the same moment Fidra rushed over to rescue the burnt porridge from the coals. "Look what you've made me do!" she cried. "Get out! I don't care where you go, just get out."

"I'm not going anywhere," Knos answered staunchly. Adding embarrassment to injury, his eight children, ranging in age from two to fourteen, were watching with interest from the ox-hide curtain separating the main room from the sleeping quarters. "Orana, you should've been watching the fire," he scolded his eldest daughter.

"Don't sidestep the question." Urope went over to comfort her chastened daughter. "Sinopi's kinsmen say you're to blame. *She* says you're to blame."

Knos threw up his hands. "How many times do I have to tell you that she's lying?" He caught himself starting to raise his voice. Like stirring a hive with a stick, shouting would only further agitate his strong-willed wives. Softening his tone, he continued, "I'm not a complete fool. I'd never dally with a chieftain's daughter. Sinopi must've heard the tall tales about me. Why, she must've given them my name to protect her real lover."

Fidra beat at the lingering smoke with her hands. "Just go, Knos."

"You don't mean that, dear."

"Yes, I do." Her broad, plain face was flushed scarlet, and she refused to look at him.

"Go stay with your kinsmen," Urope added. Bestowing a kiss on Orana's temple, she urged the girl to help Fidra roll fresh dough. "Go purify yourself and make an offering to the gods for having offended your wives."

Hariana said nothing, but her expression signaled agreement. Knos knew well enough to realize when his sweet talk had failed. There was no point in forcing the matter. Let them brood about the infidelities of men and sleep on their discontent, he decided. In the morning he would return with wildflowers, woo them with platitudes, and everything would be well.

"In that case," he said, "I'm going. But you'll miss me."

Knos made his way through the fishing village's narrow streets down to the beach, which was deserted except for a group of fishermen running their boat into the foaming surf. Dominating the sand, resting on her keel above the tidemark, was the hulk of his trading ship, a ninety foot, oar-driven vessel called *Dolphin*. He ran callused fingers along her planks, assessing by mere touch the mortise-and-tenon joints, the constricting yew lashings. *Dolphin* smelled like sun and salt, kelp and the pitch sealing her timbers, and the cypress from which she had been constructed; hers was a scent as welcome to him as that of a woman's desire. Since he had inherited her from his late father fifteen years ago, *Dolphin* had never given him a day's trouble; her sturdy construction had safely brought him and his men through gales and tempests on numerous occasions. Knos understood her, loved her, found her a more amicable mistress than the human wives who ruled his hearth.

Knos lay down in the sand beside his ship, and pillowed his head on his elbow. The sand was soft, still warm from the day's heat, and the midsummer evening was balmy. What did his wives have to complain about? Aside from that one dalliance under a canoe with a fisherman's wife on Patmos, *and* that fumbling liaison with a buxom young widow inside the sanctuary of Raziya, *and* that pleasant hour fondling a woman through her clothes on Nissiros, he had behaved. Mostly.

He could not help it that he was sensual and earthy, and that he preferred his women as uninhibited as he was. To judge from his frequent exploits, one might be forgiven for thinking that he was dashingly handsome, but outraged husbands and kinsmen were routinely shocked to discover that the infamous Knos was of middling height and appearance, a sinewy, brown man with salty gray strands threading through black hair which he wore clubbed at the nape of his neck. He kept clean-shaven, but spidery creases from constant exposure to wind and sun webbed the corners of his eyes and mouth.

His sexual adventures would have been the end of him had he not also been an exceptionally easy man to like. People were more willing to forgive a sailor his misdemeanors when he was also a merchant who brought valuable wares: obsidian tools from Melos, fine linen, medicinal herbs, animal skins and semiprecious beads, as well as news, messages from kinsmen, and stories and songs he had collected during his many voyages. Given the accessibility and traffic of the sea lanes, Knos was not the only Rhodian merchant trading with the ports of the eastern Aegean and Anatolian mainland, but among those dozens he was certainly one of the most successful.

Would that his wives appreciated that fact better! They were no longer entranced by tales of his voyages, of the foreign customs and sights he encountered. They no longer cooed over his gifts of beads and cloth as they once had. What was the matter with them, anyway? Had they taken lovers in his absence? Knos doubted that. His brothers and other kinsmen would have told him straightaway had his wives been unfaithful.

He recalled the woman by the waterfront. Bare feet and nipples painted scarlet with red ocher, and an eager mouth that would not quit. A chieftain's daughter would never paint herself thus, or behave so wantonly. Sinopi was so young—yes, he admitted, old enough for marriage to the fat, middle-aged man who was her husband—but nevertheless, barely out of childhood. It was all a misunderstanding, a false accusation. Things would sort themselves out once Sinopi started telling the truth. Slowly, his eyes closed, and he fell asleep.

Knos jolted awake from a hazy dream of three luscious widows devouring his manhood to the reality of several men attacking him, sitting on his chest and pinioning his limbs. He instinctively lashed out as his captors dragged him upright, but landed no blows. Quite the contrary, someone slapped him so hard across the face that stars exploded behind his eyes. Not his wives again. No. When he recovered enough to get a glimpse of his assailant, he found himself staring straight into a very familiar but unwelcome face. Gods, but Divos was an ugly bastard when he sneered.

"What are you doing here?" he choked.

An elbow to the gut doubled him over before he even finished his query. Retching, Knos was too preoccupied with breathing to resist the hands wrenching his arms behind his back and binding his wrists with hemp rope. Someone looped a noose around his neck and tightened the knot against the back of his neck. What was this? Divos and his bully cohorts intended to throttle him right there on the beach, did they, without a hearing from the elders?

"The council wants to see you." Divos tangled thick fingers in his hair and wrenched his head up. Knos's nose throbbed; he felt blood trickling from one nostril. "You think you can fuck my sister and get away with it?"

Knos gasped for breath. "I never touched her." Gods above, was he still dreaming? Where were his kinsmen and crew to defend him? "It's all a misunderstanding."

Divos snapped his fingers at the men behind him. "Bring him."

They dragged him stumbling from the beach into the village, which at this early hour should have been busy with women headed to the well and the beach to browse through the morning's catch. Instead, a crowd had gathered before the mudbrick structure where the village elders judged local disputes, dispensed justice, and appealed to the gods. Men and women surged toward him, jeering, shoving, and pelting him with pebbles. Amid the whirl, Knos saw no one from his own clan; they all looked like members of the Dolphin and Octopus clans.

Divos jerked the rope around his neck; the crowd roared its approval.

Knos grunted and clenched his teeth as the younger man's brutes hauled him through an ox-hide curtain into the mudbrick house.

The village's eight elders sat cross-legged in a semicircle around a plastered central hearth decorated with cross-hatching and spirals of red and yellow ocher and black. The walls were banded with colors, various shades of ocher, except around the central flue where the escaping smoke had stained the plaster with soot.

Shobai glowered at Knos from deep-set eyes under an oppressive monobrow. Obese Rabbas was perspiring heavily despite the early hour; his glistening face was drawn so tight with rage and humiliation that his treble chins quivered. Knos found Dravan, his own clan chieftain, appearing very small and insignificant in comparison with the other elders; the old man returned his gaze for a fraction of a second, then glanced away, shaking his head in dismay.

Knos was astonished by the vehemence of the opposition, both within and without. Did people actually believe that he had committed adultery with Shobai's daughter?

"What is this?" Aramo, Knos's husky elder brother, stepped forward and, shoving the nearest of Divos's companions aside, fumbled with the substantial knot tightening the noose around Knos's neck.

Aramo unfastened and removed the noose, while younger brother Rauda cut his bonds. "You assured us an hour ago," Aramo said, "that Knos would be given every opportunity to comply peacefully with the council's summons."

"I didn't do anything wrong," Knos affirmed quickly.

Abbek, Knos's first cousin, glared murderously at Divos. "Did your ruffians bother to wake him before jumping on him?"

"That *was* their idea of waking me," Knos muttered.

A hiss from behind him. "You deserve worse."

As usual, Shobai did not reprimand his eldest son; his grumbled command to come to order was intended for the rival accused and his kinsmen. "Let there be no further disruption to these proceedings, for we now stand before the all-knowing, all-powerful gods." As the high priest of his clan, he uttered his pronouncement with a typically overblown flourish. "Nidnu, do us the honor of offering the libation. Let the gods of the clans hearken to us with eyes and ears open to the truth, and hearts ready to judge."

Those deities, of molded clay in the primitive style of the mainland, occupied a plastered platform to the far left. Among them were arranged the sacred clan tokens: the skulls of the the clans' totem animals. Knos regarded the yawning eye sockets of his clan's bull skull. It was an ancient relic, yellowed with age, its left horn broken, and some of its teeth were missing. Whenever he gazed upon the skull, which was not often, Knos always sensed its silent yet potent presence, and had to suppress a surge of indignation over how diminished the most ancient of totems had become, shoved to the cobwebs, dust, and shadows of the rear while the village's more powerful clans allotted prominence to their own unimpressive relics.

Knos drew in a steadying breath. The village's most sacred enclosure stank of wood smoke, stale food, and what he immediately recognized as the smell of human fear—a distinctive juxtaposition of acrid sweat, urine, and shit. The compacted earth floor under his worn rush sandals exuded dampness. Someone had recently voided their bladder there.

Nidnu, the elder of the Cypress Clan, raised a painted cup in his hands, and intoned in his mellifluous voice, "Oh, gods of Rhodes, here is a sweet offering of milk and honey. Grant us your favor and attention. Hear the case against Knos, son of Manasi, a captain and merchant of the Bull Clan, who stands accused of committing adultery with the woman Sinopi, the late wife of Rabbas, revered elder of the Octopus Clan, and the late daughter of Shobai, high priest and elder of the Dolphin Clan." Kneeling, Nidnu touched his forehead to the shelf's plastered edge, and presented the cup.

Late wife and late daughter. Had Shobai and Rabbas already put the young woman to death, then? "I never committed adultery with your daughter, Shobai. The woman I lay with was much older. She was—"

"We ask the questions here." Spittle sprayed from Shobai's thin lips.

"You violated my wife. We should stone you right here and now." Rabbas wheezed whenever he spoke. His conspicuous rolls of fat meant he needed assistance with the most basic tasks, from sitting and standing to walking and, rumor asserted, relieving himself. How *did* a man like that fuck a virgin girl without crushing her or killing himself?

"I swear on Potnidu's testicles that I never touched her." Knos considered it a genuine shame that Rabbas was angry with him; the chieftain of the Octopus Clan was not a particularly vindictive man, merely an overindulgent and slothful one. Knos even transacted business with him on occasion, always finding him amicable and ready to barter, not to mention the fact that he maintained an excellent table. A sensible wife would not have had to try very hard to have kept him satisfied. "The woman I had never even told me her name."

"This isn't about adultery," Abbek snorted. "Gods forbid another man consummate your marriage for you!" Knos winced at his kinsman's unnecessarily callous remark, while simultaneously trying to avoid meeting Rabbas's gaze; the man's pudgy face had swelled purple with rage.

"We were told this would be a fair trial." Aramo crossed both arms over his chest.

"The verdict should not be a foregone conclusion," Dravan interjected weakly. "Custom states that Knos is entitled to—"

"We have no need to debate this matter further." Shobai bulled right over him, which he did with everyone he considered inferior. That amounted to more or less the entire island.

Aramo clenched his callused brown hands into fists. "Our chief elder and the accused have the right to speak." He drew a breath. "No one here will argue that a disobedient wife or daughter ought to be punished, but when she foolishly plays the harlot and misleads the man who lies with her, then what crime has he committed?"

"This is an insult," Rabbas wheezed, "to our dignity."

"Since when was insulting a man's pride punishable by execution?" Aramo shot back.

Knos shook his head in an effort to clear it. Had Sinopi painted herself and played the harlot to get away from her gross husband? Was that what she had done? Knos did not want to contemplate the possibility that he had been deceived.

"Quite right." The elder seated to Shobai's right stroked a black beard rancid with the animal fat he used to smooth it down. "Perhaps we can reach some sort of profitable compromise, perhaps material compensation in place of bloodshed." Knos rolled his eyes. Sarduri always awaited him on the beach whenever he returned from a voyage, in order to nose through the baskets and bundles Knos's men unloaded, and to palm whatever obsidian blades, beads, and other trinkets he fancied. Because he was head of the influential Seagull Clan, he could get away with his petty thefts. "As I recall, the Bull Clan breeds some very fine cattle." Sarduri's teeth, when he smiled, gleamed whitely despite their unevenness. "Let's say about forty or fifty head of cattle would suffice to restore good relations between the clans."

"That's outrageous!" Knos answered sharply. "Not even a chieftain's daughter is worth that much."

"We can't meet that price," Dravan croaked, "and this council knows it." Knos did not bother stifling his exasperated groan. A competent chieftain would have argued against extortion, suggested a fairer price, anything but slump his shoulders and admit defeat.

"Why are you even negotiating?" Rabbas's objection came out as a plaintive whine. "Kill Knos and be done with it."

Knos shouted, "I committed no crime!"

"The law—" Aramo started.

"Quiet!" Shobai voiced Knos's own raging thoughts. "Sarduri, your eyes are bigger than your common sense. The Bull Clan obviously doesn't *own* fifty head of cattle. Twenty-five head will have to suffice, with fifteen rams and ewes, thirty goats, and a man's weight in obsidian."

Abbek exploded, "You didn't even ask that much as a bride price for your daughter!"

"Ah," Sarduri crooned, "but we are putting a price on the Dolphin Clan's dishonor. Surely you weren't intending to cheat those your kinsman wronged!" He adopted a mask of mock horror.

A tense and anticipatory hush descended over the chamber. Knos began perspiring in that close, rank space. Were they actually contemplating hanging an innocent man? Blue-bearded Marynos, where was his crew?

"Ten head of cattle," he said, "five rams and ewes, but no obsidian and no goats." He did not care that he lacked the authority to barter with the clan's collective property, because it was obvious to him what Shobai and his cronies were trying to do. Not only was his life at stake, but the entire Bull Clan's future, and Dravan, that useless goat's asshole, could not be relied upon to help him. "That's a fair price for a chieftain's daughter."

Shobai tilted his head, his eyes shiny and cold as the precious obsidian Knos brought back from Melos. "The insult was very great." He gestured to Rabbas. "My son-in-law is now without a wife and his honor. How can he hold up his head? Where will he find a bride to replace my daughter?"

Shedding his triple chins would go a long way toward easing the burden of holding up the man's head, Knos reflected sourly. As for a wife, Rabbas needed a nursemaid, not a broodmare. "Sinopi insulted you, Rabbas. The woman on the waterfront never told me her name. She didn't look anything at all like your wife. Please, if I did any injury, I never..."

Rabbas looked away.

"Do you enjoy your life, Knos?" Shobai asked maliciously. "Is it such a sport with you, seducing and despoiling other men's wives?" Since he had begun speaking, he had not twitched a muscle, but sat there regarding his prey with viperous concentration. "Either we hang or stone you for your adultery, or you pay the thirty head of cattle."

Knos opened his mouth, but it was Abbek's voice which argued, "It was twenty-five a moment ago!"

The ghost of a smile flitted across the chieftain's mouth. "And in another moment it will be thirty-five, plus twenty rams and ewes, forty goats, and twenty-five bushels of your barley crop."

Aramo raised a hand as much to silence his outraged kinsmen as to speak. "And we contend that this charge of adultery is absurd. Why haven't you objected, Dravan?" The Bull Clan chieftain looked noncommittal. Dravan never took so much as a piss without permission from the other elders. Aramo glared at him, then continued, "Everyone knows the law. It's only adultery when—" Shobai tried to overrule him;

Aramo simply raised his voice. "When a man's wife and her lover are discovered in the act! *In the act!*" He enunciated each word by shaking his forefinger. "And then it's Rabbas who gets to execute them, not *you*, Shobai. My brother never committed adultery with Sinopi because he never realized who she—"

"*ENOUGH!*" Shobai hollered. "You will all pay for this!" Sarduri and the elder of the Goat Clan had to restrain his arms. Had the ancient traditions not prohibited violence in the presence of the gods, there might have been a brawl.

Aramo regarded the elders coolly. "That's what you really want, isn't it?" he said, once they got Shobai seated and quiet once more. "You've been stealing our livestock and goods, and encroaching on our fields for the last ten years. When we complain, nothing is done. When by chance the offenders are caught—and *somehow* they always manage to be Dolphins or Seagulls, imagine that!—they're rarely punished. So I say now, how *dare* you use Knos and your slut daughter as a pretext to continue robbing us."

Knos heard Divos mutter a warning, something about Aramo watching his big mouth. And yet, his brother was right. How many times had Knos returned from a voyage to hear about another theft, another boundary dispute, another attempt at intimidation?

"This is a question of honor!"

Abbek once again added his voice to the clamor. "Honor? Pah! You avenged your clan's honor this morning when you hung your daughter."

The tension was becoming unbearable. Knos was by now spoiling for a fight. When would his men arrive, and overpower the Dolphin ruffians holding him? To accuse him of lying with another man's wife—well, he technically *was* guilty of that—but to threaten him with death as an excuse to extort his clan? That was fucking outrageous. Would he beat Shobai's skull in first, or his son's? Or perhaps he should start with Dravan. That was the only decision he wanted to have to make in the next few minutes.

"Please! Let us work this out as reasonable men!" Rauda had not bothered opening his mouth until now; he was so superstitious that he did not think an ordinary fellow like himself ought to speak in the presence of the gods or clan totems. "Please! Shobai, would you accept an offer of ten head of cattle, five rams and ewes with their lambs, eleven goats, an infant's weight in obsidian, and a daughter of the Bull Clan to replace the wife Rabbas has lost?" His voice, squeaky at first, gained confidence as he realized that the gods were not going to strike him down for opening his mouth. "It would come from our immediate kinsmen's holdings, so the entire clan need not be punished for any wrongdoing Knos might have committed."

"No," Knos growled. Not on those terms, and certainly not by admitting to a crime which he felt he had not committed. Rauda threw him a desperate look, trying to shush him.

Shobai spat contemptuously into the hearth fire. "Our family's honor is worth more than that insignificant sum. Don't insult us with your offer of a lowly peasant woman." Rabbas's lower jaw started to tremble, setting his treble chin to jiggling; he would not meet anyone's gaze. Sinopi had been an exceptionally lovely girl. Rabbas must have been absolutely besotted with her.

Dravan raised a hand to speak. "Let's assume," he began, "that we surrender Knos to you for execution. Then would you—?"

"*WHAT?*" Aramo and Abbek roared simultaneously.

Knos lunged forward, snarling, only to have Divos's ruffians wrench him back with such force that his arms were almost dislocated from their sockets. Then a man's hand savagely cuffed his right ear, agitating the bruise Hariana had left there the night before, and Divos said menacingly, "Go ahead. Just give me an excuse to beat you senseless."

Dravan, meanwhile, seemed unperturbed by the outburst. "I want to hear the answer."

"You're a fucking traitor to the clan," Abbek spat.

"Well, let's see..." Shobai narrowed his eyes, clearly toying with them. "We could execute Knos now and be reconciled for, say, thirty head of cattle, thirty rams and ewes with their lambs, twenty-five goats, ten pigs, and a man's weight in obsidian and alabaster. You may keep your daughters."

Dravan's face fell. "I see."

The entire right side of his face throbbing, Knos glared at his chieftain. "Disappointed, you fucking bastard?" Divos made an unpleasant sound in his throat, which might have been a prelude to another beating but for the threatening stance of Aramo and Abbek, who were clearly done cooperating. Rauda looked as though he wished he were anywhere else but there.

Dravan ignored them all. Who in all the seven hells did he think he was, anyway? His power came only at the clan's sufferance. "What must be done," he said ponderously, "will be done."

What the fuck did that mean? Knos wondered. Aramo gave voice to those thoughts, and more, saying, "Your word alone isn't enough, and you certainly don't speak for the rest of us in this. Divos, there's not going to be another execution this morning, so back away from my brother."

"Go fuck yourselves," Divos retorted, and his brutes chortled. "I don't take orders from you."

"No," Shobai agreed, "he does not." Exchanging a conspiratorial smile with Rabbas and Sarduri, he added, "Knos is an accused criminal. We cannot risk his escaping judgment while you and your clansmen hatch some scheme to have him flee aboard his ship and therefore deprive us of what is owed. Divos will stay right where he is, you will take your places, and we will settle the question right here and now, before the gods."

CPSIA information can be obtained at www.ICGtesting.com
Printed in the USA
LVOW01s2135210915

455067LV00025B/564/P

9 781466 382626